THEY WOULDN'T DARE

DEANNA GREY

Cover Artist: Mumbi Munyua

Beta Reader: Cydney Humphery

Sensitivity Reader: Elwen (Bookish & Beyond)

Copy & Line Editor: Muddled Ink Editorial

AUTHOR'S NOTE

The Yara and David you will meet in this book began as side characters in an old series called *Westbrooke Angels*. That series has since been unpublished. If you've read the unpublished books, please know that this version of Westbrooke and all the characters within have been changed. Some in minor ways, others in major ways. The older works are no longer canon. I hope you enjoy this updated version of Westbrooke University. Happy reading!

CONTENT WARNINGS

Discussions and depictions of self-harm
Discussions of OCD, physical child abuse & neglect, a car
accident resulting in injury
Mention of a parent with addiction
Character previously in foster care
Sexual content

This book is intended for readers 18+

1

FALL SEMESTER | SENIOR YEAR

WESTBROOKE UNIVERSITY'S starting tight end stood at my front door, soaked from head to toe. His jaw was tense, frustration radiating heat from his gaze like the eye of an oven. Nevertheless, the warmth didn't pierce through my shield. After almost a decade of knowing him, I've insulated my walls against his weather changes. Nothing got in or out without my say-so. It was brilliant (for me) and a point of grievous annoyance (for him).

"Did you do it?" I asked, despite his clear success.

David Evans scoffed, mouth parted, and tongue poking the inside of his cheek. I'd bet good money that before knocking on my door, he'd contemplated if today was his last straw. Tried to determine if today was the day he let me win once and for all.

He raked his fingers through his hair, shoving the short brown strands off his forehead. The wrinkle between his brows resembles a well-traveled valley. David's dark brown eyes looked even more like pits of despair when he was on the verge of giving up. I straightened with a bit of hope, my back becoming a lightning rod for the endgame. But, unfortunately, the guy wasn't a quitter.

David held up a shiny dime. "Here's your year 1915."

I grabbed it to confirm the impossibility. Even tried to bend in case of fraud. He snorted at the gesture, and I knew that was the most amusement I'd get out of him tonight.

"No way!" I scratched at the metal, and a bit of polish came off the tip of my red nails. Not a metallic speck in sight. It was real. "How long did it take you?"

"Three hours," he forced through gritted teeth.

A laugh slipped from my lips. "You dived in fountains for three hours? God, David. You're something else."

"No diving necessary. I used a net," he said.

"Oh...smart." My shoulders sagged. Though I appreciated his ingenuity, I would have preferred his complete dedication to wading. But I hadn't proposed requirements for this dare, so that was on me. I'd do better next time.

I tilted my head to the side, considering. "Wait, if you used a net, why are you all wet?"

His jaw ticked once again. For a second, I didn't think he'd tell me the actual reason.

"I...slipped," David mumbled.

"I knew I should have stayed with you!" I shook my head, mourning the missed opportunity. "That lecture could have waited."

"Did you at least take notes for me?" He looked like he didn't want to ask, even though he had been asking since the semester started. In all three years at Westbrooke, my political science track surprisingly hadn't overlapped with his social work major classes. But in our senior year, my luck had run out. We shared two courses. It seemed like the university's final attempt to break me.

"You may copy my notes later. Under supervision, of

course," I offered. "Now, if you'll excuse me, I have meal-prepping to do and a discussion post to write."

As soon as I tried to close the door, David used his hand to stop it. "I need to shower."

I snorted, looking him up and down. Tiny puddles pooled underneath his grimy gray sneakers. Patches of dirt stained the hem of his blue jeans. He smelled like chemicals and wet asphalt. "Yes, you do. Who knows what filth's in a university water fountain?"

He let out a noise that was one part sigh and the other part groan. "Now, Yara. Right. Now."

I bit back a laugh after realizing what he was asking. His grip on the door loosened, but the desperation in his eyes remained firm.

"There's no way I'm letting you track water and muck all over our nice rugs." I crossed my arms over my chest. "Haven just cleansed the apartment. And you're definitely carrying around enough bad karma to undo a day's worth of goodwill. I mean, coins in fountains are wishes, right? You just stole someone's wish."

I didn't believe in cleansing, karma, or wishes, but the irritation that appeared on David's face made pretending worth it.

"You were the one who instigated a stolen wish," he said, eyes dancing with amusement when I frowned at the statement. "So, where does that leave you?"

I shook my head. "You'll have to do better than that if you want to guilt-trip me."

"Yara," David's voice went at least two octaves lower. It was a method he'd fallen back on since realizing it scratched some unknown part of my brain I had no control over. I'd given that sensitive information away years ago, when I'd been too young and naïve to know better.

"Don't make me beg." His hand fell from the door. David knew keeping me would no longer require physical effort.

I almost readied myself to give him a taste of his own medicine. But the look in his eyes reminded me of why he'd thought of the net in the first place. It was the same reason he'd panicked whenever his water bottles got mixed up with the other guys on his team. And why he'd done everything he could each year (including camping outside the dean's office for a night) to ensure he got a coveted single-bedroom on-campus housing. I could be a hard-ass, but I wasn't heartless. Not completely, at least.

"Okay." I sighed. "But you have to be quick. Haven's out. If she comes back and sees you, then I'm in for another cleanse and lecture about letting destructive energy into our space."

"Deal." He pushed past the threshold.

"Wait, hold on." I waved my hands for him to stop.

"Seriously?" He leaned his head back as if the ceiling would answer all his prayers. "Yara, could you just—"

"You're tracking in water." I hurried to the bathroom, grabbing a stack of towels.

David looked pissed but kept his commentary to himself. I laid the towels on the ground one after another. With each one placed, David stepped forward as if he were traveling on a row of lily pads.

"Slow down, slow down," I protested when he kept catching up to me.

"This is ridiculous," he complained, but stopped on one towel to give me a slight lead.

"I'm not the one who tripped." I glanced up at him.

David's hands were on his waist. The position made his soaked t-shirt (which looked a size or two too small) stretch across his chest. The dull gray of his shirt highlighted the reddish undertones of his white skin. I could make out every tight curve of his muscles. Besides being impressive on the football field, David was an avid runner. We'd bumped into one another far too many times on the nature trails back in our hometown. His wardrobe had changed little since then. Thus, the too-small t-shirt.

"Are we waiting for an alien invasion or for the polar ice caps to stop melting?" David's voice pulled me away from the foggy nature trails and a memory of him telling me to wait for him whenever the trail got too steep or too remote. He never believed in my ability to gouge an attacker's pupils using my safety keychain (despite how often I used to ruin his day at our community center karate lessons when we were in seventh grade).

"You joke, but I think we're closer to an alien invasion than not," I teased. His scowl made me laugh. I still jumped into action, though.

Our towel bridge reached the bathroom mat laid out in front of the shower. I smiled, satisfied with the outcome. David seemed more pissed than ever. Although he won his dare, I felt like the victor tonight. His disapproval was catnip to me.

"You can use my soap in the caddy." I pointed at a blue bottle.

"Lucky me," he mumbled and went to remove his shirt.

"Whoa, whoa." I slapped my hand over my eyes. He snorted.

"Well, you were taking so long to leave, I figured you wanted a peek," he teased.

"You figured wrong." I waved my hands, trying to feel my way out of the bathroom while keeping my eyes shut. David's deep laugh tugged at my core. I slammed the door behind me, only to have it open a few seconds later. He tossed a pile of clothes out.

"Excuse me?" I yelped when the clothes fell at my heels. "Are you some sort of speed undresser?"

He ignored my question. "Wash those."

"I take 'pleases' and 'thank yous' like a normal human."

The door shut again. I huffed as the shower started, the curtain rings scraping across the rod.

I'd have to wash his clothes or listen to him complain and put them in the washer himself. If the clothes didn't get in the wash now, that meant I'd have to endure his presence for even longer.

I took the L, complaining under my breath the whole time. Before picking up the wet (potentially cursed) pile, I grabbed a pair of disposable gloves from the kitchen.

"Slipped or catapulted?" I mumbled with a creased brow as I carted the dripping pieces into our small laundry area.

As usual, Haven still had a load in the wash. I switched her clothes over and poured an insane amount of detergent into the machine. I smiled at the thought of David walking around with not just his skin but clothes smelling like me ... Someone could interpret that the wrong way.

And you'd like that, wouldn't you? Especially *if he ran into anyone from home.*

I frowned. No. Absolutely not. I wanted a lot of things, but wanting to be seen as David's and vice versa had never been one of them.

I wasn't dense enough to deny attraction. He was good-looking in a way that snuck up on people. At first glance, he was strikingly average with his dark hair, strong nose, and crooked smile. Upon second glance, the dark in his eyes seemed like an ode to a Gothic hero, and the way he spoke, ever low and steady, was reminiscent of every villain from some canceled-before-its-time paranormal TV series. A third glance risked complete fascination. Luckily, I've seen all of his sides. And most of them I didn't like. Looks only got someone so far. And unfortunately for David, there were a plethora of kind lookers in the world.

After turning on the washing machine, I slipped into my room. Textbooks, notepads, and colored highlighters littered my desk. Before David's knock, I'd been deep into studying, trying to get a head start this semester, so I would have enough time to dedicate to my campus organization's events. Even though the semester just started a couple of weeks ago, my calendar was full of expectations.

As president of Westbrooke's chapter of the Black Women in Development (BWD), I had the honor of spearheading events for Black women on campus. Our organization worked to foster connections and encourage personal and professional growth through workshops, lectures, and events. And since this semester marked my final year before graduation, I wanted everything I did for the org to be big. I needed to solidify my place in its history.

My mom had been the president when she was on campus. She'd not only gotten the role as a sophomore, but she single-handedly put our chapter on the map with her incredible fundraising abilities and her (now staple) end-of-year balls.

My oldest sister, Aimee, had followed in her footsteps, making her mark by partnering with local hospitals to raise funds for research.

All the presidents before me at Westbrooke had done their part in making our chapter one of the most successful. They'd left their own unique marks. And then, I showed up.

Since becoming president, our chapter membership has been at an all-time low. Attendance at meetings was sparse. And I practically had to drag pledge members out of bed to attend events. The appeal of sorority rushing rang far louder and shone ten times brighter to new students.

I'd done everything in my power to bring the chapter back to life. Partnered with after-school programs, coordinated unhoused outreach, and silent auctions for art funds. But each endeavor had minimal success, and each semester felt like falling back down to the base of a mountain. I wouldn't admit it out loud, but on most counts, this chapter was dead. For my senior year, I was going to do everything possible to defy the odds and breathe it back to life... or die trying.

"Do you always pick the same spot?"

I started and looked over to find a bare-chested David in my doorway. He had wrapped a fluffy pink towel (somewhat loosely, very risky) around his waist.

"What?" I cleared my throat and tried not to look as startled as I felt.

David gestured at the back of his head. "Your hair. You were picking at it."

"No, I wasn't." I shot out of my seat, ignoring the churn of embarrassment in my stomach, and headed to the closet. "I might have a shirt for you."

"I'm fine."

I frowned, still rummaging through my clothes. "You're half-naked. No one's fine half-naked in a stranger's room."

"Is that what we are? After all these years? Strangers?" He was on the move now, near my dresser, where I kept most of my books. "That can't be accurate."

"Well, we're not friends," I countered, glancing his way for some sort of clarification.

"No, definitely not friends," he agreed with a nod.

"Acquaintances, probably." I pulled out a black oversized *Halloween* tee.

David didn't accept the shirt when I held it toward him. I wiggled it, doing everything short of tugging it over his head myself. Washing and drying the clothes would take forty minutes to an hour. I didn't think I could wait that long without falling into the trap of distraction. I'd started counting the freckles on his shoulders, for goodness' sake. Ten on the right, eight on the left.

"Acquaintances don't feel right either." David gestured to my books. "Are these all film novelizations?"

I raised a brow, readying for some quip. "Yes...and?"

David shook his head. "Nothing. I've never known anyone who brought these, let alone read them. And from the looks of it–" He leaned in closer, inspecting cracked spines and peeling covers. "–enjoy them."

See, this was why I never invited people into my room. Not even Haven got the chance to scan my belongings and cast judgment on their value.

I scoffed at David's assumption. "There's an entire market for them."

"Maybe in the eighties," he countered.

"I didn't say booming. I said, market."

He shrugged, unfazed by the bite in my tone. "What's your color-coding system? These little circle stickers."

I laughed, surprised he noted the inconsequential detail. "Really, David?"

"What?" He blinked, confused.

I squinted at him, searching for an ulterior motive, but there was none amidst his tired eyes and water-activated curls. "Purple's my comfort reads, blue's copies I'm willing to lend out, and red is ones I love but will never read again."

"Why keep a book if you're never going to reread it?" He seemed genuinely perplexed.

"Sentimental value." I tossed the shirt over his shoulder. Somehow, some way, even after showering with my soap, he still mostly smelled of himself: pinewood and early mornings. "Of course."

David snorted. "Didn't take you for the sentimental type. That's... interesting."

He said "interesting" as if it were a change in expectation. A disappointing awakening.

"Didn't take you for the questioning type," I shot back.

Caring about disappointing him wasn't typically high on my priority list. But a pinch of frustration burrowed its way into my chest, making itself a nice, happy home.

"Just starting a conversation," he said simply. "My questions are arbitrary and meaningless, like most during small talk."

I laughed dryly. "We're not having a conversation. You're judging me while I wash your clothes, give you something warm to wear, and offer you something to drink."

He raised a brow. "Did I miss that last part?"

"It was coming up. I'm making coffee. You want some?"

"It's a little late for caffeine, don't you think?" Thankfully, David finally tugged on the shirt. He looked funny with a towel as a bottom, but unless he wanted to wear my dolphin shorts, that'd have to do.

When I smiled at the thought of him squeezing into my shorts, he frowned at me.

"Why are you looking like that?" he asked, every word infused with suspicion.

I shook my head. "No reason. Was that a no on the coffee?"

David didn't look like he believed my lie for a second, but said, "I'll take some water."

"Coming up." I went to the door, pausing before I left to say, "Touch nothing. If you do, I'll know."

"Your sentimental clutter is safe with me." He drew an X across his chest.

I made a noise of disapproval. He winked and waved me off. It took less than five minutes to turn on my machine and slip in a flavor pod. Once I got back into the room with his cup of water, David was lounging on my bed. He'd spread a blanket and rearranged the pillows so he remained propped up. He flipped through one of my sketchbooks that'd been on the bookshelf.

"Uh, excuse me?" I snatched the sketchbook from him. My heart hammered at him, of all people, seeing my random doodles.

I was no artist. In fact, I was whatever the opposite of an artist was. But on my worst days, when the thoughts were anvils, and I was on the verge of plucking at my hair for too long to hide the damage, I had to put pen to paper.

"I said, don't touch." I pinned the book against my chest.

"You drew those?" He sat up a little straighter, which loosened his towel. I frowned at the sight. I felt as if I had swallowed ice, and it was stuck in my chest, melting painfully slowly. David's brow raised as he studied how tightly I clung to my secret relaxation tool.

"None of your business. Now, here." I shoved a glass of water in his direction, its contents almost spilling over the edge.

He took it and barely mumbled, "Thank you."

I tossed a blanket over his legs before slipping my sketchbook into a drawer and sitting back down at my desk.

He chuckled, readjusting the blanket on his lap. "What was that for?"

"Your thighs were showing. No one wants to see that."

"You sure? Because you seemed to look."

Before I could respond, my phone buzzed. I glanced at the caller ID and winced.

"What?" David asked, smelling blood in the water.

"Nothing." I shoved down the guilt about sending the call to voicemail and opened a fresh Word doc to start my homework. The phone buzzed again. The guilt grew limbs, ready to run laps across my stomach lining.

"You need to get that?" he asked.

I took a breath. "No.... maybe."

"Don't let me stop you."

"Maybe you could go into the living room?"

"Sure. And greet Haven in a towel." He nodded. I could see the wheels turning in his head. "What should I tell her happened?"

My expression darkened. "The truth."

He tsked and looked up at the ceiling to think. "That's no fun."

"She'd believe nothing else," I said, even though that might not be the case.

I'd been in this dare battle with David since our sophomore year. Haven and the rest of my friends became more curious about it with each passing semester. I couldn't blame them. If one of them swore they hated a guy since middle school, but spent copious amounts of time with him, I'd be a skeptic too.

But my dare battle with David was about principle. Something my friends didn't understand. And I couldn't blame them because I wasn't the best at explaining it just yet.

"Promise you'll be quiet?" I said when my phone buzzed with a few worried texts.

"I don't like making promises, Yara. I've accepted a long time ago that I am regrettably human and thus, will most likely break them."

"David, come on. Work with me. You owe me that much," I insisted when I grabbed my phone. I needed to take this call, especially since it was Logan. Ignoring even a text from her triggered a spiral of shame I'd spend days trying to shake off.

"Fine. I will do everything I can to speak only if necessary." His grin didn't sit well with me. "In case of fire or flood."

"I think I'd smell a fire or see a flood coming."

He shrugged. "You never know."

"But you do know..." I let out an exasperated sigh when my phone vibrated again. "Fine. But I swear to God I'll ruin you if you make the slightest noise. Swallow your sneezes and coughs. Sip your water without gulping. And scroll on your phone with the volume off."

David nodded. "Yes, ma'am."

I gave him one last look before pressing the call-back button.

"Everything okay?" It required focus to ensure my voice didn't quiver with anxiety about the answer potentially being 'no.'

"God, I was thinking I'd have to drive up there in the morning." Logan breathed out a sigh of relief. Some of the tightness in my back uncoiled.

"I was busy with something, sorry." David's gaze weighed heavily on me. My cheeks burned, so I turned to face the window.

God, I should have said, screw any misunderstanding that might have happened with Haven. Having David hear my "younger sister voice" was potentially ten times more embarrassing.

"Mom wanted to make sure you remembered we got a table at Winsor's, so wear something nice," Logan said. "And preferably white and flowy. She wants photos with the dogwood trees."

"Got it." I pulled up my calendar and added a note to the already penciled dinner with Mom and my sisters.

"Minimal jewelry, no heels. Hair done or tucked away in a nice, neutral scarf." Logan spoke in a monotone as if she were reading off a script. Knowing our mother, it was wise to take notes on whatever she said. Mom remembered everything and didn't have the time or patience to expect anything less from others.

"The topic of discussion?" I dared to ask.

"Governors' Ball, of course. Which means she's going to run through everything. And everything in your case means graduation updates. I think it's time you told her you didn't get that internship in DC. Or New York. Or...well, you get my point. Honesty."

I winced. My hand went to the back of my head immediately. I picked at a few strands of hair, waiting for Logan to continue. The springs of my bed creaked. I'd nearly forgotten about David's presence until his hand nudged my wrist. I yanked my fingers away from my hair, ashamed at being caught for the second time tonight.

"Do you think my clothes are done?" he asked at a normal volume. I muted myself, but not fast enough.

"Who's that?" Logan asked.

I glared at David. "I don't know, asshole. Check."

He didn't move an inch.

"Oh, my God..." Logan sounded awake, alert, and amused for the first time in years. "Is that a guy? Yara, do you have a guy in your room?"

I unmuted and quickly confirmed. "It's no one."

David snorted once again, loud enough for her to hear.

"Uh, I think maybe I should leave you to it," Logan offered, and I could practically hear the gossip travelling through the grapevine. The news would begin with our sisters and slowly spread to the most distant relatives, where a twice-removed cousin's partner would form an opinion to be discussed at the next family gathering.

"No." I quickly tried to think of something that would reel her back in. Something interesting enough to make her forget. "I can talk. Let's talk. How's grad school? Is that other TA still taking credit for your work?"

Her adventures as a TA were low-hanging fruit. An easy trigger to steer her into a rant.

"Not falling for that." I could hear the smile in her voice. "You know you've just made the agenda, right?"

"Lo, come on," I pleaded.

"See you next week," she sang. "Love you!"

As soon as she hung up, I turned to David and promised, "You're dead."

He gave me a warm smile that was so gentle I had to do a double-take to remember what we were.

"You can thank me later," he said.

"Excuse me?"

"You wanted off that call but were too afraid to speak up for yourself." He tilted his head. "Which is strange for you. I've never known you not to stand your ground."

I frowned, unsettled by the observation and ammunition I'd just given him. "You don't know me well enough to know what's strange for me."

David shook his head and leaned closer. My breath caught in my throat. Seriously, how did he smell so much like himself after being engulfed with my scent?

"I disagree. I think we both know one another better than most people in our lives." His voice was almost too low for me to hear. "I'm going to find a word for us. Not strangers, acquaintances, or friends. There's something more, and I'm going to find it."

His promise rang in my ears. The words weren't warm, and they were far from uncaring. And yet, David looked at me as if *I* were the mystery. I stared back, just as desperate to solve our puzzle.

2

THE DARES STARTED SOPHOMORE YEAR, when David and I finally accepted that our lives would continue to overlap, whether we liked it or not. We'd grown up in the same small town, New Harbor. Back then, our classes were barely larger than fifteen students. Teachers sat us next to each other because our last names were Every and Evans.

David had been a loner back then, a quiet, socially awkward kid who built model airplanes and drew comics. Once we'd gotten to high school, he finally had his growth spurt. His voice dropped at least five octaves, and he learned how to talk to people without abruptly leaving the conversation. David earned a spot on the varsity football team, which drew the attention of everyone who loved that sort of thing.

In high school, it was very apparent that David loved getting a rise out of anyone. He had made it his personal mission to find all the wrong buttons to press. My responses to his egging were some of his favorites. I become his go-to. David gravitated toward me without assigned seating. We bickered enough to convince our friends and every other person in our town that we'd repressed some burning desire for one another. Both of us applying and being the only people in our graduating class to go to Westbrooke University didn't help the matter.

After we moved away from home, we'd become the only source of normalcy for one another. Bumping into each other wasn't easy on a large campus like Westbrooke. And yet, we did it with ease. It didn't mean we liked one another. It meant we'd gotten so used to each other's mess that we couldn't untangle ourselves, even if we tried.

Haven was the first person to see the truth: there wasn't any untapped love between David and me.

During our freshman year, she warned me not to engage when she noticed how heated I got in his presence. But I couldn't stand around knowing how far he'd take his contrary, nonsensical opinion without providing pushback.

"Sure, nihilism has its place in society," I ranted to Haven in our kitchen. It might be too early for a philosophical debate, but David's response to my very well-thought-out discussion post had me seething.

After my call with my sister, he'd spent another forty minutes waiting for his clothes to dry. While I had been typing away on my laptop, he'd been typing away on his phone. It wasn't until after he left that I realized he'd crafted a lengthy response to my post on hope in a capitalistic society. His response was three times the required length. He'd picked apart every bit of my argument without so much as an attempt to see my side of things.

"But we're doomed if we think nothing matters," I continued.

Haven stood at the breakfast bar, balancing on one leg while her foot rested on her thigh.

"Doomed might be a strong word. Challenged, maybe," she said in a calm tone. She sipped green juice through a metal straw.

"You're on his side?" I raised a brow. Haven was Ms. Optimism. In her world, everything had a divine purpose. She loved meaning and would insist nothing happened by accident. Everything in the universe was unfolding for your good...*if* your karma was good.

"I'm not on anyone's side." She insisted as she tugged her sisterlocks into a ponytail. Haven's dark brown skin glowed with the shimmery highlight placed carefully on her high cheekbones and the wide bridge of her nose. The bracelets on her wrist jangled like morning bells. Between the comforting scented oil she wore, beautifully glowing skin, and noisy jewelry, it was impossible not to know when she was around.

"I'm just considering his viewpoint. You know, like you say, people should." She gave me a teasing smile.

I scoffed and grabbed my favorite mug. As the coffee machine hummed, I got a protein bar from the pantry to toss into my bag.

"David sees the world with a lot of sharp edges," Haven said.

"And whose fault is that?"

"Circumstances?" She shrugged. "All I'm saying is that it's difficult—and sometimes not even natural — for someone to look on the bright side."

I frowned. "I know that."

"Really? You seem to ignore the possibility. You struggle to extend grace to him — and him only. It makes me wonder..."

"Haven, don't. Just because you were a psych major for a semester doesn't mean you know how to analyze a person's actions properly. Not even professionals can do that."

"Maybe you see yourself in him?" She continued, ignoring my plea.

"Please, can we have one conversation where you're petty like me?" I groaned and stretched across the island to grab her hand, squeezing to emphasize my desperation. Placing my hand over hers reminded me that I kept forgetting to make her ten-step skincare routine a daily practice. My warm brown skin could use a bit of her dewy glow and cloud-like softness.

"Petty ranting is so, so fun. I promise you'll love it." I pulled away to grab the hand lotion in my bag. Being Ms. Go, go, go, didn't mean I had to live a life of dry knuckles.

Haven laughed. "I'm sure it is. But bringing you back to earth is even more fun."

I sighed. The coffee machine clicked, so I turned my attention to something that would go my way this morning. "Fine, whatever. I'm over it."

"Really?"

"For sure." I watched the coffee drip into my cup, its color a perfect creamy brown.

"You're outlining a five-page opposition essay in your head, aren't you?"

I chewed on my lip, ready to deny. Despite only knowing each other since freshman year orientation, Haven and I had become experts at understanding one another's tells.

"Ten-page, actually." I joined her at the island, sitting instead of standing because morning kitchen yoga had never and would never appeal to me.

"But I'm stopping now. The days of letting David Evans make me out to be some raging, argumentative know-it-all are in the past."

"Very recent past," Haven murmured with a smile.

"Besides, I have to be on my best behavior. I represent something bigger."

"Hope?" Haven asked.

"Even better." I pulled out my phone and opened the BWD sign-up form. "Check this out. Here's this year's executive board sign-ups."

Haven whistled, impressed.

"Not exactly overflowing so that we'd have to hold a vote with non-board members," I said, shoulders sagging a bit.

"Oh, how you love your politics." Haven laughed.

"A good debate will feed me for weeks," I agreed. "Regardless, we're going to have an actual team this year. And I have a good feeling about them. They're going to show up and do the work."

"That's incredible." She squeezed my bicep. "I'm proud of you. That marketing push over the summer was brilliant. Thanks to you, we have a full executive board. And though I adore being your all-rounder, I'd like to just crunch the numbers without having to worry about everything else."

Haven joined BWD as treasurer, but as attendance waned and people began to leave, she became my everything. The organization was too buttoned-up and preppy for a woman who dressed in flowy skirts, carried crystals, and communed with her ancestors. But she put on a blazer and pencil skirt for me, and that's when I knew I'd give her the world as soon as I could.

"I even got that one girl from my design class to agree to be our graphic designer," I said.

"That shy girl? Covee?" Haven raised a brow. "You've been trying to get her to talk since freshman year."

"Tell me about it." I sighed, pleased that everything seemed to be coming together.

"So, now that we have an executive board..." Haven looked a little hesitant to ask her question. "Is the ball a go?"

Low ticket sales and the withdrawal of three sponsors caused the cancellation of last year's ball.

I smiled. "I can say we're eighty percent in the clear."

Haven clapped. "Oh my God, I've been waiting for this day."

I laughed. As a former homeschooler, Haven had had no

experience with school dances. This was as close as she was going to get.

"I'm going to hold a vote on themes in a couple of weeks," I said. "Any ideas you want to toss in the ring? I'm thinking gothic or old Hollywood. A couple of the girls wanted Regency or disco."

"Masquerade, please, *please*. I've dreamed of this," she pleaded. "Masks, hidden identity, and falling for a girl I may never know in one night."

"It'll be on the list," I promised. "And we'll let democracy do its work."

I typed 'masquerade' in my notes app, adding it to the long list of ideas I'd gleaned from other board members. Before I could relock my phone, a text from Mr. Thorn In My Side came through.

DAVID

> Don't forget about tonight. A no-show means an automatic forfeit.

I scoffed and responded:

> I know what it means. I made the rule. Why don't you just worry your pretty little face about your part? K?

DAVID

> She thinks I'm pretty. I'm blushing.

The thought of David blushing had me shaking my head. Despite his pale complexion, I'd long ago learned he barely changed shades.

"Hey, don't forget an umbrella today." Haven's warning made me look up from my phone. "It's going to rain, and your hair's too nice to ruin."

I frowned because that wasn't on today's forecast. "You

sure? They said it'd be sunny all day."

"Trust," she said, and wiggled her fingers to emphasize her arthritis. "You don't want that five-hour installation to go to waste."

"Alright, thanks." I tucked my phone into my pocket and grabbed my bag. "I'm off to conquer the world. Do you need anything while I'm at it?"

"Bones of our enemies would make a good broth for tonight." Haven winked.

"Done. I'll see you for dinner."

"Love you," she said.

———

Haven didn't emphasize the rain enough for me. Halfway through the day, it felt like a full-on hurricane was passing through town. Everyone scrambled across campus, trying to get to their destinations without getting soaked to the bone. A few professors even canceled classes for commuters because of flooding on major streets.

I'd accidentally stepped in a deceptively deep puddle after my second class of the day. The water and dirt ruined the bottoms of my beige slacks. I almost cried in the bathroom at how my stain-removing stick wasn't doing anything. It took longer than I'd like to admit for me to calm down and remind myself that dry-cleaning existed for a reason. Pushing away my need to look one hundred percent presentable was a feat that zapped most of my energy.

My initial spark to take on the world this morning faded to a strained ember by the end of the day. So, I didn't exactly feel like showing up for David's dare. Especially when I realized it'd be at a bar...a cowboy-themed bar.

I had a rideshare drop me off in front of Ye-Haw Way a half hour before our meet-up time. The customer demographic seemed diverse enough at first glance. Most who filtered in and out of the building wore cowboy-themed attire. I snapped a photo of the blinking 'giddy on in' welcome sign to send to David. There was slim to no chance Ye-Haw Way wasn't his intended destination. But I still needed to try.

> This the right place?

DAVID

> Congrats. You know how to use a GPS. Do you need help finding the door as well?

I blew out an annoyed breath and grabbed the wooden door handle. After I went through the traditional door, I came to a swinging door that reminded me of old Western bar entryways.

The inside of Ye-Haw Way was loud and packed. I raised a brow at the surprisingly colorful overhead lighting. There was a live band complete with banjo and fiddle players. The lead singer was a woman with dark skin and brown wooden beads at the end of her braids. Her deep voice reminded me of the older women in the choir from my church. She was far younger than they were, but she had an "old spirit" way about her, as she swayed back and forth.

It took me a second to re-focus on my main goal: finding David, finishing his dare, and getting the hell out of here. The place wasn't as unwelcoming as I thought it'd be from the outside. I moved through the crowd easily enough. No one looked at me too weirdly, even though I felt wildly out of place in my business casual.

David sat at the bar. I paused for a second, taking in that his hair was shorter than usual. Whenever the football season was about to start, he'd get a good cut in. He wore his trademark jean jacket, which was fraying at the shoulders and along the sleeves. The cup sitting in front of him was empty, and he stared into the glass like it held the answer to life's greatest mysteries. He glanced up every so often, as if he were looking for something he'd forgotten or needed.

When I finally moved closer, a guy beat me to the punch. He wore the cutest pair of floral cowboy boots, baggy jeans, and a white linen top. He was beautiful with his curly red hair and thick beard. I was close enough to hear that he had a tempting low voice to contrast his sweet exterior.

Most people nearby seemed to have eyes for him. But he didn't seem interested in making eye contact with anyone outside of David.

I didn't blame him. His bright aesthetic would stand in brilliant contrast to David's. They'd be the pairing musicians wrote about: cute, mean guy, adorably sweet guy, and a fairy-tale ending. I lingered back to wait for things to play out.

Their exchange was brief. David didn't look up once during it. His disinterest didn't seem to deflate the guy's ego, though. He still left a piece of paper under David's cup and moved on to join what I presumed were a few friends on the dance floor.

"Not your type?" I teased as I settled onto the stool next to him. "Too good and kind for your damaged soul? Did you not want to taint him and bring him into your misery?"

David didn't look up at my words either. But his mouth twitched, which was more animation than he'd given the guy.

"Didn't come here looking for a type," he said simply and signaled to the bartender for a refill. "I'm seeing someone."

My ears perked up, shocked at this tidbit of information. David and I didn't have conversations about what we got up to outside of our hangouts. We were always too busy trying to wound each other's pride. I'm now considering how many blind spots we must have for each other. It was strange to know someone so well but not know them at all.

"Really? Who's the unfortunate lad, lass, person?" I

winced at my phrasing and the curiosity tangled with it. But it was too difficult not to wonder about his dating life. In reality, the thought of someone being with David romantically seemed impossible. Who'd lack that much self-preservation?

"Lad? Lass?" David snorted. "What are we? Bisexuals or pirates?"

"I'm not opposed to being both," I joked.

David shook his head, smiling a bit. "You really want to know who I'm seeing?"

I scoffed. "I'm not dying for the information or anything."

Though my breath caught a little when he looked at me.

"Good. I can't have your death on my hands. Haven would never forgive me." He finished his drink with no sign that he planned on answering my question. So, he was going to keep this person a secret? Fine by me.

"Let's get this over with," I said. Suddenly, the warmth of the building wasn't comforting anymore. I wanted to be back out in the rain because the cold felt more welcoming than whatever was going on between us. Like David said last night, there was no word for our relationship. Tonight, that didn't sit well with me.

"Sure, you don't want a drink first?" David stood from his stool but didn't move from the bar.

I slipped off my seat too. At six feet, David was a few inches taller than I was. I was used to being the tallest person in most rooms (which didn't say much, considering five nine wasn't exactly *super* tall). Still, I found it odd to have to tilt my head to meet someone's gaze.

Tonight, David smelled of whisky, and his eyes almost matched the color of it. The warm overhead lights were doing wonders in smoothing out his harsh features.

"I don't drink," I forced out in a stern tone.

The softer David looked, the tougher I felt I needed to be.

"A disappointment." He sighed, feigning sadness. "Drunk Yara might actually be fun to hang with."

"If I were such a chore to hang around, you wouldn't be blowing up my phone every other day," I countered.

His expression changed. For a second, I thought I had made a decent shot.

"Correct me if I'm wrong," he said in a voice that indicated he never once believed that was a possibility. "But you're the one who started texting me."

My jaw tightened as I remembered our first back and forth when we'd gotten to campus. I'd been at rock bottom, and he'd been familiar.

"Why are we here, David?" I asked instead of going down that rabbit hole with him. My boots were too wet to be comfortable, and the ends of my twists were still dripping water onto the back of my blouse. I need a warm shower, a cup of coffee, and a crappy reality TV show to veg out on immediately.

"Follow me." He pushed away from the bar with a dark smile that sent a spark through my veins. This spark didn't feel as ominous as it usually did...In fact, it kind of felt exciting.

What the hell was there to be excited about in David's presence?

"Hope you remember rule number two," I called after him. The place had gotten harder to navigate. I bumped into a few people as I tried to keep up with him. It looked like the band was switching out. A guy with a charming grin took the place of the soulful singer from before. His opening word to the crowd was 'howdy.' I started at the roaring response it received.

"Of course I remember," David tossed the words over his shoulder. "You remind me every time. You really that scared?"

"Truly," I had to yell over the crowd to confirm.

After our first few dares, we came up with a set of rules

neither of us could break. First, never dare one another to do something illegal. No stealing from stores, committing fraud, yada yada. Occasional trespassing might be acceptable, depending on the context.

Rule number two: we couldn't dare one another to do something that could physically harm ourselves or others.

Rule number three: Dares couldn't be sexual. No daring to hug, kiss, or sleep with someone...or each other.

As we neared his destination, my stomach dropped, and my mind immediately went to rule two. I said as much out loud, which earned me a laugh from David.

"You're not going to hurt yourself," David said as soon as the current rider on the mechanical bull fell off headfirst. They rolled off the padding, rubbing their neck.

"Well...as long as you hold on or fall with grace," he added with a shrug.

I took in the large, brown-saddled bull. Every part of me twisted at the thought of mounting that thing. My clothes would get more wrinkled than they were currently. And my twists would whip in every direction. I swallowed at the thought of how ridiculous I'd look. When I glanced at David, he was looking back at me with a smile. He knew. He knew I wasn't just scared of falling. David understood how much I adored looking put together and in control of every aspect of my appearance. He knew how ridiculous this would make me look and feel. He had found the perfect activity to ensure maximum embarrassment and discomfort. Payback for the fountain slip.

"I didn't dare you to get in the water." I crossed my arms over my chest.

"I know. But I am daring you to get on the bull... or, are you putting an end to this once and for all?"

The first one of us to refuse a dare meant the game was

over, and that person owed the other person anything. Anything on David's terms was dangerous.

"Absolutely not," I snapped and pulled a hair tie from my pocket. He watched with a smug look on his face as I unbuttoned the sleeves of my silk top and rolled them up.

"Just be happy I'm not setting a time limit," he said. "Originally, I wanted you up there for at least a minute."

I rolled my eyes. "Oh, thank you for your benevolence."

"For you? Always."

"Who's next?" The operator called, looking around the crowd for a willing participant.

I squared my shoulders, cracked my knuckles, and declared, "Me."

"You?" The operator's eyebrow lifted. He readjusted his cowboy hat as if he were having trouble seeing me. "Are you sure, sweetheart?"

I scoffed at the overly familiar pet name. "More sure than you'll be if you call me that again."

The operator chuckled and opened the gate for me. "My apologies... Miss."

As I crossed the threshold, the operator called out, "Alrighty, here's how it's gonna go, you control how fast this is. If you're good, you signal me a thumbs up. Stop's a thumbs down."

"Inventive," I said under my breath.

"Unless a yell or scream comes first," he joked. "Just give whatever you can."

"You can count on it," I promised.

"You should try for the record. Maybe you'll surprise yourself," David called in a mocking tone once I stepped onto the padding. I had to take my boots off. My wet socks squeaked against the plastic underneath me.

"And what's that?" I played along even though there was

no way in hell I'd stay on this thing for more than a millisecond.

"Seven minutes." David gestured to the clock behind me, pointing to the record time beneath the current timer. "You get free drinks for a year."

"Well, in that case..." I gripped the handlebars near the "head" of the bull and wrapped my arm around its "body." With a deep breath, I pushed myself up to swing my leg over. The operator was polite enough to look the other way, hiding his laugh. David? Not so much.

"Might want to use the stirrup." David rested his elbows on the wooden gate surrounding the bull. He looked entirely too entertained. The only thing missing was a bucket of popcorn.

My cheeks burned when I noticed the very convenient stirrup. I didn't know how I had overlooked it before. Maybe it was the nerves coursing through my veins, or that David hadn't torn his gaze from me once. I was approaching full-panic mode.

With a determined inhale, I gave myself a quick mini pep talk. In moments of doubt, I imagined myself to be someone else. And tonight, I needed to be a rough-and-tumble Yara—a girl who rolled with the punches and mounted bulls like a champ.

My second attempt at the bull went much smoother. I yelped in celebration, tossing both arms in the air like I was a ref calling a touchdown. A few people nearby clapped for me, too. My business-casual attire had garnered attention. Could a cubicle worker stay on a bull longer than a seasoned rider? Stay tuned to find out.

David gave me a clap, too. It was slow and mocking, matching the glint in his eyes. He was so ready for my fall.

"All good?" the operator asked when I finally stopped squirming around to find a decent position.

"Not much traction," I complained, mostly to myself.

"That's the point," David reminded me.

The operator chuckled and nodded in agreement. "You ready to start?"

"One sec." I held my middle finger up to David. He laughed and returned the gesture. "Okay, now I'm good to go."

The machine kicked into motion. Despite the slow, steady back-and-forth at the beginning, I squealed enough for the operator to ask repeatedly if I wanted to stop.

"No, no!" I gripped the strap so tight I thought my wrist might pop out of the socket. "I can do this."

Somewhere along the line, I decided I was genuinely going to try for the record. Yes, I had a bad habit of being one of the densest women in the world. But when push came to shove, I always went big before going home.

A few onlookers whistled and cheered for me when they realized I hadn't gone flying off the bull in the first second. Instinctively, my legs tightened, and my body moved in rhythm with the rocking. I was moving too fast to make out anyone, least of all David. But I knew he was still watching and waiting.

The operator asked if I wanted to go up a notch, and I gave him a thumbs-up. Bad idea.

My neck whipped around enough that I knew I'd feel soreness in the morning. And my ass cheeks... God, I thought my upper body would get most of the workout during this process.

As expected, I felt like a fool on this silly machine. Had to look like one, too. Was there any way to look good on a bull? There had to be some kind of technique because the up and down appeared erotic when I'd watched clips of people doing this in the past.

Once again, the operator asked if I wanted to go up a

notch. I gave him another thumbs up, and my hand barely went back down before I got thrown onto the mat.

Thankfully, I landed on my side and not my head. The impact was hard enough to knock the wind out of me. My small crowd cheered. I stayed flat on my back, not moving for a second as my brain caught up with my body.

"You okay, miss?" the operator asked, sounding concerned, but it was David who joined me on the mat.

His head appeared over mine. I got an upside-down view of his face. He placed his hands on either side of my head, leaning in to get a better look at me. The worry in his eyes was new. It bloomed, traveling to his jaw, tightening the muscles. I have invoked many emotions in David over the years. Mainly those that sparked arguments and fueled grudges. But this emotion looked ready to trigger an apology session. A plea for forgiveness. Even some groveling.

"You going to help me up? Or did you just need a good excuse to gawk up close and personal?" I reached out my hand, trying to see if this new mood would stick around. Maybe my near-death experience would make him finally offer me a kind word.

David stared at my outstretched palm as if it were poisonous. His worry melted into nothingness when he saw my smile.

"Get up," he ordered in a hard voice. "You're holding up the line."

I scowled and pushed myself into a sitting position. Sure enough, people willingly queued up to get yanked around until their brains rattled. I fumbled my way off the mat, nearly tripping when I realized how dizzy I felt. My boots were gone from the spot I left them. The operator nudged his chin toward David, who was a few paces away.

"Nice work. Nowhere near record level but..." The operator shrugged and handed me a drink voucher. There was a number written on the back of it. "This one's on me."

The wink he gave me before I left went straight to my head. I guess I didn't look too foolish on the bull.

"You know what?" I said as soon as I caught up with David.

He raised a brow as if he couldn't care less. My boots were in his hands, and I left them there for the time being, enjoying the idea of having a personal caddy for the night.

"I think I'm going to have that drink," I said, waving my voucher in his face. "Got to celebrate my victory after all."

David looked unimpressed but still said, "Fine. After you."

3

"IT WAS ONLY FORTY-FIVE SECONDS," David said. "Relax, Daredevil."

He sipped on another whisky while I tried a bourbon, a la *The Vampire Diaries*... it didn't taste as good as a vampire made it look.

"Don't be such a bad sport." I set my drink down, giving up on it. "Just admit you thought you were going to get me with that one."

"I did get you."

"How so?" I laughed and pointed back at the mechanical bull. "I not only got on that thing for the first time, but stayed on for nearly a minute. Come on, even you have to admit that's impressive."

David snorted before finishing his drink. He had that look he usually got when he used to get up and leave a conversation at a moment's notice. I used to play a game with myself: how long could I make David Evans remain interested? I consistently beat everyone I knew.

"What's more impressive was your face," he said.

When I frowned, confused, he pulled out his phone and

36

opened his camera roll. My ears burned, and my stomach dropped when he clicked play on his newest video.

"You've got to be kidding me." I reached for the phone only to stumble when he held it out of reach. "Why did you record that?"

He chuckled at my high-pitched panic voice. "Thought it might come in handy one day."

"Delete it," I ordered.

From the few seconds of the video I saw, my appearance was much more disheveled than I initially thought. Oil from my twists had dripped onto my shirt, leaving massive yellow stains. Smudges of mascara on my eyelids highlighted the terror in my eyes. I looked like I was a raccoon on the run from an angry mob of homeowners who were tired of me digging through their trash.

"I don't think so." David locked his phone and slid it into his back pocket. I scowled at the unreachable, off-limits position. Even if I were brave enough to touch this guy's ass, I still wouldn't know how to unlock the phone.

"I will end you," I threatened with a narrowed gaze. I tried to stand taller so that at least the top of my head met his chin.

"You've been saying that for years now." His brown eyes danced. "Love to see you try."

He ate up my fury. Practically lived off my disapproval.

"Screw you," I grumbled and grabbed my drink. I finished it in two big gulps. It burned my throat and left my taste buds in agony. David chuckled when I coughed and waved the bartender down for a glass of water.

"I see why you don't drink," David noted as I fanned myself in an admittedly dramatic manner. As soon as the bartender set down the water, I nearly drowned myself. Some of it dripped down the corners of my mouth. I suppose I'd given up all attempts at grace and poise tonight. My mother would be so proud.

"After spending so much time in your presence, I'm thinking it's a necessity." I wiped my mouth with the back of my hand. "See why you do it so much. It's a shame you can't take a break from yourself."

Instead of throwing a jab back, David said, "Put your shoes on. I'm ready to go. I'll take you back to campus."

He nudged over the boots he'd been guarding for me. My shoulders sagged when I thought about slipping back into the damp leather. He noticed my reluctance but figured it was for the wrong reason.

"You prefer ordering a rideshare?" he asked. "Because I don't care either way. I just thought I'd offer."

"No, no rideshare," I said quickly. "You're the lesser of two evils."

"Lucky me," he said in a dry tone. "So, let's get a move on."

When I didn't move, he added, "What's wrong?"

"Nothing." I reached for my uncomfortable boots. "I just hate wet socks in wet shoes."

Before I could pick them up, David beat me to the punch. My brows furrowed as he grabbed a handful of napkins and stuffed them into the boot. He pulled out the napkins after a few seconds and then stuffed them in the other shoe. David repeated the process three more times before unlacing the boots and laying them before me.

He said nothing as he pushed away from the bar and started toward the exit. I hurried, not even having time to tie the laces as I tried to catch up properly. When he noticed I was lagging, he slowed down, and once we reached the doors, he motioned for me to sit on a stool.

"What are you...?" I asked, trailing off when he kneeled to tie my shoes. He pulled the laces tight, knotting them firm enough so they wouldn't come undone easily.

Was he being... considerate? I hesitated to call it anything positive because David always thought three steps ahead. He'd helped me with my shoes for a reason. And that reason might be something I didn't figure out until a few weeks from now.

No, I decided. What he did hadn't been considerate. It'd been the groundwork for a long game. And I'd be ready for whatever he had in store.

The rain drizzled when we stepped out of the bar. The wind had picked up a bit. A chill seeped through my shirt, raising goosebumps on my skin. I hugged myself while shifting my weight from one foot to the other. David paused on the sidewalk, looking toward the parking lot.

"What's the hold-up?" I asked after a beat. "Go get your car."

He looked at me, confusion making his brow knit. "You're not coming?"

"I'm soaked from head to toe in wet shoes," I said. "The least you could do is be a gentleman and bring the car up."

David blinked, his confusion evolving into amusement. "You want me to be a gentleman?"

"It's all I dream of," I said deadpan. "Is that a foreign concept for you? Perhaps a new vocab word? I know how much you football players love skipping classes. I tutor for a small fee, you know?"

He laughed, his eyes wrinkled around the corners as he offered me a rare, genuine smile. I stopped shivering at the sight of it. He looked sweet, like someone I could curl up next to and receive soothing back rubs while they told me how much I meant to them.

"You're so irritating," David said, interrupting my fantasy as soon as I constructed it. He pulled out his car keys.

"Took the words right out of my mouth," I said, and gestured him toward the parking lot like I was dismissing him from class. I watched him jog off into the darkness. As soon as I lost sight of him in the rows of cars, the rain picked up. The drops sounded louder on the concrete, almost like hail.

I waited on the sidewalk for what felt like ages. A few times, some people came out of the bar only to see the downpour and hurried back inside. When David's car didn't pull up for a while, I considered that he might have left me.

He's not that *rude*, I told myself. But honestly, who was I kidding? David had disappeared on even his closest friends in their time of need. With that thought, I pulled out my phone.

Just as I was about to order a ride, David pulled up in front of me. I blew out a breath, thankful I wouldn't have to pay for two rides tonight. Since my parents changed my weekly allowance to a monthly one, my cash flow has been on the lighter side.

"Took you long enough," I grumbled as I slid into the passenger's seat. A thick towel was draped across the seat, and the heat was on full blast.

David's only response was a grunt. He waited for me to settle in before pulling away from the curb. I checked my email as he headed to the highway. He didn't turn on the radio, so the silence between us felt like rising water.

Naturally, his car smelled of him. All spicy and cool with a hint of mint. He kept his dashboard spotless. The black would sparkle if the soft material reflected any light. He'd hung two of those tree-shaped car fresheners on the rearview mirror. His scent of choice was Summer Linen.

Other than the fresheners, there were no personal touches in David's ride. No leftover receipts in the cup holders or discarded sweatshirts in the backseat. I was acutely aware of all the space. Absence told just as much of a story as clutter did. But one had to look much more closely to figure out the details of the story. I didn't have the patience to look closer. I needed some other clues.

My gaze turned to his radio. I wondered if he had pretuned stations. Surely his taste in music would tell me more about him than his cleaning habits could.

"Don't touch it," he said in a firm voice when I reached for the volume knob.

I frowned, hand frozen in the air. "It's quiet."

"What's wrong with the quiet?"

"It's awkward."

"Not to me." He flicked on his signal before merging onto a ramp. Before switching lanes, David checked his side mirror and then looked over his shoulder to be sure no one was in his blind spot. I bit my tongue, trying not to cite how dangerous it was to glance over his shoulder. Being a backseat driver was something I'd been actively working on since I got so many complaints about riding with Haven.

I could barely make out David's expression in the night's darkness. The streetlights cast a blue glow on us. The color made him look like someone from a Van Gogh painting. His wet hair, curlier than usual, stuck to his forehead. He was all swirls, blurred edges, and muted colors. I watched a raindrop slide down the bridge of his sharp nose. As soon as he caught me staring, I whipped my gaze out the window.

"Very awkward," I insisted in a mumble.

"That's because you're making it."

"I'm not making this awkward. You're not playing music. Most people play something in the car when they have company."

"That's because most people are like you, afraid of being uncomfortable for even a second." He opened his console and pulled out a dry washcloth.

My brow raised when he offered it to me.

"Your hair's dripping all over my seat. I just got it steam-washed a few days ago," David said, nudging the cloth closer to me.

I took it and grabbed a handful of twists to dry. "It's kind of your fault."

"My fault?" He shook his head. "Oh, I'm going to love hearing the logic behind this one. What is it? Do I control the weather now?"

"Probably did some kind of blood sacrifice." I used the remaining dry part of the towel to wipe my neck.

"You got me. The cat's out of the bag now."

I snorted. "Anyway, you can make it up to me."

"Which is all I ever want to do in life."

"My executive board and I need a ride to the beach this weekend."

He started shaking his head before I even finished the sentence.

"I wouldn't ask if I could get someone else," I add quickly. "But Haven's car broke down last week. It's still in the shop."

"I'm not taking you and your org on a joyride."

"It's not a joyride; it's for our new headshots," I defended. "And it won't be the whole org. Just the four of us. Our secretary has a car but can't take everyone without making multiple trips."

"What happened to your car?"

"What car?"

His forehead wrinkled. "You don't have a car? Doesn't your family own like half of our town?"

"Just a couple of local businesses." I waved my hand. "And that doesn't equate to having a car...especially when I don't have a license."

"Huh?"

I made a face and repeated louder, "I don't have a license."

"You don't have your license?" he asked in shock. "After we've moved hundreds of miles away from home to a large commuter school, you don't have your license?"

"It's on the to-do list."

"My God, for how long?"

"Can we get back to the topic at hand?"

He laughed. "Sure. Lucky for you, I heard the school's bus route takes you halfway there."

I scowled. "I know that. But the other half is just highway. No bus stop for miles."

David nudged his chin to my feet. "Better wear walking shoes next time."

I pressed my molars together, leaning back in my seat as I brainstormed other options. If we all chipped in, we could rent a car for the day. But the under-25 insurance fee would be a nuisance.

As my mind buzzed, I latched onto something that made me slowly smile. David sensed my change of mood in a heartbeat.

"Shit," he mumbled under his breath.

"I have your next dare," I taunted with a grin and paused for dramatic effect.

David motioned for me to continue. "Go on then."

"I dare you to be an honorable BWD member this weekend."

He looked unimpressed. "That sounds impossible."

I shook my head. "Not at all. Our group isn't exclusive. We're focused on the development of Black women on campus, but are welcoming to allies."

David glanced at me. "Honorable member means...?"

"Help prep and attend any events. And what do you know, we have one this weekend!"

"Yay," he mock-cheered. "Exactly how I wanted to spend my day off."

I smiled. "This will be perfect. You'll pick us up in the library parking lot at eight."

"Nine," he bartered. "There's a team run at seven. I need time to shower."

"Fine. Nine," I agreed with a sigh and mentally recalculated the schedule. "I expect you to bring a great attitude. My members must meet a high standard. I'll expect no different from you."

"You realize you've just invited me on a day trip, right? The nearest beach is two hours away. And that's without traffic."

My forehead wrinkled. "Of course I know that..."

David smiled at me. Seeing the smug curl of his lips made me rethink what I'd gotten myself into.

"What are you... what's the problem?" I asked, knowing he wouldn't share but hoping there was some sense of kindness left in his cold, little heart.

"No problem. I'm just looking forward to spending some extra time with you," he said. "Have you ever realized we only ever hang out at night?"

"I suppose. It's the only time we're free," I said, trying to suss out where he was going with this.

David nodded, humming in agreement. "Guess you're right. It'll be nice to see you in daylight, though."

"I don't see how that's going to change anything."

"It does, Daredevil," he said. "Trust me, it does."

4

I WAS the first to arrive at the agreed meet-up spot for my org. I stepped into the library as the sun barely peeked over the horizon. Though the cafe wasn't open, the seating area was. The scent of coffee lingered in the air from late-night orders. The cafe's walls were sandy white, and the tile was a few shades darker. It required focus not to slip each time my heels came in contact with the freshly mopped floor. I slowed my pace, doing my best not to face-plant before getting to one of the plush yellow couches. As soon as I sat down, I opened my laptop to get some work done.

As always, I knew precisely which girls would show up first. My VP, Indie Layne, came into the cafe, claiming the seat next to me. Her outfit was a toned-down version of mine: a nice, frilly top, a cream blazer, and dark-wash jeans. Indie's skin was a deep shade of dark brown. Her round cheeks were aglow with her signature purple blush. She wore black hearing aids to help with her progressive hearing loss. Indie was over six feet tall, with thick thighs and a round belly. She'd grown up as a beauty pageant queen who spent her last two years of high school being homeschooled while modeling in New

York. We'd all been excited to find out she guest-starred in some TV shows we'd watched growing up. Hellish was the only word she used to describe her experience. She had no interest in delving into behind-the-scenes stories, so we all stopped asking for them a long time ago.

"It's weirdly burning out," Indie noted as she pulled her black goddess braids into a loose ponytail.

"The season flip-flops around here," I said. "Can't decide if it wants to be fall or not."

She frowned in disapproval. "If that's the case, are you sure we shouldn't start in our shorts?"

I shook my head, only looking up from the document I was editing for a second. "Nope. I want to get the business casual out of the way. We need as much morning light as possible for the headshots. Plus, the casual photos aren't a priority."

"I suppose you're right." Indie blew out a breath and fanned herself. No matter how hot she claimed to get, she never broke a sweat. It was a trick I'm convinced she learned during her pageant days. One day, I was going to get it out of her.

Haven joined us next. She'd tucked her locs into a loose bun and wore one of my pencil skirts. The wince on her face when she tried to sit down in it made me equally sorry and amused.

"You look great," I offered and tossed my cardigan over for her legs. She was used to showing off her toned arms but typically hid her equally toned legs under tiered skirts. The hint of calf made her self-conscious.

"How do you always walk so fast in these?" she asked.

"It's in the hips and the stride," I said.

"Got to take quick baby steps," Indie suggested as she started filing her nails. "It helps you fall into a rhythm."

"Morning, everyone." Our last addition, Covee Bailey,

greeted us as if this were our first time meeting. She was a tall girl (only an inch or so shorter than Indie) with golden brown skin, wide hips, and a soft belly. Her tight, thick coils were braided into a crown. Covee was quiet in a polite way. Gentle in everything from her sweet smile to how she handled her role as our social media manager. In our group chat, she always asked everyone involved whether they were comfortable with how they looked in the image before posting. And if not, she found another shot. When that didn't work, she brought her editing skills to the table. I wanted the chance to get to know her better, but she had an invisible force field up. A strict line she wouldn't let anyone cross over. Covee was happy doing most of this college thing on her own. I admired that.

"How was your study date last night?" Indie asked.

I looked up to see who the question was for. There was no way in hell Haven had a date without telling me.

Covee's brow twitched, but she managed to regain a neutral expression in the blink of an eye. "Study date?"

"With that tall blond guy I told to fuck off before you gave me the green light," Indie prompted, holding her hand above her head to indicate height. "From our design class."

Covee remained silent, looking slightly confused.

"I saw you two in the library." Indie shrugged and smiled. "Looked pretty cozy and cute together."

"Are you talking about Weston Briggs? The guy on all those posters in the student center?" Haven chimed in with a furrowed brow. "I tutored him last year in Spanish."

Indie snapped her fingers and nodded. "That's him! The quarterback with that tattoo sleeve that matches those other players... Do you think they're in a cult?"

"Who?" Haven asked.

"Weston and the others with the sleeve."

Haven laughed. "Of course they are. They're on the football team."

I itched to shut my laptop and join in the conversation. But I'd made a rule for myself as soon as I became the president of BWD: I wouldn't get buddy-buddy with the girls while we were in org mode.

I needed to be someone they looked up to and trusted to lead. You don't trust a sitting president if they spent all night partying next to you. You don't trust the boss who spent their morning gossiping with the rest of the co-workers around the water cooler.

"I didn't go on a date with Weston Briggs," Covee promised quietly and then gracefully changed the subject. "Were you guys able to see my scheduled post? Any objections to the caption?"

Indie sighed, disappointed she hadn't gotten any morning drama. But she should know better than to source her entertainment from our most private member.

"The caption is brilliant," Haven assured. "As always."

"No notes," Indie agreed and then glanced at her phone. "Who are we waiting for again? I thought Emmy and the others had headed out?"

Emmy Jackson was our secretary and our photographer (for the day). She'd picked up the board members who lived on her side of campus and had already started toward the beach a half hour ago.

"Our ride should be here any minute now." I dug into my bag to retrieve a few manila folders. "If you're bored, you can run through next week's agenda with me."

Indie eyed the folders. "I'm not bored. I'm having the time of my life. Don't I look it?"

Laughing, Haven shook her head and accepted the folders from me, passing them to Covee and Indie.

"We should use this time to be productive," I said when Covee and Indie hesitantly glanced at their pages. "We don't have much time to prepare for the semester's first meeting."

"Didn't we talk about the benefits of slow mornings last year?" Indie mused.

Covee hummed, softly adding, "I was in charge of that discussion. Lots of merits."

"Merits left, right, and center," Indie agreed.

"I *was* looking forward to gradually working my way into a road trip kind of mood," Haven said.

I glared at her. If anyone were going to be on my side, it'd be her.

Haven shrugged. "I made a playlist and everything."

"I made one too." Indie tossed her folder onto the coffee table. "Send me the link. We can make a mashup. You don't have any boy bands, do you?"

"What's wrong with boy bands?" Covee wondered.

"Ladies, come on," I interrupted. Witnessing them continually get off track this early in the morning — when they were supposed to be at their most alert — gave me concern for later on. "Let's focus on what we're here to do. The music can wait. Besides, I doubt David will let us play anything."

"You got David to agree to drive us?" Haven laughed, impressed. "What'd that cost you?"

"His usual rate, a piece of my soul," I said.

"So this one's sneaking between bookshelves with the quarterback," Indie gestured to Covee.

"I'm not..." Covee murmured, unable to make eye contact.

"And this one's–" Indie pointed at me "—Got the tight end chauffeuring her around the city. You two are way better than me. You wouldn't be able to get me to shut up if I had half as interesting a love life."

"Love life's a stretch," Covee murmured as she kept her gaze averted.

"David and love in the same sentence is a stretch," I added with a scoff.

"Oh, come on," Indie said to me. "How long are you going to pretend that's not your man?"

I raise a brow. "Excuse me? In what world would David ever be my man?"

David and I were positive and negative charges, pinned together due to coincidence and a small town's dwindling population.

"You should see them for more than a couple of minutes together," Haven came to my defense. "Their back and forth gives me the migraine of a mother of five under five."

"Hm." Indie studied me for a moment and shook her head. "I don't know; I'm usually pretty good at these things. I used to read palms, you know? That was my special talent. The only thing I actually enjoyed about being on stage."

"No shit?" Haven scooted to the end of her seat, holding her hand out to Indie. "Do me!"

Covee leaned forward in her seat, too, curious but too cautious to ask for a turn.

I sighed, feeling a mix of relief and acceptance when I realized they wouldn't follow our agenda. Hey, as long as the topic of David was out, I didn't mind.

"You guys?" Covee's quiet voice cut through Indie's musing about life lines and future love matches. "I think he's here."

I turned to see David getting out of his car with his phone in hand. His hair was still wet from his shower, drops trailing down his neck and onto his collar. Even from afar, I could see the clenching of his sharp jaw. He pressed his lips together as he typed something into his phone. My phone buzzed. I didn't have to look to know it was a snarky text about my needing to hurry. I lingered in my seat while the girls gathered their things to head to the door.

My lag in response wasn't because I wanted to annoy him — not this time, anyway. No, I didn't move instantly because of how the sun caught in his hair, making the brown appear almost golden. I smiled a little at how his eyes glared when the rays hit him, like he was suspicious that the heat was out to get him. His chest rose and fell in a sigh. He ducked back into his car for a quick second and came back out with a pair of sunglasses balanced on his nose. Strangely, the glasses made him seem less intimidating and like someone who would kindly give directions or patiently point out an untied shoe.

"Hey, you ready, Prez?" Indie asked from the cafe's entry-way. She gave me a knowing smile that practically sang *'your man, your man'.*

I tore my gaze away from David, cheeks ablaze. "Of course! Let's get this show on the road."

5

DAVID not only let the girls play their music but also accepted their request with an easy, charming, "Of course."

I nearly choked on my tongue when he opened the door for them, offered to carry their things to his trunk, and patiently helped Indie link her phone to his car's Bluetooth. She struggled during the process, so David turned off his engine to ensure she was connecting to the correct system.

"Someone's had their coffee this morning," I mumbled once we were finally on the road.

Haven did, in fact, have boy bands on her playlist. But Indie didn't object. And without David's usual griping, we listened to bubblegum pop anthems while we sped down the highway. Indie and Haven sang along. In the rearview mirror, I caught Covee smiling at them and mouthing along whenever the chorus came around.

David pulled his gaze away from the road for a second to look at me. "I don't drink coffee, remember?"

He rested his elbow on the console, coming a bit too close to pressing his bare arm against my blazer sleeve. The car smelled of him, warm and fresh with a hint of mint. His face was clean-shaven. The aftershave he wore was new, with a calming scent that encouraged closer inspection. My stomach clenched when I realized I had noticed a minor change in his routine. I tugged my hands in my lap, forcing myself to think of anything other than wanting to press my nose against his cheek.

"Well, something has put you in a good mood," I said in a dry voice.

He smiled. "You pissed at me already, Daredevil? It's only 9 a.m."

"I'm not pissed." I glanced at the rearview to see if our conversation was being too disruptive. The heartthrob's loud singing and Indie's failed attempts to teach the girls harmonizing kept them from noticing my conversation with David.

"Something's got your lips puckered." David chuckled when I instantly relaxed my mouth. "You told me to bring my best attitude, so here I am. Now, you have a problem with my good mood?"

"I don't have a problem."

"Then why are you holding a fist? You look ready to throw a punch."

I let out a breath and unfolded my fingers. David's gaze lingered on my hand. He went quiet, distracted as he watched me flex my fingers. The car in the lane to our left merged in front of us. David nearly grazed their bumper since he'd been looking at me. One of the girls yelped once he slammed on the brakes, jerking us all forward. His arm reached out to act as a bar, keeping me from getting thrown against the dashboard. His fingers burned on my skin. David's touch was an oven radiating obscene heat. He clutched my arm as if I'd slipped off the edge of a cliff, like he'd be more than willing to fall off with me before letting me go.

"That was close. Are you good?" Indie asked him, her

hands braced on our headrests, knees shoved into the back of the console.

David nodded, mouth barely opening as he said, "Fine. You guys?"

"We'll live." Haven fanned herself, trying to calm down.

"This time," Indie muttered, and they all tightened their seatbelts in unison, as if it were a practiced action.

David chuckled. There was a hitch in the sound, a hint of uncharacteristic anxiety.

The girls eventually calmed down enough to sing again when another song came on. I cleared my throat after a beat when David's protective hold lingered on me. He snatched his hand away when he realized. A hint of red crept up his neck. The fingers that'd been holding onto me flexed a bit before returning to the steering wheel.

"Are you...are you okay?" he asked in a low voice only I could hear. He sounded almost shy, and his gaze remained glued to the road.

"All good," I promised in a voice even lower than his had been. I glanced down at my arm, expecting I'd find evidence of his hand on me: an outline or imprint. There was nothing, of course. No sign he'd ever crossed an unspoken threshold and touched me.

For people who'd known one another since middle school, I could count on one hand how many times we'd touched. Each one was an accident. Brushed fingers while walking side by side. Mashed shoulders in crowded rooms. Never intentional. Never lingered.

"Always ready to throw the first punch," David said, trying to restart our normal conversation after his not-so-normal protective grip.

His husky tone attached to a part of me that needed comfort. I closed my eyes for a second, recalling Haven's meditation chants to center myself. This upcoming semester was going to be stressful for me. It made perfect sense that my mind would go to reach for some kind of relief. But David wasn't that relief.

"I'd never punch someone," I said. "I'm not going to start with you."

"Not physically," he agreed. "But verbally, you swing like an MMA fighter on steroids."

My laugh made David glance away from the road again to study me. He didn't linger, already having learned his lesson from before. But he took in enough of me to make it feel like I'd given him something when he looked away.

"Verbal punches are your specialty." I unbuttoned my blazer. It was high time I settled into the ride and stopped sweating.

"Maybe," he agreed. "But there's no denying you can keep up."

I mock-gasp. "Is that admiration in David Evans' tone? Admiration for little ol' me?"

He smiled. "Don't get your hopes up, Daredevil. It takes a lot more than a little back and forth for me to admire you."

"You keep telling yourself that. But it doesn't take a genius to see I've already done more than enough to garner your admiration."

"That so?"

"Yeah, otherwise you'd have stopped these dares a long time ago. You're entangled with me till graduation," I said. Or longer? Could we keep this up when we inevitably went our separate ways? This was the first time I had considered it, and an odd tightening in my chest made me frown.

"Entangled," he repeated as if he were tasting the word for the first time. "Now that's a good one. Closer to what we are to each other. But not enough. Not just right. But we're getting there."

———

WHEN WE FINALLY ARRIVED AT the beach, Emmy and the others were already there. David parked beside them, and we climbed out of the car, stretching our arms and complaining about our numb legs.

"How was the drive?" Emmy asked when I joined her side. She'd done the big chop and dyed it red the first week of the semester. The new look was courtesy of a brief post-breakup identity crisis. The only makeup she wore was a hint of blue eyeliner. Emmy was a short, curvy, doe-eyed woman who never shied away from saying what was on her mind and only occasionally regretted it afterward.

"That good?" Emmy teased when I blew out a breath. She held out a paper bag of dried mangoes. I grabbed a handful.

"We almost got into an accident," I said loud enough for David to hear.

He stood at the trunk of his car, helping the girls unload. My salty declaration made him scoff, and he said, "We got here in one piece, didn't we?"

"Nice to see we're all in good spirits." Emmy snapped a few quick photos of our pissed expressions. Then, in a voice low enough for only me to hear, she said, "So, I scoped out a few locations last weekend. I think I have the perfect spot for headshots, and six options for group photos. Maybe we could take some candid ones on the walk over, too? The sky's perfect today, so natural lighting's going to be incredible."

"Whatever you prefer is what we do." The best thing about being on BWD was being a part of this team. My girls– though chaotic–rose to the occasion. I'd trust them with my over-priced planner any day.

Emmy fidgeted with her camera strap. She only ever chewed on her lip when the camera hung around her neck.

Otherwise, she was all full-steam ahead, listening to the sound of no other drum but her own.

"Okay..." She pressed her lips together as she scanned the shoreline. Instinct told me to jump in. Map out a clear route for the day because heaven knew I'd already done so a million times the night before. But all my ideas were deep in the Plan C territory. If three semesters of leadership taught me anything, it was when to back off. The act didn't come without a fight. In fact, my lips quivered with unspoken orders.

Emmy was more than capable of leading this shoot. Her past relationship had stolen her self-belief. What good was BWD for, if not to help her take it back?

"I don't know," she whispered with a look asking for guidance.

I shook my head and smiled. "You do know, you just told me, and it sounded perfect."

Emmy's shoulders relaxed, but the tension in her brow lingered.

The girls were already complaining about their heels and polyester skirts. With a loud clap, I gained everyone's attention and directed them toward the boardwalk.

"We're going to make this as smooth as possible while still having a little fun," I promised with a smile. I always loved photo day at school. My mom used each one as an excuse to dress my sisters, my brother, and me up in our Sunday best. Even though the skirts constantly itched and my braids were too tight, dressing up never failed to make me feel like I was home.

Emmy led the trek down the wooden staircase to the beach. Once on the sand, most of us removed our shoes. I looked around for David and found him talking to Indie. He wasn't exactly smiling, but the smoothness of his brow was atypical. I ignored the clench in my chest and pushed aside the *'how dare he have fun doing a task that's supposed to be akin to torture'* feeling.

I said I wanted him to be an "honorable member." Talking to the girls was a good thing. Not frowning was a good thing. And hey, maybe he'd learn some manners from Indie... or some patience from Covee... or some chill from Haven. If anyone could smooth out that asshole's hard edges, it'd be those three.

I hurried to catch up with Emmy, who was already snapping photos of us walking through the sand.

"All good?" she asked in a distracted voice as she got a shot of Haven splashing Covee with water. She took shots quickly, as if she were afraid even blinking would make her miss the perfect moment.

I bit my tongue, forcing myself to swallow a command for the girls to stay out of the water so they remained dry. Toeing the line between bossy and too bossy was a conscious effort.

"All great." I nodded. "I actually wanted to check in with you about our panel. Sorry to pile all this stuff on you, but I'm trying to narrow down dates and conference room schedules."

Emmy smiled and put her camera down, turning to be sure I could see the honesty in her eyes. She kept moving, never missing a step as she said, "You know, maybe you should try to relax today. It's a sunny day. We're at the beach. I'm... trying to lead the shoot."

"You're doing a wonderful job."

Emmy laughed a little. "Thanks. What I meant to say is, all you really have to worry about today is... smile."

She took a photo of me without warning. I nervously pressed my hand to the top of my head. I didn't check whether my edges were still laid and my bun was still centered.

Emmy noticed my discomfort and stopped walking backward so that she was beside me. "What's the matter? David really getting to you? He seems chill enough today."

I shook my head. "No, it isn't David. I'm just... my head's spinning, and relaxing isn't exactly in my vocab. Plus, this year's panels are going to be a pretty big deal for a lot of women on campus. I want to bring my A-game."

"Whoa, Yara." Emmy placed a hand on my shoulder. "Slow down. You're breathing really fast."

I stopped talking long enough to swallow and, sure enough, it felt like I was heaving air in and out.

Emmy frowned. "Are you taking time for yourself? Like regular breaks. TV veg-out days? Because from our group chat, you always have something in the pipeline. It worries me. It worries all of us."

"I do." The lie easily slipped off my lips, so silky smooth. I hated the taste of it, but I was in love with how it felt. "I just don't talk about the mundane stuff much."

She studied me for a second. "Okay, sure. But if you get too overwhelmed, you should talk to one of us. Indie's really great at understanding pressure and anxiety, and Covee was super helpful whenever I got lonely over the summer break. We're all here to help. Sisterhood, remember?"

My shoulder relaxed at the reminder. It was nice to have friends so willing to have my back... even when I was bent on climbing mountains alone. "Definitely. I'll reach out if I need to... But I don't right now. So how about that panel confirmation?"

Emmy smiled, giving in. "I'll be there to talk about my shot putting."

"And your cousin's girlfriend?" I crossed my fingers, praying my luck wouldn't run out.

"Aderyn's on board," she confirmed. "Ready and willing to talk about Black women in hockey. And she has a friend who can talk about Black women in streaming, too."

I let out a sigh of relief—another thing to check off my to-do list. I was addicted to the color-coded high of those little boxes. "God, thank you. This panel's going to be incredible. Black woman taking up space in uncharted waters. Minorities in potentially hostile environments."

"Fun stuff," Emmy teased.

"Amazing stuff," I insisted. "It'll be one of those moments where in a decade people will say, 'Hey, I knew them before they were famous'."

Emmy laughed, her eyes alight. "I hope so. With your energy, maybe I will make the Olympic team before my joints give out."

"How much longer?" Indie called. "I'm not a big fan of sand between my... everything."

"Just a few more yards, Anakin," Emmy said.

Covee snorted, with Indie grumbling under her breath about not knowing who Anakin was.

"At those rocks," Emmy said to me, gesturing in the distance. "I have an idea, but it's going to take some effort. It'll be worth it, though... I hope."

My forehead wrinkled as I looked at the large black rocks. "Sounds great. As long as we aren't climbing them."

Emmy chewed on her bottom lip and busied herself with readjusting some settings on her camera.

"Emmy?" I stopped walking. "My top's cashmere."

She snapped another candid of me and smiled. "It's going to be good, Yara... or, I hope it will. In my head, it's brilliant. We don't actually have to do it. There are some cute benches on the pier..."

I sighed, remembering that this was supposed to help rebuild her confidence. I was supposed to be her cheerleader. "No, Emmy. If you want to climb the rocks, we're climbing the rocks."

6

"Hold these." I didn't wait for David to respond before I shoved my heels into his hand. He was already carrying Emmy's camera bag, Indie's duffel, and Haven's backpack.

To my surprise, he hadn't uttered a single complaint on the walk over. In fact, he looked as calm and content as he could be. Calm for David still involved a pensive glare. But no eye rolls. No snarky scoffs.

"What?" I asked when he studied me in silence. David lingered at my side. Even though we had plenty of space on the nearly empty beach, when he stood next to me, I felt like we were in a closed room. I shifted my weight from one leg to another, reminding myself there was still enough air to breathe even if it felt like he was sucking it all up.

Emmy helped everyone pick their rocks, citing the need to choose something that represented them. Indie volunteered to go first, selecting the tallest one in the bunch. She needed help climbing it, so a few girls spotted her. They held up their hands, doing their best to make sure she didn't slip. While they got into position and chatted among themselves, I tried to estimate how long it would take us to finish the group photo. If we were back on campus within the next couple of hours, I could fit in a study session before meeting with my academic adviser. Internal planning typically grounded me, but with every small gust of wind, I got a hint of David's scent. My teeth clenched as I struggled to maintain focus.

"You're pissed," David noted, his voice unusually low. Intimately low. We may as well be sitting across from one another in a candlelit restaurant. He raised a brow when he caught me glancing at his mouth. I took a deep breath, averting my gaze.

The sand, a dark brown with crushed orange and yellow shells mixed in, dug into the arches of my bare feet. White seagulls glided so far apart they looked like polka dots on the cloudless blue sky. The air smelled of salt and... David. There was no escaping the tiny observation that he looked good in the morning sun. The desire to study him grew until not looking at him felt impossible, because maybe, just maybe, another glance would confirm my original assessment was incorrect.

"At me?" he continued, sounding more and more pleased with each syllable that rolled off his tongue. "For not causing trouble."

I laughed and crossed my arms over my chest. "Contrary to popular belief, not everything is about you."

"Then, if it's not me, what's got you all hot and bothered?" He maintained his low voice.

"Nothing." I brushed my hands on the back of my pants, trying to get rid of the sweat on my palms. A part of me wished I had listened to Indie. It would have been nice to start in our casual outfits.

"If you keep pouting, you'll ruin this fun day for the rest of us," David said.

My brow raised in disbelief. "Fun? You're having fun?"

His smile lit up his eyes, making his face more beautiful. I wondered if his awkward phase in high school was ever really that awkward, or were we all just annoying teens who believed if you weren't perfect, you weren't nice to look at.

"Of course. I'm having a blast being the group's pack mule. Are you not having fun? The peaceful sound of waves, cold sand between your toes, and a personal chauffeur not doing it for you?"

"Oh, I'm living the dream." Right as I said that, a spray of sea salt landed on my tongue. I coughed and moved so my back was to the ocean, which meant I'd turned entirely into David.

"You don't bullshit well." He shook his head and looked away for a moment as if he were bored with the conversation. Or me. My money was on both. "You know, if you want to go into politics, you're going to need to clean that up."

I wrinkled my nose. "Who said I wanted to go into politics?"

David's gaze settled on my buttoned blazer. "Uh, your matching-set wardrobe. You were born in freshly pressed slacks, weren't you?"

"I'd rather be over-dressed than under," I defended, looking him up and down. His blue jeans and thin cotton long-sleeve shirt had seen better days.

"You've almost fine-tuned every one of your expressions."

I frowned. "Excuse me?"

He gestured at my face. "It's impressive how perfect you look all the time."

I almost took that as a compliment, forgetting David had the unique skill of turning the nicest things inside out.

"It's very disingenuous," he continued. "You'd be a wonderful politician if you learned how to lie better. Tip: stop your right eye from twitching."

I bit down on my inner cheek, holding back from sharing

my knee-jerk retort. The satisfaction of biting back would keep me fed all week. But I needed to be more mature than that, at least in front of my org members. "I'm a lot of things, David. Disingenuous isn't one of them. You, on the other hand..."

"What?" He tilted his head to the side when I paused. "Oh, come on. Don't get all shy on me now, Daredevil. What am I? Give me something new this time. Asshole is tired. Jerk's elementary. I want something you can really sink your teeth into. Something that stabs me right in the soul."

"Fuck off," I said under my breath.

"Big, bad Yara's run out of insults. Another tip to add to your practice sheet: go for the jugular. Debate opponents are ruthless. You know, it's a good thing you have me around. I'll get you sharpened up."

"I have a lot of insults," I promised. "None of which are appropriate for me to say in front of my org. I respect the people on my team."

"That so?"

"I do my best to make sure others aren't uncomfortable in my presence. Can you say the same?"

David whistled long and steadily. "God, it kills me how much you fascinate me. You and all that energy you put into being this version of yourself that you've crafted. It's the one thing I can't wrap my head around. I can't understand why it works and why, like everyone else, I'm—"

David stopped himself. I frowned, confused at the abrupt cut-off, but ultimately took advantage of it.

"Person I've crafted? What about you?" I asked.

He frowned. "What about me?"

"You're telling me you're naturally a nuisance?"

David shrugged. "Some people find their destiny along the way. Others are born with it."

I laughed. "So you were born to be a pain in the ass? That tracks."

"Disagreeable," he corrected with a smile. "I prefer the term disagreeable."

"Do you like that destiny?" I watched him closely as he responded. We were half joking, but in all of our back and forths, there was always a small inkling of realness. And when I was lucky —which was rare— I could pick through the bullshit to find it.

"It's fun," David confirmed. "Getting to rummage through everyone's genuine emotions is fun."

My brow furrowed as I considered his words. "Genuine emotions?"

David nudged his chin toward the girls. They were laughing and squealing at their failed attempts to get comfortable on the rocks. "They're not going to show you who they really are if you're nice and agreeable all the time. People rarely show you who they truly are unless under pressure."

"I disagree. I think you can tell a lot about a person in how they respond to kindness."

He rocked his head back and forth, considering my words. "Maybe. But you learn even more about someone by how they respond to strife."

I laughed, even though he had a point. I didn't mean for it to sound like I wasn't taking him seriously, but from the cloud that appeared across his face, I could tell my intentions didn't matter.

When David didn't feel like he was being taken seriously, he sniffed twice. I'm not sure if he knew it was his tell. The first sniff was barely audible. The second sounded like he was trying to fight off a sneeze... or the urge to charge like a bull; the odds were fifty-fifty.

"Your personal philosophy is kind of sad," I said, my smile fading slightly.

"Yours is sadder."

"What is mine, exactly?"

"Push and push until you're bone tired. Smile your way through it all until you get what you want. Fake it till you make it. Play happy until you learn how not to be so sad."

My smile was gone entirely. David had dug around in my brain, shining a light on all the dark, secret corners. I didn't know how to disinvite him, so I stood my ground. "I'm not playing happy. I am."

"Are you?" Another gust of wind blew against us, carrying his scent under my nose. Swirling his presence all around me until it was all I felt and wanted. Fury and desire were an infuriating combination.

"Because I think if you were," he said. "You'd have told me to fuck off a long time ago. You wouldn't keep texting me. You wouldn't have looked for me on campus. You wouldn't have wasted a dare to invite me today."

I tried to laugh, but there was no air left in my lungs to breathe it into existence. "I tell you to fuck off every day."

"Yeah, but have you ever really meant it?" he challenged. "Be honest."

"Yara!" Emmy called.

I jumped, not ready for how close she'd been behind us. David smiled at my surprise and stepped away from me.

"You ready?" Emmy asked, looking between the two of us. Thankfully, she knew well enough not to ask questions.

I nodded, shaking my hands out as if that were enough to ward off whatever feeling David left in my bones. "Ready."

"Great." She bounced on her toes, then directed her next comment to David. "Stop distracting her, yeah? I'm pretty sure you were just invited to carry things and look pretty."

David winked at her. "Ay, ay, captain. Carrying things and looking pretty is my specialty."

I rolled my eyes and followed Emmy.

"You good for a little climb?" she asked when we got near the rocks.

"Of course." I swallowed, having a hard time feeling my toes. "Just tell me which one you think I should go for."

Emmy pointed to a large rock in the middle of the rest. "That one's the perfect height. Plus, the sun's hitting it at an amazing angle right now. Don't you think so?"

"Definitely." I inwardly groaned at the thought of scrambling all the way up there. But I couldn't complain. Or rather, wouldn't.

As soon as I took a step forward, placing my foot on a smaller rock, I felt the heat of someone by my side. I glanced over, thinking it'd be Emmy or one of the other girls offering me help. Instead, I found David.

"I'm fine," I said, ignoring his offer to stabilize me.

"And I'm just here to have a front-row seat to your fall," he assured.

I waved the hand away.

"Come on," David insisted in a more serious tone. He stretched his arm toward me. "I don't actually want you to fall."

"You were singing a different tune the other night."

"Yeah, well, that was the other night and a dare. I was banking on entertainment."

"Keep banking." I reached for the next rock up. It was cold and sticky underneath my palm. I tried to keep a straight face when a slimy substance coated my fingers.

I got more confident with each step I took without David's aid. Emmy called out encouragement as I neared her rock of choice. Right when I was about to take the last step, my foot slipped on the green slug that marred most of the rocks.

It was the kind of fall that happened in a heartbeat but felt like it was happening in slow motion. A part of me thought I could recover in an instant. But my brain and body were on two different pages, leaving me stunned and barreling toward my death. David's reflexes were decisive. Like me, he had little time to think. Unlike me, he knew exactly how to react.

I shouldn't have been so impressed. He was a football player, for goodness' sake. An athlete who'd spent copious amounts of hours fine-tuning his response time. Years of sculpting his body to withstand full-force hits from guys twice my weight.

When his arms wrapped around me, my heart jumped into my throat. Not because I'd almost cracked my skull onto some rock, but because I was in David's embrace. As soon as he caught me, he pulled me into his chest, so he'd have an easier time steadying us both. One hand cupped my head, protective of its vulnerability. His warm fingers covered my ear, muffling the sound of my executive board in a panic, yelling as they scrambled over the rocks to assure we were okay. I couldn't focus on what they were saying because David's other hand encircled my waist, his grip firm and confident enough to feel like it'd been there before. Like it was coming home.

"Fine, huh?" he said in a voice so low I could barely make out the words over the waves. I blinked at how soft his shirt felt underneath my palm. I felt no sign of his heart racing. My sudden fall and David's sudden save didn't result in even a slight uptick. Why was that so captivating? That he could do all that without hesitation or fear clouding his judgment.

His hair had long since dried in the sun, and I got the disgusting urge to brush the short strands off his forehead. I curled my fingers into a fist, trapping some of his shirt inside.

"Throw a punch." His eyes flickered to my fist.

"Is that an official dare?" I asked, all breathy and confused.

His playful smile sent me spiraling. "You can't give me a freebie?"

"Shit," Emmy hissed. She was the first to reach us. "Are you hurt?"

"I'm fine." I tried to stand up without David's help, but my legs nearly gave out from adrenaline and his grip on my waist.

"Give your body a moment to catch up. Shock's got your brain in overload." David kept hold of me. "Add that to the list of things you'll have to fix, Madam President."

He had a faint set of freckles on his nose. How had I never noticed them before? This close, David had fewer jagged edges and a softer center when I could see those freckles paired with his usual smirk.

"My brain's fine," I whispered, trying to stand on my own again.

He chuckled and looked down at my fist. "You sure?"

"I'm uncomfortable," I lied. "You're holding me really tight."

"Should I let go then?" he asked.

"Yes," I snapped, even though if he let me go now at this angle, I'd probably slip between the rocks. My feet were bare, but he wore a respectable pair of sneakers.

"I will," he promised. "In a second."

David slipped his arm underneath the back of my knees. I gasped when he lifted my feet off the rock.

"Oh, my God." I clung to him, nails digging into his shoulder blades as he started our descent. I squeezed my eyes shut as we moved. "Be careful, please, be careful. If you lose your balance, David–"

"Shh, you're fine," he promised in a surprisingly comforting tone. "We're almost down."

He made it back to the sand and gently lowered me. Once he'd completely detangled himself from me, the girls surrounded me. They fussed over me, noting the rip in my slacks and the cuts on my ankles and arm.

"We have a first aid kit," Covee said as she rummaged through her bag.

"I'm so sorry, Yara," Emmy pressed her hand to my arm. "I shouldn't have asked you to climb so high."

"Did you bring a pair of sneakers?" Haven asked, frowning at my bare feet. "Or even flip-flops? You can't wear heels to walk back."

I was overwhelmed by the attention and care, and by the fact that I missed the feel of David's chest beneath my hand. He'd been so solid and warm, the opposite of the shifting, cold sand underneath my feet.

"It's fine," I said hollowly. "I'm fine."

"Thank God David was close," Indie said.

"I'll say," Haven agreed.

Their attention extended to him when they noticed a cut on the back of his elbow. It was far deeper than my little abrasions.

"You were so quick," Indie said, her hand lingering on his bicep.

"I don't know how you got her back down that fast," Haven agreed, sounding almost suspicious. In her defense, we did once theorize he was a vampire.

Covee assessed both of our wounds. When she met my gaze, asking for silent permission, I nodded and said, "Of course. He's first. It's way worse than mine."

She moved, not hearing the rest of my sentiment. David seemed uncomfortable with their comforting words and warm admiration. His cheeks went red at the praise. He tried to smile, but it didn't quite pass the wincing stage. Amid it all, David looked at me. We held one another's gaze, and I'm shocked at the nerves in his eyes. He was shy because a bunch of hot women surrounded him, and he was used to eating lunch all by himself in the school cafeteria.

And there it was, David didn't realize he was —to some—

a very attractive man. A catch, if you were into football players who were made of sarcasm, nihilism, and a hint of keen observation skills. His eyes read, '*save me,*' but I left him to simmer as I gleaned more material to use for future sparring matches. Unfortunately, it took an almost neck-breaking fall to get this information. The steep price was worth it.

7

WHILE THE REST of the board went to the restrooms to change for the casual photos, David and I found our way back to his car to nurse our wounds. There was a heavy silence between us that I'm only used to experiencing with people I want to like me. Whenever we accidentally made eye contact, we both looked away.

"Great," I grumbled under my breath as I searched through my bag for the thousandth time for a pair of socks. I was more than ready and willing to abandon my heels for sneakers.

"What?" David didn't look up from the cooler he'd been reorganizing in the trunk. Apparently, he had enough fore-thought to pack us cold drinks and sandwiches for the day. He was taking his honorary member role seriously. It almost made me want to thank him. But since he was only doing this because of the dare and his burning desire to one-up me, I wouldn't waste gratitude on forced attendance.

"I forgot my socks." I sighed and tossed my things back into the bag.

"Check the glove compartment," David said without looking up.

I made a face. "Are you confessing to having a sock fetish and stealing mine?"

He chuckled. "Maybe. Maybe I have all kinds of things in there just waiting for you to see and hold against me till the end of time. You know how I adore giving you the power to neg."

"I knew you were a kinky guy," I teased and opened the compartment. Inside, there was a neat stack of notepads and pens, a box of tissues, hand sanitizer, a copy of his car registration and insurance,... and a pack of unopened black ankle socks.

"Well, aren't I a lucky girl?" I asked, grabbing the pair in awe and rueful appreciation. "First, you swoop me into your arms like some comic hero, and now, you're offering me your just-in-case socks."

David shut the trunk and came before me with two water bottles in hand.

"You take care of me so well," I teased, accepting the water.

He didn't respond, cracking open his own bottle to take a few sips. We both were well aware that it was best to strike while the others' defenses were down. And for some reason, David had lowered the bridge and opened his iron gates.

"Are they one of my members?" I asked.

David frowned. "What?"

"The person you're seeing." I waved the socks around. "First, opening the doors, helping them down the beach, and now, you have a woman's pair of socks?"

"They're unisex." His tone was flat.

"They're small," I said. "Too small for you."

"Now who's the one with the fetish?" he teased. "Been checking out the size of my feet, Daredevil? If you were curious, you could have just asked."

"You wish."

"This is the second time you've inquired about my love life," he said. "Doesn't seem like I'm the one doing the wishing."

"Just making conversation," I mimicked his tone. "My questions are meaningless, like most."

He laughed. Silence settled between us once more as I pulled on the socks. He watched me shrug out of my blazer and take my twists out of my hair tie.

"What is it?" I asked, pulling on my blue Westbrooke University sweatshirt.

"Nothing." David blinked and turned to look at the ocean. I figured we'd leave it there, give ourselves a brief break to recuperate from being in one another's faces for so long. But he turned back to me with a question in his eyes and hesitation on his lips.

"Are you good?" I asked, studying him with a mix of concern and suspicion.

"Definitely," he said, voice low with defensiveness.

"'You sure? I saw how hard it was for you to get all that attention." I gave him a look. "You do realize people like guys who play football? It doesn't make sense to me, but they do. And somehow you've stumbled into recognition and easily earned awe, and yet, you act like you're some socially inept eighth grader with a body odor problem."

"I seem to remember that was once the case," he said, self-deprecation infused in his smile.

"I figured your bleak outlook on existence shunned the idea of being stuck in the past," I teased.

"It does," he confirmed.

"So why are you knee-deep in it?"

"How do you figure I am?"

"Because of our entangled history. I know what you looked like in middle school." I stood up and shut the car door. "I know what mini David Evans looked like when people realized you weren't so weird after all. You get red when you're nervous. A cliché, bright, burning red, that makes your nonchalance shed like the farce it is."

"I wasn't nervous," he said. "I was…"

I raised a brow. "Was?"

"Worried," he mumbled and took another sip of water.

"Worried? About what?"

He shrugged. "How were you going to manage not being the center of attention for more than a few seconds? My heart was in utter shambles for you because I know how much you need it to survive. I remember what you looked like in middle school, too."

I laughed and bent down to check my reflection in the car's side mirror. "You're an ass."

"Need help walking over this gravel?" he asked. "It gets a little hairy the closer we get to the sand. And, well, you've proven to be delicate."

"Nice try, but you're not going to get another excuse to touch me today. Sorry, I know you were looking forward to it now that you've got a taste."

"No worries. I'm sure you'll come up with something for me soon enough."

"Always piggybacking off my labor," I teased. "You know, post-college, you'll have to do your own work. I'm not going to be around to offer you lecture notes."

"From experience, I know if I ask the right way, you'll give them to me anyway."

My expression darkened at the mention of how easy it'd become for him to get what he wanted from me. "I'll be thousands of miles away. No matter how much you ask, I won't hear you."

"Going somewhere phones don't work?"

"Nope, just losing your number. I've had my share of David Evans. Enough for a lifetime."

He stepped closer, making the air between us dense with his warmth. "I'd like to see you try to stay away from me."

"Is that a dare?" I cocked my brow.

"Oh, wouldn't that be interesting?" he said, pausing for a second as if he was actually considering. "It is my turn, after all."

I swallowed when he moved even closer. His water bottle grazed the back of my hand. I didn't dislike the chill; it was a strange sort of connection to him. The cold was disconcerting and tempting at the same time... like David. He was an arrogant man whom I knew I shouldn't want to touch again, and yet, I still couldn't seem to stop picturing it.

"So?" I asked, realizing that if he did this dare, it could be the end of this. And part of me pre-maturely mourned because we hadn't even figured out a name for us yet. Surely he'd want to stick around long enough to do that at least.

David's gaze scanned my face, and I knew he picked up on my concern. He sensed my dread. I cringed, bracing for him to use it, to point out that, yes, I indeed wanted this, and in some ways, I wanted him.

"Maybe later," he said. "For now, I'm working on something a bit more entertaining. Since you plan on moving someplace unreachable by modern technology, I'll have to take advantage of the present and get all the fun I can out of you."

I tried not to sigh too loudly, to keep my face neutral as relief warmed my skin.

8

I WAS the youngest and shortest of my siblings. My toes were used to repetitive strain whenever I tried to make myself big enough to be seen in a crowd that was my sisters and a brother. Being surrounded by excellence was a privilege. Drowning in it was a byproduct.

As kids, we weren't ever expected or encouraged to compete. Our parents were self-aware enough to refuse to compare. And yet, the side-by-side notes snuck into our lives anyway from outside sources. Impressing viewers through glass panes became a sport for me. Getting pats on the back from my older siblings was my equivalent of the Olympics. I would pole vault, high dive, and butterfly my way to victory. It didn't matter if I didn't care for sports; it mattered that I fit in my family's perfect puzzle. It mattered that I wasn't the one who dropped a stitch in an otherwise perfect silky sweater.

I pushed through the pain of exhaustion to keep up. And I'd been doing so well up until senior year of high school because that was when shards of metal tore through bone.

My past mistake was a patchwork quilt, draped over my shoulders every time I slowed down for even a second, so I had no choice but to keep moving. Maybe I could keep myself busy enough to forget my wrongdoing, or push myself hard enough to earn forgiveness. I allowed myself four hours of sleep before waking up to prepare for a student org meeting that could undo some of those patches. Maybe it could lighten some of the weight.

During a long day of classes, I slipped in and out of restrooms to stuff paper towels under my armpits. My breathing was shallow when I left the stall for the last time. Tonight, I was meeting with the president of the Black Student Union, the president of Women in Business, and the president of Minorities in STEM. It'd taken some hardcore convincing to get them all in one place at the same time. The window was small: thirty minutes. But I was determined to make this work. I needed to get them to work with me, and possibly convince them to pull a little more weight than I initially let on.

You can do this. I repeated the mantra to my reflection in the mirror. The plum purple on my lips had disappeared from all my coffee guzzling. I swiped on my lip gloss for a quick touch-up. My hair was still in decent shape, pulled into a high ponytail. The blush on my skin had long faded, leaving my brown skin looking a little lifeless. I searched through my purse, hoping to find something to liven up my complexion, but the only makeup I had besides my lipstick was mascara.

It's going to be fine. You look as put-together as anyone could be this late.

The words didn't provide much comfort as I exited the bathroom and moved down the hall. I tried to find shelter in them anyway because it was better than weathering the storm unarmed.

Turquoise carpeted floors and endless hallways filled the student center. The building had six floors, and the middle three housed meeting rooms. And tonight, every one of those rooms was fully booked. Westbrooke ranked among the highest for on-campus activities nationwide. Since I couldn't secure a booking in time, I'd asked the other to meet me at one of the tables in the hall.

I thought I'd calmed myself enough to come face-to-face with them, but as soon as I turned the corner and saw all three of them already at the table, my stomach dropped. I ducked behind the wall, pressing my back against the cold plaster as I tried to steady my breathing.

What's wrong with you?

My chest had never been this heavy when talking to people. Talking was the place I thrived, where I could run circles around the best.

I let my hand find its way to my kitchen and gave myself permission to pick at the hair there for a couple of breaths. My phone buzzed in my bag, interrupting the unfolding panic attack. I pulled it out and saw David's name flash on the screen. My sigh of relief left me conflicted. A David-shaped distraction was exactly what I needed. Seeing his name reminded me that there were more people on campus than the three I wanted to impress. But who was I becoming to find comfort in his interruption?

DAVID

I have my dare. Where are you?

I snorted and typed,

'Student Center.' But I have a meeting, so I can't talk to you right now.

DAVID

After. What floor are you on?

Do NOT come find me. Wait on the first floor. I'll come to you.

When he didn't reply, I figured he'd listen to my command for once. But in case he didn't internalize the order, I sent a follow-up text that said,

> I mean it. I'll find you in 30 mins.

Though I regrettably appreciated the digital distraction, I didn't need David here in flesh and blood. I didn't want him to see me like this. I didn't want anyone I knew to see me. I was a half-blob of a human right now, melting with every minute that passed.

With a last roll of my shoulders, I pushed off the wall and started toward the table.

The president of Women in Business, Hana Yosef, was the only one who looked up from her laptop when I came into sight. She offered me a smile that made her already warm exterior inviting. The muted blue hijab she wore highlighted the smoky gray shade of her eyes.

"Yara, hi," Hana greeted as she removed her bag from the only other chair that wasn't occupied. "So great to meet you in person. It's nice to finally put a face to the email."

My other two guests (jurors?) looked up. Anthony Follow, the president of BSU, raised a brow at me. He had starter locs with red tips and wore black-framed glasses that slid down his nose when he took a not-so-subtle glance at his watch.

Like me, he was a stickler for time. We'd collaborated on a couple of projects in the past, and every time I worked with him, I experienced what it was like to be the slacker in the group project. The guy could write a ten-page paper in a night while also getting a run in, cooking a healthy dinner, and organizing a successful panel. I'd witnessed it all first-hand and reconsidered all my hopes and dreams.

"This should take just thirty minutes, correct?" he asked, voice coated in a kind of heavy exhaustion I'm sure all of us could relate to, even though this semester was just getting started.

"Correct. I'll have you guys out of here in no time." I attempted a smile, but the corners of my lips fought me every second of it. Thankfully, I sounded steadier than my balance felt. I quickly sat down and pulled out my tablet.

Olivia Johnson fanned herself with a brochure for the new grocery store opening up on campus. Her brown skin had a flawless complexion that celebrities often claimed to achieve naturally. Her ponytail, made with honey-dyed curls, easily fit under a worn baseball cap.

During our first year at Westbrooke, Olivia was Haven and I's third roommate. We'd set out to revive BWD together. But once she met some girls from her STEM courses, she converted. We were friendly whenever we ran into each other, but never '*stay up late gossiping, do you want to make a late-night run for ice cream*' close.

"I read your write-up." Olivia's dark eyes never left mine. Her tone was a flat, low-effort noise. Post-freshman year, with rose-colored glasses removed, it was nearly impossible to elicit any kind of feeling from Olivia other than moderate intrigue.

For the past couple of semesters, I've reached out to her for event collaboration. She'd passed every single time with a simple: not interested. When she agreed to this meeting, I couldn't believe it. And honestly, I'd accidentally asked because her email remained on my mailing list of student orgs I thought would give us the time of day.

A part of me figured maybe she humored me because this was our final year as Presidents. And perhaps some part of her felt guilty for ditching our goals and essentially our friendship... but from the slight frown of her round lips, I'd say guilt was the farthest thing from her mind.

"What did you think?" My stomach twisted to prepare for the incoming rejection. I remembered enough about Olivia to understand that once she touched the top of her tongue against her upper lip before speaking, whatever response she was going to give wouldn't be constructive.

She leaned back in her chair, glancing at the ceiling for a second. "It's a lot of work."

"Most of which, Yara says she has covered," Anthony countered. He rested his hand underneath his chin, gaze on Olivia. "Seems simple enough on our end."

He sounded like he was on my side, but the way he brushed his pinky across his bottom lip revealed Olivia could persuade him to think differently if she moved the correct chess piece.

"I agree with Ant." Hana shrugged. "We post a few things on our socials. Sell a few tickets at our meetings. Attend a handful of fundraisers. Sounds easy to me."

"But the money from the tickets we sell goes right into the BWD's account, right?" Olivia looked at me for clarity.

I swallowed. My throat felt like the abrasive side of a sponge. When I reached for my water bottle, it was empty. I felt silly holding the empty bottle, but I was too nervous to set it back down. "We will keep the income, yes. Most of which will go towards the event cost and an elementary after-school program charity. This isn't a cash grab—"

"So, sounds like we're basically your street team," Olivia mused as she closed her planner. She'd been using one of the same styles since freshman year. It was red and glittery, with stickers of '90s cartoons.

Hana frowned at her comment. "And what's wrong with that?"

"Nothing," Olivia said. "It just feels a little one-sided. BWD doesn't have a quarter of our following online. Or the amount of trust we've built with students. So, if we're hitching ourselves to her wagon and something goes wrong, we'll be in the mud along with her. If she fails—and let's be honest, BWD's track record hasn't even been impressive—it'll fall on our shoulders too."

Ouch. I'd failed to raise enough money for the ball my sophomore year and tried to put on a small event during junior year, but lost half of my board by the time the event was supposed to take place. But it wasn't like every decision I'd made had been terrible. I'd been dealt a fairly crappy hand. I didn't say that, though. *Only losers make excuses*, my mom's voice rang in my head. *Winners create opportunities.*

"You won't hurt for members since you're always hurting for members. But, if we're seen failing with you, our org loses credibility," Olivia noted.

Anthony and Hana exchanged looks, their expressions clouded as they considered their social status at risk.

"Collaborators. You'll be my collaborators," I said, quickly trying to pivot. Had Olivia come here just to turn down my idea? To infect the other two with her doubt?

My phone buzzed in my bag. I ignored it, taking a deep breath, and straightening my shoulders. I was an Every woman for goodness' sake. My grandmother was a lawyer in an era when women were barely allowed on college campuses. My mother was a politician who was a keynote speaker at too many conferences to keep track of. And my sisters were leaders in their respective fields. If they could break down barriers, I could stand my ground in a meeting of three people.

"You all will get your organizations' names on all the posters, flyers, and social media posts," I continued without faltering. "You're getting your name on the official banners. Your executive board members will get free tickets. The event's straightforward, with a low margin for error. You'll see the projected cost and potential growth on the spreadsheets in the email. It'll be all our event, even though my girls and I will be the only ones clocking in hours."

I was supposed to revise that last part. We needed more

hands on deck. But I was losing them. Without their support, there was a ninety percent chance we'd have a repeat of last year, and I'd officially go down in BWD history as the president who put a nail into the Westbrooke University's chapter coffin.

Hana was the first to speak, smiling as she did and making the dimple in her chin deepen. "Free food and a fun night for our members for the low, low price of telling everyone at meetings to show up? I'm in."

My chest loosened. "Thank you. Anthony?"

He took a second, glancing at his laptop where my write-up was on the screen. He brushed his thumb across his beard as he thought. "You don't have a location yet, do you?"

"I'll have it finalized next week," I promised.

"Text me then, and I'll have an answer," he decided. With a last look in Olivia's direction, he shut his laptop and started packing up. "For now, you can put BSU down as a tentative yes."

I bit down on my inner cheek, trying my best not to look too excited. They knew good and well they were doing me a colossal favor, I didn't need to remind them.

When Anthony started packing up, the girls began doing the same. His impending absence was their cue to follow suit, even though I still had fifteen minutes of their time.

I stood too, not wanting to be the only one hanging around, despite still needing Olivia's answer. She waited until the other two were down the hall to give it to me.

"Yara," she started with a slight smile that didn't reach her eyes. "You really think you can successfully put on this big of an event by the end of the semester?"

I tugged my bag over my shoulder, nails digging deep into the leather. "Of course."

"Because if we put our name on it and the event is your typical BWD event—"

"Typical BWD event?" Why did the phrase sound familiar coming out of her mouth? It sounded like she used it enough to refine every vowel.

Olivia pressed her lips together, pausing for a moment to gather her thoughts.

"Liv," I said, trying to appeal to her kinder side with the nickname. "Come on, you aren't really this upset about us using your clout."

"Reputation is everything," she said point-blank. "And you know I won't ask my org to promote something that doesn't align with our vision."

"An end-of-semester ball doesn't align with your vision?" I almost scoffed, but swallowed it. Professionalism was sometimes a thorn in my side.

"Being associated with an uninteresting org that puts on lackluster events doesn't align with our vision," she corrected.

I blinked, stomach churning with the shame that'd made its way into every vein. "You could have just said no and been done with it then. Why even show up?" My tone was as hard as my expression.

"Just thought I'd be the honest one. Those two weren't going to do it, and you need constructive feedback," she said. "They're too nice to tell you BWD's a lost cause. You should have jumped ship after freshman year. Unfortunately, your talent's going to waste. Your opportunities to network with people who are actually going to have a voice in the world after we graduate are dwindling."

I laughed under my breath at her assertions. "I'm sure I'll manage just fine."

She raised a brow. "Yeah?"

I thought about my girls. My silly, easily distracted, incredibly sweet girls. They talked to one another daily, either in person or through text. They'd come to our meetings venting about their problems with loneliness on campus. Their experiences with microaggressions. Struggles with dating people who want them for themselves and not as part of some weird college experiment. BWD gave them a safe space to be themselves, free from judgment, in a world that would always hold them to ridiculous standards.

"I'll put you down as a hard no," I said.

Olivia sighed as if to say, *'you're not getting it.'* She looked at me with a patronizing smile as if I were some kid who once again skipped a few letters in the alphabet. "How about this? STEM will host the ball. Your board will be in charge of set-up and fundraising. We'll put both our names on the flyers — obviously, ours will be larger, but you'll still get credit. Your mom will find it respectable. Hey, she might even have you in the bragging section on her lunch agenda."

My chest caved in. Olivia was one of the few people who knew that being president of BWD was my attempt to make up for the harm I'd caused, to prove I could offer something more than derailment and shame to my family.

"No," I said gently, though the storm in my brain raged on. "We'll do it on our own."

Olivia's face fell. It's childish, but I felt vindicated at the sight. She wanted this ball because she knew it had the potential to work. It could be something that'd have the entire campus vying for a ticket. Her poorly concealed desire was enough to motivate me to press forward.

"Alright, then." Olivia nodded and even tried to smile as she accepted my refusal. "Good luck, Yara. You'll need it."

"I won't," I promised.

9

I HURRIED down the staircase of the student center, heels slamming against the carpeted floor. Because of my frustration and annoyance, everything around me blurred. My mind raced with new ideas for how to ensure this ball was an undeniable success. I had a list of ways to make Olivia regret ever thinking of giving me a pitiful stare.

In my blind fury, my shoulder knocked into someone else's. As soon as the familiar scent of summer linen hit my nose, I swallowed my impending apology.

"Took you long enough," David said, mouth turned down in disapproval.

"Shut up," I muttered and continued toward the doors.

He didn't hesitate, falling into step right after me. David caught the heavy door that I had failed to hold up for him. His chuckle made me shoot him a hard, piercing glance.

"I see your meeting went well." He wore baggy gray sweats and a loose white tee. His sneakers looked as if he'd dragged them through the mud one too many times. And one of them had duct tape wrapped around the toe.

"Went just as planned." I itched to rant and complain

about Olivia and my failure to establish a better reputation for BWD. Instead of spilling my guts to a guy who didn't give a damn, I continued down the sidewalk. My hips switched, and my chin tilted upward as I channeled a newfound determination.

"Perfect, even," I continued, only half-talking to David. I wanted to hash things out myself. But it was frowned upon to talk to myself in public (something I learned the hard way). So, his presence was helpful for once.

"Sure sounds like it," David agreed. He was so close I could feel the warmth radiating from his body. The chill of fall lingered in the air, the wind coaxing orange and red leaves from the branches above.

We walked underneath black iron lampposts, heading toward my bus stop. Only a handful of students were outside. Most people found themselves in warmer places like the library or dorms.

"Uninteresting?" I grumbled. "Her last event was a dinner themed after the periodic table. No speakers. Just cupcakes and scientific notation. And I'm uninteresting? A whole ball on a college campus is uninteresting?"

David blew against my hand. I didn't realize I'd reached for my hair, twisting the strands tightly around my index finger. I winced and pulled away. He was supposed to be a silent observer.

"I can guarantee without knowing what you're going on about that you're stressed over something that won't mean a thing in the next year," David said.

I scowled. "I didn't ask for your opinion."

"Since when do I care whether you asked?"

"Can you be quiet for once and just pretend to be my friend? Lord knows I've done it enough times for you."

He chuckled. "When was this? Was I there?"

My stop was abrupt. So was his. Those goddamn reflexes.

"When you called me up after midterms last year—" I crossed my arms over my chest. "—whining about your water bottles."

A muscle in his jaw flexed. "I don't whine."

I laughed at his inability to deny what had happened. "You whine all the time. It's your second language."

David had begged me to bring him extra water bottles, insisting it was an emergency. And I'd gotten out of my warm, safe bed to catch a bus to retrieve his water bottles from a corner store.

"Everyone else I knew was at the stadium. No one likes leaving during a game," he defended. "You were my only option."

"I don't care about the reason. All I care about is that I was exhibiting peak friend-like behavior. It wouldn't kill you to do the same."

"It might," he joked under his breath.

"Then we'll both be put out of our misery. A win-win," I said.

We were silent, glaring so hard we could probably burn through the red-brick buildings and cobblestone walkway.

"Fine," David said through gritted teeth.

"Fine?" I blinked, and my shoulders loosened ever so slightly.

"What's this about the periodic table and disinterest?" He gestured with his hand, indicating I had the floor.

I frowned and started walking again.

He didn't miss a beat, following back into step with me. "What? Now you don't want me to ask?"

"No, I don't want you to ask because you don't actually care. You've been forced into it."

I was going in circles; I knew it. But with the twister of emotion building in my chest, I couldn't figure out how to plant my feet back on the ground.

"Aren't most people?" he asked. The dose of genuine curiosity in his tone made me glance at him. "To maintain a friendship, people feel like they have to ask questions about stuff they don't care about. That's being forced into it. Maybe in a less obvious way, but still not of their own volition."

My laugh lacked any sense of amusement. "You can't be serious. What anti-social boot camp did your folks put you in?"

The muscle in David's jaw ticked as he directed his gaze forward, expression half-pained, half-furious. For the first time in a long time, I wished I could take a jab back. I didn't understand why my words settled under his skin, but I did know they'd dug in deep. David remained quiet for the rest of the walk, his presence a waning ember that I feel horrible for nearly snuffing out.

"I'm sorry."

Those words should have been coming from my mouth, but he'd said them. I looked up at him to find that the color had come back into his cheeks, and his eyes weren't so hard.

I shook my head. "David, I..."

"I don't know if I ever said thank you for the bottles." He stuffed his hands into his pockets. "You were a friend to me that day. And you're right, I could do better at returning the favor since we spend so much time together. It's only fair."

It all sounded so logical and to the point. I appreciated it. But I craved something more. I wanted something colorful and connecting. It'd be nice to be on the same side for once in our lives. Because honestly, over the past few years, I *have* considered being David's friend. And unfortunately, there were merits to the idea.

For one, David was focused. He could—and most of the time preferred— to stick to a routine. He ate lunch at 1 p.m. , dinner in the café at 9 p.m, was up at 6 a.m. every week to run, and 7:30 a.m. on the weekends.

He didn't waver in the wind. Every one of his opinions (regardless of how irritating they could be) was steady. He stood in his belief without the fear of standing out in a crowd. No one could talk him out of something unless they had definite evidence of his being wrong, and David wasn't so far up his own ass that he couldn't admit when he was wrong.

And on our best days, our conversations made me get out of my head and into the present. His nihilism was an anchor to the present—something I often abandoned for the what-if.

"Thank you, Yara," he said. "Really. I was going through a rough time, and you pulled through for me."

My cheeks burned because his brown eyes softened as he looked at me. There was genuine gratitude in his voice. My eyes flickered to his lips, mind rewinding to a few minutes ago when he'd blown on my hand to disrupt my nervous tick. He hadn't used the picking against me yet. Something told me he never would.

What the hell was happening? Why did he sound nice? Seemed like someone I could hold hands with down this cobbled walkway?

"You're... welcome." I cleared my throat and looked toward the trees, street lamps, and anything else that wouldn't make me feel like I was struggling for air.

We were at my bus stop now. There were a couple of students sitting on the bench, so we lingered a few feet away. Whether it was maintaining our own privacy or respecting theirs, I'm not sure.

"It's about five minutes out," I told David after checking the schedule on my phone. "So if you have something to say or a dare to impart, now's your time."

"You should come to this party I'm planning," he said.

I scoffed so hard I started coughing. The students on the bus bench glanced at me, concerned. But David said nothing, watching me with his resumed unbothered gaze. We waded back to normalcy.

"A party?" I asked.

"You'll be fine," he said.

I laughed at his attempt to encourage me. "Of course I will. Will you?"

"I'm hosting it, so it'd be concerning if I weren't."

"David Evans, hosting a party?" I teased. "What bet did you lose?"

"As you're aware, I don't make a habit of losing." He pulled out his phone to text me the details.

I eyed the off-campus address. "What is it for?"

"Why does it have to be for anything?" He feigned offense. "Can't I just host a party?"

"You can't just do anything."

David paused for a moment, watching me with a small smile. "A friend. It's for a friend."

"David Evans hosting a party for a friend?" My teasing tone melted into surprise. Between football, schoolwork, and our dares, I didn't think he had much time (or interest) in socializing. But once again, I was reminded that despite how much we knew about each other, we didn't *know* each other.

He seemed to sense my thoughts, or somewhere along the line of them. "I'm just offering you a chance to relax around halfway decent humans. Don't read too much into it."

I nodded, still trying to read between the lines and uncover everything he hid from me by just staring into his eyes. The bus rolled up, forcing me to let it go prematurely.

"Okay, fine," I said. "I guess I'll see you at your party."

He nodded and waited for me to get on. I claimed a spot at the window, glancing at the place where I had left him on the sidewalk. He was already walking away, back to me, and focused once more on whatever he did outside of us.

10

—————

"IF WE CUT BACK to finger foods." Haven untangled her locs with one hand and punched numbers into a calculator with the other. "And make them ourselves, we could save the eight hundred on catering."

I chewed on my pen cap, staring at the whiteboard we'd been moving stuff around on for hours. Event logistics were more of a hassle than anticipated since I didn't have the resources of the three other orgs. Women in Business excelled at hosting small gatherings, but their roster of connections was almost as thin as ours.

"That's a lot of hand-rolled pigs in a blanket," I said.

She shrugged. "Beats an over-charged credit card."

"You're right." I sighed and erased the caterer from the board. "Maybe we can make it into a bonding event for the board and members."

"We'll have much more control over the menu that way," Haven said around a yawn as she updated our finance tracking sheet.

"You want to call it for the night?" I asked.

She shook her head. "No way. I'm having the time of my

life. We haven't even dived into the exorbitant amount of money our potential locations want as a down payment. Not to mention their insurance fees. Did you know most of these places give you one week after booking to cancel, and then, you're locked in? No matter how far away the event is. Did I mention I'm having the time of my life?"

Groaning, I fell onto the couch, face-first. "I just wanted to do a cute little ball. I don't think that's too much to ask."

Haven patted my head. "It's not too much; it's just... a lot."

"What's the difference?"

"One's exhausting; the other's obtainable with a bit of elbow grease."

My phone alarm went off. I sighed, pulling it out of my back pocket. "Of course, this is tonight."

"What's tonight?" Haven pushed herself off the floor and went to the kitchen, on the hunt for leftovers.

"David's having a party," I said.

She laughed. "A party? That should be interesting. Think he'll dance?"

"I hadn't even considered that as an option, but now that you've mentioned it, I don't think I can afford to miss this."

"You're really considering going?" She twirled a pair of unopened chopsticks between her fingers as she waited for her noodles to reheat.

I pushed myself into a sitting position. "I... yeah."

"Why? David's the reason your blood pressure was so high last year."

"My blood pressure has always been high," I said. "It's genetic."

"Well, hanging around him can't be helping."

"When he invited me, I think... Haven, I think he was trying to be nice."

"Nice? David was trying to be nice?"

"He even said thank you for the water fiasco last year," I said. "And get this, he apologized for not pretending to be a friend sometimes, like I do."

Her nose wrinkled. "Did he have any weird marks on him?"

I frowned. "What?"

"Like hints of being injected." She gestured to the back of her neck. "You know, for the probing."

I pressed my lips together, trying not to laugh or engage with anything to do with aliens. Once Haven and I got on this train, it was difficult to jump off.

"Speaking of probing," Haven said, realizing her joke would not be enough to pull me in. "There's a new season of *Out There* available. Want me to heat your chicken and rice? I could get the weighted blankets, too. Maybe some lavender tea after we finish eating, and we can start theorizing?"

"Tempting, but I'm going to this party." I pushed off the couch and went to the laundry room to dig through the dryer. "And you're coming too."

She laughed. "I only half-support your venture deeper into the world of David. But I will not partake in that journey. My intuition screams run the other way."

"We don't go to parties." I retrieved my fleece-lined tights. "We've never gone to parties. Don't you want to tell your children about the wild stuff you got up to in college?"

"No, because A: I won't be having any."

"Right." I had forgotten about her decision to remain child-free.

"And B: I don't need to go to some unknown location with drunk strangers to feel like my college experience was worthwhile. I didn't think you needed to either."

"I don't. I'm mostly going to be nosy." I leaned against the laundry room's door frame, twirling the tights in a circle. "David's throwing the party for his friend."

She raised a brow. "You could have led with that. Is this someone from where you guys grew up?"

I shook my head. "No one from where we grew up wanted to leave."

"Aw, well, it's baby's first friend then?"

"Seems like it. So, what do you say? It's off campus. In that fancy neighborhood with the locked gates and grass that's always two and a half inches tall. We could dip in, see how many times a football player can use the word 'bro' and dip out to get fries and pick apart theories on *I Believe* forums."

Haven chewed her noodles slowly, considering. "Will you throw in a trip with me to the RV lot?"

After college, Haven was determined to move into an RV and travel across the US for a couple of years. "I will gawk over prices and try to haggle for you until the lot closes."

She smiled. "Did you see my good skirt in the dryer?"

———

A CODE WAS REQUIRED to open the gate. A code David failed to share after multiple texts. I eventually called him. It took two times before he finally picked up. And once he did, I was greeted with a lackluster, "Yeah?"

I closed my eyes to avoid rolling them because Haven was in the driver's seat, and she would turn her car around the second she sniffed unnecessary conflict.

"The gate code, David," I said flatly.

"Shit." He muted.

We waited for about a minute. Haven drummed on the steering wheel, leaning forward to read the gaudy residential name.

"Baymount Springs," she said with a wrinkled nose. "Do you think people who live in places like these actually like these big houses with no personality and golf-cart-plagued crosswalks? Or have they just convinced themselves it's better because it's behind a gate, which, mind you, is a false sense of security because even I could climb over that?"

I shrugged, swallowing down my response of actually liking neighborhoods like these. It was like the one I grew up in. The large bay windows on most of the houses reminded me of winters spent tracing snowflakes on glass. I'd spent plenty of summers riding around the neighborhood in my parents' golf cart. They'd trusted me enough to take the thing out as a preteen. My friends and I would drive it to the far corners of the golf course to count the number of misplaced balls and see if we could sneak in a few holes without getting caught.

Haven knew I came from money. Sure, it wasn't the upper echelon, rubbing elbows with world leaders' kind of money, but it was still the fine china, trust fund, multiple vacations, we'll load up your debit card if you want, you can get both pairs of shoes kind of money.

Haven didn't know I got nostalgic about it. She didn't understand that manicured lawns and animal-shaped bushes made me feel at home. And I never attempted to explain, too embarrassed and guilt-ridden about enjoying what most would consider soulless or too extravagant.

"2543," David said as soon as he came back on the line.

Haven punched in the number, and the gate creaked open.

"Good?" he asked.

"Yeah, all good. Thank—"

He hung up. Haven gave me a look, and I shook my head. "Don't say it."

"I'm not going to say it," she promised and, in a lower voice, added, "Yet."

"We're here to gather crucial dancing-David evidence, stuff our bags with over-priced snacks, and maybe make a few contacts for the ball. Everything else is irrelevant."

"Alright, alright." Haven parked right alongside the sidewalk. There were already a handful of cars on the circular driveway. When we got out, we saw a brown-skinned woman walking her dog and talking on the phone. She smiled at us and gave us a small wave before carrying on.

"Evening," an old, gray-haired man who was cruising by on a bike greeted with a serene smile.

"Evening," Haven and I said in awkward unison.

My best friend ran around the car to meet me on the sidewalk and tucked her arm through mine. "Aren't they supposed to be side-eyeing my dump of a car? Asking if we're lost? Or are we safe because they smell the new money on you? I'm sure your parents used to bathe you in it."

"I don't think that's it, considering the money baths only happen on my birthday," I said. "The smell fades after a few months."

Haven watched our six as I led us up the walk to a surprisingly quiet house. I checked the number on the door twice to be sure we were at the right place. When I knocked, there was a squeal, a crash, and a flutter at the curtain.

"Relax, relax." A tall, broad-shouldered guy with one of the famous tattoo sleeves opened the door. "It's not him. It's... Yara?"

I smiled and wiggled out of Haven's grip to hug him. "Hart."

Hart Hwong lifted me off my feet and carried me past the threshold. Last semester, we were the only two minorities in a course called Cultural History through the Lens of Film. I backed him and his demand for more Korean films to be added to the watchlist. And he was my right-hand man whenever I pushed for more queer Black media to be included in our discussions on intersectionality.

"Where have you been?" Hart asked. I ignored the curious gazes of his friends. They slowly began going back to what they were doing: taping up a 'Happy Birthday!' banner, setting out food, and scattering confetti on the marble floor.

"Where I usually am." I laughed when he gave me a last squeeze and set me down. "Library and slash or student center. What about you?"

We'd made promises to stay in touch. Sent a few texts about how we missed each other and would try to meet up during the summer. But our lives didn't quite overlap... or, maybe we just didn't work too hard to make them overlap. Hart was on the football team with David. He was a guard: large, fearless, and steady. He had a type of calm confidence I admired and envied.

"Football field, gym, bed." As he spoke, we kept our arms wrapped around each other, too excited to realize how odd it might be. But we were both huggers and hand warmers, and whatever involved comforting touch.

Haven cleared her throat, too polite to tell him to get his hands off her designated security friend.

"This is my best friend." I reached out, tugging Haven into our little world.

Hart's eyes brightened. "The one who surfs?"

I nodded. "And wants to travel for a living after school."

"Wicked," he said and smiled at her.

She tried to smile back, but the lack of people distracted her. "Very wicked...so, where's the party? I thought we'd be swinging off banisters and doing keg stands."

"Oh, no, that was last week," Hart teased. "Sorry you missed it. Tonight, we're more of a small group who argue over orange and red properties or who did what in the study room with the candlestick."

When Haven gave him a confused look, and he returned it, I laughed and became their translator. "He's talking about board games. She didn't grow up with board games or TV unless it was late-night cable."

"I'm very proficient in *I Dream of Jeanie*," Haven offered.

I slipped out of Hart's embrace when he asked about classic American television, and got a glimpse of David disappearing into the kitchen. I smiled at the strangers in the living room, who offered me obligatory waves and polite 'hellos.'

The kitchen was an outrageous display of wealth. The glossy finery made me wonder whether people actually cooked inside, or if it was as useless as an IKEA display. One thing that my siblings and I could ruin in our family home was the kitchen. Mom even had a TV installed above one of the counters so we could watch cartoons while helping her bake. Another wave of nostalgia engulfed me. Big houses with small rituals were the source of most of my homesickness.

A guy with gold-wire framed glasses, dark brown skin, and a look of absolute concentration carefully placed a couple of candles around the edge of a sheet cake. Based on my current catering knowledge, I estimate the trays of food on the island cost about $300. On the ground were pot after pot of houseplants. The space was one part fine dining, one part greenhouse.

"Hi," I greeted.

The guy looked up, confused for a moment before offering me a warm smile. "Hello."

It was quiet for a second as he continued placing the candles, and I stood in the doorway, awkwardly watching.

"I'm Yara."

"Nathaniel," he said without looking up.

"Nice to meet you."

He nodded. More silence.

"I'm a frie—David invited me," I explained my presence. "I thought I saw him come in here."

"Bathroom," Nathaniel nudged his chin toward a long hallway leading into the back of the house. There were at least six visible doors, each closed with light filtering out from underneath.

"Right." I clasped my hands behind my back. "Mind if I wait here for him?"

"Not at all." He moved to get more candles. I took a seat at the counter on the lush, green-threaded barstool.

Nathaniel's fresh fade and thick biceps conjure images of a smiling athlete pinned to the dining hall's bulletin board. He'd been on the school website's front page more times than any of his fellow teammates combined. He was a true golden boy of Westbrooke's dreams.

"I remember you made that winning touchdown last year," I said. "They say you broke the school's losing curse."

"Lucky catch." He shrugged, offered me a shy smile before pushing his glasses on top of his head. Nathaniel moved some plants from one side of the room to another. He even lifted the large pots with one hand and little to no effort.

"Rumor has it you once won the lottery and survived two plane accidents. People say that's why they recruited you. Apparently, whatever you touch turns to gold," I teased, trying to trigger a conversation.

According to my stealthy Google search underneath the table, Nathaniel held the all-time best receiving record in the NCAA. Westbrooke hadn't even qualified for the playoffs until last year, when Nathaniel stepped on campus. After his arrival, they'd lost only two games in the entire season, a nearly impossible feat.

Nathaniel was a fantastic contender for the annual picnic basket fundraiser BWD hosted, featuring a handful of eligible Black men on campus. Charming smile, incredible arms, and a winning record. His basket would undoubtedly spark a bidding war. If I could get him to open up and trust me, maybe I could convince him to get involved in a worthy cause.

He offered me the smile one might offer a little kid who was word vomiting, and said, "That so?"

"Very so," I assured.

A hint of ink peeking out of his grey long sleeve marked him as the second guy in the trio of tattoo sleeves. In the handful of times I've seen him around campus, he barely opened his mouth. Nathaniel seemed perfectly content in the silence. Not interested in the slightest in bragging about his talent and victories.

Unsure of what to say next, I fell back on what was most comfortable:

"I'm the president of a student org." I dug into my bag, looking for the business cards Haven insisted were a waste of money. But nothing said you meant business like a glossy logo. "I would love to connect and talk about potential collaboration opportunities."

"Yara," a warning voice appeared from the doorway behind Nathaniel. "Don't work my teammates."

"What? We're just talking." I shrugged.

"I didn't invite you to pressure people into extracurricular activities." David began helping his friend move the plants from one end of the room to the other. "Don't worry about her. She'll talk your ear off if you let her. Don't let her."

Nathaniel chuckled and came over to grab the business card from me. It's then that I realize how much taller he was than me. Shoulders broad, jawline sharp, wide nose stunning. "It's cool. I like talkers."

My cheeks burned at his genuine smile and the kind tone of his voice. I gave David a look that said, *'See, some people appreciate me.'*

"I'll have my people contact your people," Nathaniel said.

I nodded, still feeling a bit lightheaded at his full attention. He had this way about him that I'm sure could only be captured on some genius's canvas or a poet's prized notebook. "I'm my people."

"Me too." His laugh was deep and soothing. Now I'm the shy one, too stunned to speak.

"I need to grab a couple more pots from my car," he said to David before giving me a polite nod and smiling goodbye. "It was nice meeting you."

I watched him leave, only to be pulled back down to earth when David cleared his throat.

"Sorry." I blinked and shook my head. "He's just...wow. And...wow."

"Tell me about it." David nodded, reminding me we had similar tastes in men. "But I need you to leave the networking alone. I was trying to be nice, inviting you here, but if you keep trying to broker deals, I'm going to have to see you out."

"I'm just starting a conversation. I can't help it if it naturally flows into things like events. Events are my thing."

David stood at the sink, scrubbing his hands. There were clouds of steam from how hot the water was, but it didn't seem to bother him.

"Nothing naturally flows with you," he said, still scrubbing. I could see his blurry reflection in the window over the sink. The ghost of a smile lingered on his lips.

"If I didn't know any better, I'd say you're in a good mood," I teased. "Thanks to my arrival, right?"

He scoffed and glanced over his shoulder for a second. "Yeah, I'm so thrilled to see you for the fifth time this week."

"Who wouldn't be?" I smiled. "What's with all the foliage?"

"Nat's moving in for the semester. These are his children," he said.

"Moving in?" I looked up at the chandelier. "A college athlete can afford this kind of rent? I knew I should have kept running."

"This is Weston's family's house... one of four." He finally stopped washing his hands, grabbed a napkin to dry them, and paid careful attention to the space between his fingers. "They only use this one every other summer. Six beds, four baths, a sauna, and a mini golf course in the back—because the community one wasn't enough."

I laughed. "Wait, so, you're friends with this guy but give me the side-eye because I'm used to getting my clothes dry-cleaned and spent a few summers in the Maldives?"

He gave me a half-shoulder shrug. "I gave Weston shit for it at first, too."

"At first?" I noted. "So, why exactly have I not transitioned into reverent respect?"

"Who says I don't reverently respect you?"

I frowned. "Really?"

"I'm not trying to start an argument," he promised with a hand to his heart. "Not this time. I actually do reverently respect you. Why wouldn't I? You work hard. Grind. And put a lot of pressure on yourself. Too much for someone of your background. So, I figure you're trying to make up for where you come from. It's admirable. And unnecessary. Those seem to be your calling cards."

My mouth was open, but nothing came out. David seriously said something nice. Something not laced in disappointment or disapproval. I'd long ago released the desire to glean his approval. But now that it was here, I couldn't help but bask in its warmth.

"That's... charitable of you," I managed.

"Yeah, well, don't get used to it," he warned with a smile. "I still think you're annoying."

I laughed, thankful for his lifting of the soft veil that'd somehow draped over us for a moment, making our exchange feel like coming home after a trip that went on far too long.

"How do you have friends like this, anyway?" I gestured

with my thumb over my shoulder. "Nathaniel seems kind. And Hart's a big, beautiful sweetheart. I think one of my org members is involved with Weston, so that's a good seal of approval for me."

"Contrary to your very limited belief," David said. "I can be fun to be around."

I laughed. "I'd kill to see some of that fun."

"I have to be around people who bring the best out of me."

David gave me a knowing smile, and my mind conjured up the memory of us on the rocks. I'm right back to his arms around my waist, with his lips just a breath away from my ear, and I can't be properly annoyed because I'm properly confused. He stared back at me, also confused about why I didn't parry his remark.

His phone buzzed on the counter, freeing me from his gaze and the possibility of being seen right through. Whatever was on the screen made him smile.

"Weston's running a bit late," David said. "We've got about another forty-five minutes until he'll show up. More than enough time for a dare."

My stomach caved. "Now? You don't have more streamers to hang or caviar to plate?"

David held out his hand. "Give me your phone."

I pulled my bag closer to my chest as if he demanded to take all I was worth. "Why?"

"It's part of the dare," he said. "I dare you to let me text anyone in your contacts."

11

"Phone?" he asked. "Or forfeit?"

My jaw tightened as I considered all the havoc he could wreak with one message. David offered me a dark smile, knowing I was running through scenarios.

"Can we set some ground rules?" I asked.

He shook his head. "We already have rules, Yara. You can't keep adding to them anytime you're scared. I'm not going to remember a ten-page document's worth of dos and don'ts."

He had a point. The more we had to remember, the more prone we'd be to forget. As much as I loved a good tabbed document, our back-and-forth didn't warrant such attention to detail.

"Fine." I slapped the device into his palm.

"Honestly, I thought I might have had you," David said.

I gave him a fake smile. "It's going to take more than the threat of a silly little message to have me give up all this groundwork."

When I let go of my phone, David reached for my hand. I gasped at his warm fingers pressed against my skin—a reaction way more dramatic than I intended. David laughed at the noise. He'd laugh at how my heart leaped into my throat, too, if he were privy to it.

"What are you..." I watched as he gently straightened my thumb and pressed it to the phone to unlock it. As soon as he let me go, I tugged my hand into my lap, massaging out the buzzing sensation he'd left behind.

"You could have asked for the passcode," I said.

"I could have," he agreed, voice quiet and distracted as he swiped across my screen.

"So, you needed an excuse to touch me?" I tried to come back to my senses and feel less like I was about to come undone. David was just some guy from high school who liked to preach stoicism and judge intellect on his own moral scales.

"You know I'm always looking for a good excuse," he murmured as he typed. "I got a taste of it at the beach, and now, I can't get enough."

I would have scoffed if I weren't taken aback by the fact that he brought up that moment. He could have referenced anything. He could have left it alone. And yet, his mind lingered on something I was also stuck on every time we came face-to-face now.

His brief comment sparked a moment of deep reflection. As I weighed the likelihood of seriousness underlying his teasing, David's forehead furrowed at whatever was on the screen.

His confused, hushed "*shit*" sent off immediate alarm bells.

My smile faded. Visions of sugarplum sandcastles washed off the shore. "What?"

"I didn't realize she was going to respond so quickly..." His brow knitted. "And angrily."

"Give it to me." When I reached for my phone, he pulled it back.

"Yara, give me a second to…"

"To?" I shook my head, waiting for an explanation that'd calm my nerves. "What the hell did you do?"

"It'll be a temporary misunderstanding," he promised, though the unsure tilt of his brow told another story.

"Give. It. To. Me," I ordered through gritted teeth.

David took a deep breath and handed me the phone. As soon as I saw the name at the top of the text thread, my heart dropped. But that was just the tip of the iceberg. The text David sent made bright dots cloud my vision.

"What the hell is wrong with you?" I chewed on my thumbnail as I watched the text dots disappear and reappear, then disappear again. God, she was still responding.

"This is my ex," I hissed at David.

"Well, that was the point," he said in an admittedly remorseful tone. If I weren't so furious, I would have noted how he winced with regret, how his fingers pushed through his hair in a slow and steady motion, how the small bit of color in his cheeks stretched toward his neck.

"You sent an 'I've been thinking about you' text to my ex." My breathing was shallow.

"In my defense…"

I stared at him, waiting for a valid explanation. After a few seconds of floundering, David couldn't come up with a single thing.

"Yeah, I thought so." I groaned as Ren's text finally came through. I squinted, hoping limited visibility would lessen the sting. It didn't.

YARA (DAVID):

Hey, I've been thinking about you. And us.

REN

Are you being serious? This is so weird and inappropriate. You know I'm with Rose. She's in the room right now. What if she had my phone?

REN

Have your sisters not mentioned the proposal? Is that why you're sending this??

I almost threw up while reading the last part. No one had mentioned any proposal. That news must have been stuck somewhere in the grapevine... Uncle Kevin, probably. He could sit on a secret for weeks.

"The Rose she's talking about wouldn't happen to be..." David stopped as if he'd rather not know the answer.

"My sister, genius." My hands trembled as I tried to type a response. Ren and Rose had been together for three years. They were madly in love and had no guilt about it. Not that they should... even though I wouldn't have minded a bit of groveling from either party.

Every time I typed up a response, it sounded too try-hard. Too fake.

How the hell was I supposed to get her to believe me through text? None of my sentences felt strong enough to convey how much Ren *hadn't* been on my mind. Nothing written could convey an honest denial as well as my tone. But calling wasn't an option. She'd probably put me on speaker for Rose to hear. They were probably cuddling on the couch or whatever a three-year, live-in couple did.

"Your sister's about to be engaged to your ex?" David asked.

I waved him away, not wanting to field a question. "You're done, David. Go away while I try to fix this."

I texted,

> Sorry, it was a joke. Someone I know wanted to prank me. I did not send that text.

REN

> You expect me to believe that?

Oh, fuck her. I groaned and shoved my phone face down on the table.

"Are you cool with it?" David asked.

"Am I cool with you leaving?" I rubbed my hand over my face. "More than cool. Enthused. Obsessed with the idea. Nothing would satisfy me more than you getting out of my face."

"No, the engagement."

I frowned. "I don't care about any engagement. I care about the fact that the girl I date for *two* months, maybe three max, thinks I'm still obsessed with her."

I'd worked years to convince them both that I didn't care about their whirlwind romance that happened on the one family vacation I couldn't go on because I'd been heartbroken and battling the flu. The flu had been more painful than the heartbreak but my family couldn't be convinced otherwise as they coddled me through the early days of Ren and Rose's romance.

David blinked, quiet for a second before saying, "A simple yes would have sufficed."

I'd challenge him to a goddamn fight so fast if I weren't in a skirt, a few inches shorter than him, and no longer lifted weights regularly. I'd challenge him so hard that I'd make it an event, sell tickets, and order t-shirts. Every vs. Evans. It'd be the match of the century.

David reached toward me. He grabbed my phone before I knew what he was doing.

"Are you kidding me?" I tugged at his elbow when he turned his back to me.

"I got it. Trust me, I got it."

"Nothing you say or do is going to help me at this point." I kept grabbing for my phone. David held it just out of reach. I strained closer, my body pressed against his in a way that lit up a dormant part of my brain.

Our bodies fit well together. It was a thought that sent my skin ablaze because what did that mean? Yes, maybe my head could rest perfectly on his shoulder, and he'd be able to rest his chin easily on top of my head. But what did that matter when he also ruined my mood every other time we locked gazes?

"Yara," David protested with a laugh when I flicked his neck to intimidate him. How dare he have fun while my stomach continued to do backflips. "Relax. You're going to make me drop your phone."

"You wouldn't be close to dropping it, if you hadn't picked it up." I continued reaching.

In one swift, confident movement, David grabbed my wrists, locking me in his firm grip. To keep me more easily in place, he pinned our entwined hands at his waist. My breath got stuck in my chest. His gaze remained on my phone, utterly oblivious to my internal war of emotions and a burning desire between my legs as he typed with one hand.

"Oh...umm..." Nathaniel was back, eyes wide at the sight of David and me so close and entangled.

"Sorry to interrupt," he said.

"No worries, what's going on?" David remained unfazed. He didn't move an inch away from me or look up from my phone.

"I just needed to grab this." Nathaniel offered us an apologetic smile and picked up a spray bottle of water before quickly departing.

"You've got to be kidding me," I said once Nathaniel was out of earshot.

"Ssh." David's deep tone stilled me. I swallowed and attempted to remind myself of my overwhelming hatred of him. Unfortunately, lies were hard to pull off when you were chest to chest with someone, which made it nearly impossible for you to breathe without wanting them to notice.

"I got this," David promised again.

We remained in the same position as he pulled the phone to his mouth.

"What are you—"

"Hey, Ren," David started in a steady voice.

My eyes widened. I pressed my lips together, keeping all my protests at bay, once I caught sight of the screen. He wasn't on a call, thank God. He was recording a voice message.

"Sorry about that text. This is David. I'm Yara's..." The weighty pause and a glance down at me said too much and too little. His grip on me loosened, but the shift in his hips aligned us so I could feel the seam of his jeans against my core.

David's gaze flickered to my lips and remained there as he continued, "... anyway, I don't know if you remember, but I used to go to school with you two. Yara and I were messing around. I have this thing for testing out social dynamics, and old exes of Type-A people are infinitely intriguing. It was a shitty joke. I promise, Yara wasn't in on it."

As soon as he let go of the record button, David released my wrists. But I didn't move, and neither did he.

"What?" he asked, eyes on my chest now, unabashed in his observation. I'm covered up in a long-sleeve shirt, but that didn't seem to stop him from taking his time.

"You..." My unfinished response coaxed his attention back to my face. His breath smelled of spearmint. I wondered if he'd taste like it too.

David's hand was on my wrist again, but instead of

pinning it to his side, he urged my palm open. I didn't pay much attention to the movement, too enthralled with how our breath intermingled. He leaned close enough that his nose brushed along the side of mine. Our eyes were barely open as we tested the strength of our fortified barrier. Turns out, we had several weak points.

"Is this... are we doing...?" David's gaze locked on my parted lips.

My breath shuddered, but I nodded. "Think so."

"Damn it," David whispered against my lips as he let go of his last bit of resolve.

The world around us went silent when his lips pressed against mine. The touch was featherlike, a dream almost fading before it truly began. He stopped for a second, waiting for a reply. I offered him another kiss. Another dream. It was just as soft and timid as his. David's response to my offer was something firmer, longer, greedier. His hand cupped my jaw, tilting my head back as he parted my mouth with his. The tip of his tongue brushed mine, giving me a preview of what would be possible with him kneeling between my thighs.

I've dreamed of this once or twice, and it always ended with me waking in a cold sweat while a chill ran down my spine. David wasn't the man of my dreams, but he'd found his way in there somehow. Now, I understand why. I didn't know how I'd convinced myself he wouldn't belong.

David was hard, the imprint of him pressed against my thigh. He backed me into the island, the cold marble surface offering a beautiful contrast to the heat of his body. A moan lingered in my throat, but I refused to release it. Some parts of my brain still had a concept of time. A rational part of me considered self-preservation.

Something crashed in the living room, and a group of people laughed. There were footsteps in the hallway. The threat of someone seeing us made my desire taste sweeter.

David seemed to agree. He kissed me until the last moment; every second made us more frantic and hungry. When we finally pulled away from one another, my lips were swollen, and his were red.

"Hey, David," a bright-eyed, unassuming raven-haired girl greeted. "Know where I can find a broom?"

"Third door on the left." He gestured to the long hall behind us, turning himself slightly away from her so she couldn't see the hardness in his crotch area.

"Thanks." She smiled at us both before disappearing for a moment.

"Here." He held out my phone. "I'll let you decide if you want to send it or not."

There was no acknowledgment of his lips on mine or his arousal pinned against me mere seconds ago. If he didn't brush his fingers across his bottom lip as if he were reliving the whole thing, I'd assume I'd had a walking dream. Or nightmare, depending on the outcome.

I snatched the device and pressed send without a second thought. My heart pumped blood to my erogenous zones, so thrilled something like this was finally happening after a year of self-pleasure. "Of course I want to send it. It's possibly the only thing that'll clear my name."

David snorted, pulled his hand away from his mouth, and placed it in his hair. He used both hands to brush his strands back. There was an easy smile on his lips, but from the frantic way he gripped the hair at the nape of his neck, I suspected his calm was a lovely mirage. "You're welcome."

"Oh, thank you," I said in a mocking tone, covering up my own internal crisis. "Thank you for fixing what you broke. For cleaning up the mess you made. Thank you so much."

He held back a laugh, biting down on his bottom lip. I wanted a chance to do that to him. David's hand gripped his neck as he massaged circles on his pulse. I wanted him to have an opportunity to do that to me. Harder, though.

Oh, you're screwed.

"New rule," I decided in a stern voice. "Just a simple one."

He continued to massage his neck as he said, "Let's hear it."

"No contacting exes."

He nodded. "Fair enough, Daredevil. Fair enough."

In the spring semester of my sophomore year at Westbrooke, I had hit a low unlike any other. The days had started blending, a muddy mosaic of uninspired creation. Homesickness became the film through which I saw the world. I could have gone home. My parents wouldn't have minded. And my siblings would only tease me for as long as I could keep my tears in–and at that point, my record was thirty seconds.

I didn't leave campus. A window for a bus ticket remained open on my laptop, though. And the number for a private car service was written on my wrist every morning. I walked through campus with a smile and an inescapable ache in my stomach. I went on like that for a month before seeing David outside of the student center. He was hurrying across the quad, a gym bag swung over one shoulder, books stacked in his hands. His tongue poked the inside of his cheek, and the familiarity of the gesture offered temporary relief to my constant ache. The way his hair fell in his eyes made my lips twitch. It wasn't a smile, not yet. But it was enough to remind me I once had the capability of feeling something other than wayward and isolated.

David looked like home. He wore a worn tee from a local seafood restaurant where he'd bussed tables all junior and senior year. The braid bracelet on his wrist came from an older woman who sold handfuls of them to hiking tourists every summer season. If I got close enough, he'd probably smell like the mountains. Westbrooke smelled so much of salt and sea that I missed the pine needles and oak trees.

I didn't move closer, but I did pull out my phone. We'd exchanged numbers years ago for some group project that'd meant the world then and absolutely nothing now.

My finger had hovered over the send button. A message this late into our college career would be weird and perhaps a little desperate. What exactly did I want? And why did I think David Evans of all people could provide it?

But sending the text felt no less or more painful than the days I went through on autopilot. Seconds after I sent it, David pulled out his phone and stopped dead in his tracks. He stared at the screen for a moment before a small smile appeared.

DAVID

Told you you'd miss me.

I snorted, recalling his warning when I vowed never to speak to him again after graduation.

It was a simple question. Doesn't mean I miss you.

And I hadn't. I'd missed our gray-bricked high school, rugged hiking trails, star-gazing watch parties, and community movie nights in the park. But I couldn't have that and grow up, so talking to him would get me close enough.

DAVID

You want tickets to a football game? You
hate football.

I'm giving it a second chance.

DAVID

Being away from the rest of the royal family
forced you to expand your horizons, huh?

Careful.

DAVID

Careful? You threatening me?

Possibly.

DAVID

With what?

You want to risk finding out?

DAVID

Yes, one thousand percent.

I'd bit my lip, fighting off a full smile. This was what I
wanted, what I needed.

He'd taken my pause as a retreat and tried to reel me back
in by texting,

I dare you.

There'd be no retreat. David and I were just getting
started.

———

THE LAGOON WAS a restaurant made wholly of stained-glass windows and overpriced poached eggs. It was the halfway point between Westbrooke and my hometown, a place my mother had heavily vetted as a worthy replacement for the usual place we "held court."

Dad and my older brother, Adam, had an open invitation, but they never used it, citing that "court" was for those in charge, and they simply got in the way. The real reason was that they loathed the idea of being up on a weekend any time before 11 a.m..

On the other hand, my sisters and I were well-oiled cogs. All of us focused on becoming the best of the best and being regimented. And though I'd been picking at my hair all week, on the morning of breakfast, I felt no urge to reach for the thinning patch at the back of my head. Because even if I still felt like a bumbling loser for not having the ball neatly laid out and my hiccup with Ren haunting every other thought, I knew Mom was going to wrap me into her arms like I was the reason the stars shone so bright. My oldest sister, Aimee, would hum in approval of all my ideas. She was basically a second mother, and that made her perpetually impressed with anything I accomplished since she'd known me during the time when I couldn't hold my head up. Logan would ask if I was getting enough sun and suggest I replace coffee with Haven's green juice in my morning routine. And Rose...

Well, Rose and I stood on almost the same playing field. At exactly eleven months older than me, she was more prone to take whatever I was doing and hold it up next to her to-do list to see if we aligned. We shared the same temperament, which led to the same hang-ups. If I were to argue with a family member —which was almost concerningly rare considering how often we got together— it would be her ninety-eight percent of the time. Today, especially, I prepped for a battle, manning myself with a freshly steamed blouse and white skirt.

"I'll never understand the need to dress up to go to breakfast with family," Haven said around a yawn as I was on my way out.

"It's what we're most comfortable with." I shrugged. We'd tried doing a casual, sweatshirt and loose jeans kind of meal, and the whole time we'd fidgeted and lost track of where the conversation had been going.

"Never understand," she repeated, lying her head back down on her pillow to catch a few more hours of sleep.

The morning sky was painted pink when Logan's black sedan pulled up on the curb to get me.

"Sorry, traffic's a nightmare," she said, an explanation for her two-minute lateness.

"There's a game on campus this afternoon." I slipped into the seat.

"Jeez." She pulled back onto the road slowly, ever cautious, ever vigilant.

"You got this." I clicked on my seatbelt, watching the rearview with her as a fast car nearly clipped our side.

Logan chewed on her bottom lip, going silent so she could focus on making it out of the university area and onto the highway. I dug my fingers into my seat until we were safely merged and in the flow of traffic. Logan was a highway driver, far more confident going eighty miles per hour on a long stretch of road than thirty-five miles per hour on a local street. My shoulders relaxed, and the unspoken, no-talking rule disappeared, blowing away with the blasting heat of the AC.

One day, I would be brave enough to talk about why she was hesitant behind the wheel and why it was my fault. One day, maybe we'd admit that despite getting along so well, we also fueled one another's anxieties and fears in a way no one else ever could. Not today. The pain was still too heavy to lift off my shoulders today.

"I should warn you." Logan reached to turn on the radio. Comforting smooth jazz flowed into the space.

Great. She was trying to keep my heart rate down.

"Why do people say that?" I wondered out loud. "Why don't they just warn you?"

"Courtesy." Logan shrugged. "It's only polite."

Every women lived for politeness. Politeness was like a second skin for us. And it came as easily as breathing to me... except when I was with a certain someone. And since I'd got a taste of the opposite side of the coin, I craved it in moments like this. David's blunt rudeness released me from any leading anxiety. I could never admit this out loud, but it was freeing in a way. No tiptoeing around corners to avoid hard edges.

My lips stung at the memory of us in the kitchen. His hand on my jaw, mouth coaxing me to let him in. We hadn't spoken since then. One week. It's the longest we've gone without talking since we started texting again. I hated it. I needed the space, but I hated it. Missing him was embarrassing, wanting him was confusing.

"Mom knows about the text," Logan said.

My sister's warning temporarily eclipsed my worrying about my awkward standing with David. I slouched in my seat, wiping my hands over my face.

"But I don't think it's going to be that big of a deal." Logan reached over in an attempt to pat my head, but snatched it away when she realized someone was trying to merge in front of her.

"Rose didn't even say anything to me." I unlocked my phone and scrolled through our texts just in case I'd missed something. In case we had some heart-to-heart I'd forgotten about.

"From what I can tell, it was a last-minute slip," Logan said.

"From what you can tell? Were you there when she said it?"

She nodded. "We were shopping for engagement dresses."

"Engagement dresses?" I asked. "So, I'm really the last person to hear that Ren's proposing?"

Logan winced, ashamed of the secret. "It was a touchy subject and a very new development. We all wanted to wait until we could be together to tell you in person. So we could be there for you both."

I sighed. "I don't need anyone to be there for me. I don't care about Ren and Rose. Also, who buys an engagement dress? Aren't engagements a surprise?"

Logan gave me a look. "You know Rose would never in a million years stoop to being surprised."

"Not even for something romantic?" I asked, though it was a lost cause. Rose had been planning her own birthday parties since she was six years old. She made color-coded activity sheets for vacations. And placed name cards on tables for big family get-togethers.

"She's nervous about seeing you," Logan said. "That's why she told Mom about the text. Rose thinks you're mad at her."

"I'm a little annoyed, that's all." Once upon a time, we'd been so glued at the hip we'd been mistaken for twins. We called ourselves twins until Ren and Rose's relationship.

"Was it really a prank?" Logan asked, glancing my way to gauge my honesty.

I pushed myself back up straight. "Of course, it was a prank. Even if I were still into Ren, I would never in a million years do that to Rose... and it hurts that any of you would even consider that."

Logan chewed on her bottom lip and reached over once

more to squeeze my hand. "Tell her that. Be honest, and I'm sure eventually everything will work itself out."

———

"Yara." Whenever Mom said my name, it sounded fancier than it was. My name became a flowery lyric or obscure poetry title. Her accent was a beautiful mix of Southern charm and the decade she'd spent in France as a young girl.

"My wonder." She didn't get up from her seat but did tilt her head so we could kiss one another's cheeks. Mom patted the empty seat next to her as she turned to give Logan her typical greeting of, "My storm."

All of us had our own larger-than-life comparisons that Mom had given us as kids. She was insistent that the moment she laid eyes on each of us, she saw something large and powerful. It was a lovely sentiment that constructed the foundation for our self-esteem at a young age. I couldn't say it helped me much since high school, though. These days, being called a wonder felt like a joke.

Aimee, on the other side of me, waited until I settled in my seat to straighten out my twists and offer me a side hug. "How have you been?"

Her voice was soft enough to find solace in, and her smile was warmer than the sunlight that reached through the windows in front of us. Aimee wore her hair short, the soft curls dyed a chestnut brown that brought warmth to her dark skin. She still shaved her eyebrows completely off —had been doing that since college— and still pulled it off in a way that made one wonder if eyebrows were even necessary. The answer for me was yes, very necessary. I used to do anything and everything I could to make myself look like Aimee.

I smiled and shrugged. "Busy."

"Good busy?"

"Always," I promised, the lie so flimsy I had to look away before she called me out.

My gaze fell to Rose on the opposite end of the table. She wore a wavy lace-front wig with curtain bangs that framed her round face perfectly. Her lips were glossy red, and her nose was dotted with faux freckles. She was deep into something on her phone and had barely looked up when she heard Logan and me joining them. Rose finally looked up when Logan sat down beside her, offering our sister an enthusiastic hug and asking about her TA workload.

"Three of the assistants I'm working with are dating each other —it's a love triangle kind of thing— and the other one doesn't realize it's obvious that he's sleeping with the professor," Logan said, eyes alight with the chance to relax and gossip.

"You should pitch this as a reality show. Or maybe write a comedy." Rose laid her phone face down, ready and willing to probe into college department drama. She lived vicariously through all our college experiences, since she'd opted to complete her degree online so she could audition for shows at theatres full-time in New York City.

The server came by to offer us drinks and take our orders. As we waited, Rose kept pressing Logan for department gossip, then eventually asked Aimee how her clinical trials were going and Mom about the community garden. It wasn't until the food was at the table and the drinks had been refilled twice that Rose decided to address the elephant in the room.

She didn't look up from her omelet as she asked, "How have you been, Yara?"

"Great, thanks for asking," I spoke as if every word was a landmine. "You?"

"Couldn't be better."

"Oh, yeah?" I asked.

"So much has been going on." She nodded, cutting her egg into small pieces. "So much has been changing."

Aimee took a long sip of her drink, trying to hide her smile. If anyone was going to find amusement from disagreements, it was her. She still saw us all as children fighting over our favorite toys and TV time. The quiet lull over our table made me itchy. I clawed at my wrist as I decided to go for broke. "I think we should talk about it. Get it over with."

Rose looked at me, expression blank in that creepy way she always did as a child when I didn't do what she wanted. It'd taken me years to figure her out. Even when we were close, she had moments where her walls went up, and her sirens remained on full alert.

"I think that's a great idea," Mom chimed in. Once we were old enough to venture out of the house on our own, she'd decided we were old enough to work through our issues with one another. She only interfered to play the occasional referee or cheerleader.

"The "it" you're referring to is my girlfriend, right?" Rose asked.

My girlfriend. The words were laced with barbed wire and soaked in venom. I pressed my molars together, jaw tight at how possessive she sounded, how her words made me sound like I'd shot the first warning arrow.

"Ren showed me your text," Rose continued.

Logan readjusted in her seat, gaze scanning the room as if looking for a decent reason to excuse herself. Aimee rested her hand under her chin, watching us with interest. I wouldn't be shocked if she'd pulled out a notepad and started scribbling down our behavior for a future research project.

"Did she play the voice note too?"

"She did." Rose nodded, expression remained unchanged. "You're hanging out with David Evans these days?"

Logan's attention snapped back. "David Evans...wait, was that the guy in your room that night?"

"In your room." Aimee whistled, impressed. "Not you having late-night company."

Mom wasn't impressed or stunned. The wrinkles on her brow indicated disapproval. As a woman who got married before attending university and then divorced before getting the opportunity to enroll, she was a stickler for education first.

"I'm a senior," I reminded them. "I'm old enough to have people over after bedtime."

"David's that football player, right?" Aimee pivoted. "The one who almost got kicked off the team?"

Logan nodded in confirmation. "A lot of kids got into some trouble for vandalism. The school board had a whole meeting about it. Mom and I went to the open forum. The whole thing was a pitchforks and let's burn the witches vibe."

"And yet, he avoided getting arrested multiple times during senior year," Rose said. "Everyone loves a problematic pretty boy with a good throwing arm."

"David had a rough patch. Not everyone had a healthy home life," I said. "And his arm's not that great; he's a tight end."

They all looked at me blankly.

"His specialty is blocking and receiving. So that makes him a pretty boy with good blocking and receiving ability."

"Okay..." Rose shook her head, not caring.

My defense of David was automatic. I didn't like how Rose's nose wrinkled when she recalled who he was. Or the slight hint of judgment in Aimee's tone when she mentioned him almost getting kicked off the team. They hadn't seen this guy in years and talked about him as if they had him all figured out. I was the one who'd spent countless hours a week going back and forth with the guy, disagreeing with him until my head hurt and my patience ran thin. If anyone had the right to act like they knew him, it was me. And I'd never claim to know half of who that guy was because he never actually let me see him.

"Whatever he is, he doesn't have a good sense of humor," Rose said. "Sending my soon-to-be fiancé a 'I still want you' text is the furthest thing from funny. Which makes it hard to believe that it was a joke."

My gaze hardened. "But it was. I'd never say something like that to Ren. I'd never in a million years go behind your back."

"Alright, sure." She nodded, sounding nowhere near understanding. "But you can't blame me if I'm a little worried. Because in every joke, there's some truth."

Aimee hummed in agreement, but when I glanced at her, she stopped and mouthed, 'Sorry.'

I scratched the back of my neck, frustration like a rash spreading across my skin. "Maybe, but I didn't tell the joke. Thus, making your logic flawed because no part of my truth was in those words."

Rose blinked, unconvinced. "You know, we never talked about it. All the stuff that happened with Ren and me. It was so fast, and we never got to discuss how it made you feel."

There was a pause when they all looked at me, genuine in their curiosity about my headspace.

"We did talk," I reminded her of the hurried conversation we'd had back home when she was still a gorgeous, deep brown from the Italian sun, and I was coughing up the last bits of flu. Rose had confessed her whirlwind romance in a single, run-on sentence. Her nails had been bitten down as far as they could be on her trip back home. I would have been furious and hurt if I hadn't already seen that she'd mentally battled that version of me already on her twelve-hour flight. It hadn't seemed fair to put her through more anguish, and to be honest, I'd just wanted her out of my face so I could throw up in peace.

"But not *talk* talk," Rose insisted.

"You know I support you two," I said. "I helped throw her birthday party last year. "

"A birthday party's different from a wedding," Rose said. "Ren's going to be a permanent fixture in this family. I want to make sure there's nothing underneath the surface. Not just for you, but for everyone."

Her gaze scanned our sisters and Mom. But honestly, what protest would they have made? Everyone loved Ren. She was a six-one goddess who played beach volleyball and modelled for Nike. The woman spoke three languages and wanted to become a biotech engineer after she attempted to make the US Olympic Team. She never forgot a birthday or anniversary, and was the type to send roses just because.

Okay, yes, maybe I had some lingering jealousy. But that wasn't because I was in love with Ren. I got over her as soon as I realized she wasn't ever going to be in love with me. I did feel some type of way that while my sisters seemed to be moving forward, full-steam ahead, I was stuck, struggling with the same hurdles I'd been trying to clear since freshman year. I haven't had a successful fundraiser, a promising internship, a fellowship, or a loving partner to show for the past four years.

"I'd rather have any lingering resentment bubble up now than while we're at the altar," Rose continued.

"There's no resentment," I promised, focusing hard on keeping my voice steady and sure. "I've moved on completely... I'm seeing someone."

Rose blinked in surprise. "You're seeing someone?"

"Why didn't you say anything?" Logan asked, suspicious,

given her earlier attempt to help me prep for this confrontation.

"It still feels new," I said.

"How new?" Aimee asked around between bites of danish.

"Since the summer," I said, because none of them had been home during the summer. With no one around to confirm, they'd never be able to figure out that I'd spent most of my time tagging along with Haven to the beach and watching her get hit on while I scribbled ideas in my sketchbook.

"So, what's their name?" Mom asked.

"Their name..." I hesitated as if it were a math question.

Rose scoffed, and Logan shot me a sympathetic look.

Mom laughed, oblivious to any kind of suspicion. "Yes, I assume they have one?"

"It's David," I said, because it seemed like the most logical next move. Logan had already heard his voice in my room. And Rose heard his voice note. It was clear we'd been spending time together. Since we went to Westbrooke together, it made sense that maybe we'd found solace in one another... I almost laughed at the thought, but kept myself together under the curious stares. There had been an actual kiss between us after all. So, some chemistry (no matter how minuscule) existed underneath the depths of our shared disdain.

It may not be that deep.

"You sure?" Rose asked.

"What do you mean, am I sure?" I frowned, trying my best not to snap at her. So, Ren chose her over me. So, she'd been able to reach her dreams at breakneck speed. So, she'll be married by next year. Was it really so difficult to believe that someone would be interested in me once again?

"David's a great guy," I continued, forcing myself to think of more nice things to say about him and our nonexistent relationship. "He's matured since high school. Really dedicated to his team. And he... pushes me to try new things. I'm pretty sure I'm in love."

The last part had been unnecessary. But I wanted to emphasize I had my own world outside of them. While their world kept spinning, mine did too. I was growing, changing, and falling in love.

"Really in love this time. Not the first time, puppy love stuff with Ren. She was sweet but... well, with David it's different," I said, and that seemed to drive the point home. They exchanged looks, and the consensus seemed to be they were willing to move David to the next stage in Every women approval. They needed to vet him for themselves.

"You should bring David to the engagement dinner, then," Rose offered with a smile.

"I think that's a lovely idea." Mom held up her glass of orange juice to salute Rose. "I think this is the first time all of you girls have partners simultaneously."

"The engagement dinner...?" I asked, my skin itchy again. Aimee noticed my nails as I went to work, placing her hand on top of mine under the table. My cheeks burned, but she didn't say anything to everyone else. She simply patted me and went back to finishing her danish.

"It'll be nice to have everyone together," Rose said.

"Okay, yeah, I'll ask, but it's the beginning of the season, so... he's swamped."

"He can't take one night off to go to dinner with his girl-friend?" Rose raised a brow, a challenge.

I swallowed and forced myself to smile, trying to make it look as natural and easy as possible. "I'll bring him. He'll be there."

"Perfect." Rose beamed, and it was her turn to salute me with her glass. "To love. New and old."

"New and old," I said, hollow and a million miles away.

David had started this mess, but I'd dug myself deeper. I was at the core of the earth, and my only way back up may be a temperamental asshole with a penchant for making me work for it.

13

I'D GONE to sleep that night hoping a better option would present itself in my dreams. I'd solved plenty of nightmare scenarios in the comfort of my subconscious. But no matter how many times I hit snooze, my options remained the same:

1. Come clean and start another uncomfortable, unnecessary point of tension between my soon-to-be-engaged sister.

2. Convince David to play nice and pretend to be my boyfriend for the entire engagement and the wedding.

You should have kept your mouth shut, I scolded myself as I got off the bus at the football stadium's stop. I was hunting for David since he'd been ignoring my texts all morning. He still had his location sharing on from eight dares ago when we'd ventured to a town over for a music festival and crowd surfing.

There was no way for a normie like me to get on the field with the guys unless one of them had given someone express instructions to let me in. So, I was stuck heading for the stands and scanning the crowd of sweaty guys in a shirts and skins scrimmage.

"Yara," a voice called from down the field. Hart jogged to

where I was in the stands. Sweat or water, or both, slicked back his black hair. Shirtless, it was clear he was far larger than I'd ever given him credit for. He was built like a boulder, wide and impenetrable. His gaze contrasted with the intimidating reality that he could probably punch through a wall. Hart's smile possessed a gentle welcomeness. I leaned on the stand's fence, trying to make it easier for him to hear me.

"Morning," I greeted.

"Good morning." His smile brightened. "What brings you to our side of town?"

"Looking for..." I trailed off when Hart climbed. It was concerning at first because I couldn't see a path up. But he moved without abandon, a clear sign he'd done this plenty of times before. I laughed when he reached me, his hands on the outside of mine and his face right in front of me.

"For?" Hart probed with a smile, rocking himself back and forth as he balanced.

"This feels a little dangerous and unnecessary," I noted. We were close enough that I could smell the grass on him, see sweat in his hairline, and feel the weight of his curious gaze.

"I couldn't hear you all the way down there," Hart said, offering me a one-shoulder shrug.

I smiled. "I'm looking for David."

"Right." He tilted his head to the side, studying me. "Are you two a thing?"

"No." I laughed a little. "Never."

Well, technically never.

"You sure?" Hart squinted with a smile as he pretended he could see right through me. My plans to have David as my plus one for the next three months seemed to be written on my forehead.

"He's not my type," I promised.

"So why are you two always hanging out?"

"We're one another's karma," I said simply. It would feel almost unethical not be there to shove David in the direction of optimism. And I'm sure he felt the same about his attempts at flooding my brain with pessimistic sentiment.

"Sounds intense," Hart noted.

"Only at the beginning. Now, it's as mundane as a morning shower. I wake up, go to class, and think of ways to make sure David remembers he's not the center of the universe. It gets uninteresting and repetitive, but someone's got to do it."

Hart chuckled. "How long have you two known each other?"

"Since middle school."

"Really? He never talks about you," he said voice low, almost as if he were talking to himself. It was a simple statement. One that didn't surprise me but somehow settled on my skin, making everything hot and unwelcoming.

"Oh, yeah?" I asked, trying to sound uninterested, as thousands of questions about what or who David had shared filled my mind. "Would you consider him a friend?"

Because of course David wouldn't talk about me to an acquaintance—

"I'd say he's one of my closest friends." Hart's declaration gave me pause.

My assumption came toppling onto my head, leaving a swollen bruise to my ego. "You're joking."

He shook his head. "He'd take a bullet for me."

"David Arthur Evans would take a bullet for you." I laughed because it's nonsensical to think he'd even take a bus ride for someone.

"And I'd do the same for him," Hart said without a moment's hesitation.

My laughter faded, and I'm faced with the possibility that

maybe it's just me who remained at arm's length from David. Back home, he'd done that to everyone, but here at Westbrooke, anytime I'd come across someone who knew David, they liked him. Not in a 'oh, he's a decent guy' way, but in a 'I really respect and admire who he is' way. Where was this respectable and admirable version of David when I was with him?

"Which is why I wanted to be sure you two aren't seeing each other," Hart continued while I was still trying to catch up to the whole, David genuinely can't stand me because he sure as hell would never take a bullet for me, despite knowing me since we were in braces.

"I don't understand the correlation," I said.

"Being into the same person can get messy for friends," he explained.

My stomach flipped once my mind got back on track.

"Before the season starts, the team always has this field day kind of thing," Hart continued. He scratched the back of his neck. "It's not exclusive for team members."

I nodded, too nervous to offer any kind of encouragement to continue on this quest of asking me out.

"Would you be interested in coming?" Hart asked. "With me?"

I took a breath. My fingers tightened on the cold steel of the fence. My hands were still between his, benefiting from the warmth his body radiated.

It had been a year since someone asked me out. I had given little consideration to the prospect of dating. School and the org filled my calendar so well that even my thoughts barely had time off to dream or fantasize about dates, kissing, dorm room sleepovers, and morning afters.

I took too long to answer. But this didn't feel like something I should rush. Hart was cute, and his beliefs aligned with mine, and I could see us kissing, and me not completely being bored by the idea like I had with everyone else I dated since Ren.

But I couldn't bring myself to say the simple, easy yes. Not because I didn't like him, but because I hadn't had time to consider liking him more.

A sharp, loud whistle called for our attention. One of the assistant coaches was demanding a huddle. Hart let out a sigh but accepted his fate with a simple, "Think about it?"

"Of course."

"I'll find you later?" he requested, giving me a chance to say, *no, you don't have to give me a second chance to answer your simple question.*

"Of course," I repeated because my brain malfunctioned. I'd forgotten how to consider romance, to imagine myself in someone's arms and want to be there. The memory of David's hand on my waist was a hot, heavy taunt. My throat went dry from the longing the vision tugged straight from my chest.

Hart climbed back down, tossing me one last smile before heading back on the field. I watched, losing myself in a replay of his proposed date. With my attention in the depths of delayed embarrassment, David's appearance below didn't register until he offered an impersonal, "What are you doing here?"

My heart felt like it restarted from the frozen state Hart had left it in. I glanced down to find the reason for my appearance in a thin tank, the sides long and wide enough to provide plenty of content for future daydreams. I had to ignore a vision of him shoving me against that large marble island in that tank. Seeing a side view of his pecs would surely be my downfall.

"You," I said, trying to make my voice hard. But I've now moved on from the *'why would he ask me'* portion of figuring out Hart's question to the *'why did it make me feel soft and vulnerable'*? Now, it was just an open wound, ready to be poked and prodded by the one person who never let up.

"That so?" David moved closer to the fence but didn't climb it like Hart. He didn't seem concerned about losing my words to the wind.

"You need to help me," I said as I regained feeling in my fingers and toes.

"I need to help you?" He laughed and crossed his arms over his chest. "Need. A very dangerous word. I don't think you should use it so flippantly."

"As much as I would love to delve into the philosophies of word choice," I said. "I don't have the time or care to make it."

"All I'm saying is I don't *need* to do anything. You, on the other hand…"

"One day you'll learn that unsolicited edits aren't the right way to get to a girl's heart," I said dryly.

"You don't say. Does scaling fences do it for you then?"

I smiled and studied David closer. He'd seen Hart and me talking. No, he'd *watched* Hart and me talking. And from the wrinkle in his brow and the way his gaze kept consistent hold of mine, he was searching for something. Who was in need now?

"Perhaps." I rested my elbows on the railing, bending as far as I could to get a better look at him.

David shook his head, feigning disinterest even though I saw his eyes change. Curiosity was David's default state. Whether he liked to admit it or not, he enjoyed learning about people. He pushed buttons because he was interested in the way the gears worked. It wasn't always for annoyance's sake, I'd realized. Sometimes, he truly didn't understand.

"What do I need to do, Yara?" he asked, still stone-faced, but the hardness in his voice had melted.

"My sister didn't believe me about the text."

"Did she listen to the voice note?"

"Yes, and knowing me, she probably considered that maybe you'd made it under duress."

He laughed. "I'd like to see you force me into something."

"Well, today's your lucky day. You're going to help me fix this."

"I already did. I can't control whether your sister believes the truth. Neither can you, so my suggestion would be to let it go. Let it play out."

"I told them I was with you, David. That we were dating."

His smile evaporated. "Why the hell would you say that?"

"Because —at the time— it was the smartest way through."

"That makes no sense."

I closed my eyes for a second. "David, listen…"

"You've made an absolute mess of this." He released a humorless laugh. "The voice note was fine. I could have recorded a follow-up if things were that fucked."

"*We* made a mess of this," I corrected.

David shook his head. "I don't remember being at this exchange. I don't remember giving you the green light to tell your family I'm your boyfriend."

My fingers curled into a fist as I tried to grasp onto my final semblance of patience. "I'm not going to an engagement dinner, wedding rehearsal, and ceremony with the tiny inception of a text you sent."

"Get someone else to do it," he said. "Or, better yet, get an actual partner. You already have one person in line."

His tone had enough grit in the last sentence to make me do a double-take. "Isn't Hart your friend?"

"What does that have to do with anything?"

The look of sheer annoyance and disgust on his face was what it had to do with everything. He disapproved. He loathed the idea. Maybe I didn't know his friends or how he spent his free time. But I knew when he was a hairpin trigger away from being pissed as all get out.

"I gave them your name," I said, trying to reel him back in. "It'd set off a million and one alarm bells if I showed up on someone else's arm. I'm trying to get them to believe me, not push myself deeper into suspect territory. Besides, I don't want to taint the possibility of actually dating Hart."

"You plan on dating Hart?"

"He asked me out, so it's on the table," I said.

The quiet between us was heavy. I waited for a snarky comeback about not being interesting enough for Hart.

"Okay."

I frowned. "Okay?"

"I'll do it."

My fingers unfolded, the marks in my palms getting much-needed relief. "You will?"

"Don't look so grateful," he muttered. "It makes me second think."

I tried to fix my face into something less *'thank god I don't have to scramble to come up with a solid Plan B.'* It got easier to frown when I remembered the person he'd been seeing.

"This won't get in the way of whoever you're dating… right?" I asked, more hopeful he'd finally tell me who it was, so I'd better work through my odd bout of jealousy.

He was quiet for a beat before shaking his head. "No."

"No?"

"No," he repeated, point-blank.

"Alright then." I removed the joy from my voice, replacing it with the seriousness this deserved. "This isn't tit for tat, alright? You're doing this favor because you are the sole reason I'm in this web."

He gave me a look. "Not the sole reason. But I'll accept being the catalyst."

"Call it what you want."

"This is just until the wedding," he reminded me. "Not something we're going to drag on for your family's entertainment."

"Of course. Dating a guy like you for too long would be devastating." I wasn't confident he was buying it, but I needed to try to put in the effort. "I'll have to get Haven to cleanse my spirit as soon as possible."

"Exactly." He smiled. "Glad we're on the same page."

14

Hart's declaration of potential self-sacrifice in the name of friendship heightened the priority of my learning more about David. Knowledge of the middle school version of him wouldn't cut it if we planned on becoming a believable couple. If a guy he met three years prior could boast about being best friends, I believed David could share decent aspects of his personality.

I made a list of questions for him, ranging from favorite food to opinions on the known universe. After our football stadium agreement, David promised to meet me on-campus Saturday.

DAVID

Rivere at 6 PM. I only have an hour
window.

It's Saturday, you can't give me two?

DAVID

I'm leaving at 7

Fine.

I'd do everything I could to squeeze as much as possible out of him in those sixty minutes. On the way to the cafe, I got a text from him saying,

Need to reschedule. Come at 7.

I'm already on the way.

DAVID

so turn around?

I scoffed and continued down my path. I'd ridden the bus for half an hour to get down here. By the time I took it back, I would only have fifteen minutes at my apartment before having to hop back on the bus again. There would be no turning back.

Rivere was an underground cafe right on the edge of campus. The cobblestone steps led into a stuffy room littered with stained wood tables and Pepsi on tap. Most of the tables were full, students welcoming the weekend with karaoke and dart boards. Everyone was in either jeans or sweats. My matching plaid skirt set aged me in a way I wasn't sure I was ready to address.

My gaze landed on the prick of the hour tucked in a booth on the far end of the cafe. I poked my tongue against the inside of my cheek, letting out a disbelieving exhale. David was in his typical attire, a baggy gray sweatshirt and matching bottoms. A bunch of guys who were sipping beer and talking with their hands surrounded him. Every single one of them had a smile on their face, including Satan himself. My gaze narrowed when I saw him laugh, an honest-to-God, belly laugh, and I had half a mind to consider the existence of doppelgangers.

I recognized three of the guys at the table. Hart sat on the end, one foot out of the booth because he was too big to squeeze in completely. Nathaniel was next to him, chunky reading glasses on top of his head. Weston Briggs was next to him, a dirty blond quarterback who I'd seen a handful of times on campus. He was the type of beautiful old Hollywood used to produce in droves.

The other three guys with them look a couple of years older. They were dressed in grey polos and khakis. Despite their varying skin tones, they somehow look like clones of one another, in some kind of time-share company or religious order way.

I grabbed a stool at the bar and asked for a ginger ale before texting David:

> You realize you're not the only one with a schedule, right? Try warning me earlier next time.

When I glanced back over at David, I caught him looking at his phone for a second and typing a quick response before setting it face down on the table.

DAVID

> sorry.

It was half-hearted at best. I blew out a breath and tugged my laptop out of my bag. Fuck him. I wouldn't waste a walk down here. I'd finish one of my papers and then come up with a new game plan. Maybe I could convince Haven to be my plus one. Our relationship could be realistic considering we'd been roommates forever. She wouldn't give me half the headache David would, and she'd actually appreciate the company of my family.

Falling into a work rhythm was easy despite all the

surrounding noise. I'd almost forgotten how much I loved having the buzz of conversation around me while writing. After two ginger ales, one awkward date refusal with an awkward CS major, and a brief conversation with the bartender about climate change, I'd nearly forgotten all about my David problem. I had almost let it go until Weston Briggs appeared by my side to remind me.

He'd come to the bar for a refill and did a double-take when he saw me.

"Hi." His smile was lopsided and cute, front teeth slightly crooked in a way that made no sense, but also made him more approachable.

"Hello." My voice sounded a little suspect. I glanced over his shoulder at David, considering maybe this was some odd chess move. But David was still too enmeshed in conversation to direct his attention outside his booth.

"I'm Weston." He offered me his hand. It was large, veiny, and possibly worthy of an art study. "And you're Yara."

I accepted the handshake. He didn't squeeze my fingers to death like some guys did when they were trying to prove a domineering point. He teetered toward the okay side of my first impressions meter.

"David's mentioned you," he said.

My brow quirked up. "Really?"

Weston nodded, taking a seat next to me. When he rested his arm on the bar counter, his sleeve rode up slightly, revealing the last set from the tattoo trio. I tried not to stare or ask the question burning on my tongue, because if the gossip mill was even slightly accurate, the reasoning behind those tattoos wasn't something you brought up casually.

"All terrible things, I'm sure," I joked, but his silence made me frown and repeat, "*All* terrible things?"

He chuckled. "Not all."

"But some, which is more than enough." It took concentrated effort not scowl. "Care to share? Or are you also in the camp of taking a bullet for him and thus, loyal to a fault?"

"I don't make my mind up about people based on second-hand accounts," he said, a gentle assurance that I wasn't already on his bad side. "No matter how much I trust the... accounter?"

"Accounty?" I tried.

"Accountant?"

We shared a laugh.

"I think you scare him," Weston said once our laughter faded.

"What?"

"You're very put-together." He took in my outfit and leather handbag. "And you answer all his calls. He's not used to the attention."

I laughed. "Yeah, okay."

"Your counter?" Weston rested his chin on his hand, settling in for a long haul.

"He doesn't get scared."

"What makes you say that?"

I shrugged. "He's a bank vault of a human being. Nothing gets in or out."

"Plenty gets in," Weston argued. "What do you think the tellers are for?"

"You saying I'm a teller?"

He shook his head. "Oh, far more important. I'm a teller. You're the bank manager."

"Doubt David would ever trust me with any kind of lock combo," I said. "We used to sneak expired eggs and old tuna in each other's lockers."

"A budding love language if I've ever heard of one."

I snorted. "David doesn't believe in love."

Weston frowned in disbelief. "Did he say that?"

"Every other month," I promised. "He doesn't think it's "practical.""

"Practical." The word pulled out another laugh from him. "Jesus."

"Do you?" I asked, curious about the amusement in his eyes and disbelief in his tone.

"Do I?"

"Believe in love?"

He took a moment to think it over, fingers drumming on the counter. "Sometimes, yes. Most of the time, I really want to. With every fiber of my being, I want to."

There was a thread of sadness in his words that he glossed over with another one of his crooked smiles. Now, there was a guy under rubble. He was masking in a way that was so professional, I assumed he'd done it his entire life. I knew that game well. It was how I'd kept my picking a secret from my family. It was why I ran around campus like a woman on a mission, when inside I was tucked in some corner, wondering if and how I was going to make it out of my darkness alive.

"Why are you friends with him?" I wondered out loud because I couldn't take it anymore. First Hart and Nathaniel. Now, after talking to Weston, a seemingly well-adjusted (as much as a twenty-something college athlete could be) guy, I couldn't fit David's puzzle piece with theirs.

"We like each other." Weston shrugged as if it were that simple.

And then I considered maybe it was. Maybe all this time, David wasn't some guy who hated every person he'd come across. Maybe it was the opposite.

"Wow," I whispered to myself.

Weston's brow furrowed. "What?"

"I think I'm the only person David doesn't like." It was a cold, hard realization that coaxed a humorless laugh from me.

For years, I'd wholeheartedly believed David was as difficult and callous with everyone he met. My interactions with him were standard, not an exception.

But then there came the kiss... why had he kissed me? Some delayed attempt to connect? Hate manifesting into something physical? I never believed people when they said they could have hate sex, but now, I could see the possibility as clearly as I could see my hand in front of my face.

Weston didn't refute my claim, but he didn't look too convinced either. "I wouldn't say he doesn't like you."

"Then what would you say?"

He took a moment. When he couldn't find an answer, he puffed out his cheeks and blew out a weary breath. "I'd say he needs some time to warm up."

"Almost a decade of knowing each other should be enough time to warm up," I said flatly.

Weston tilted his head back and forth, considering. "Sometimes, depending on the circumstances, one might need a bit more time."

I laughed. I appreciated the attempt to comfort. The lie was structured to mend a fence he had no hand in building or breaking. But it was clear as day that David liked everyone else —and they seemed to return the sentiment without hesitation— but he hated me with consistent dedication.

"This has been enlightening." I started packing up my bag.

"Sorry... what?" Weston frowned as I stood up. "Are you leaving?"

"I've finished all I wanted to." I nodded. "And I don't want to stick around and wait for a guy who doesn't want me around."

"David wants you around." Weston stood up, but didn't block the exit. His gaze flickered over my shoulder for a second before landing back on me, pleading in those green eyes. "Trust me."

"I don't know you. I barely know him," I said.

"And you're trying to change that."

I froze, eyes narrowed. "What?"

Weston rubbed the back of his neck. "The dare thing... the kitchen thing."

My heart dropped. "David told you about that? *All* of that?"

Not only did he have friends, but he shared stuff about us with them. This entire time he'd been acting like once out of sight, I was out of mind.

"Look, why don't you come hang out? I'll buy you a drink," Weston offered. "Those recruiters are gone, so the conversation is more relaxed."

"Hard pass."

"I feel like I said something wrong." His shoulders sagged. "That wasn't my intention. Far from it."

My gaze softened a bit as I looked at him and saw a guy who just wanted to help his jerk of a friend out. "Don't worry about it. You've helped me more than you know."

"He's good at that," an unamused voice interrupted.

Weston and I glanced over my shoulder to find David. He had his hands in his pockets, a suspicious gaze toggling between both of us. "What exactly did he help you with?"

"Clarity," I said, offering only Weston a smile before leaving.

I didn't even make it up the stairs before I felt David at my elbow.

"Where are you going?" he asked so casually you'd think we were at an airport terminal, waiting to be shuttled to our gate.

"Home." I'm growing fond of one-word answers. They provided a kind of freedom. Maybe I didn't owe anyone an extensive explanation of the split-second decision. Maybe I had the right to change my mind and goal.

"And the one-on-one?" David kept in step with me, an easy feat considering his legs were longer and he was in better shape than me. It was vital that I started running regularly again. What I could recall from our cross-country days, I had more endurance than he did.

"You're relieved of your duties." I dared to look at him, and I was just in time to see a flash of confusion color his eyes.

"You came clean?" he asked, sounding impressed.

"No." I frowned, irritated that his admiration had been within reach for a second, and I'd wanted to grab hold. "I decided I'm dating Haven."

He chuckled. "Oh, yeah?"

"Yeah."

"You two would be a nice couple."

"I thought so."

"So, how did we break up?" he asked.

I wrinkled my nose and stopped walking. "What's it to you? You're free. Released from duty. Go do whatever it is you do."

"When I go back home, I'd like to have some sort of inkling of what the gossip mill will be touting," he said.

I sighed because, with the way people talked back home, I'd want to know the same thing. "Fine. I'm thinking of saying you cheated, and I cried to Haven, and she nursed me back to health and into a deep, more profound love."

"Cute," he said flatly. "But I'm not a cheater."

"It's fiction."

David shook his head. "You're not telling people I cheated on you. Next."

I scoffed. "Next?"

"Next scenario."

We glared at one another, gazes burning as we stood our ground.

"Fine," I gave in. "You didn't know anything about me and weren't interested in learning."

"What?"

"A disinterested boyfriend," I said. "Not a cheater but standoffish. It fits."

"It does not."

"David, it fits," I snapped, frustrated that he was fighting this hard.

"You prefer the in-between moments in seasons, when spring's still cold and winter days are bright with sunshine. The quilt on your bed was a project you finished with your grandma, made up of your favorite childhood clothes. On weekends, you don't get out of bed until eleven, but spend the rest of the day feeling guilty, so you cram in a boatload of things on your to-do list. You binge the same show every fall. It's called *The 100*. You skip the last season, though, because a character named Bellamy doesn't get his due justice, and it makes you cry. And I'm fairly sure you have an anxiety disorder that results in excessive picking. You hide it concerningly well."

My ears roared as if I were trapped behind a waterfall. Before I could resurface, he continued.

"You tell everyone you want to work in politics or the nonprofit sphere, but from the looks of your multiple sketchbooks, you want to create something new, not work in someone else's old system," he said. "But you lack natural talent and, for some reason, you won't enlist your drive. When you get tired, you wink, one eye after the next, because you think it helps energize you. Your sisters treat you like the baby because you are, and you like coddling, but don't enjoy the aftermath of them looking down on you. You can be a leader, but something about them makes you always defer. I can't tell if you're unable to trust your potential or if you believe they're smarter than you. They're not; you're one of the smartest people I know. One of the most intriguing people I know. Your favorite color is orange."

My head was spinning. I didn't know whether to address the TV show, sketchbooks, picking, or favorite color.

"I'm not a disinterested boyfriend," David said firmly. "Next."

15

THIS MAN HAD a dossier about me. And here I was, drawing blanks on what he did when he wasn't coming up with dares and catching a football.

"This was supposed to be a get to know each other meeting?" I whispered, the question more for me than him. Shame burned in my cheeks as I realized I was severely outmatched.

David watched me. It was the perfect time to gloat, and yet he remained silent. He didn't shove the long list of facts he'd collected on my life and personality in my face when he had every right to do so.

"If you need a fake partner," David said, voice slower and almost gentle. "I'm better than most. I know your family dynamics, understand your idiosyncrasies, and can anticipate your disapproval. The interaction would be seamless. Damage to psyche, minimal. The gossip mill would be bored with us in two seconds because I'm not fresh meat like Haven. They've already gotten a taste of me and have spat me out."

"You still want to... do it?" My guilt chewed through my carotid arteries, set on seeing me bleed out. I had half a mind to give in. I'd gone on about us not knowing each other and him not caring, and now look at me, standing in front of a table he'd set with delicate details of my life.

"I'm willing," he said. "Want is a whole other matter I didn't plan on factoring in."

He had the upper hand, stood on the high ground, and I couldn't figure out how to switch things. What bothered me more was I couldn't figure out why he wasn't rubbing this in my face. He wasn't jumping at the chance to make me feel like a jerk for not being able to say half the amount of things he'd shared about me.

"It's going to rain." David's gaze upturned, taking in the cloudy night sky. "What's it going to be?"

"I... I'm willing to not to break up prematurely," I said. "Now that you've expressed... interest in this relationship."

He scoffed and a smile played on his lips. "Alright, let's go."

Instead of heading back to the cafe, David started in the opposite direction.

"Where are we going?" I jogged to catch up.

"My place is around the corner," he said.

"Your place?" Another white blob of a thing in my map of his world. My stomach jumped in excitement to see something of his that was tangible, proof he existed outside of the bubble we warred in.

Rain started to trickle down when we neared the athletes' row. The buildings here were newer, brighter, and cleaner, and iron plates engraved with donors' names and dates paved their walk.

"Keep up," he warned when I lingered at a gray fountain made of marble and home to an impressive football statue shooting out water from atop his helmet.

"Did you find the 1915 there?" I teased, my smile growing when he glared and held the door open for me.

Their lobby smelled of Pine-Sol and pears. When the

elevator opened for us, we faced a mirror, and I couldn't help but note our stark differences and the climb we'd have to make to become a cohesive couple. His messy hair and my 'no flyaways' policy signaled a discrepancy. David's shoulders slouched from his high school wallpaper years. My posture was tall, thanks to classes in manners and etiquette that began as soon as I could form a sentence.

"How do you feel about color coordinating?" I asked.

"What?"

"I'm brainstorming ways to make us look like we fit together."

David hadn't glanced in the mirror before, but he was staring at us in it now. "We look fine together."

"Fine and fitting are two very different things."

He continued to stare and surprised me by moving closer until he stood behind me. I could feel the heat of his body, a solid energy. There was a lump in my throat when he looked down at me. I kept my gaze straight, transfixed on the curious way he was scanning my profile. When he looked at me like that, we looked fine. Great, even. It didn't make any sense, but we were a mismatched outfit that somehow worked.

I pulled my gaze from the mirror and met his. We were face-to-face for a second, close enough that our breaths mingled. Was it possible to miss something I'd only experienced one time?

David's gaze fell on my lips, studying them as if he were trying to read words before I uttered them. His hand pressed gently on my lower back as if to keep me in place for a second. I didn't feel like I was on solid ground anymore. The aimless floating didn't induce panic. I was as safe as I'd ever been.

I leaned closer to him as if some force tugged me. My heart was in my throat. Right when my nose brushed his, the elevator dinged. David pulled away, walking out unceremoniously, completely unfazed.

I laughed at myself in the mirror, rubbing my hand on my burning cheek. It took a couple of seconds to regain my composure. Once I did, I followed him to the end of the hall. All the doors had bubble letters and stickers from bands or movies on them. I knew which one was David's before we reached it. The door was blank, as if no one had moved in yet.

"Love what you've done with the place," I said under my breath when he opened the door, revealing a clean, nearly empty studio. I kid not, there was a sparkle on his kitchen appliances, their cleanliness somewhat historical.

"Take off your shoes," he said, gesturing to his own pair near the door.

I did as he said, still scanning the space as if I'd only get a couple of minutes to memorize everything before being told to leave.

His bed set was deep green, with the sheets tucked tightly underneath the mattress. The comforter folded perfectly, draped over the bottom of the bed. David had two pieces of art on the walls. One: a print of Mount Rainier. The colors were bright and saturated, and the texture was like oil. The other print was of a very sad-looking, anamorphic bird.

"Are you thirsty?"

I jumped at his voice, so lost in wondering why the contrasting prints felt so him. "Huh?"

David raised a brow and held up two choices: a water and a sports drink.

I shook my head and shrugged out of my blazer. "I'm fine."

"Here." David hurried over before I could rest it on the back of his couch.

I let him have it, figuring it was something he needed to be particular about. "Should I sit or wait for a bedsheet or something?"

"What?" David flashed me a confused look as he tugged

my blazer over a wooden hanger and carefully set it on the rack. The crisp pink plaid stood out amongst his black and blue collection of sweatshirts. I had the urge to add more to the mix, to make it an even amount. Level the playing field. Make it easier to see how it'd look if we lived together...

Relax, Yara. It was one kiss.

I didn't even know what I meant about living together. I wouldn't be able to stand anyone other than Haven as a roommate.

"I had an aunt like you," I said, careful with every word that left my lips because, just like my picking, this was uncharted territory for both of us. "She didn't like us sitting on her furniture with outside clothes on. And she couldn't — not for lack of trying— get us to wash up and change into fresh clothes every time we visited. So, she wrapped everything in plastic."

"I don't care if you sit on my couch, Yara." He sounded exhausted, and I frowned. Well, screw me for trying to be considerate.

I plopped down on his couch and dumped my bag down beside me. He eyed the bag but didn't say a thing as he took a seat on the edge of his bed.

The space between us was small, filled only by a circular wooden coffee table. There were a couple of textbooks stacked neatly, accompanied by a straight line of pens and pencils. I unloaded my laptop, pulling up the document I'd set up for our deep dive. David cracked open a water bottle. I watched his neck bob as he took a few sips. The veins in his hand were prominent as he clutched the bottle. I traced those veins down his forearm, all the way to his elbow.

"Yara," his voice tugged my gaze back to his face.

I blinked and looked back down at my screen as if I hadn't been burning a hole through his skin.

"You ready?" The amusement in his voice set my skin aflame.

"Yeah, just waiting for you to rehydrate," I muttered. "You gulp like a goat."

"What was that?"

"Let's start from the top." I cleared my throat. "Shall we?"

He chuckled and gestured for me to continue.

"Favorite holiday?" I asked.

David's brow furrowed. "How is that at the top?"

"Just answer the question," I said. "Mine's New Year's Eve."

"Why?"

I shrugged. "New beginnings. Fresh starts. It's fun creating mood boards. Everything feels possible right after the clock changes."

David nodded. "Of course. I should have guessed that one."

I didn't react to his disparaging sigh because I'm the bigger person. And I'm also the person in need, so I let the pettiness go for the night.

"I don't like holidays," he said simply.

I swallowed a sigh and tried to smile. "That's... valid."

It killed me not to argue. David grinned and leaned back on his hands. I didn't look at the small bit of skin revealed when his shirt lifted. Or rather, I didn't look long.

"You really think so?"

My gaze flickered to the new shape his arms made in this position. I shifted my weight on the cushion, testing out a better position.

"I do." I typed down his answer, taking more time than necessary because I couldn't quite get my fingers to work with my brain.

"Next question," I said, a little breathy. "Any allergies?"

"Chocolate. You?"

"Fish," I said. "What did you want to be growing up?"

"A landscaper," David said simply.

I paused. "Landscaper?"

"Yeah." He nodded, not looking like he was going to elaborate until I removed my hands from the keyboard and tucked them under my thighs in wait.

"I looked up to the guys who rode around all day on lawnmowers. It seemed fun. And I enjoyed being outside back then, so... it just felt right."

"That's... kind of cute," I said after a few seconds of silence.

He scoffed. "Yeah, okay, Yara. Next question."

"I'm not messing with you. I swear."

"What about you?" He sounded more than ready to turn the attention away from himself. "What did little Yara want to be? Let me guess, Madam President?"

"That's a little on the nose, don't you think?" I asked, tone flat.

"I'm right, aren't I?" He smiled when I hesitated.

"Cute," he mimicked me. Or at least I thought he meant to mimic me. But there was a bit of softness in his tone that hinted at something honest.

"Okay, but it was only for like two years in elementary," I defended. "The rest of the time I wanted to be an acrobat."

"You were terrified of hurdles that one time Coach Connor asked you to try out for the track team," David noted. "You refused to do the high jump."

I frowned, surprised he remembered. "You were there?"

"I was on the team, Yara."

"No, I know that," I said. "I meant at that practice. I hardly ever remember you being around."

"You're not that observant, no," he said as if I'd given him something to agree with.

My jaw clenched, but I continued. "Tell me about your folks."

When putting this list together, I realized I hadn't known a thing about David's parents. There had been some drama with him in his freshman year that led his parents to come on campus to pick him up. I didn't remember actually seeing them, though. They were like the teacher in Charlie Brown, headless and speaking fluent gibberish.

"Next question," he said.

I sighed. "David—"

"Next question," he said more sternly.

I studied him, seeing hardness return to his eyes. This wasn't a door I should even pretend to reach for and open.

"Fine," I said in a low voice. "What do I say if someone brings it up?"

"You're more creative than you think." He took a couple more sips of his water.

Surely, I knew who his parents were at some point. Or someone from school had to. I made a mental list of people I was still in contact with from our high school and considered messaging the one with the most discretion.

"These questions are very... surface level," he broke the silence.

"Isn't the surface all that we could explore in the..." I made a show of looking at my watch. "An hour and a half since we started dating?"

"Just thought you'd have more hard-hitters."

"Like?"

"Like my obvious OCD and your potential OCD," he said. "We, for once, could be a matching set."

I frowned. The plan had been to gloss over my most secret issue completely in exchange for the easier ones. I'd rather talk about my poor art skills and my dreams of working some-where with casual Mondays and a bring-your-dog-to-work policy. Even my lack of a love life could be on the table—it was a bland meal, but we could pick at it, nonetheless. The calories were still there. Besides, David usually derived pleasure from shoving food around his plate with no real goal other than to see how it'd hold up.

"Would you like to share your gritty details, or shall I go first?" I asked. When he gestured to me, my stomach turned. I shut my laptop and set it to the side.

"Whenever you're ready," he said after a couple of minutes of silence.

"I'm getting there," I said. "Sorry, it's taking me a bit to gather my thoughts on something I haven't even spoken about with a therapist."

His smile faded. "You don't actually have to tell me anything. I mostly—"

"I don't realize I'm doing it most of the time," I interrupted. Truth was, no matter how dark and scary this part of me felt, I did want to show it to someone. Then I could make them agree I was some odd, twisted thing that needed to be looked at and fixed. I didn't always plan to hide the picking. My family believed I stopped doing it after the school counselor in middle school sat me down and said, "You should stop. You're messing up your beautiful hair." After that, I pretended that the pursuit of beauty was enough for me. It had been for a while. But that was before the accident restarted the cycle.

Who better to tell than the guy who could only stand me in bite-sized pieces? David's judgment would wash right over me because I'd developed skin that was repellent to his particular brand of analysis.

"One moment I'm thinking a million things at once, and the next I've started a new bald spot." I shrugged as if I told him I didn't hand-wash my delicates (I did), or get my yearly checkup (bi-yearly, thank you very much). "Once I start on the spot, I have to at least pluck three strands. More means better luck... fewer means I'm asking for trouble. I need the luck so I don't... fuck things up more than I already have."

David nodded, understanding. My stomach was contending with a full-on storm as I tried to read his expression. Admitting fault had me ready to run for the door. I could hide in a closet for the rest of the semester and still want to throw up from how sick inadequacy made me.

"Is a therapist on the agenda?" he asked, gaze never leaving mine. I waited for the joke, the teasing. But all that existed was a sober curiosity.

"Is a therapist on *your* agenda?" I shot back.

He blinked, unfazed by the hard retort. I'd snapped us back into place, away from this open and warm back and forth that almost felt nice. Could have felt nice if I weren't so prone to ruining a good thing before it began.

"Here I was, thinking you were handling this so well." David sighed, disappointed.

My fingers curled into a fist. "I am."

"How convinced are you really?" he asked. "Are you the kind of person who tries to bring things into existence by sheer belief?"

"Are you asking if I believe in manifestation?"

"Sure, whatever you want to call it."

I frowned, knowing this was a set-up, but stepping forward anyway. "Yes, I believe that the words we speak—most of all to ourselves— are powerful. You?"

He smiled. "Definitely."

David's response was cold water poured down my top in the dead of winter.

"Really?" I asked, confused about where this thread would lead. Surely not us agreeing for once in our lives.

"I've spent more than half my life trying to mold my body into a perfect machine for a sport that can and will leave me with permanent brain damage," he said. "Of course, I believe in positive self-talk. There's no escaping the mind when it's the only thing left to keep you company."

"How astute," I mused. "Why then? Why do you play a sport that kills the mind?"

He smiled and offered me a one-shoulder shrug. "It's fun."

"Fun?" I asked, unconvinced it could be so simple.

"Yes, have you tried that before?"

I sighed and reopened my laptop, typing out how he found the risk of football worth it because of "fun."

"I think I have enough to convince my family we're semi-involved," I decided.

"You sure?" He tilted his head to the side. The softness of his eyes almost showed disappointment. Had he meant to get more out of me? Did he think he'd somehow coax my anxious tics out in the open to be dissected by his icy fingers?

"Positive." I slipped my laptop into my bag. "Or, at least, for the first event next weekend. It's dinner at my parents' place. Business casual. Don't wear gray."

"What?"

"Business casual. Don't wear gray," I repeated. "My mom hates gray. It's a bad omen in our house."

David chuckled and shook his head. "God, what have I gotten myself into?"

16

―――――

"WHAT ARE WE LOOKING AT?" Anthony had one arm crossed over his chest and a hand rubbing the side of his face. Hana stood beside him, trying her best to maintain a smile.

I moved in front of them, briefly blocking the view of the rusty, rundown warehouse we'd walked twenty minutes to see. The smell of fish hung heavily in the air. Seagulls continued doing their business on the white-stained sidewalk. Old dinghies and center console boats swayed up and down on the dock behind us.

"I know it's not what we envisioned–" I started.

"It's not what you sold us." Anthony shook his head, gesturing to the building as if it were a bag of trash someone had forgotten to take to the curb. "Not even close."

"Hey." Hana raised her brow at him. "Let's hear her out."

She didn't look hopeful, but I appreciated her attempt.

"I sold you a high-class ball." I closed my eyes for a second and nodded. "But I swear, this is going to be better."

It took only a few meetings with my board for us to accept the impossibility of booking a grand ballroom. The quotes I'd gotten over the summer had risen nearly fifty percent. I thought we would have time to book something four months out because Westbrooke's surrounding area wasn't exactly known for hosting expensive events. I was wrong.

"Most students can't afford a gown or know where to rent a tux," I continued. "A strict dress code will have people second-guessing when buying tickets."

"That was your idea, though," Anthony reminded me. "I thought you were going to figure it out."

"I did, and I think a masquerade *party* will be better. Costumes and hidden identities. Not some stuffy hotel glitz and glam. Something that feels like an escape. No gown or tux required. Just a mask."

Anthony sighed and glanced at Hana to see if she was buying it. From the way she twisted her mouth to the side, it seemed negative.

"We're going to be coming fresh off of Halloween," I said quickly. "I'm still going to market it as an elegant event. But also something far more relaxed. Think a hole-in-the-wall speakeasy with vampires. The theme's immortal and classic."

"Vampires *are* always in," Hana said with a shrug.

"That's debatable," Anthony said.

I took a breath and brought out the big guns. "This is a great deal, Anthony. No labor on your part. One fundraiser in which I need a couple of your members to attend—and you have hundreds, so that should be cake, right?"

Hana laughed when Anthony ruefully nodded.

"You're getting marketing, networking opportunities, and a chance for free tickets to the event of the year."

He whistled, but there was a smile growing on his face. "Event of the year. You're already claiming it, huh?"

"I don't sit around hoping success falls into my lap. When I need to get something done, I get it done," I said. "So? Are you a yes yet? I have the president of the Historical Society in my inbox. He's offering a full account takeover for a week and covering the drink bill."

Anthony's jaw ticked. The president of the Historical Society, Luther, was his ex. Once a power couple, now rivals who continued to step on one another's toes every chance they got. Luther had caught me in the student center a couple of days ago after he'd caught wind of my fragile alliance with BSU. I knew I was just a tool to step on his ex's toes, but I didn't underestimate the power of revenge.

"And Hana's doing decor," I added. "So, your involvement is getting more and more questionable. I mean, what are you really offering?"

I crossed my arms over my chest, feeling the cool breeze of the high ground. Anthony frowned at Hana. She responded with a shy shrug.

"It felt right," she defended. "We've got tons left over from last year's charity dinner."

"I offer reach," Anthony said simply, but instead of pressing for more details, he held out his hand. "Without it, you'll be lucky to get a handful of people through the door."

I wanted to argue, but he was right. And though I could be a sore loser, I was smart enough to only whine about things behind closed doors. I accepted his handshake.

"Looking forward to doing business with you," I said with a smile.

———

WITH LESS THAN seventy-two hours until David had dinner with my family and the looming deadline of a million and one things on the masquerade party checklist, my stomach remained trapped in a cycle of constant backflips. Only time would help the masquerade anxiety. But I could do something about my racing heart when it came to preparing David. I spent most of Friday texting him things like:

> Don't bring up the Marvel Cinematic Universe. It'll start an argument about capitalism.

> Try not to get up too much during dinner. One bathroom break is usually the limit; otherwise, they might think you're hiding something…

> One of my sisters dated a guy who used to steal. My brother caught him trying to take my grandma's china, between turns of Monopoly.

> Speaking of Monopoly! Just in case they ask you to play the Heads Up game, you need to research musicians. It'll particularly impress them if you can name people from the eighties.

He didn't respond all day. I couldn't even get a measly reaction. A simple emoji would've been nice. So, when I texted my final reminder that I'd be seeing him tonight at the field day thing Hart invited me to, I was shocked to receive a reply:

> Just seeing this now, I couldn't have my phone on. Today's been big for me. Will read all your previous messages later.

> See you tonight.

Today was big for him? Talk about an impressive adjective. Big. The word simple, yet vulnerable, for a guy like him.

"When a stoic texts you their day's been big, what do you think?" I asked Haven. I was doing the most, but it always made everything a little more fun that way. I glanced at her through our bathroom mirror. She was kind enough to help with my wash day, putting my hair into mini twists to tide me over until my next appointment.

"That their day was big." She shrugged, too disinterested to delve into a conspiracy with me. "What did he do this time?"

"Nothing. After nearly twenty-four hours of ignoring me, he said he'll see me tonight."

"Do you want to stage a fight?" she asked. "I'm still down to be your fake rebound girlfriend after your fake last-minute boyfriend."

I took a breath, trying to pretend to be put out by this whole endeavor. But the memory of David's relaxed smile while we were in his apartment planted a seed of endearment in my chest. I'd grown dangerously fond of the idea of having him by my side for dinner. If not for anything but the chance to give me an entertaining sparring partner.

"Let's leave that option open." I reached for a hairband to tie the twists up, but Haven placed her hand over mine, stopping me.

"You have some serious breakage." She gently pressed two fingers on the crown of my head. "Right here. I know they're your signature, but you'd better cool it on the high ponytails."

I smiled, doing my best to keep my embarrassment to a minimum. I hadn't checked the spot in weeks. In fact, I actively ignored it.

I'd shoved David's observation that I had OCD into a corner along with the picking. I'd happily keep it there if this weren't the second time someone had brought it up.

Two people knew about the spot. One was a guy who often thought of ways to ruin me mentally. And the other, my best friend, who didn't yet sense the red flag, but once she did, would surely implement a six-part recovery plan. I didn't have time to war with the two greatest fighters I knew, so I decided I was quitting cold turkey.

"Are you driving, or should we take the bus?" I slipped on an oversized jean jacket that Haven was letting me borrow. It was a little too stiff for my liking, but the casualness was a necessity since I was trying to impress Hart. I wanted to show him another side of me that didn't involve academia, because he was a cute guy with a romantic interest in me. And I could work with that. I wanted to work with that. I'd love to break out of the monotony of university life and have something else to think about for once.

"Driving," she said. "I need to see if the battery's holding up. The best place to break down is on campus."

I nodded in agreement. It didn't take her more than a few minutes to tuck her hair into a headscarf and dab a bit of pink blush on her cheeks.

By the time we got to the location Hart had sent me, most people had arrived. The soccer fields were muddy from the earlier evening rain. No one seemed to care as they set up their lawn chairs and coolers. There were hordes of gaming supplies, things like tug-of-war and ring toss.

"It's actually a field day." I crossed my arms over my chest, examining the set-up.

"What were you expecting?" Haven tugged a lawn chair out of her trunk, along with her own mini cooler and a baseball cap.

"For it to be a metaphor. An excuse to drink and aimlessly kick a ball around before campus security told us to leave." I gestured to the cap. "How are you going to get that over your scarf?"

Haven undid the back clasp and hooked it on her shoulder strap. "Go team."

I laughed. "Why?"

"I can have school spirit, can't I?"

My shoulders sagged when I realized what that meant. "You're not playing any of the games?"

She gave me a smile and dragged her chair behind her toward the field.

I hurried after her, giving up on finding a step to take that didn't result in a muddy sole. "Then you didn't have to come just because of me."

Haven laughed and whipped her chair open. "How presumptuous. I may or may not be interested in socializing."

"You want to socialize with football players?"

"They're very close to the girls on the softball team." She flipped open her fan with dramatic flair.

"Ahh." I smiled as I watched her take it all in. The sunset, the open field, the short shorts.

"Go get me something to drink and bring back some gossip," Haven instructed as she relaxed into her chair and pulled out her phone.

"Alright, auntie." I laughed and started toward the open coolers. Small groups of people clustered together. I scanned for Hart while I grabbed a couple of iced bottled waters. When I couldn't find him on my preliminary search, I texted:

> Trying to report for duty. Where are you?

HART

> Sorry! Traffic off campus is horrible. Pulling up now.

I glanced over in time to see David's silver car pulling into the lot. Hart and Weston hopped out of the back seat while Nathaniel and David climbed out of the front.

I knew it would be far more logical to follow Hart's journey onto the field. But my eyes cast their vote on David's easy stride, his furrowed brow. His dark hair fell into his eyes, and he continually shoved it off his forehead.

David was in conversation with Weston, their expressions far more serious than one may expect during what was supposed to be a low-stakes evening. Hart and Nathaniel broke away from the two, B-lining to the coolers and me.

"You came." Hart smiled and held his arms up, but didn't step closer, giving me the final decision to accept the hug.

"Wouldn't miss it." I hugged him. He smelled of aloe and spicy aftershave. A bit of his wet hair pressed against my temple, leaving a cool imprint that I tried to wipe away discreetly. I waited for nerves to coil in my belly or for warmth to bloom on my cheeks, or for my heart to race even a little. A full-body scan showed no immediate changes in my body, which wasn't necessarily a bad sign. No change could mean I was comfortable with Hart. And since I hadn't gone on a date in forever, comfortable felt good. Safe.

"Yeah?" Hart chuckled at my statement and nudged his chin to a large group gathering on the field. "Have they named the teams yet? The game should start soon."

"I don't know; I just got here." I shrugged. "Haven't had the chance to ask."

"I'll make sure we're together," he promised. "Ready?"

"One second." I waved the dripping water bottle to indicate I needed to make a detour.

Haven smiled, grateful for the water and my presence. "Who should I be cheering for?"

"Me, obviously."

"I like to be on the winning side."

I snorted and glanced over my shoulder, looking for Hart, but my gaze somehow immediately locked in on David. He was on the field, hands on his head as he talked to a few people. There was a smile on his face now, small but effective. He looked happy to be there, interacting.

My staring went on for far too long to be normal. David, probably feeling the weight of my gaze, glanced over. When our gazes met, his smile faded a little. But I wasn't offended. The slight change in expression indicated something honest. His chest rose and fell as he took a deep breath before being the first to look away. His group regained the attention I craved.

"You realize you can say hi first." Haven's smiling up at me, the rim of her water bottle pressed against her lips.

I frowned and shed my jacket. "What?"

"To your fake boyfriend. You're allowed to say hi first."

"I don't need to say hi." I tossed the jacket beside her, and she tugged it onto her lap, using it as a blanket. "I talk to him all the time. All day through text, in fact."

"And yet you really want to do it some more." Her smile would annoy me if it didn't reveal her cute dimples and make me want to pinch her cheeks.

"Film me?" I needed to change the subject, stat. "I want a record of doing something that's not inside school walls so the next time my family complains about my nose being in a book, I have ample evidence."

I tossed her my phone and jogged back to the field. Hart was easy to find with his broad shoulders and height. He was also looking for me, which was plenty of reason for a spark to run up my spine or breathing to take a brief intermission. Neither of which happened but it was still early.

"You, Nat, and I are blue." Hart smiled wide. He offered me a blue vest that smelled of sweat and grass. I tried not to wrinkle my nose, swallowing down a "no, thanks" when I saw everyone else tugging on their vests without protest.

"What's the game?" I clicked myself into the vest.

It was Nathaniel's quiet voice that explained, "Flag football."

"Fitting," I murmured.

Hart stepped closer to help me tighten the sides of my vest. "Do you know how to play?"

"Is it like normal football?" I asked.

Hart nodded. "Yeah, sort of."

"Then no, I know nothing."

He chuckled, and even Nathaniel smiled a little.

"It's no-contact," Hart said. "That's the biggest difference from football. You can't tackle, dive, or block."

I nodded. "Good, because I wouldn't know how to do any of those things."

"You see where the ball is?" Hart pointed to a football placed on one of the spray-painted white lines in the grass. "That's the line of scrimmage. It'll move forward or back depending on where the play ends. It's a starting point. Picking up where we left off."

I frowned, already a bit confused as to how to accurately track the change.

"Okay, so what—" I cut off when a jacked softball player appeared with an armful of belts that sported fabric strips velcroed across. She passed them to each of us. My stomach twisted when I remembered I was among Division I athletes. They were on track to do this for a living. Some of them would make millions doing this for a living. And here I was, in baggy jeans and a dream. Maybe I should have cheered from the sidelines? Had Hart actually invited me out here anyway? Had the invite been just to spectate? I couldn't remember.

"This won't be serious." Nathaniel smiled at me, a gentle acknowledgement that he'd noticed my internal panic. "We bend the rules all the time. No need to worry about getting it right because there isn't a right with this bunch."

I nodded, only half-calmed by the assurance. My eyes strayed to David, a couple of yards away. A yellow vest hugged his torso. His arms crossed over his chest, emphasizing the broadness I used to overlook. I missed overlooking. Everything felt easier that way.

"You sure?" I joked. Half-joked. The other half panicked. I

wished I had time to run over to Haven and grab my phone. I needed to find a short crash course on all things flag football and ingest every detail in the next four to five minutes. "The yellow team looks stacked and determined."

Nathaniel shook his head. "Promise. They're all bark. This is all for fun. No one wants to get hurt before the season's over."

"Makes sense." I nodded, and a few of the knots in my shoulders unwound.

David's gaze found me again in the crowd, and he raised a questioning brow. I frowned back, sending an unspoken, *what?* He wasn't well-versed in telepathy. Nor did he have an interest in learning it on the fly. He mouthed, *you okay?*

The concern in his brow made my chest tighten. I fought the urge to walk right up to him and ask him what was so big and important about his day.

Fine, I mouthed back.

He nodded, satisfied, and turned back to strategizing with his team.

"You ran in high school, right?" Hart's question shattered my delusion that the only people on this field were David and I.

"Cross country and track." I nodded. "I was better at track."

Small, quick bursts of energy earned me a spot on varsity all four years in high school.

"How much better?" Hart asked.

"Fifth in the state during my junior year in the 800 meters." I placed my hands on my hips; it was still something I was proud of. "And third, during my senior year."

"Thinking what I'm thinking?" Hart gave Nat a knowing smile.

Nat returned it, not as convinced but still amused. "You know who's going to want to cover her."

"Yara can take him." Hart waved his hand, dismissive of the warning.

I raised a brow. "Take who?"

"He's going to hold back," Hart promised. "If you're one of our wide receivers, David won't work half as hard."

"It's a decent strategy," Nat agreed.

Hart nodded and winked at us both before calling over the softball player from before. Her tight, coily brown hair was tousled from the wind or wrestling. Maybe both. Her dark brown skin was dotted with acne scarring, and her sharp jaw was the envy of movie stars of all ages, I'm sure.

"Rissa, this is Yara." Hart gestured to me. "Yara, Rissa. She's the captain of the softball team and the captain of our flag football team."

Rissa smiled and offered an elbow to bump. "Yara... have I seen you at the Rivere?"

"Maybe." I nodded. "It's my favorite place to sulk between classes."

She laughed, flashing a gorgeous smile that rendered Hart, Nat, and me temporarily speechless.

"David's Yara," Hart said in a, *'you get what I'm talking about'* tone.

Rissa's brows lifted with recognition. "No shit?"

The title, "David's Yara," wrapped around my shoulders. I shouldn't like how it felt like a perfect fit. I didn't jump to correct them. I rationalized the need to practice getting used to it for at least the next couple of months. To my family, I *would* be David's Yara... or he'd be Yara's David —a title which felt even nicer. I was going to be sick.

"And she's a track star," he said.

"Former," I amended, still reeling from being seen as anyone's anything. Hart had gone from telling me David didn't bring me up to calling me his on a date. This was a date... wasn't it? Or the preface to one? I studied Hart as if I could read his mind and confirm we're romantically linked, even by the smallest thread. But from the moment he scaled the gate at the football field, I had felt little of anything except the budding friendship we'd cultivated last semester.

"Any experience is more than enough," Rissa said. "You're a receiver, kid. If you want the position, of course."

The three of them looked at me, expectant. If they thought, even for a second, I could help them win against David's team, I was game.

"Position filled," I decided. "Just tell me what you need me to do."

17

RISSA, Hart, and Nat made everything very clear. But my brain translated their detailed explanations to something far simpler: get the ball across that white line. A white line that was at least fifty yards away. A white line guarded by seven soon-to-be pro football and softball players.

I glanced over at Haven on the sidelines just in time to see her hold up a pink, glittery sign that read, *Go Yara!* I laughed as she waved it back and forth with a grin on her face. When she had time to make it and sneak it into the van, I had no idea.

"Got your own fan club already." David was on my side of the field.

After our team's strategy meeting and break, we'd split up to our designated places. The yellow team took longer to discuss. Their captain, Weston, kept his team in a tight circle, and his gaze continued to flicker to his friends and me as he spoke.

"He knows our plan," Hart had murmured in disappointment.

"Doesn't mean it won't work." Rissa had nudged him in

the side. "Don't pout; it'll make them think they already won. We're going to make them work hard for this."

We'd waited fifteen minutes before Rissa got impatient enough to start shouting teasing taunts about them being afraid of our team. That seemed to nudge them right along with hopes she'd eat her words.

"So do you," I said, and glanced over at the group of students on the sidelines who seemed like Haven, friends of friends of athletes. They couldn't keep their eyes off him.

"I can't believe he convinced you to run." David moved closer, a couple of feet between us. He'd found a headband. It was yellow with an embroidered flower. Its whimsy suggested it wasn't his. This hinted that someone, once more, liked him enough to lend him favors, and he was comfortable enough to ask.

I could have gotten him a headband.

The silly desire made me want to crawl under a rock. What was different after that night in his apartment? Nothing, really. No amount of interpersonal knowledge should change the fact that David and I were oil and water. And yet, when we found ourselves close enough to feel each other's warmth, I finally felt that spark, a buzzing on my fingertips that carried the type of voltage that could wipe out a city grid. I wanted to touch him: needed to wipe the blade of grass off his shoulder, readjust the headband so it pushed all his hair back, or trace my thumb across his bottom lip. The feel of him faded a little more from my memory every day, and I was holding on to the replay of our kiss for dear life.

"I wanted to run," I said, instead of hooking my fingers around his.

"You haven't run since senior year," David said.

"I run all the time."

"Really?"

"Do you have access to an all-seeing eye?" I asked. "Some CCTV cams you log into outside of my apartment building?"

"No, I just know you don't run anymore."

I scoffed. "And I'm telling you, I do. How is this factual tidbit of my life an argument? You really believe you're this much of a know-it-all about me? You just memorized a few facts."

He scoffed. "Oh, come on. It was more than a few. Admit it, you're upset I'm actually interested in people. In you."

In you. My heart was in my throat, and I could barely get words around it. "Why would I be upset if you're interested?"

"Probably because it'd reveal how jaded you are about me," he said. "How much you need me to be the bad guy, so you don't have to deal with anything other than manufactured contempt when you see me."

I laughed dryly. "Nothing about my contempt is manufactured."

"Keep telling yourself that." David chuckled.

"Alright!" Weston called from the middle of the field, where most of our teammates had lined up on a white line. "Everyone ready? First to five? House rules."

Multiple people cheered, confirming their readiness. I tried to move a few feet away from David, and he followed.

"Back off," I warned.

"It's man-to-man," he explained with an amused smile.

I tried to move again, but he was like gum on a shoe. David closed the distance between us right as Weston stood on the line to say something to our team's quarterback. As they talked, David grabbed the hem of my shirt, holding me in place.

"Stop cheating, asshole." I swatted at his hand.

"If you stand too far to the left," David whispered in my ear. "You'll get caught between Jacob and Mike. They're sore losers, so trust me when I say they won't go easy on you just because this is supposed to be a casual game."

"Why are you giving me tips?" I was more shocked at how close he had gotten, how incredible his spicy aftershave mixed with his natural scent smelled, and how gentle his voice was in my ear. Instead of wanting to run, I'm tempted to lean back on my heels because I know my back would meet the solid form of his chest. Who cared about a ball and a touchdown? I wanted to know how it'd feel to have David's arm wrapped around my waist again. Or maybe how his hand felt around my neck. Options. There were so many options.

Was it knowing about you? Was that really all it took?

No, that had been the icing. The cake was how, despite everything, David always talked to me like this when he thought I needed it. He was soft when he felt I'd slipped and needed some place to land. I hadn't noticed this shift before. I focused too much on our disagreements. But it'd always been like this when I flipped through our memories, going as far back as high school. David could and would be soft when I needed it.

So you like that about him? Big deal. Doesn't mean he likes anything about you.

And there it was. The kicker. David didn't like me. His smiles for me were few and far between. An eye roll was a customary greeting for me. Hell, I had to beg the guy to fake date me.

Yeah, squashing this flicker of a growing crush was of the utmost importance.

"I'm making sure you don't embarrass yourself." David's hold on my shirt loosened but didn't release. "Or hurt yourself."

"I could yell foul," I said. "You know, for touching me."

His voice was still low and breath tickling my ear. "Go ahead and do it. I dare you."

It took everything to mask the shiver that ran down my spine. "It's not your turn."

"Hurry and come up with something then. It's been weeks."

"I enjoy taking my time, thank you very much," I said.

"Well, so do I, but at a certain point, all this edging becomes a bit trite. Don't you think?"

He meant nothing more than what we were talking about. There was no depth to his words —David had warned me of that himself plenty of times. And yet. And yet.

I dared to glance over my shoulder at him. He met my gaze, daring me to do something else. Say what I'm sure he could clearly see in my eyes.

"You're cheating," I repeated, my voice a whisper, almost drowned out by Rissa calling the play.

David let go of my shirt then and stepped a few paces back. There was a ghost of a smile on his face when he warned one final time, "Keep away from Mike and Jacob."

"Got it," I murmured, too overwhelmed and frustrated with the warmth in all my erogenous zones to care about being defiant.

The second Rissa handed the ball off to a red-haired woman who tossed it to me, I was supposed to take off. I had faith that my team would guard me well enough to keep others off my trail. All I really had to worry about was David.

When I caught the ball (by the grace of some divine being), I headed straight for the touchdown line. No gimmicks was what Rissa had told us in our huddle. Apparently, Weston liked flourish. Simplicity was what would trip him and his plan up.

I wasn't delusional enough to think I could outrun David. That was why I'd done what he told me not to do and gone straight toward the middle. Hart had already warned me about

Mike and Jacob, and Rissa already had a plan to neutralize them.

Once I was clear of the fray, I glanced over my shoulder to see a still very upright, hot on my tail, David.

Plan B: The Yara effect. Rissa and Hart's name, but I enjoyed the ring of it.

I stopped dead in my tracks, and David nearly tripped over his feet, trying not to run into me.

"Hey!" someone on the sidelines yelled. "What are you doing?"

"Run!" another voice said this time, I think it was Haven.

"You still have a little way to go." David gestured behind me.

"I'm aware." I tossed the ball from hand to hand. "But come on, you and I both know I can't outrun you."

"You're selling yourself short."

When I raised a brow, he chuckled.

"Fine, what is this?" David shook his head, confused.

"My team and I made a bet you wouldn't pull my flag," I said.

"And why wouldn't I do that?" David took a tentative step closer, and I took one back, my heart racing just slightly because maybe we were wrong.

I offered a half-shoulder shrug. "The reasons vary."

"Grab her flag, man!" someone from his team urged.

"Focus, David!"

"Get the ball!"

"Aren't you two adorable?" That was Rissa's mocking.

David held his hand up, telling everyone to keep their distance. This was his issue to handle. The heckling didn't faze him. His gaze never wavered from mine. This undivided attention felt like gold. Fool's gold, perhaps, but still pretty enough to admire.

"Give me your reason," David challenged.

"You still think I have cooties," I teased, taking another step back.

David followed me, not one who was easily distracted. "Hardly."

"In the four years since we've been here," I said. "You've touched me, what, twice? I'm practically radioactive."

He scoffed. "That's not why I don't touch you."

"Then why don't you?"

"For the same reason you kissed me like that in Weston's kitchen."

My smile faded. "What?"

"You know what I'm talking about," he promised. "Like I said, you're one of the smartest people I know."

"And what if I don't know?" I didn't. Not really. Not officially. Not wholeheartedly.

Unofficially, I knew David was far less despicable to be around the older we got. I knew his defiance was hot, and his refusal to lie down and let me barrel forward without an obstacle was what I wanted in a partner. I knew the way his hair fell in his face was less annoying and more endearing these days. And my fingers running through them were, in some weird way, my sworn destiny.

"Yara!" Rissa's voice snapped me out of my David fog. The next step of the plan came back to me in a blink.

She was lateral to me, with a couple of yards in between us.

"David!" someone yelled. I think it was Weston. But it was too late. David moved closer, reaching for a flag. His hand made contact the second after I launched the ball over to Rissa. She took off as soon as the ball hit her hands. With her head start, there was no way anyone could catch her, but that didn't mean they didn't try.

David couldn't stop the momentum of his lunge toward me. He did his best to minimize the contact, though. His hands lightly gripped my hips, holding me away from him like he was the danger.

"See what I mean. Cooties," I teased, even though this swift removal of his hand made my stomach twist. Now, I was considering what was so wrong with me, other than my obviously smart-mouthed, argumentative speaking style. If I could look past his glum, surely he'd be able to accept how often I ran my mouth.

David laughed under his breath, watching as Rissa passed the touchdown line and did a celebratory dance.

"Fine," he said. "Maybe you're right. Maybe you're radioactive."

"Maybe you should get over it."

"I'm going to have to, aren't I?" He started backing away toward his team to regroup.

"Yeah?"

"Tonight especially," he said. "I am your boyfriend. Kind of need not to have an aversion to touching my girlfriend."

My forehead wrinkled. "Tonight?"

He stopped backing away. Our teams were arguing in the background. Someone was complaining about a flag, Hart was defending the house rules, and Weston looked like an exhausted dad who just wanted to go home.

"Afterparty," David said as if this wasn't news to me. "We're going. We need practice being a couple. And I figured if we could convince my friends, we have a decent shot at convincing your family."

I tilted my head to the side when I realized this was what they'd meant by "David's Yara."

"Wait... did you tell your friends we're dating?" I whispered to him. "Like *actually* dating?"

He shrugged. "Figured if we could trick the people who know me best, we had a pretty good shot of tricking the people who know you best."

I laughed a little. "Whoa... you do know Hart invited me here, right?"

"Sure," David said, unbothered.

"Sure?" I scoffed. "So you're okay with one of your closest friends asking your supposed girlfriend out?"

"I don't mind the competition, and neither does Hart," David said. "We hashed it out. I told him we were new and if he wanted a chance and you were willing to give it, who was I to stand in the way?"

My lips parted, but nothing but an exhale came out.

"What do you say?" He asked, moving on from the tar pit I was still stuck in. "Trial run?"

"I think... I'd appreciate that."

"I'm sure you will." He turned to go back to his team.

With him gone, I finally had a moment to catch my breath, relax my shoulders, and stop thinking so hard about what was going on with my hormones.

"Alright!" Rissa cheered as she came in for a double high-five. Nathaniel was right next to her and offered me a fist pump.

"Execution was flawless," he said in his calm, nature documentary narrator voice.

"Brilliant," Hart agreed, coming into focus and offering me a wide smile.

"Thanks." I tried to smile back and not look so taken apart.

"It'll only work once," Rissa said. "But that's more than enough. Weston's going to try and use that pretty head to be creative."

"Well, that's his specialty," Nat warned.

"Yeah, but now, while he's running through millions of possibilities—" Rissa squeezed his shoulder. "——we can sit back and play it by the book. Gotta shake things up and then return to normal. That always confuses an opponent. Now, come on, guys. Places!"

I hung back with Hart, taking my time before scrambling into position. I needed a few more minutes to recover physically and mentally.

"That was quite a Yara effect," Hart teased. He was a little less smiley but not an ounce less friendly.

I look up at him, chest tight with words I'd eventually have to say.

"Rissa's right," he said with a half-shrug as if accepting something. "You and David look nice together."

It's a simple release from our maybe, could-be, almost romantic relationship.

I smiled, grateful for the ease of this transition. "Not really."

"You just don't see it yet."

And that's where he was wrong.

18

THE BLUE TEAM WON, and Hart, Nat, and I didn't let David and Weston hear the end of it on the ride to a beachside bar.

"You got lucky," David said with an amused glint in his eyes.

"And you got distracted," Weston teased. Their gazes met in the rearview for a second, and I would have given away my lecture notes for free just to understand what passed between them. Whatever did resulted in red on David's neck, and a muffled laugh from Weston's lips.

I had piled into David's car after the game because Haven had found herself deep in conversation with Rissa. My best friend swatted me away with her hand behind her back when I mentioned needing a ride to the bar, where almost everyone agreed to meet up after.

My phone finally buzzed with a text from her as we were pulling up into the bar's parking lot:

HAVEN

She wants surfing lessons! She's beautiful and sweet, and she wants me to teach her how to surf.

Sorry I couldn't drive you! I got tunnel vision.

No worries! I get it. Are you coming to the restaurant?

HAVEN

Yes...

Because she'll be here?

HAVEN

...I love you. See you soon!

I chewed on my bottom lip, trying not to laugh out loud. Haven hadn't gone on a date in ages. From experience, seeing her fall for someone was one of the sweetest things ever. I looked forward to early-morning humming and heart-shaped sugar cookies for dessert.

"I think the shortest person should be the designated middle seater," Hart was complaining. Seeing them shoved in the tight space was both comical and impressive.

"Exactly," Weston agreed, voice low from distraction as he typed something on his phone. "So, we're right on track."

"I'm not shorter than you," Hart said before Nat could point it out.

"You are," Nat promised.

"We get a full write-up of everything from body fat to shoe size," Weston reminded him. "You're the shortest."

"I'd been slouching that day," Hart tried.

"You slouch every day," Weston countered.

"Alright." David put the car in park. "I'm too tired to listen to you all go back and forth. Get out of my car."

"Tired? You barely broke a sweat today," Hart muttered under his breath, earning a chuckle from Weston and a smile from Nat. They followed David's order regardless, continuing their disagreement outside. Before I could join them, David made a low hum of disapproval and reached over to pull my door shut. I swallowed at his large arm and how good it looked stretched over me.

"Not you," he said simply as he leaned back into his seat.

I pressed my lips together to assure my mouth wasn't agape. The guys glanced back at us, curious about our delay. But Weston said something that pulled their attention to the restaurant. Hart was the only one to give us one more glance before disappearing inside with the others.

I frowned at David. "What was that for?"

"Just because we're new and I'm letting another guy have a shot, doesn't mean I wouldn't show some bouts of selfishness," he explained. "If I were really into you, I'd want you to myself any chance I'd get."

"Right..." I couldn't feel my face.

"So, how are we playing this?" he asked. "What should we practice?"

I shook my head, trying to think of anything besides his lips on mine. "Just... being near each other. And nice. Being nice to each other."

He smiled. "Low-hanging fruit."

"I'll say," I agreed.

"Come here?" He motioned with his finger for me to move closer.

I blinked, mouth going dry. "What?"

"Come here."

Some of my natural defiance finally leaked back into my

veins, thank god. I managed a, "If you want something, you come to me. I'm not going to follow your orders just cause we're supposedly a couple."

David shook his head, but disapproval was nowhere in sight. He leaned over the console and took my chin between his fingers.

"So, a couple more of my teammates have shown up and just parked across the way," he explained.

When I tried to look, he made a low noise of disapproval.

"Look at me like you wish we didn't have to be here," he said. "Like you're asking to go back to my place."

"I told you." It took maximum effort to speak through all the buzzing heat between my thighs. "I'm not blindly following your lead. That's not the kind of person I've ever been in relationships."

"Fine." He took a breath, but there weren't any echoes of annoyance. Instead, David seemed pleased. "Who would you be?"

"I'd be the girl you'd beg to take home."

The smile that spread across his lips made the ache in my chest reach a level of unbearable I didn't know I could survive.

"So, do it. Make me look like I'm begging," he encouraged. "Sell it."

I closed the distance, my nose brushing against his. David took a breath but didn't let it out. We hadn't been this close since our kiss. We hadn't even talked about our kiss. All the weight threatened to spill over now. His gaze flickered to my mouth, and I knew without a doubt he wanted to do it again just as much as I did. The confirmation left me with more questions. The biggest question was which one of us would be the first to officially break. Did it matter who held out when the reward would be complete and utter relief?

"You've thought of me since then, haven't you?" I whispered. My voice was steady, leaning on the solid post that was seduction.

"Since...?" he prompted, needing me to say.

"Since our kiss."

David swallowed but showed no other sign of arousal. "Hardly."

"Liar." My lips almost touched his, but not quite. We didn't need to kiss to prove we were dating. "You've thought of it like I have."

His jaw ticked, but he offered a half-shrug. "I guess."

"Did you do it in bed? Like me?"

The red was back, creeping up his cheeks, and I went for broke.

"Touch yourself to it like me?" I asked.

He let out a heavy breath, his body nearly shivering at my words. "Are you fucking serious?"

I smiled and shook my head. "I don't know. All I know is I'm making you beg for it."

"That's not...you're..." It was rare to render David speechless. I reveled in the ability to do so while being so off-kilter. Once my gaze flickered down to his sweats and I saw a nicely hardened outline, we both knew denial would do him no favors.

"So... beg." I wrapped my hand around his wrist, holding him in place where he still gripped my chin.

"Please," he whispered, eyes soft with desperation a woman could only dream of.

For a second, I froze, confused whether this was still the game or if we'd crossed some line. But more of his teammates were showing up outside. And the only reason he held me back was to play this up. David wasn't actually asking to be taken home.

"No," I said, equally directed to myself as it was to him.

I pulled away from his grasp and opened the door. He

didn't stop me this time. Stepping outside into the crisp air calmed the heat of my skin. The few teammates who had been curiously watching the exchange quickly turned away, pretending to have no interest in their tight end's love life. I rubbed my fingers across my lips as I started up the wooden stairs to the bar. Any doubt of successfully feigning attraction was decimated.

———

I WAS in my third game of pool with Weston and Hart when Haven showed up. She'd waved at me from the bar, where she claimed a spot by Nat, Rissa, and David. I smiled back, trying my best not to get distracted by my fake boyfriend and his habit of watching me like I was the only person in the room.

"You're scary good at this," Hart said after my turn. He'd tried the whole, *'want me to show you how to hit the ball'* thing. I ended up coaching him on his form after they witnessed what I could do. All three times, I'd beaten them in a landslide.

"And we most definitely suck." Weston laughed when Hart missed an easy shot, once more cementing me as the winner. "You shouldn't have bet."

"*We* shouldn't have," Hart corrected as he dug in his pocket to fork up the cash.

"I haven't won yet." I smiled as I got into position for my last shot.

"Well, let's have it." Hart gestured with dollar bills, signaling me to seal the deal. Once I did it with ease, Weston whistled. Hart just smiled at me indulgently. He held out the cash, but when I reached for it, he kept it out of reach.

"What's exactly going on with you and David?" he asked as he held my winnings hostage.

"Hart," Weston warned in a singsong voice as he placed his cue back on the rack.

"What exactly do you think's going on with David and me?" I crossed my arms over my chest, trying to mask the heavy thumping of my heart. Was he somehow onto us? What if David and I didn't look as desperate as it all felt? Was that more or less embarrassing than actually feeling desperate for David?

"I don't know. Whatever it is, it's cute," Hart said. I smiled at how genuine the assessment sounded.

Weston snatched the money out of Hart's hands and offered it to me. "One more round? I need a little extra cash for the bar."

"*You* need cash for the bar?" I laughed and made a show of counting out my earnings.

Weston smiled and shrugged. "I left my cards at home. Trying to curb spending habits."

"You're on," I said, and then, to Hart, "You really think we're cute?"

"Sure." He nodded. "Not as cute as you and I could be, but there's still potential there."

"Has nearly four seasons of NCAA football taught you nothing? You know if you want something someone else has, you shouldn't talk up the opponent, right?" Weston gestured over his shoulder toward David.

"I'm not so insecure that I have to trash-talk someone behind their back." Hart shrugged. The confidence was sexy, and if I weren't so entangled with a guy I've known since middle school, I may have let him pretend to teach me about form this round.

"But I also know when to bow out gracefully," Hart directed that statement to me.

My cheeks burned, but before I could comment, a hand pressed on my lower back.

"You okay?" David asked me, but his gaze was on Hart. The hardness there, though manufactured, was flattering.

"Are *you*?" Hart asked with a teasing smile. David's glare didn't bother him for a second.

"Great." I waved my money back and forth. "I'm winning."

"I see." David pulled his gaze from Hart and onto me. His expression softened noticeably. My stomach fluttered when he hooked two fingers around my belt loop. Hart's gaze flickered there for a second, and his brow twitched, a micro-expression of annoyance.

"As to be expected," David continued. "Take a break and come sit with me."

"She's a bit busy," Hart said, voice still lighthearted, even though the look in his eyes wasn't.

"Not when it comes to me." David met his friend's gaze with a look of warning. His fake jealousy did wonders for his jawline. And it was dangerous for my growing desire.

"I'm... going one more round with Weston," I said in a voice barely louder than a whisper.

"Actually..." Weston had his phone out, texting someone with intense focus. "I think I'm out of here."

"You're leaving?" Hart frowned, worried.

"Yeah." Weston looked up at us and tried not to smile too much as he said, "I need to pick something up."

"For you know who?" David asked with a brow raised. Hart and I exchanged looks since neither of us had a clue what was going on. "Congrats."

"Shut up," Weston told David, allowing himself to smile this time. "And you two, be civil. Don't scare Yara away. You're lucky she's talking to either of you."

I smiled, liking this quarterback more and more. We said our goodbyes, and Weston made me promise to let him have another match later.

With Weston gone, the tension was back—mostly on David's end. After a beat, Hart simply smiled and said, "Very cute. I really can't complain."

While David frowned in confusion, I laughed. As far as I was concerned, Hart's observation was a seal of approval regarding the validity of our "relationship."

19

"After what happened at the bar... I think we should discuss our boundaries. Physical and otherwise. So that things don't get muddled."

We were two hours into a three-hour drive when David finally interrupted my spiel of my family tree. I started with my great-grandma, her move from New Orleans, and how she met great-granddad on an orange farm in Florida. Reciting family history soothed the nerves that'd followed me all the way home after the flag football, in my sleep, and through my morning routine.

The heat was on. Leaves were red and orange, falling across the near-empty two-lane highway out of Westbrooke. I was comfortable enough to have my shoes off. My legs were covered in a blanket David so happened to have put in the backseat. Allegedly, he'd forgotten to take it inside after prepping for a tailgate with a few of his friends. Seeing through his lies was getting a little bit easier.

"Boundaries. Muddled," I said, cheeks ablaze as I thought of the things I'd said the last time I leaned on his console. And how his fingers hooked on my belt loop had been more than enough to have me going straight to my room once I got back to my apartment for some quality time with my vibrator. "Great idea."

David's brow wrinkled as he glanced at me. He'd suspected something all morning but had yet to question me. Harboring a secret crush on him was strange. Despite this developing soft spot, I still wanted to get under his skin. Poke the bear until he growled back. It's a desire now mixed up in a need for his attention. To be heard, seen, and... taken care of. Damn, I wanted him to take care of me in a multitude of ways.

As David changed the radio dial, I sank into my chair, afraid that something could capture my thoughts in the air or on some radio frequency.

"What the hell is going on?" he mumbled to himself when all he could find was snow.

"Dead zone," I reminded him with my collar pulled over my mouth to keep out the longing sentiments behind some kind of blockade.

There was always a weak signal during this part of the drive. I didn't know if it was the height of the trees or the lack of houses.

"What kind of couple are we?" David started fumbling with the AC instead, turning on the heat. "Affection-wise."

"I don't know." I straightened to look less defeated.

He took a deep breath. "What kind have you been a part of in the past?"

"You first."

David frowned. He thought I was deflecting when I was really just fishing. I didn't want to be the first one to suggest we should hold hands. It was a childish thing to get butterflies over, and yet, I was ready to burst.

"I don't mind holding hands when it fits the occasion," he said.

I snorted. "When it fits the occasion? What do qualified occasions look like?"

"Crossing the street, going up or down a staircase, in a crowded room, at theme parks."

"So, practical hand-holding," I summarized. "Not romantic. David, we're supposed to be romantically involved."

"I'm aware."

"Which means sometimes we may hold hands just for the heck of it."

"Every couple's different."

"If you don't want to hold hands, you should just say that. We're discussing boundaries. You can make it your boundary," I reminded him as I relaxed again in my seat. The warmth from the vents helped calm my edgy nerves.

"I don't mind holding your hand," he said with little if any thought.

"You sure?"

He nodded. "Positive."

"Wonderful to know you'd deign to interlace your fingers with mine," I mumbled sarcastically. "How are we with hugging? Hand on the waist. Shoulders?"

"I can hug. My waist and shoulders are fine."

"Same." I pressed my lips together, treading carefully as I continued. "As my boyfriend, my family will not expect you to make out aggressively with me or anything. But a little thumb on cheek brush or hip grab would sell things."

"And we don't want to go out of business too early."

I flipped down the mirror and checked my makeup. I needed something to do with my hands, and my phone still barely had a signal. "Exactly."

"Speaking of kissing," David said.

My stomach's in hell, but I barely blinked. "What about it?"

"Obviously, we'll try to avoid the lips at all costs," he continued.

I laughed, all anxiety, no amusement. "Obviously."

"What about other places?"

That shouldn't have sounded so dirty and shouldn't have set my skin on fire.

"Yara?" David asked when I took too long to calm my thoughts. "Are you..."

Oh no. No, no, no. I've shown my hand.

David smiled, satisfied with his ammo. He was a starved man stepping foot back into civilization.

"You are," he decided with a low exhale. The noise wasn't mocking; it was intrigued.

"I'm not." I flipped up the mirror with enough force to raise concerns about its structural integrity. David would typically scold me for being so rough with his belongings. But not this time.

"You're imagining me kissing you somewhere else," he said.

I want to be a butterfly at this point. Weightless. Free. Able to escape this car and find some safe flowers in a field far, far away from this man.

"'Course I was. I was mapping out all the logical points at which a boyfriend would kiss his girlfriend." Sometimes it was best to fight his fire with nonchalance. David backed off when he realized something didn't bother you.

"Where exactly would those be?"

"Cheeks, temple, forehead." I touched each spot as I spoke, as if he needed help to figure out where everything was. "All of which is fine with me, so engage as you see fit. Especially when my sister or Ren are in sight."

"Got it." He nodded. "Anywhere else?"

I frowned. "I don't know. How about you tell me, since

you seem so interested in the topic? Where else would you like to kiss me, David?"

"Like's not the word I'm looking for," he said.

"Oh? When you figure out your vocab, please share. I'm still waiting on pins and needles for what you decide to call us."

"I'm working on it," he promised and looked over at me with a smile. David's gaze lingered. He didn't turn away even when I raised a questioning brow.

The radio came back on, giving me a jump scare. David blinked, the spell breaking as he cranked down the volume.

"We're an hour out," he announced. "We've got hand-holding, waist grabs, shoulder grabs, and mapped out kissing zones all in the green. Anything we're missing?"

I chewed on my lip and shook my head. "You?"

"Alright, let's move on to red zones. I have only one. Don't shove me right here and we're good." David gestured to his chest area.

My brows furrowed. "There would never be a need to, but... why not?"

"It's a boundary," he said firmly. "Just don't do it."

"Got you." I stared at the area. "You said shove. What about touching it? Casual like. Gentle."

The chest covered a large area. I needed to know if I should avoid it altogether.

"I'm fine with gentle touch," he promised. "A soft pat, rub, you can even rest your hand there. Just nothing with too much force... my foster dad used to shove a lot there. It's a trigger... I'm working through it, but not there yet."

My shoulders sagged at the tidbit. Much like in his room, I was hungry for more about him. David hadn't faked throughout high school, but he minimized. Made his life seem like such a void, bland and empty when it was everything but.

"Red zones for you?" David asked.

I cleared my throat, reminding myself he didn't owe me anything about his life. No matter how many dares and time we shared, if David wanted to keep certain things to himself, that was his right. I'd respect it. Mourn it. Contemplate ways to help him understand that I could be a safe place. But ultimately, let him decide.

"No boob or butt grabs, and I'm golden," I said.

"You got it. Now what about safe words?" he asked.

"What about them? We're not... partaking in anything that adventurous."

He gave me an amused look. "Regardless, better safe than sorry. If I do something like kiss you one too many times and you can't tell me to back off because someone else is around—"

"Again with the kissing. You're really looking forward to that part, aren't you?" I rested my elbow on the console and my chin in my palm as I smiled at him.

He chuckled. "Your projection's your largest tell, you know that?"

"I learned from the best."

"Uh huh." David laughed again. I'm on a roll with these. My head grew larger at the sound of each one. There was no denying that David enjoyed my company now. Even when he looked disapproving, I could easily make him smile. And I'd long since released the idea of hating his presence. Annoyance still shoved its way in between us sometimes, like a toddler in need of attention. But I loved the interruptions. Love annoyance's cute, constant presence, all soft and familiar and full of potential love.

Love. Not the romantic, head over heels, I can't live without you love. Not now. Nowhere near now. But someday? One day. I wanted it one day.

Holy crap. We've just now decided to hold hands.

I pushed away from the console, turning my gaze out the window.

"Yara?" David noted my change in energy.

"I'll ask you to call Haven," I said.

"That's a phrase, not a word."

"It's less suspicious. And I assume the scenario won't be heated. I'll have plenty of time to get it out."

He was silent for a second before finally saying, "Mine will be, call Weston, then."

"Best friends to the rescue," I murmured.

"I guess," he agreed, quieter as he got lost in his own thoughts.

———

"WAIT for me to open the door." David unbuckled his seat belt and turned off the car.

When we pulled into my family's U-drive, there was already a large assortment of cars parked. Most of which were my siblings' and their partners'. But I noticed a couple of cousins', aunts', and uncles' vehicles, too. The majority of my family still lived in New Harbor, so simple dinners often became mini family reunions. And since my parents owned one of the largest homes in town, equipped with a basketball court and a pool, they rarely received declined invitations.

"No one's..." I sighed when he shut the door and came around to my side.

"It took two seconds," David noted flatly when he saw my disapproving stare.

"I counted ten," I said. "And no one's watching. Besides, you don't have to lay it on thick. My family's not going to grade..."

David brushed a twist behind my ear, his thumb lingering

on the lobe. Nothing about it should be sexual, and yet, it was as if he'd pinned me against the car door to kiss me breathless.

"Someone is watching," he whispered, leaning closer. Our height difference was a non-factor most days. He wasn't much taller than I was. But while cupping my jaw and keeping my gaze upward, I was keenly aware of how easily he could block the sun's heat and keep me cool and protected from the elements.

"Ever since we pulled in." David's lips were by my ear, hand on the roof of the car, keeping me between him and the door. It should feel claustrophobic. Despite that, I want to reach out and grab his shirt. Suffocate myself in his familiar scent. That wouldn't be a bad way to die. In fact, I thought it might be preferable. I also thought I was losing all common sense.

"Second-floor, third window on the right." David pulled back just a little so I could meet his gaze. There was no sign of dismay in his eyes. No hitch in breath. No dilated pupils.

The best part about being at odds with David was that I was never alone. Together, we were stranded on an island, finding cover in a shoddy shelter from the ground up. Somewhere along the lines, I'd discovered a new stretch of land not too far off. I'd swum here on my own, and it was painfully lonely. I preferred disagreements over this. Jabs. Taunts. Anything not to be this lonely.

"That's the third floor," I whispered, keeping my voice steady as I glanced up to find the window he was talking about. "Probably one of my sisters. Rose's room is up there. It's the only one my mom didn't convert into some house project."

"She converted your room into something else?" David frowned. "Why? There's like fifty of them."

"Only eight."

"Only eight," David repeated with a low, disbelieving laugh. "Three floors and only eight rooms, pardon me."

"Sorry." I took a breath. "I wasn't trying to…"

His expression softened. "I was teasing, Daredevil."

David's hand was still on my jaw, thumb massaging circles on what were now tense muscles.

"I know where you come from," he said. "I'm not trying to make you feel bad about it."

I scoffed in disagreement. "That's quite a change of tune."

"I only ever wanted you to admit things were nice on this side of town." With his thumb on my chin now, tilting my head higher so I'll hold his gaze. "That you were royalty in this town."

"Royalty's a stretch."

"Your mom's the mayor and your dad's a lawyer who owns like half of the restaurants."

"She was voted in, and kings don't exactly own chain cafes and law firms, last I checked."

"You're practically a princess." David wouldn't budge in his stance. He stepped back, though, giving me enough space to duck into the car and grab my bag. I straightened up in time to see his gaze on my ass.

"Were you checking me out?" I laughed, cheeks burning at being noticed by him. In all our years, David's gaze never strayed in curiosity or admiration… at least, not that I've seen.

"Felt appropriate." He shut the door behind me. "We're still in our honeymoon stage. As a new couple, it makes sense for us not to keep our eyes off each other." David's all matter-of-fact and even-toned.

"All couples are different." Heat sparked through my stomach when he tucked a twist behind my other ear. His fingers didn't linger this time.

"Fair." David nodded. There was a little red in his cheeks,

but I wasn't sure if it was because of the conversation or the chill in the air. "If you'd prefer I didn't, I won't."

"I don't mind," I said a little too quickly. "I was just surprised. It's strange. We're not exactly each other's type and—"

"Since when?" David frowned.

I raised a brow. "Since the dawn of time."

"You have a bad habit of making sweeping statements." He looked genuinely pissed. "You should get in the habit of speaking for yourself. We've already proven you don't know enough about me to know my type."

I opened my mouth, but nothing came out.

"So? What's your rebuttal? I know you have one."

There would be no argument from me. He was right; I didn't know enough about him to make a decent claim of knowing his type.

"Maybe if you opened up a little and gave me a fighting chance, I'd have one. Maybe I'd know your type." I tilted my head to the side, studying him and considering the best way to get him to take on the challenge. "I dare you. Open up."

He scoffed and shook his head. "How would you like me to do that exactly? Which part of me do you want to see?"

I shrugged, too embarrassed to let David know I was interested in every dark corner and closed door.

"You don't have any parameters?" he asked, unconvinced.

"Only one is to be honest," I said. "Tell me what you've told your friends on the team. Tell me enough about you to make me understand why they'd speak so highly after only knowing you for four years."

"Four years is a long enough time to be close to someone."

"Nine's longer," I countered with a bit of fire in my tone. "Are you forfeiting or not?"

"Not," he assured. "Never."

20

———

My dad was the first one to greet us at the door. He was a big guy, which should give him an aura of intimidation. But he was as soft and welcoming as a luxury hotel bed.

"Yara." Dad wrapped me in his arms the second I stepped into the foyer. For a second, I'm eight years old again with my feet off the ground and my dad lifting any and every weight off my shoulders. "I've missed you."

"I missed you, too." I laughed once he stopped spinning me around, and I stepped back to see his beaming face.

He kissed my forehead and directed his gaze toward my plus one. "And is this the Louis kid? The one who used to give you all his extra candy after Halloween?"

I raised a brow, surprised he remembered that and even more surprised I'd forgotten. The memory slipped right out of the cracked door of my subconscious. David dumped a bag of Starbursts on my desk because he knew I'd have a collection of Almond Joys I couldn't wait to pawn off to the highest bidder.

My brow furrowed at how clear the memory was now that it was back. How much of David had I forgotten? What memories of him remained tucked in the far corners of my mind, stuck there until someone triggered them.

"We bartered." David smiled at my dad and offered his hand. "And it's Evans. I lived with the Louis family, but I'm an Evans, sir."

I frowned. The Louis family. I'd assumed they were Evans. They looked like David, all stoic expressions and dark hair. But David had been a foster kid. I'd only learned that much an hour ago. Again, the shame of it all made my stomach sour. As a teen, I'd just assume we all had parents we pretended not to like, went home to beds where we got ample sleep, and came to school without the haunting of home life holding us back. I hated myself for it. For not asking. Not knowing.

"Got it." Dad accepted David's hand and offered him a hearty shake. "You're a starter for the Angels, aren't you? I'm more of a basketball guy, but Westbrooke's football team is easier to cheer for."

"You can still cheer on losers," I joked. "They're the ones who need it the most."

Dad laughed while David's brows furrowed.

"She never had much luck in little league, poor thing," Dad explained as he wrapped an arm around my shoulder, pulling me into his side.

I rolled my eyes good-naturedly. "We never had a carrier."

"Carrier?" David asked.

"Someone talented enough to carry the entire team. There's always a handful of those when you're that young."

David nodded. "I was one of them."

I laughed. "Brag much?"

My fake boyfriend actually looked a little embarrassed and dismayed. Dad swooped in with the save, noting, "A man who knows his worth. Got to respect the confidence."

"Yara!" We were interrupted by a group of aunts and cousins. They introduced themselves, becoming instantly smitten by David's smile and nonchalant attitude about being *so* talented. They fawned over his story about last year's championship, which most of them had a viewing party for because they were football fans. I'd missed the family memo.

"This is the guy?" My older brother, Adam, appeared behind me, leaning against the sitting room's doorframe and watching everyone take the turn to 'oh' and 'ah' over David. "I thought you hated jocks?"

Adam was all long limbs and brain. The shade of his brown skin matched mine to a tee, which made him swear off makeup store trips with me. He had plans on publishing an eight-book series about dragons and time travel, but only after he finished his sidequest of opening an anime-themed restaurant two towns over with his friends.

"I do." I pressed my back against the wall next to him.

"So what's different about this one?" Adam and I weren't the golden children who could revel in reaching goals like our sisters. We worked tirelessly to achieve successes that our parents would note (because they weren't assholes), but wouldn't quite shine as bright as Amiee, Logan, and Rose's stars. Comparison came from our small-town community, not our four walls. Still, the *"what about you?"* and *"your sisters must be a huge inspiration"* seeped underneath our floorboards, rising high enough to graze our ankles.

Because we often brainstorm in corners on how to keep up in this sibling race, I planned to tell Adam my relationship was all for show. That a guy like David and a girl like me were like oil and water, and no kiss or amount of flirting could fix that. Adam could already sense it. I could tell by the unconvinced tilt of his head when he looked down at me, waiting for an answer.

I considered how to give him a hint about the subterfuge, but when I locked eyes with David for a second, my chest tightened. "Sometimes you just want something different."

I couldn't blow our cover just yet, even with Adam, because a small (slowly growing) part of me enjoyed being the talking point of the evening. Enjoyed people thinking his gaze finding mine alluded to budding love and admiration. A deep, embarrassing part of me longed for everyone's attention and approval. Something to show everyone, hey, I'm worth getting to know. I may not be as smart as Logan, as talented as Adam, as agreeable as Aimee, or as pretty as Rose. But I could be worth something to someone as successful as David.

"I feel like I have to be intimidating," Adam confessed. "Dad's in his palm and Mom's bound to be the same. Where's the instinct to defend their nest? I think if we were actually birds and there were wolves, they'd invite them over for dinner and cocktails."

I laughed, watching Dad brag to my aunts about how good David was on the field, even though he'd only seen him between commercial breaks of basketball game reruns. "You don't have to be intimidating."

"I do." Adam nudged his chin toward David. "Look at him. He's too comfortable this early in the game."

An outsider would assume David was in his element. He wore an easy smile and answered all questions in a calm, even tone and laughed at a few jokes about the upcoming draft. But a glance at his white knuckles from a tight fist revealed anxiety. Red inched up his neck, hot and threatening.

"Be nice to him," I told Adam.

He gave me a *'you know better than to expect that'* look. "We'll see if he deserves nice, and I'll reassess from there."

Before pushing away from the wall, I had to ask, "Do you know if Logan's coming tonight?"

Guilt ate me alive as I crossed my fingers for 'no.' It was a disheartening space to be in, loving someone so much, yet not wanting to see them, because then everything buried threatened to be unearthed. My headspace wasn't strong enough to balance family, David, and the past all in one night.

"No, she has some paper she's behind on writing," Adam said with a shrug, none the wiser about my fear. "She'll be in town next week if you want to drop by."

I smiled and nodded. "Maybe."

My smile vanished when I caught David's eye again and saw a plea for help. I went to his side in an instant. I reached for his fist, massaging circles on the back of his palm until he released his fingers. They intertwined with mine, clasping hold like I was the only thing keeping him on solid ground.

"I want to show David the house," I interrupted Aunt Clare's recount of her time dating a quarterback in the nineties.

"Remember our doors open policy," Dad reminded as I tugged David to the staircase. He chuckled, joking but not really. Adam was half-wrong; Dad had at least a bit of protective instinct.

"I'm aware," I said. Never mind the fact that all his children were twenty-one and up. Their house, their rules.

It wasn't until we'd cleared the staircase that David took a breath. I raised a brow, questioning this sudden bout of anxiety.

"Are you okay?" I wanted to make a joke, but he looked so far from okay, I thought it'd be downright cruel to tease him.

"Fine." David unbuttoned his collar. He'd really tried to get dressed up for this dinner. His usually unruly hair was slicked back with a bit of product. And his slacks —though not perfectly tailored, and a little worn around the knees— hung nicely on his waist. He was handsome. And terrified.

"You're red in the face."

"It's warm in here." He swallowed and looked around the hall as if he were hunting for the source of heat.

I smiled and resisted the urge to rub his arm. "Have you ever done the 'meet the parents' thing?"

"Have you?" he responded quickly. An immediate flash of remorse crossed his face. "Sorry... maybe I'm... just a little overstimulated. Out of my element."

My shoulders sagged with empathy. "My folks can be a lot. But I promise they're harmless. And very accepting. They love you already if that's any comfort."

He chuckled. "Only because I can successfully catch a ball over and over again."

"Maybe." I shrugged. "Still impressive. You're on a team that has earned Westbrooke back a championship title. There's pride in that."

"Pride's risky business."

"So is being someone's fake boyfriend, but you're doing just fine so far."

"So far."

I grabbed his hand even though there was no one around. No audience to play to. I grabbed David's hand because his face was still red, his breath still uneven, and touching him seemed to calm us both down.

He looked down at our fingers for a second. "Has this house gotten bigger?"

I laughed. "What?"

"It was big as a kid." David looked around the long hallway, taking in the embellished gold-plated frames, statues Mom had purchased in a museum auction, and vases from elected officials who'd wanted endorsements or just Christmas party invites.

"But, it feels bigger," he said.

"They did add a guest house." I shrugged. "But it's in the back, near the lake. You can't see it from the house."

"Near the lake," David repeated in a whisper. "I don't think I'm meant to be here."

My smile dropped. "What? You're... here. There's no way you're backing out of this now."

David shook his head. "I'm not backing out."

"Then what are you talking about?"

"Nothing." His eyes lingered on a family portrait Dad commissioned one Easter. "Just talking. Meaningless small talk."

There was no chance in hell he was telling the truth. But I let him have it due to his anxious state and the fragility of the line we were towing between fake partners and occasional flirts.

"You want a look into what's left of my childhood?" I asked.

"Of course," he said, still distracted by the decor. "I'll need the canon fodder for later."

I rolled my eyes and started walking. My room was at the end of the hallway, a glorified art gallery with a full-size, four-poster bed with curtains that closed. The bed was the only thing my mom and I agreed would never be moved out of my room.

"What was it like before?" David scanned the space as if he were trying to see through some glamour.

"My boy band posters were over here." I gestured to the wall on the right. "A shrine to a mermaid series I was obsessed over used to be there. My mounted TV was covered in rhinestones. And a couple of shag rugs overlapped each other."

David nodded, releasing my hand as he walked toward the bay windows. Mom placed new white cushions and over-stuffed brown pillows on the seat.

"I'm sure it was nice." He sat down in the bay window seat, massaging the hand I'd grabbed.

"Do you..." I gestured to his hand and took a seat beside him, keeping a respectable two pillows in between us. "Need to wash your hands?"

"No." David smiled, seemingly thankful as he shook his head. "I'm not... it's unnecessary. Or at least that's what I'm trying to tell myself."

I'm quiet, waiting for him to expound, but he continued massaging and studying my room in silence.

"Remember the dare?" I smiled and nudged my shoe gently against his. "You're supposed to be open."

"I think it needs at least a time parameter." He turned back to me. "It's not fair if I have to be open with you indefinitely."

"Why couldn't it be indefinite?" It was supposed to sound teasing, but there was a weight in my words. I hoped that David would consider me as more than the person he pestered for a couple of hours before disappearing into the void. "We talk almost every day. You're sitting in my childhood bedroom. We used to barter for candy in elementary school. David, I hate to say this —you know I hate to say this— but I think we're friends. Not the best of friends, don't get me wrong. But friends."

He sighed and shook his head.

"No?" I asked, urging him to say whatever rejection he was thinking.

"We didn't barter," he said. "Your dad was right. I just didn't want him to think I'd been crushing on you for that long when I hadn't."

I blinked. "We definitely bartered."

"I'm allergic to chocolate, remember? But you liked Starbursts. And you wouldn't take anything from me then without offering something in return."

"I did like things to be even," I agreed with a nod. Even back then, my sense of justice overshadowed the bliss of sugar highs.

"So I gave them to you for Almond Joys."

"Why?"

"Because you liked Starbursts." He still massaged his hand, gaze trained outside to a couple of other cars pulling into the driveway.

"Right, but that was... kind."

He looked at me again, unamused. "I've always been kind to you."

I snorted. "David, come on."

"Fine, cordial," he said.

"I can't believe you took something you're allergic to."

"Is that open enough for you?" he asked.

I shook my head. "What did you get? From the entire exchange, what did you get?"

It had to be something. Ever since we started at Westbrooke and these dares, David had gained something from our interactions, whether it was a laugh or an ego boost.

David was quiet as he considered his response, thinking so loud that I could barely focus on the voice in my head.

"It's not because you had a crush on me?" I asked, teasing, joking, hoping.

"Sorry to burst your bubble, but no. Did you have one on me?"

I scoffed, only slightly disappointed and mostly relieved because my answer was also, "No. Not even close."

"I can't remember the exact reason," he confessed. "But I know I enjoyed talking to you —if only for the reminder that we couldn't stand each other. It was entertaining."

I laughed. "You risked going into anaphylactic shock to talk to me because arguing was fun?"

"The candy was wrapped in plastic, so the risk was minimal," he said. "And worth it because sometimes you and I were on the same page. The more we interacted, the more chances we got to agree. And sometimes agreeing was just as fun as arguing. Not wanting to bite another's head off was nice. Like now."

"Now is nice?" I shouldn't tease him. This was the longest we've gotten along in years. The first time we feel like we're on the same team.

"To me," David amended. "It's nice to me."

And there it was, a show of maturity I could have never mustered to express first. David stood in his honesty. Or maybe it was the dare talking. Either way, my heart drummed hard enough to be felt in my fingertips.

"Me too," I said before I could rethink it. Before some weird, jeering comment spilled from my lips and pushed him away.

"I figured." His statement should be a joke. My launching pad to something more our speed, like below-the-belt jabs or petty observations. Instead, I smiled and looked away for a second with burning cheeks as if I were some young girl whose first crush just spoke to her on the playground.

There were voices on the stairs, growing louder as the group moved closer to my room. I could tell it was Aimee, Adam, and a couple of my cousins. I cleared my throat and scooted away from David to put even more space between us. David did the opposite, inching closer and resting a hand on my knee. When my eyes widened with a question, he asked, "Trust me?"

"Maybe," I whispered back.

"I need a yes if I'm going to continue," he said.

"Yes," I offered, my voice breathy. There wasn't much of a window to overthink. And I'd be tossing and turning all night after this, frustrated at not knowing what it was that David wanted me to trust him with.

Right before my family was close enough to push the cracked door completely open, David placed his hand on my cheek. His hand covered the bottom half of my face, so when he leaned in, it was impossible to see that his lips never touched mine. He got close, though. The edge of his mouth hovered over mine. He smelled of spearmint and felt like the setting sun.

"Just to sell it," he whispered against my mouth. The movement of his lips was like fire on my skin. It was the most heart-stopping non-kiss, leaving my throat dry and body aching for the real thing. How I had experienced the real thing and lived to tell the tale, I had no idea.

As soon as the door opened, David pressed his cheek against mine for an inhale. My body was abuzz with the desire to turn my head slightly and make contact. I would never, but I could dream. I would dream, I'm sure, to the end of time. He pulled back when Aimee stumbled over her apology.

"I didn't think..." She pressed her hands to her cheeks, trying to figure out a way to retrace everyone's steps, go back in time, and knock. "Sorry, that was rude of us. We didn't mean to interrupt."

"The door's supposed to be open. All the way." Adam made a show of pushing the door wide enough so the hall was in full view. Two of my cousins were giggling with one another. They were young enough to swoon over David openly and without shame. I smiled because they got to express what I felt on the inside. All the fawning and sighing. At least someone could let it out.

Was this how it would have to be from now on? Would I always have to suppress what I felt about David, no matter what that feeling was, to appear nonchalant? First, it was my disdain. Now, it was my attraction. The switch—though nicer —was frustrating to contain. And all for what? To one-up him? To pretend he didn't affect me when he had been doing just that for almost a decade.

"Sorry." David took his time putting a bit of space between us. But he didn't remove his hand from my knee. "That was my fault."

David supposedly closed the door, made out with me, and took the blame for a broken rule. He even sounded a little breathless from the kissing and the embarrassment of being caught. Talk about selling. And my siblings were buying.

Adam frowned, growing more protective by the second. Aimee and our younger cousins sighed, excited to see me finally with someone after Ren.

"Dinner's ready," Aimee said, gesturing over her shoulder. "Yara, you've graduated from the kids' table this year."

"All it took was a football-playing boyfriend. I'll take it." I brushed at my skirt and stood up as if I weren't lightheaded and craving the feel of David against me. David only partially satisfied my desire when he placed his hand on the small of my back as we followed everyone out of the room and downstairs.

"I'm Adam," my brother introduced once we were at the bottom of the staircase.

"David. Your buddy Xavier used to be my mentor back when I was in grade seven."

"I remember." Adam nodded. "He said you were hard to get along with."

I attempted to make eye contact with Adam, but he promptly ignored me.

"I am." David nodded. "It's one of the things I'm working on."

"Good," Adam said. "I'm sure the list is long now that you're with Yara."

"Adam," I said, not waiting for eye contact this time. "Relax."

"Just being honest. If he wants an Every, he'll have to learn how to be with one."

I shook my head. "Stop it. David's more than capable of being with an Every. Whatever that means."

It was the first time I was protective of him. Underneath David's smile was a host of nerves and a need to impress a house full of strangers who would spread gossip to the rest of our not-so-nice small town. He didn't deserve that. His people weren't here to defend him and shout his praises. So I would have to do that for him. It wasn't the fake girlfriend in me that was motivated; it was the part of me that'd spent every weeknight and weekend with him. It was the part of me who texted him before I went to bed and when I woke up, who was saved by him at the beach and coached by him on the football field. I wanted to back up the guy who gently chided whenever he caught me picking at my hair and kept it secret. David never made me feel like I was broken for doing it. The least I could do was present a united front.

"Just being with one Every, though, right?" Adam asked, unconvinced. "Because hopping around isn't cute."

Adam hated the idea of Ren and Rose. The beginning of their relationship caused a rift in the family that lasted a couple of months. It was the longest we'd all been on awkward terms with one another. But I was quick to forgive, and it made little sense for Adam to continue to carry the grudge if it had nothing to do with him.

"She's the only person I'm interested in," David promised, his hand still on my back, tracing small circles on my spine. "Every or not."

Adam smiled, not convinced but at least amused. "Nice answer. I guess time will tell."

My brother patted David roughly on the shoulder and gently pinched my cheek before starting into the dining room.

"Sorry about him." I turned to David and busied my hands with straightening his collar. "He's trying to make up for my parents being lax. And the whole Ren thing. He's firmly on my side —if there were sides. There shouldn't be sides."

"But sometimes there are, and I get it." David placed his hands underneath my elbows as I continued to fidget. It shouldn't feel this natural being this close to him. "I like him."

I smiled, surprised and pleased. "He just chewed you out for no reason."

"He's looking out for you," David whispered as a few more of my family passed us to go into the dining room. The table was set with everything, spanning from a meat lover's dream to a vegan oasis. Mom made it her mission to ensure everyone had a well-rounded meal while under her roof.

"I like that," David said. "You deserve that."

I stopped fidgeting and rested my hands on his shoulders. He felt solid underneath me. Steady and stable. My mind wandered to all the times David had looked out for me on campus, even though I'd pulled away every time.

"What's wrong?" he asked when I paused for a beat too long.

I frowned and pulled away from him. "Nothing. Let's... get in there. If we do this right, you won't ever have to come to one of these things again."

"Let's do it right then." He was supposed to sound ready, excited to get this over with. Instead, David didn't move a muscle, lingering in the hall as if to stall for time. Maybe he wasn't moving because, like me, his mind was stuck back upstairs, playing our non-kiss on repeat. Maybe he wasn't moving because this hadn't been hell on earth. We haven't been one another's worst nightmare. In fact, we've become a glimpse of a dream.

"What's wrong?" I'm the one who asked this time. And once again, he beat me in the category of maturity.

"I think you know what," he said, voice low and steady.

I swallowed and shook my head.

"It's different." He looked down at me. "Us being here. All this pretending... Yara, it isn't hard."

My chest burned, and his confession was a soothing salve. "Isn't it?"

David frowned, but was steadfast in his honesty and openness. "No, not for me."

21

THERE WASN'T any time to dissect David's confession. At least, not out loud. So, I sat at my family's long, crowded table set with fine china and lacy tablecloths. I listened to aunts and uncles talking about new jobs. My sisters discussed our annual Paris trip. My parents complimented David on his ability to balance football and academia (he'd maintained his 4.2 GPA since high school, of course). Of course, he was smart, polite to parents, and easy on the eyes, and he made my family fall in love with him. Of course.

I sat there through all of that, knowing that he found this easy. Being mine wasn't hard.

"Yara?" Amiee called my name, bringing me back to Earth. I blinked twice, clearing away the fog of David. Once my vision returned, I realized everyone at the table had their cups raised. They all looked at me, waiting for me to pick up my glass as well.

Ren was standing. She'd gotten to the dinner late and taken her place next to Rose with little fanfare. With the attention on David, I could tell my sister and her fiancé (as of this morning, it'd become official in my parents' backyard) were itching for some eyes on them. Hence the attempted cheers.

I quickly grabbed my cup and numbly held it up. Adam raised his brow at me from across the table, questioning if I was okay. And a few of my other family members exchanged looks, well acquainted with the lore of Ren, Rose, and me.

I hated that we had lore. I hated that my hesitation made it seem like I was focused on my ex-girlfriend and sister's engagement when, really, I was panicking because I wanted to kiss David.

Sensing my unease, David casually rested his arm on the back of my chair and leaned in to whisper, "Give it another half hour, and I'll figure out an excuse to get us out of here."

I smiled, grateful for the confirmed escape and convincing partner act. David placed his hand on the back of my neck, massaging gentle circles to release the built-up tension. I'd wanted to pick at the space. He'd sensed that and stopped it with ease. The soothing pressure of his thumb was eons better than the sting of self-punishment.

Gazes moved back to the newly engaged couple. I could hear the gossip now: *Yara didn't even want to raise her glass. Her boyfriend had to tell her to keep it up. How sad. How unfortunate. I wonder what she did to deserve it.*

That last one was me. An old haunt that reared its head as soon as Ren began talking.

"I want to thank you all for joining us to celebrate." Ren held onto Rose's hand as she spoke. "This has been a long time coming, so it's nice to be here with everyone we love finally."

Ren's hair was longer than the last time I saw her. The loose brown curls swayed down her back. Her brown skin had a beautiful tan. She held her head higher than she used to when we were in high school, all youthful insecurity gone out the window. She smiled down at Rose, knowing precisely what she wanted and who she wanted.

I waited for the lingering emotion of betrayal to burn through my chest. I steeled myself for the frustration of my first girlfriend breaking up with me, only to ask my sister out two months later. Steeled myself to feel the hurt about my sister going on the date first and coming to me after.

"I've loved you from the moment I saw you," Ren continued.

That should be an arrow. Knife to the chest. I felt nothing.

"And I'm so excited and honored I have the privilege of being yours and calling you mine."

Rose was in tears. And I was happy for her. She looked in love. She was in love. I'd never experienced that with Ren.

"Good?" David whispered. Concern made his jaw stiff.

I gave him a grateful smile and subtle nod before whispering back, "Good."

Before tonight, a small part of me had wondered, *what if?* What if I wasn't really okay with Ren and Rose being together? What if the text David sent was something I'd secretly wanted to send all along, and the universe had made it happen? What if Ren was my one true love, and I'd have to spend the rest of my life seeing her at family dinners and on family trips and suffering in silence because my sister was so happy? What if?

The bubble popped, and I'm freed from that fear. We all raised our glasses a little higher when Ren finished her speech. There was a collective hum of "cheers" and "congratulations."

And I was okay. Maybe even better than okay, because I was never in love with Ren. Never destined to be some forlorn ex, living in the shadows of her happily married sister.

I hadn't been in love then, which meant I had that to look forward to now.

When we all lowered our glasses, David accidentally knocked his against his soup bowl. From the moment we sat down, he'd been slow to touch everything. Any time his fingers made contact with something, he held it as if it would shatter in his hands. The overcorrection birthed an excess of nerves. While he'd easily comforted me, he couldn't do the same for himself.

David's glass tipped over, red wine staining the white linen. My aunt, sitting next to him, yelped and popped up before the liquid could get on the vintage fur coat she'd rested in her lap. Her quick motion disturbed the table, making a small bowl of soup splash over into a plate of olives.

David apologized quickly, trying to grab a cloth napkin, but in the process, knocked over my wine as well. The red stained my wool skirt. He was beet red, fingers shaking. His gaze immediately snapped to my parents, as if he expected a scolding. What he found was laughter instead.

Most of the people at the table smiled and waved off his apologies. A couple of cousins got up to grab more napkins and new glasses for us.

"I didn't... I'm sorry." David lowered himself into his seat, looking defeated as our silverware got replaced.

"Your reflexes are better with a football, son," Dad noted, still chuckling.

"It's fine," I whispered and rubbed his back. I wanted to laugh too, but when we locked eyes, I could tell something was off. He wasn't recovering from the embarrassment, the red darkening on his cheeks.

"Sorry," he repeated, again, sounding like he deserved some kind of penance.

I frowned, my hand frozen on his back. "It's fine. It was an accident."

"Yeah." He nodded as if trying to convince himself. "It's just... it all looks very... expensive."

"We have plenty more tablecloths and glasses," Mom assured from her side of the table with a genuine smile.

Someone commented that it was extra to have the cloth on the table anyway, setting off our family's recurring debate about fine dining at home.

With the attention off of him, I hoped David would relax. Instead, I caught him tucking his shaking hands underneath the tablecloth. He wouldn't meet my gaze anymore, retreating into his own world. My brother caught my gaze, though, sending a wordless inquiry about my boyfriend's issue. Adam temporarily set aside judgment for empathy.

"It's fine," I mouthed, stomach clenching at how not fine it felt.

———

I WAS desperate to get David alone and check on him after dinner. But before I could, Rose pulled me aside when we were all done eating, and everyone moved into the backyard for dessert by the pool. The heat from so many people inside dissipated. And the younger cousins kept going back and forth outside, letting the chill fall air find its way through the first floor.

"How are you?" Rose asked.

It felt like a silly question. Even though I wasn't upset with her anymore, there was a slight twinge of annoyance in my gut. Rose didn't want to broach the topic. She would just poke at it to see if it would give.

"I'm great." I offered her a small smile. "Congrats. I know you two are going to be happy together."

"Thank you." Her eyes lit up at my stamp of approval. "You really think so?"

"Of course, don't you?" My brows wrinkled when she hesitated.

She shook her head but still tried to smile. "I do, I do. I just... it's all so surreal, you know? And you and I never really talked about how Ren and I happened. We hardly talk about anything anymore."

Rose and I had the least close relationship of our siblings. It could be the eleven-month age gap, the constant external comparison, or that we're more alike than we'd like to admit. Either way, I didn't think we would ever be best friends, but we could be there for each other.

"I'm happy the two of you happened because you're happy." I grabbed her hand and gave it a gentle squeeze. "You light up when she looks at you. It's beautiful."

She squeezed my hand back. "You don't know how nervous I was to see you."

"Why?"

"I didn't think you were actually over Ren. I can't imagine anyone being over her."

When I laughed, Rose frowned. She looked almost offended. I reeled back in. Just because we were working toward common ground didn't mean we would throw out years of baggage.

"You can't imagine it because you're in love," I reminded her. "But I never was."

"*Really*?" Her eyes grew big. The relief in her voice was palpable. "Ren swore you were."

"We were only together for two months. Besides, Ren swears a lot of things," I muttered.

"She does," Rose agreed and laughed with me this time.

"The point is, I wasn't. I was only hurt that she asked you out, because I thought maybe the whole time you two were into each other, and I was just in the way. No one wants to be the foil in someone's romance story. Least of all your own sister's."

"And here I was thinking I was the foil to yours." Her shoulders relaxed, freed from the burden of a guilty conscience.

"For a moment I thought maybe you were, but..." I shrugged and glanced toward the sliding glass door that led outside. I saw David, with Adam and Aimee, on the porch. He held two plates of cake as he waited for me. David looked mostly recovered from the wine tipping incident. His only tell of nerves was his struggle to maintain eye contact for more than a couple of seconds. I needed to go to him.

"I know for sure that was never the case," I finished.

Rose glanced over her shoulder for a second, turning back to me with a smile. "I never in a million years thought you'd like David. Let alone go out with him. That's why I couldn't believe it when you said you two were dating. But now..."

"Now?"

"He looks at you like you're everything he's ever dreamed of." Rose poked out her bottom lip. "It's so sweet."

"Very sweet." I nodded and swallowed a sigh. David and I were so entangled that I didn't know where to start. We didn't have a proper beginning to our friendship. How would that translate into a relationship? More importantly, would that translate? He said it wasn't hard being with me, but that didn't exactly mean he wanted to date me for real.

"You should tell him," Rose said in a lower voice as if our rowdy family could hear us over their buzzing conversations and the music blaring from someone's portable speaker.

"What?" My gaze snapped back to Rose, suspicious of potential mind-reading abilities.

She gave me a knowing smile. "You should tell him you think he's sweet. I know you. You can be so hard and stand-offish when it comes to romance."

"I'm not." My defenses went up even though she wasn't exactly wrong. I'd never been a heart-eyed, hand-holding girl-friend... maybe because I'd never been with the right person? Because nowadays, I want to hold David's hand all the time.

"Tell him, Yara," Rose said firmly. "He seems like a good

guy. And if he's the right guy, let him know. It'll do you both some good."

I swallowed a retort about not needing her relationship advice. This was a nice day. A good dinner with the family and a hurdle I cleared with David's help. Everyone believed he was my boyfriend. He'd played the role so well that he convinced us both, too. I would not ruin the vibe with my stubbornness. So, I smiled, nodded, and told Rose, "I will. I'll tell him."

22

We flew too close to the fake-relationship sun, earning ourselves an invitation to a double date with my parents.

"We'll have a car pick you up next Friday," Mom said, half distracted by typing out an email. Flooding at the high school auditorium led to the cancellation of the last town hall meeting. Dozens of people used her inbox to express their grievances.

"At Yara's apartment. 8 p.m. sounds good?" Mom asked, walking away before either of us could answer.

"Sorry," I said as soon as she was out of earshot. "We've done so well today that I could come up with an excuse to get us out of that later."

"It's fine," David said simply. He sat down on the bench in the gazebo my enthused mother had trapped us in. The sun had long since set, solar yard lights lining the walkway. Sixties jazz music played from one of my cousins' portable speakers. They were waiting for the older folks to clear out before switching it to something obnoxiously contemporary.

"Fine, as in, you're not overwhelmed?" I joined him on the

bench, keeping my distance because our audience wasn't hungry for an encore. "Or fine as in, you don't mind going."

"Both."

I studied the dark brown of his eyes, looking for any sarcasm underneath. David further raised suspicion when he added, "Your family's not terrible to be around. I like them."

"You're joking?" I smiled, folding my legs to the side with my knees pointed toward him. The air smelled of fire from the pit Aimee insisted on lighting. Burnt marshmallows and melted chocolate weaved into the smoke, making it feel like a proper welcome to fall, even though we were halfway through it.

"It's not a joke," he promised. David picked at his nails as he watched my family argue over who would get their turn in horseshoes next and who would help clean everything before the night was over.

"Can I ask what happened earlier?" I whispered, an attempt to remain gentle and avoid triggering his guard. "When you knocked over your glass at the table?"

David's jaw clenched. He remained quiet as he watched my brother urge my mom to dance with him. She was still on the phone, trying not to laugh at his attempts at distraction.

Instead of answering my question, David said, "Despite all of this–" He gestured to the house and my family. "—I think we're more alike than we are different."

He met my gaze, eyes holding a kind of seriousness that did away with my need to force gentleness. I should know by now that David didn't need me to be lighthearted. Smoothed edges didn't impress him.

"And that's why I couldn't stand you all those years," he said.

I snorted, only a bit offended, mostly amused.

"And probably why you couldn't stand me," David continued.

"So how did we get here?" I was anxious about this side of us. It was so new and impossible. It was like a weird dream of your childhood celebrity being so madly in love with you that you weren't sure you could actually handle that reality.

"I'm not sure," David matched my tone, all hushed and curious.

I waited for more. When nothing came, and his attention was redirected once more to my family, I felt my heart rate pick up. If he wouldn't say more about it tonight, then it was up to me. I'd have to bridge our final gap.

"David, I think we should..." My throat constricted as the words struggled to push past my chest. "What I mean is... I like this feeling of... us."

He took a beat before confessing, "So do I."

Those three words calmed the riptide. My head resurfaced above the water.

"I've been thinking about how we've known each other for such a long time and maybe... maybe the universe kept pulling us together so we could get to this moment," he finished.

I laughed a little because it was strange to hear him say something like that. "You don't really believe in that. In the universe's intervention?"

He smiled and shook his head. "No, and yes."

"You can't have both."

"But that's what we feel like," he said without hesitation. "And I've always wanted to believe in the universe. Or something. Anything. But that always felt impossible until you started showing up everywhere. And so, I started looking for you. We started doing this, and it started feeling like the only thing that made sense. Being with you is the only thing I can guarantee I will seek out."

"I don't know what to do next," I confessed. "Do you?"

His forehead wrinkled. "Do we have to know?"

My laugh was dry. "That would be nice, wouldn't it?"

"I don't see the point."

"Of understanding your emotions? Knowing how to interpret them so you can make the best decision for yourself? There's no point in that?"

David shook his head. "We don't need to come up with a five-year plan to justify a feeling, Yara. Have you ever just leapt?"

"Plenty of times. But with a parachute."

"Some of us weren't fortunate enough to grab one before we were pushed out."

"I don't mind sharing."

He chuckled. I didn't know how I ever sat next to him while he did that and didn't feel some type of want. The ache in my chest spread through my veins, pleading with me to either satisfy my urge or figure out another way to sedate it.

"I have a dare," David said.

I took a deep breath, curious but slightly disappointed in the potential change in topic. "What have you got for me this time?"

"There's this team dinner," he said, dipping his gaze down to his hands for a second. "Very important and daunting. I'm not great with... charm. You are. And you make me less afraid."

The flattery bypassed my head and went straight to my heart.

"Be mine for the night," he said. "I dare you."

It's not a request for a date or a clear step to a relationship. But somehow it was even more promising. More hopeful. More than us.

———

WE PASSED our old middle school on the way back home. The park across the street had been updated: the swing set, see-saws, replaced with a mini rock climb, and a metal slide for a plastic one. The aching nostalgia didn't haunt just me.

David pulled into the parking lot and wordlessly unbuckled his seatbelt. When I gave him a questioning look, he asked, "Remember when you cheated in that monkey bar race?"

I scoffed and unbuckled my seatbelt. "I did not. Why are you lying about a monkey bar race?"

"Why would you cheat?"

"Is this your way of asking for a rematch?" I opened my door, and he did the same with his.

"Fair's fair." He hopped out of the car.

The night's too cold for the skirt-and-stockings pairing I have on. But I ignored the chill in favor of seeing David's face light up. We walked toward the bars, slow at first. But then, he picked up the pace, and I matched his energy. When he does it again, I enlist my arms to help push me through an impromptu speed walk.

"Remember that walking race in middle school?" David's breath was a white cloud, his arm pumping just as fast and steady as mine.

"Yeah." I was already huffing and puffing.

"Heel, toe," he reminded me, and then kicked into his third gear.

I cursed under my breath, remembering the technique our gym teacher had tried to hammer into our brains. But no amount of heel or toe could help me contend with a starting university tight end.

"You... suck..." My lungs burned when I finally made it to the bars. David stood tall with his hands on his hips as I placed my hands on my knees, trying to catch my breath.

"We've got to get you back on the trails, Daredevil," he said. "You used to dominate."

"I've... been... a little... busy." I needed water. Or an oxygen mask.

"Why did you stop?"

I held up a finger, practically begging him to give me a moment. He chuckled but let me have a quiet recovery.

"I stopped because I didn't qualify for Westbrooke's track team," I said. "And I was a little salty about the whole thing."

"Sounds like more than a little," he teased.

"Would you still play football if Westbrooke didn't take you on?"

He nodded without hesitation. "I'd find some kind of rec league."

"Really?" I asked in surprise.

"It's the only thing I can do to fully get out of my head and escape my repetitive thoughts," he said. "The only thing that helps me avoid hand washing for a couple of hours. Playing's the reason I've survived this long."

My face softened. I stood up straight again. "That's... thank you for sharing that."

His smile was small and a little sad. But he moved on, reaching for a monkey bar and swinging back and forth. "So, are we racing or are you too winded?"

Despite my dry laugh and the growing stitch in my side, I went over the other end of the bars. Since there was only one monkey bar when we were kids, we'd race to see who'd get to the center first. A thinning area marked the middle of the mulch where other kids had taken over the tradition.

"Ready?" he called, still showing off by swinging back and forth.

I grabbed onto the cold metal and tried to suppress my wince at the slight burn. "Ready!"

"On three?"

"Three," I agreed.

David counted us down with an obnoxious amount of energy. It was a turn-on. His energy, his smile, his willingness to do something so random just because it reminded him of old times. Of us.

"Three!" As expected, he was fast out of the gate. I tried to match his speed, but holding on was far harder as an adult. My legs had to curl up far more not to touch the ground, and my palms didn't have the calluses I so carefully built up as a twelve-year-old with a title to defend.

David beat me by three bars, laughing as I cursed under my breath once I finally met him in the middle. We remained hanging for a second, our knees knocking into each other, a breath apart.

"Are you trying to hang on longer than me?" he figured after a couple of seconds.

"Maybe..." I managed through a strained breath.

"You are really something." He was smiling brighter than ever.

"Trying to win at something tonight," I grumbled.

"Fair." David held on for a bit longer and even did a couple of pull-ups to show off before he decided, "I'm letting go. I could do this all night, but I'm afraid you're going to hurt yourself to prove a point."

"Coward," I said half-heartedly as he dropped back down to the ground. I let go, too, trying not to let the relief show on my face.

"Let me see." David's voice was soft, a hint of protectiveness in the tone when he saw me massaging my palm.

"It's fine," I said, but offered him the hand. His touch was tender, thumb brushing across the screaming red on my fingers. My breathing became heavy as I took in his cologne. His freckles were lighter because of the fall, barely noticeable constellations on his skin. I was so invested in memorizing the curve of his cheekbones that I didn't notice him reaching a tender spot between my thumb and index finger. I hissed involuntarily. He pulled away from it in an instant and frowned at me.

"See," he said, disapproving. "You hurt yourself."

"It's fine..." I repeated, trailing off when he lifted my hand to his lips to press a gentle kiss on my knuckles. My heart stopped as it contemplated what it needed to sacrifice to offer itself to him.

"I was..." David's brow wrinkled as he considered his following words. "I was scared after knocking over the wine. As a kid, I used to go to extreme lengths to avoid making a mistake. It didn't matter how painful holding out was, I did everything I could to be good..."

He looked at me then, searching my eyes for judgment. Instead, I offered encouragement.

"For your foster family?" I asked.

"Yeah." David nodded. "Mary was my cousin. Second or third. My closest living relationship after my mom died when I was eight."

"I thought... I thought Mary was your mom."

"It was easier to call her that at school," he said. "I didn't exactly like having to rehash the story of losing my mom to an overdose and never knowing if my dad was a biker from Maine or a truck driver from Utah."

I raised a questioning brow.

He smiled a little. "They both sent Christmas cards until I was eighteen. The day after my birthday, they completely cut me off."

"Assholes," I muttered.

"Kind of," he agreed. "Mary was the bigger one, though, so everything else pales in comparison. But the biggest, well, that went to Riley, her boyfriend. My foster dad."

My shoulders sagged. "The one who... who'd shove you?"

"Shove, kick, punch." David looked down at my palm again, centering himself by lightly tracing the lines on my skin. "If I did so much as forget to dry the dishes, chaos would begin. So, making a mess was like declaring war. And I fought back when I was little. Argued. But eventually, I learned it was best just to do what they wanted. They didn't yell if I didn't spill something. So, I decided I'd stop making mistakes. A daunting goal, but I managed to achieve it most of the time. And when I couldn't... I'd clean things. Make stuff look nice to make up for my mistakes. Count the cracks in the sidewalk, because if I tallied them all, the shouting would be over by then. Tapped the edge of the table before leaving because that made me lucky enough that nothing toppled over."

I imagined a younger, smaller version of David. The one who watched the ground whenever he walked to school. He used to sit in the back, scowling at his notebook as he drew on his arm. People teased him. I ignored him. I would come to school after a wonderful night's rest, kind parents, and a stable household, and not give him a second glance.

"David, I–"

"Don't." His eyes hardened. "Don't apologize; you weren't an adult back then."

"But still..."

"There's no but. Yara, you couldn't have helped me."

"I could have said something to you. Been kind. Or your friend. I could have tried harder."

"So could I. What middle schooler with any sense of survival instinct would talk to a guy in all-black, moping in some corner alone?"

I shook my head but said nothing.

"Yara, you were kind. You traded me for the Almond Joys." A faint smile returned to his lips. "Then you started challenging me to monkey bar races. Rolled your eyes when I came first in the race during field day. Called me an asshole for taking your front seat in English class."

I poked his shoulder. "You weren't a front-row kid."

His smile grew. "I know. I just loved the way you wrinkled your nose and pretended not to care. Coming to school got better so that I could mess with the hot, rich girl who had an attitude."

It was my turn to smile. "Hot?"

"It's a fact," he said simply.

I'm high on the simple compliment.

David cupped my cheek, bringing us back to something more serious. "You treated me like a human. Like someone normal. One of the other kids."

It hurt that he was grateful for something like that. Something everyone deserved to experience, especially as a child.

"Just not soon enough," I murmured.

He hummed in disagreement. "Yara, you're right on time."

23

ALMOST A WEEK PASSED until I saw David again. During that time, we barely exchanged more than a few texts with each other. The busyness of university, something I typically thrived in, became an annoying hindrance.

So, I was practically a baby deer, stumbling over my knobby knees when he picked me up for dinner. I was severely out of practice at conversing with him. And severely anxious for his attention. The sky was a reddish pink, and the trees above the sidewalk cast long shadows over the cement when he finally pulled into the lot.

"Hey," David said as he stepped out of his car. The freshly-ironed creases in his button-down were endearing. He was freshly shaven, his jawline sharp.

I'd been waiting for him to pick me up for twenty minutes. Sitting inside had become impossible, so I'd come downstairs in the hope that the cold air and real world would center me. It didn't. The fact wouldn't be so frustrating if David didn't look so unbothered. He'd probably spent his day like he usually did: unfazed by the knowledge he was seeing me later. He probably ate his breakfast without keeping an eye out for a specific text notification. I bet he went to class without wondering if I was in the student center.

"How long have you been out here?" He went to the passenger side of the car. And just like when he picked me up to go to my parents' house, he opened the door for me.

"Not long." I refused to give any indication of dwindling sanity. "You?"

It was a nonsensical question that lost me credibility in a heartbeat. David smiled, knowing.

"You could have texted if you missed me," he said. "I would have made time for you."

David rested his hands on top of the car door like he had all the time in the world.

"I didn't want your time." I placed a hand in between his, as I paused before getting in.

"Then what was it you wanted?"

"Nothing you're willing to give," I said after a second.

"And how do you know that?"

I shrugged. "I know you."

I slipped into the car before he could respond. And David didn't offer any protest until he was back in the driver's seat.

"You don't know what I'd give you." He started the car and pulled onto the road. There was a soft hum of pop music playing and a warm cup of coffee from the school's cafe in the cup holder. I didn't have to ask if it was for me because my name was already on it, written in cursive.

"Many things, I'm sure," I mused under my breath. "The first and most frequent being a headache."

He laughed. "What's it going to take to get you in a better mood for dinner?"

"I'm in a great mood." I picked up the cup and took a tentative sip. It was the perfect temperature.

David looked at me for a second. I gestured for him to keep his gaze on the road.

"Why do you look so nervous anytime you're in a car?" he asked. "Is it because your driver sucks?"

"My driver?"

"You have a family driver," he reminded me.

"Oh." I waved my hand. "We don't have a family driver... we request them from the same company. Nine times out of ten, it's a different person."

"Fine, family driving *company*." He shook his head with an entertained smile lighting up his face. "Whatever. Is it because of them? Because I've never gotten close to getting in an accident while you were in here with me."

I scoffed. "You nearly rear-ended someone on the way to the beach."

"I had it under control."

"Illusion of control, sure."

"Come on, Yara. I think we're past the subterfuge and three steps ahead of planning part of our relationship," he said. "I've been your other half, and now, you're playing mine. We've kissed. It's hardly a secret we hate that we like each other."

I took another sip of my drink, grappling with his casual confession. David spoke as if all those things were weather changes or postponed assignment due dates. The ease should be comforting. Instead, it grated on my nerves. There was no solid ground to stand on.

"I don't like cars." My confession was heavy with shame. "I... I got in an accident when I was learning to drive–that's why I still don't have my license. It was pretty bad. My folks haven't trusted me behind the wheel since. They stopped teaching me."

"They stopped teaching you." David's forehead deeply creased, a valley of concern and disapproval.

"Yeah, and honestly, I stopped asking."

"You're rich," he said. "Stop asking and hire someone."

I frowned. "I can't just hire someone."

"Why not?"

"Because I..." There was a reason, surely. And I'd find it.

"You?"

"I'm not sure I should do it." My fingers itched to pluck at my crown. The warmth of David's hand covered mine right as I was about to reach up. His fingers interlaced with mine.

"I could teach you." His offer sent a spark up my arm.

"You would teach me?" I studied his profile in the hunt for the catch. "You're offering to teach me how to drive?"

"Of course." He laughed a little at my disbelief. "Why not?"

"I don't know. I just didn't think you'd ever do something like that for me unprompted."

David's smile faded. "You still don't get it, do you?"

"Get what?"

"I'd do anything you'd ask."

I scoffed. "How sweet. You're a cute liar."

"I've done everything you've asked."

"Sure, with a lot of convincing, bribing, and guilt-tripping."

"I like seeing you work for it. But don't act like you don't enjoy doing the same to me."

"I...don't..."

David shook his head in disagreement. "The only difference between you and me is that I don't mind working for it. But that's only because you're calling the shots."

"Well, of course," I said, pretending like this was all obvious, known, and understood.

We were silent for a moment. I was lost in thought and the anxious 'what-ifs' buzzing in my chest. David seemed unbothered, taking his last turn into the parking lot of an Italian chain restaurant. It wasn't until he put the car in park that he said, "So are you in? Driving lessons."

I tried to smile as I shook my head. "I don't think it's worth your time."

"Why don't you let me decide that?" There was something earnest and wanting in his voice. I wanted to kiss him so badly it hurt.

"Alright," I whispered, too confused to protest. "David?"

His hand paused before he opened the door.

"Why is this the simplest and hardest thing we've done?" I gestured between him and me.

David smiled and gave a lazy shrug. "Because it's fun. It's us."

THE RESTAURANT WAS DIMLY LIT, a slight contrast to the bustling energy of patrons inside. Kids ran back and forth from table to table, occasionally knocking into David and me as we made our way through the building. People left chairs pushed out, making the walkway an obstacle course. And the high volume of classical music made me wonder whether they wanted to encourage people to go to clear the traffic jam at the hostess's booth.

"David," Weston greeted, finding us meandering through the throng of people.

"Where's everyone?" David scanned the place in disapproval.

"That building beyond the courtyard." Weston pointed toward the stained-glass doors, propped open, letting the breeze in and the smell of pasta out.

"Didn't realize the party was this big." David's words nearly got buried beneath the squeals of rampant grade-schoolers. But his friend didn't notice, turning his attention to me.

"Yara." Weston smiled. "It's good to see you. Glad you're here."

And it actually sounded like he meant it. I returned his smile, a sense of calm settling over my shoulder that at least one person wouldn't side-eye my attendance. Being a football player's (fake) girlfriend came with expectations. The players' partners were their extensions, potential chess pieces in a grand marketing story.

"Next time we scrimmage, you're on my team, yeah?" Weston asked.

My smile grew wider. "No promises I'll be a great asset. I had only one trick up my sleeve."

"It was a great trick." Weston patted a very distracted David's shoulder. "All good?"

My brows pinched when David shook his head. I opened my mouth to say something, but Weston beat me to the punch. "Yara, do you mind giving us a second? The court-yard's a good place for air. A couple of the guys are out there now."

An easy, polite dismissal. It shouldn't irritate me, and yet, I release a heavy sigh after David and Weston start toward the opposite end of the restaurant.

Why hadn't he told me he was nervous?

Why didn't you ask?

The phone worked both ways. And though David and I had become in sync in pissing one another off, being there for each other would take effort. I resolved to do as much. David wasn't the person to spill out all his worries unprompted. But I could be the person who prompted.

The courtyard was home to a mini garden, with dying flowers and browning leaves. There were a handful of guys talking near the fountain, like Weston said, but none of them looked familiar. I wasn't in the mood for introductions. But that didn't matter too much when I saw Covee Bailey sitting by herself on a bench in front of a man-made waterfall. I perked up.

"Hey, girl." I stopped in front of her.

Covee looked up, eyes squinted with confusion, before a smile lit up her eyes. "Yara?"

She was up, hugging me before I could get another word out. I laughed, wrapping my arms around her as if we were long-lost cousins.

"What are you doing here?" I asked once we finally released each other. Last I'd seen her, she was sitting in the back of an org meeting with her nose in her laptop and a stern look on her face. She was far more relaxed now. Hair out of her braids and coiling around her cheeks, dress hugging at her waist before flowing down her long legs.

She shrugged. "With Weston."

"With Weston?" I stepped back, exaggerating my surprise.

Covee laughed and waved her hand. "It's... a long story."

"I knew it," I said. "So are you two...?"

"Long," she repeated, grabbing my hand and tugging me back toward the bench with her. "But I've been meaning to talk to you."

I raised my brow, sobering. The story about Weston could wait. Covee looked worried.

"What is it?" I was already prepared to brainstorm and get her whatever she needed.

"Nothing bad," Covee was quick to assure. "Yara, relax."

I didn't realize the tension in my shoulders and the '*let's get to work*' tilt of my head until she rested her hand on mine.

"That's what I've been meaning to talk to you about," Covee said with a sweet smile. "You."

"Me?" I frowned.

"I wanted to apologize for how distant I've been this year." She tried to maintain eye contact but dipped her gaze down to her lap after a couple of seconds. "And thank you for always checking in on me. I know it couldn't have been easy, but... you don't know how much that means to me. Knowing I'd get a text from you about an event or an invitation made school bearable. My depression made everything so bleak, and the org is one of my only lights... sorry to dump all of this."

"No, no." I shook my head, trying to quickly assure her that everything was perfect. She was perfect. "This isn't a dump at all. This is what I'm here for. What we're all here for. If you didn't tell me, I hope you feel comfortable enough to tell someone else."

I had always wanted to be a safe space in Covee's world. In all of my girls' world. They were the sole reason I lasted this long as president. Seeing them grow and thrive, being able to offer them a shoulder to lean on, and a place to go when the rest of campus felt so hostile was all I ever dreamed of. There would be so many places in the world where no one looked out for us. We would be overlooked and expected to survive without help. We were expected to be strong enough to weather any storm while still having enough supplies for our neighbors. If a Black woman couldn't look to another Black woman for empathy, comfort, help, and love, what hope did we have?

"I wanted to be better this year," she whispered. "But I couldn't quite get there, and you didn't mind. You never minded how I showed up."

"Of course not." My voice was gentle as my hand rested on top of hers. "I never care how. I just like when you're around."

"That's what I could never understand."

I poked out my bottom lip and shrugged. "I took that sister oath to heart when I signed on as a member. Covee, I knew you were doing all you could, and that was more than enough. This season of life was one where you kept to yourself; there's nothing wrong with that."

There were tears in her eyes, but they didn't fall. She brushed at her cheeks anyway, preparing for them.

"I wish I could have been more present this semester," she confessed. "For you and for everyone. I was so lost."

"Are you back on the path now?"

Covee nodded. "Getting there. Ready to start asking for more help."

"Then this is exactly how it should have happened," I promised.

———

TIMING HAD NEVER BEEN David and I's strong suit. I considered that when we were seated at a table three times as long as the one at my parents' house. Every starting player, significant other (if applicable), and the assistant and head coaches were in attendance. Sprinkled throughout the team were recruiters, guys who had bright futures in the palms of their sun-damaged hands.

Before we could talk, someone ushered David and me to sit down and order our food. I kept looking at him, only to find he was still going back and forth with Weston, who'd sat beside him.

I picked at my appetiser while trying to figure out what I was doing here. My job description was: charm. But charming who, that wasn't exactly clear. And to what extent I don't know.

We got about twenty minutes into the meal before the man next to me spoke up,

"These things are a proper obstacle course."

He had a faint Irish accent. I couldn't tell if he was talking to himself, the woman on his right, or the guys across from him. But I answered anyway because I was dying on my island of one.

"You're telling me." I glanced at the head of the table. "Seems like everyone's trying to talk without saying anything."

He smiled at me, dimples deepening in his cheeks. There was a sprinkle of red freckles across his cheeks. His red curls fall over his ears. He looked no older than me, so I assumed he was a player. Maybe he was on the defensive team because he had a stocky build, and I didn't see him say a single word to David or Weston. The football team comprised over a hundred guys. Not all of them were here tonight —a grand impossibility— and not all of them actually knew each other.

"Aggression on the field but tiptoeing off," he noted. "It's extremely fascinating and extremely frustrating."

I nodded. "I grew up in a family of politicians. All dinners were a psychologist's dream."

He chuckled. "I bet. I'm Rory, by the way."

"Yara." I offered my hand.

"What's your poison, Yara? Player, recruiter, or coach?"

I laughed. "You think I'm part of the team? How flattering... I think?"

"You could run offense for all I know," he said. "I've seen plenty of women outshine guys like this."

"So kind of you, but I'm a plus one."

"Full time?" he joked.

"When I'm not attending lovely, entertaining dinners such as this one, I moonlight as a PoliSci major."

"Ah, I could have guessed."

"What?"

"You have the look of someone who knows how to take the lead," he explained. "Which was why my money was on the offensive assistant coach."

I smiled, happy to finally have some amusement. A hand on my knee distracted me for the briefest of seconds. David gave me a gentle squeeze without even turning away from his conversation. His hand lingered, as if he were looking for some comfort. I offered it to him, enclosing my hand over his. It was a show of unity that couldn't be seen underneath the tablecloth. My stomach greeted butterflies.

"What about you?" My voice was surprisingly steady as David traced circles between my thumb and index finger. "Linebacker? Kicker? I've never seen you around the offensive team."

Rory gave me a one-shoulder shrug. "I was late, and this was the only spot left. The best decision I've made so far tonight. Hopefully, I'll continue the streak."

I couldn't tell if he was flirting. But David sensed something because he turned his attention to me. To us.

"Sorry, I don't think we've met." Instead of reaching his hand out to shake Rory's hand, David stretched his arm out behind my chair. It was a subtle territorial marking. Rory's gaze flickered to it for a second. He didn't lose his smile.

"Rory Haynes," he said. "I was telling your assistant coach about the dance."

David's forehead wrinkled. "Dance?"

"Everyone's doing it." Rory waved toward the buzzing conversations around us. "Not as fun to watch as it is to take part."

"Is that so?" David tilted his head to the side, a telltale sign (for me anyway) that he didn't trust this guy as far as he could throw him.

"So," Rory confirmed. "Know any steps?"

"Dancing isn't my thing."

"What about you?" Rory roped me back into the conversation with an easy smile.

"Born and raised to dance, unfortunately," I said. "And sing too. Showgirl through and through."

It was supposed to be a joke, but there was a bitter truth wrapped up in it.

"I'm sure you're great at it," Rory said.

I nodded. "Brilliant at anything I do."

Rory was amused. David was annoyed.

"I haven't seen you around here," David noted.

"Well, that's because I just got in yesterday."

David and I remained silent and confused. Rory dipped his hand into his suit pocket and pulled out a card. He offered it to David, but I got a glimpse of the shiny, metallic finish of "recruiter."

"California Bucks," David read in a low voice. That was the top team on his list. I remembered, back in high school, he'd wear red jerseys in celebration with the rest of the town when the team won. New Harbor didn't care about our state team; everyone was obsessed with the Bucks.

"Is this your girlfriend?" Rory asked.

"I am," I answered for him.

Rory smiled and nodded. "Just my luck."

Despite David's fanboy past, his expression darkened at the comment. Thankfully, Rory didn't notice as he continued, "Well, if you can convince him to talk with us, I'd very much appreciate it. Cali's a beautiful place to live, and you'll find plenty of opportunities to be politically active."

"I'll consider it," I promised.

"More than what I could ask for," Rory said. "We'd be honored to have you... both."

I chewed on my bottom lip, holding back a laugh when David looked near ready to clock the guy.

"I'm sure you will," David said with the calm that came from years of practice.

2 4

"How the hell did you do that?"

At first, I thought David was upset. So I readied my guard, willing and able to provide my defense like always.

"I did what you asked," I said. "Pretended to be your girlfriend. One who was ignored most of the night, by the way—"

"Yara, you were incredible."

I paused. We were in the parking lot. There were still plenty of cars as people filtered out of the closing restaurant. We'd parked so far away from the entrance that streetlights were more helpful than the glow of the restaurant's warm windows. I studied the blue shadows on David's skin. The admiration in his eyes.

"Incredible—" I yelped when he pulled me into a hug. My arms wrapped around his neck in an automatic response, and he spun me around.

"How the hell did you get Rory Haynes to talk to you?" David asked once he put me down.

I gasped for air, trying to catch up to the fact that my feet were back on the ground even though my head was still spinning. David's hands still gripped my waist, holding me close enough that I could feel his chest rise and fall. The air was charged with the decades between us. The kiss at Weston's house. Our back and forth, I'm now considering a kind of foreplay. Who needed a decade of foreplay? Me. Him. Us. Damn. We were ridiculous.

"I think he just... wanted to flirt with the only person close enough." I shrugged, still breathless.

David's smile waned a little. "Did he make you uncomfortable?"

"No, he was nice," I insisted.

He nodded more seriously. "Did I make you uncomfortable?"

My eyes widened. "No, David. Not even almost."

"I wasn't trying to ignore you," he said. "I kept reaching for you and... no. I'm sorry. This is a moment for sorry."

I laughed a little. "Are you becoming sentient? Aware of others' emotions and the need to connect?"

"I'm trying." His cheeks were a bit red. "I'm sorry it doesn't come naturally to me."

"David, it's fine. Promise."

"It wasn't just because you're beautiful," he said.

My heart was racing a mile a minute. "What?"

"It's because you make people feel like they know you. Or could know you. There isn't an ounce of judgment in your voice when you talk to people."

"You've told me the opposite."

"Because it's always been the opposite for me." He pressed his hand against my cheek, not needing to pretend he was brushing away a twist because my hair was pulled back.

"Only because you've always been so..." I couldn't find the right word. I used to have a million and one words to describe David, but all of them seem unfair and unfounded. Maybe some of those words fit still, but he was so much more.

"So what?" He was close enough to brush his nose against

mine. His breath was warm and smelled of peppermint. I parted my lips, ready to respond with words I didn't yet have.

"You."

"And that's a bad thing."

I shook my head. "Not all the time. Not anymore."

"Yara?" he whispered, and I nodded, knowing the million and one words he had for me didn't quite fit anymore. Understanding we didn't need to find the word for us if we could experience the feeling instead.

He pressed his lips against mine, and like the other times, the world outside faded. This kiss wasn't as hesitant or confused as our others. Not on his end anyway. David knew what he wanted, coaxing my lips apart, gazing his tongue against mine.

Every one of my nerve-endings screamed for him. Begged me to get closer, kiss harder, give more.

David backed me up onto the side of his car. My spine pressed against the cold window. He tugged my thigh up around his waist. The hardness between us made me moan into his mouth. And the sound of my response to his arousal made David reply with equal desperation.

"Thank you for tonight," he whispered against my lips when we split for a breath. "For being here with me. For being mine."

"I did it for the dare," I reminded him with a smile and another kiss.

He shook his head. "Not all of it."

"How do you know that?"

"I know you." He pressed himself against me, applying the pressure I craved. It'd been forever since I had done this with someone, so every sensation felt new. I'd forgotten what it was like to breathe in sync. Wanting someone so badly both soothed my soul and set me on fire like no other.

"I'm going to have to keep reminding Rory you're mine,"

he said. I thought it was supposed to be a question, but I couldn't really focus on words when he slipped his hand underneath my butt, pressing me firmly against him. I rocked against him, trying to resolve my growing desire.

David's eyes darkened. "Hart, too."

"Is that what you want?" I smiled against his lips.

"It's what I need." His mouth was on mine again, hot and hungry. And when I needed a break for air, he continued, his lips painting fire against my jaw and neck. Teeth grazing my pulse and tongue, making the sting all better.

"What about you?" David asked, desperation making his voice low. "Do you want me to make sure I'm the only name on your lips every time you moan? Or do you want to be there to be others?"

"You'd share?" I asked, surprised.

"Not happily." He shook his head. "But for you, I'd try. For you, I'd take anything you offered. No matter how small. You are more than I ever thought I deserved."

"You can't be serious." I tried to smile, but it didn't quite work. The longing in his voice was the stuff of daydreams. David would never lay himself bare to anyone. I never for a second believed he'd do as much for me. But hell, it was a lovely fantasy.

Before David could respond, the car behind me beeped. I jumped, startled, and confused about how his doors locked when he didn't have the key in hand. My answer came in the form of Westbrooke's offensive coordinator, Lukas. I'd seen him once or twice before. He'd been the one to let me in the arena when David needed his change of water bottles.

"Sir." David moved back so I could step away from the car that was clearly not his.

"David." Lukas offered him a smile and me an unimpressed once-over. "Nice work in there tonight. A couple of guys were asking about you. Things are looking bright."

"Yeah. Yes." David nodded. His arm was still around my waist, pinning me to his side in a protective stance. "Thank you, sir."

"Make sure you keep your head in the game." Lukas gave me another glance. "You're this close to the finish line."

"Right, thanks." David's voice was a little harder, jaw tight as Lukas gave him a small smile and opened his car door.

"Night, kids," he said. "Don't stay out too late."

Once the car sped off and the heavy cloud Lukas had carried dispersed, I turned to David.

"What was that about?"

David watched as the car disappeared down the street. "He's just an asshole."

"No, I know assholes," I reminded him. "That was something else."

He let out a heavy breath. "Yara, let's not—"

"Let's get something straight."

"Didn't think either of us was capable of that," he joked. When I didn't smile, he sighed.

"I don't want to be the woman you come to just for some physical exchange."

"Physical exchange?" He chuckled. "You mean sex? How old are you?"

"Old enough to know when a guy's emotionally stunted," I said.

He blinked, all humor washed away.

"If you want this to work, I want to know you. Need to."

"Alright," he said simply.

"Alright?" I squeaked, surprised at how simple he'd made it.

"Only if the same applies to you," he said. "I want to know you. Not the version you've kept on display. The Yara who sketches in secret books and hides them in dark corners."

There's no taking it back now. "Fair is fair."

25

"Yara, what did I say? *Always* check your mirrors." David sat in the passenger seat of his car, one hand tightened around the grab handle. The other hand white-knuckle gripped the console.

"I did." My trembling hand readjusted the rearview mirror for the third time since I had backed up onto a curb.

The litter-infested parking lot of a long-abandoned Martie Mart was the perfect place for a twenty-something, non-learner's permit-having, anxiety-prone woman to learn the driving basics.

I hadn't thought I'd get behind the wheel during my first lesson. But David insisted one learned better by doing. I'd warned him of the potential pitfalls, and now, he pressed his lips together, regretful of writing me off.

"Can you see out of them?" he asked.

I scoffed. "Of course, I can see out of them. I'm not that... inept."

The side mirror on the right remained slightly turned in, dripping in morning dew. I chewed on my bottom lip and moved the tiny knob David had shown me before I got into the car, adjusting it so I could see the tree's reflection on the curb. If I had seen that before, his poor tires wouldn't have been at risk.

David blew out a breath, but when I stole a quick look at him, it wasn't anger that shadowed across his face. He brushed the back of his hand across his lips and turned his gaze outside. From the haggard way he took in air, I'd bet he was holding in a laugh.

He'd given me a complete walkthrough of everything from the tire tread to popping the hood and pointing out oil and coolant. I spaced out when he went into great detail about motors and the sounds that I should understand. So, once we got to mirrors, I'd mentally moved on to organizing the masquerade decor supplies in the living room. Haven would not be pleased with the incessant amount of clutter we'd have to live with for the rest of the semester.

"I can see through it now," I mumbled as I put the car in drive.

David cleared his throat. "It's the one thing I ask of you. If you do nothing else, do that."

I nodded and gave the gas a light tap. We jerked forward when I panicked and slammed on the brakes at the sight of a stray dog running across the parking lot.

"I almost hit him," I said in a low, rushed voice.

David chuckled. "He's at least fifteen yards away."

"But he's running."

"Away from us."

"But I'm faster. If I went from zero to eighty—" My heart slammed against my ribcage at the thought.

"My car can barely pick up to fifty on a good day. I think you're safe from hyper-speed."

"—then I could have hit him. He was in my pathway."

"Yara." David's smile melted when he noticed my labored breath. "Relax. You didn't hit the dog. You would have never hit the dog. And once you learn how to adjust your mirrors, you'll—rarely—hit a curb."

When I frowned at him, David added, "Everyone hits curbs. It's a very human thing to do. There will always be a margin for error when you're behind the wheel."

"See, and that's what I don't like." I shoved the car into park and unbuckled my seatbelt so it was easier to breathe.

"You don't like adjusting your mirrors?" His brows pulled down, confused and concerned about that being the hill on which I would die.

I looked in the back seat for my bag, rummaging through the pockets in search of gum. My fingers itched to pick, and I'd read online that giving my body something else to focus on would help quell the urge. So far, no dice. Quitting cold turkey had been easier said than done. Regardless, I had to try—especially when I was with David, who would notice.

"The margin for error," I said once I'd found two rogue pieces of gum sandwiched between my wallet and travel first aid kit.

"Everything has a margin for error, Daredevil." His features softened as he watched me shove the gum into my mouth one after the other.

"Not with stakes this high." I waved my hand toward the empty spot where the dog had been. "I could kill something... someone."

"You're not going to kill something or someone."

"But I could," I insisted. "I don't like those odds."

"They're small."

"Doesn't matter, they exist."

We were silent for a moment, watching the sun rise over the horizon, waking up our sleepy college town. I replayed what I had said in my mind, embarrassment catching up to me as I realized David was getting prolonged exposure to the irrational side of me. The board up all the windows, tin foil hat, no one can be trusted (not even myself), side of me.

"Your car accident," his words poked at the silence, gentle and cautious. "How bad was it?"

My throat tightened. I shook my head as if it were nothing of note. Like my ears weren't burning from the shame.

"You don't have to tell me," David said. "But if you wanted to... well, I'm not going to tease you for it. I'd never joke about something that's caused you this kind of stress."

"I know that." Because if I knew nothing else, I knew David didn't actually like to see me hurt. Annoyed, maybe. Frustrated, most definitely. But not hurt.

"Before Westbrooke," David continued. "I don't remember you ever picking at your hair. I know we weren't besties—"

I laughed a little, and it undid some of the tension between my shoulder blades.

"—but I don't remember you ever being this afraid to make a mistake."

I met his gaze. Those dark brown eyes, a source of familiarity, I think I'd crave for all eternity and then, another century for the hell of it.

"Am I wrong?" he asked, offering me the floor with grace.

"No." I shook my head and couldn't help but add teasingly, "For once. We should probably alert the press. We could make good money off this story."

He sighed, the sides of his mouth twitching in an almost smile. "Appreciate the acknowledgement."

"Don't get used to it," I warned and directed my attention out the windshield to avoid the awkwardness of meeting his gaze as I confessed, "My accident involved me, my sister, another car, and a ditch. It was my fault. I... it was rainy, and I was going too fast. Logan was trying to help me get some experience on the highway. When it rained, she wanted me to pull off to the side. But no, I was... me. I thought it couldn't be that dangerous. When we started hydroplaning, I turned away from the skid. I knew I should have turned in. I read everything I could before the written test. Repeated all the warnings to myself day after day. But information means nothing if your body won't.... won't listen to you when it's time."

The wind outside picked up, pressing against our doors loudly as if it wanted to be let in. A cold seeped through the windows, drowning our shared silence and my hot shame.

"I wasn't hurt too badly. Just a couple of bruises." My voice lowered, weighed down by recollection of the bloody cut on the side of Logan's head. "But my sister... she'd hit her head and didn't wake up till the next day in the hospital. She had a concussion. And messed up her hand so much that she had to take a semester off from school. She's better now, but... I can see it in her eyes every time she gets behind the wheel. Logan's not where she wants to be in school. She says it's just because grad school's difficult, but I know that's not the only thing. I know that accident took something from her I can never give back."

I sucked in a breath. Oxygen lodged in my throat, strained against the muscles as it made way to my lungs.

"Yara." David's hand covered mine, calloused fingers offering me a protective squeeze. "It was—"

"An accident," I interrupted, eyes hot with tears. "Yeah, I know. I know. Everyone has told me that over and over. And that it could have happened to anyone. And it's not my fault."

"Maybe it was your fault," he said.

My gaze snapped to him, chest tightening so much I expected a crack. His words gave me a kind of frustrating shock I couldn't process.

"I can't dance around it," he reminded me.

"Right." I may as well bury myself in the darkness.

"But that doesn't mean you can't or shouldn't forgive

yourself for it," David continued. "Doesn't mean you can't move forward. More importantly, it doesn't mean you don't deserve to move forward. A mistake doesn't make you any less than, Yara. Just because something may have been your fault doesn't mean you don't deserve to heal."

I wanted to believe that. Him. Prayed his words broke shame's ironclad grip. But anxiety remained lodged in my throat. I parted my lips, breathing through my mouth in hopes it'd breed better results.

"Doesn't it, though?" I blinked more than necessary, looking everywhere but him.

"It doesn't." David squeezed my hand again to affirm the new belief. "What you don't deserve is what you've been doing. The picking. The terror. The self-doubt. None of that will change what happened. But it will change who you are."

I twisted my mouth to the side, giving it everything I had not to break down in front of him.

"The Yara I know lets nothing get between her and the goalpost," he said. "It's the Yara I've learned to like. The Yara I want to love. The Yara I plan to protect."

I met his gaze then, a million and one sparks traveling through my bloodstream.

"Don't let this change who you are. Who you want to be. You deserve to move on, no matter what happened," he said. "I know it's easier said than done, but it is possible. With some help, it's possible."

"I've tried to get help. And talk about it. And do all the meditations, exercises, and journaling. But none of it works like...when I pick," I confessed. "The repetition, the pain, it's a ritual. If I do it enough times, I'll..."

My skin burned as I realized how open I'd become. I vowed forever ago to lock away this version of myself, in fear that whoever came across it would insist I needed to be locked away, isolated in case I was contagious. I wouldn't blame them.

"You'll?" David encouraged me.

"Pay penance. And earn another chance to be worth it. When I do it, I'm consistent. I'm not forgetting what happened. I'm—"

"You're punishing yourself," David said firmly. "Again and again. Tell me, when will it be enough? How long? How much harm will you inflict before it's enough?"

I shook my head, chin trembling. The words wouldn't make it out of my mouth, so I just shrugged.

"If one of your sisters or your brother were doing something like this to themselves, taking on judge, juror, and executioner all day, every day, what would you think? How would you feel?"

"I'd... feel awful... and I'd want to make sure they didn't feel so alone. I'd do anything to make sure they weren't hurting." I traced the bumpy stitches on the leather console, trying to ground myself.

"And what makes you so different that you don't deserve the same?"

David raised a brow as I tried to come up with something substantial, something that made sense. And when I tried for too long, he gave me the sweetest '*I told you so*' look. And I wanted to cry, laugh, and burrow my face into his neck and never let go.

"The answer was 'nothing,'" he provided.

"Such a know-it-all," I complained in a whisper.

"Nothing," David repeated, the time it sounded like a promise.

26

THE WAREHOUSE HADN'T TRANSFORMED in the magical, fairy-godmother sense of the word. The walls were still plated with rust, the windows were decorated with a patchwork of tape, and the concrete floors were stained with oil and years of neglect.

But the magic came in the colossal floral carpets Haven found at an open market right outside of town. I convinced my mom to donate the set of black, circular dining tables for the night. Indie scored us buffet tables with vintage serving bowls and cups. Emmy brought in old Halloween decor from her parents' closed-down holiday store. And Covee designed the banners and posters that would put most marketing companies to shame.

"Well?" Indie asked when she noticed I'd stepped back to the front door to marvel at what all our guests would take in next week.

"Stuff of dreams?" Haven teased as she joined my side. Her smile faded into something more serious when she took a proper look at how the space had transformed.

I folded my arms over my chest, trying not to sound too

prideful because my parents had drilled it into my skull that pride comes before the fall. And I couldn't afford a fall this deep into the semester. "I think they're going to love it."

Indie scoffed, shaking her head. "You think?"

"She's being modest," Haven murmured, eyes still sparkling in awe. "You know who's going to kick themselves till the cows come home?"

"Olivia Noel Johnson," I said with a smile. This time, I couldn't avoid tipping my chin up in pride. Hopefully, the fall came as a slight stumble. I could bear the embarrassment of tripping over my feet.

"Do you think she'll show?" Indie asked.

"For sure," Haven and I said at the same time without hesitation.

"She'll want a first-row seat, and a chance to tell me I should have listened to her." I took a deep breath, relieved that her dream wouldn't happen. We still had a boatload of things to complete: finalizing the stage, doing a sound check for the band, and ensuring every member knew what they had to cook and how soon they'd have to cook it. But mostly, this back-aching, headache-inducing, beautiful, exciting masquerade party was going to happen with more than enough time to spare. And even some extra cash to donate to the local women's shelter.

"So!" I clapped, reinvigorated by the hint of success within reach. "Which one of you is going to stick around and help me figure out the stage?"

Indie whipped out her phone like it had been ringing. "Oh, no. I have to make a tutoring session."

"You're a straight-A student," I said.

"And why do you think that is?" She squeezed my shoulder before going to grab her bag. "Nice work, Prez. Thanks to you, we'll live to party another day."

I sighed but turned to Haven with hope. She was already shaking her head.

"I have to drive you both back to campus," she reminded me. "My show's streaming at five."

"Won't it still be streaming at six?" I asked.

She shook her head. "Who knows? No one knows these things, so it's best to enjoy them as soon as possible."

I laughed. "You two are unbelievable."

"Come on, let the woman enjoy her show." Indie tossed her arm around my shoulder. "Me enjoy studying. And you enjoy that cute tight end of yours. Don't you two have a date?"

The tips of my ears burned, but my expression remained stoic. I hadn't seen David outside of lectures since our driving lessons last weekend. He'd been swamped with practice and training and trying to keep his head above water in classes. And I'd delved into org work... not far enough to avoid checking my messages every hour. But enough so that I could push his smile, the memory of his touch, and how his lips felt on mine to the back of my mind for an impressive five minutes at a time. Indie's mention of him just ruined my current streak.

"A meeting," I said.

"Ooh, a meeting?" Indie asked with a laugh. "Sexy."

"Shut up." I bit back a smile and pulled out my phone to check my messages. Technically, David and I had a meeting scheduled in our calendars for one another. And the only reason it was there was because he'd texted me halfway through week:

I really need to see you.

My initial concerned response was:

what happened? What's wrong?

DAVID

I just need to see you.

It'd taken me a second to puzzle together that this was a social text, and this was David's way of saying he missed me.

I'd joked:

I could pencil you in. Send you a calendar invite.

His response was:

Perfect. Do that, please.

I didn't know what triggered the politeness and the lack of patience. I knew I appreciated it because I'd spent days trying to figure out a decent enough dare to have an excuse to see him.

My heart jumped when I saw a message notification with his name on it. Blocking off the stage became as low priority to me as it was to Haven and Indie.

They noticed and instantly started aww'ing me.

"Alright, alright." I waved them away. "He's picking me up."

"How far is he?" Indie asked.

I checked his location. "Twenty-five minutes."

"We'll wait with you," Haven offered.

"You know, that gives us plenty of time to move a couple of boxes—" I tried.

"Outside," Indie interrupted and started herding us to the door. "We're all waiting for him outside. You need to get away from this place, Yara. It's got a hold on you."

"The grip's tight," Haven agreed as she stared around the

warehouse with the look she got when she wanted to burn incense around the house.

I let them corral me outside. The air was biting now that we were nearing the end of fall. We hurried to Haven's car for warmth while we waited. David somehow turned a twenty-five-minute drive into a fifteen-minute drive.

"Someone's excited," Haven said under her breath when she saw his car pull into the lot. She still wasn't convinced he was good for me, but she'd been open to changing that belief when I told her about his attempt at teaching me how to drive. A man who helped someone gain more autonomy was one worthy of respect in her book.

"Have fun." Indie winked at me. "Don't do anything I wouldn't do."

"Of course not." I hopped out of the car, giving them a final wave before hurrying over to David's car. He got out as soon as he saw me coming, meeting me on the passenger side. I stopped a couple of feet away, buzzing at the sight of him.

David wore a gray Henley underneath his worn black jean jacket. His hair stuck out from underneath a green beanie, the strands curling from a recent wash.

"Hi," I greeted, not knowing what to do with my hands, so I stuffed them into my jacket pockets. A shield of unfamiliar shyness went up around me, making it difficult to meet David's eyes. I blamed it on Haven and Indie. They were watching us from the van. I waved my hand behind my back, trying to gesture for them to go away. The car's engine remained rumbling in the background.

"What's going on with them?" David raised a brow, glancing over my shoulder.

I shrugged. "They're... curious."

He leaned against the car, making it that much more tempting to wrap my arms around his neck and pull him down for a kiss. "About?"

"If we're actually real. If you're good for me. If we'll last."
The last one was more me.

"I have a solid answer for two out of three."

I squinted. "Which two?"

"Come here." He gestured me over with two fingers.

I didn't move an inch. "Which two, David?"

He chuckled and shook his head. "You never humor me."

I gave him a '*come on*' eye roll. "You don't like to be humored."

"I'd like it if you're doing it. I like a lot of things more when you're doing it."

It was hard to swallow. His deep voice settled nicely on my skin, eliciting the burning desire to feel his mouth on me. It didn't matter where, only for how long... I entertained the idea of forever. Impractical, but I wasn't sure anything else would suffice.

David pushed off the car, tired of waiting for me to come to him. My breath caught in my throat when he placed one hand on my cheek and tucked his fingers around my belt loop, pulling me against him. It was embarrassing how quickly my clit screamed for attention.

"You're never going to listen," he whispered against my lips. "Are you?"

"What incentive do I have?" I was proud that my words came out in one coherent take. I could hear my heart in my ears, nearly blotting out the noise of Haven's van finally driving away.

David chuckled as he watched them go. "They didn't want to see the rest of the show?"

"Is that what you're doing?" I asked, my hands clutching his biceps. I wanted to give in to him with reckless abandon. "Putting on a show?"

He shrugged. "I don't know; I've been wondering if that's the only way we work."

My forehead wrinkled. "You think so?"

"Maybe I should have said fear." His gaze flickered to my lips.

I smiled, stomach fluttering with hope. "You're afraid of us? The real us?"

He nodded. "Of course. I'm afraid of going back to what we were. What about you?"

"Terrified," I promised without hesitation. We shared a laugh.

"I hated this week," he confessed. "Thinking about you from sunrise to sunset. Trying to figure out how to get out of practice just to see you. Yara, you live so far away. Has it always been that far?"

"Since sophomore year," I said, still laughing, still feeling so wanted and desired.

"So inconvenient," he mumbled and then closed the gap to kiss me. I wrapped my arms around his neck as my lips parted. David's thumb brushed tender circles on my cheek while his tongue promised something far more explicit.

"Standing out in this cold's inconvenient," I said when we broke away for a second.

"Am I not doing a good job at warming you up?" he teased and pulled me closer for another kiss. This one lit me up from the inside, burning any caution I had lingering about me, him, or us. Who cared about maybe when every part of me screamed to just enjoy this moment? This man. This wonderfully frustrating, contrary, bullheaded, incomprehensibly beautiful man.

"Passable," I said through heavy breaths.

"Passable?" The vibration from his chuckle would have felt so much better on my clit. "Your body says otherwise."

I smiled against his mouth. "I don't care what my body says. What I say is, I don't want to be this horny in the cold. Take me somewhere warm."

He took a breath and kissed my forehead. "Sorry to break it to you..."

I frowned, afraid he was going to say he needed to go somewhere after this. That our window is just large enough for this short-lived makeout. "What?"

"Our meeting takes place outside," he said.

I laughed, but when he didn't so much as smile, the noise faded out. "Seriously? You... this is an actual meeting?"

"If that's code for date, then yes."

My stomach jumped with excitement. "You're taking me on a date?"

"Why are you so surprised?"

"I didn't think dates were your vibe."

"Remember when I said you needed to stop assuming things about me?"

I closed one eye, embarrassed. "Sorry, sorry."

He chuckled and shook his head. "It's okay. We're both learning."

THE PARKING LOT of Horrorville was littered with old cars and costumed attendees. There was a proper crispness in the air that burned my lungs but offered infinite amounts of comfort. We followed the heavy flow of foot traffic to the pumpkin-framed entrance. I could already hear the music and pre-taped screams from this side of the fence.

"So?" David watched me as I bit back my smile. "Good pick?"

I was a horror girl through and through, who'd grown up in a household that couldn't even stand sitcom Halloween specials. Horrorville was an annual pop-up event that boosted the best haunted houses on this side of the country. The tickets reflected that accomplishment tenfold, which was why I had to pass on going this year, since my funds were limited.

"Eh." I shrugged and tucked my hand underneath David's arm.

"Come on." He pressed a kiss on my temple. "You got to give credit where credit's due."

I looked up at him, stomach fluttering with every kind of

thrill known to man. "I've been wanting to go here since the temperature dropped."

David nodded with a grin. "I knew it."

"But..." I sobered. "The tickets are almost a hundred dollars more than they were last year. I don't think—"

He shook his head. "It's fine. I've got you covered."

"No, I mean... you don't have to have me covered. I know between football and school, money's got to be—"

"Yara," he interrupted, tone clipped. "I can afford to take you on a date."

My grip on his arm loosened. "I didn't say you couldn't."

"No, you insinuated."

"I... I didn't mean to," I said in a whisper. No part of me wanted to poke an unhealed wound right after we had mended our fences. "I'm sorry."

David took a deep breath and shook his head. "No, I am. I... it's been weird, thinking about where this is going. Where we're going."

"Where we're going?" I repeated.

"You're going to make me spell it out, aren't you?" His smile reappeared.

"I dare you."

"What a waste of a dare." David tsked. "You've gone soft on me, Daredevil."

"And what do you call what you're doing?" I raised a brow. "Picking me up, taking me out, buying me dinner."

David chuckled. "I don't remember throwing in dinner."

"You were getting to it," I insisted as I smiled up at him.

His eyes softened. "I suppose I was."

"So?" I stopped walking before reaching the ropes to line up in the queue, sidestepping so we'd be out of everyone's way. "Spell it out. I know it's not your strength. But I'm not opposed to giving As for effort."

As I spoke, I grabbed onto David's jacket, opening it a

little so I could more easily press myself against his chest. His hands encircled my waist as if it were second nature. We'd made a habit of leaning into one another.

"So soft," he chastised before kissing me. My grip on his jacket tightened as I steeled my resolve not to beg for more.

"We're going toward a relationship that I have no intention of leaving anytime soon," he whispered against my mouth. "Does that sound okay? Like someplace you want to be?"

I swallowed, trying to get my mouth to produce noise again. It quickly proved to be a lost cause, so I simply nodded.

"I figured." David's low, knowing chuckle should trigger a snarky retort. I couldn't let this man get too bigheaded. But if I opened my mouth now, who knew what mushy nonsense would spill out?

"Ready to go in?" David asked, pulling back enough to let cold air filter between us.

My mouth stayed shut as I nodded. He wouldn't get my unbridled confession of admiration. My frustrating desire to have him pull me back into his chest and never let go. I wouldn't give him the satisfaction of knowing I was falling fast... yet.

"Born ready," I finally said.

———

"WE HAVE to get a scare band for this one," I said when we stood outside the largest house of the night. David and I had gone through three houses, starting with a low-scare tier: a wicked-witch one. And building up to the creepier demon possessions and masked murder houses. My adrenaline was pumping, and my cheeks ached from laughing so much.

"Lead the way," David permitted. He let me tug him over

to the worker handing out bands that told the scare actors we consented to being touched.

When I wrapped the bracelet around his wrist, I noticed the red in his cheeks didn't hint toward amusement. David's eyes went big when he realized what I'd realized.

"Come on," he said quickly and turned toward the house's line.

"David." I hurried after him, smiling as I hugged his bicep to keep his pace aligned with mine. "Look at me."

He turned his head, so all I saw was the back of his beanie. I laughed and switched over to his other side. He turned away—but not before I could see a smile tugging at his lips.

"You don't have to wear the band if you're scared. I won't judge you." I slipped to his other side and this time, caught his gaze. My lips pressed together as I tried not to laugh.

David leaned down so our foreheads touched as he whispered, "You're already judging me, liar."

"Not harshly," I promised. "Not in the way I would have months or even weeks back."

"How comforting," he muttered deadpan.

"It's okay to be afraid." I tugged at the bracelet on his wrist, but he waved me away.

"I'm fine," he promised. "You know I'm fine."

Sure, he hadn't screamed once in any of the houses we walked through so far. In fact, the man barely blinked as a very well-done headless monster fell onto the walkway. The actor didn't move, so we had to step over him. I freaked out, and David briefly picked me up to carry me over the obstacle. It was all very *thank-you-for-saving-me-want-to-have-sex* vibes after that. I quelled that feeling with about a liter of apple cider and a bucket of caramel popcorn.

"Is it the scare rating?" I asked. "You know, most of it's just preference. High ratings don't guarantee you'll be afraid. You've been doing so well, so far."

David shook his head, keeping his gaze on the start of the line. Since the sun had long dipped under the horizon, the night was full of mosquitoes and bats. Fewer people lingered in the queues. The crowds were thinning, migrating either to the parking lot or the food court. End of night meant peak time for getting into the best houses at record speed.

"Promise me you won't use this against me." The seriousness in his tone had me straighten at attention. I held up my pinky.

David raised a brow. "I mean, really promise."

"What do you think this means?" I asked and wiggled my finger. "I'm not so coldhearted as to break this kind of promise. Besides, what are you so afraid of? You know enough about me to retaliate if it comes to that."

He hooked his pinky around mine. We didn't unhook our fingers, even after we lowered our hands.

"I hate aliens," he said.

I frowned and glanced at the house's sign, The Last Abduction. "Aliens? Really?"

As far as my ranking of horror went, aliens were on the lowest tier, along with evil gnomes and chaotic birds. I couldn't think of any truly devastating horror alien movies (besides the obvious sci-fi one) that'd come out in the last decade. As far as the larger collective consciousness went, aliens seemed low on that pole as well.

"One of my foster brothers swore he'd been abducted, and the evidence—" David shook his head as if it were disgraceful not to believe— "was damning."

I swallowed a laugh because this was real and serious. Something rooted in his childhood. "What kind of evidence?"

"Creepy." He sniffed, looking around the queue line as we started moving faster to the entrance.

"Care to elaborate?"

David shook his head. "Not really. Unearthing deep-rooted fears doesn't seem wise when one is about to face said fears, you know?"

I pressed my shoulder against his. "I won't leave your side."

"Promise?" he asked, half-teasing.

"We're locked and loaded, aren't we?" I tugged on my pinky that was still curled around his. "And we can toss these bracelets."

"You wanted the bracelets, so we're doing the bracelets."

"But—"

"Don't argue," he said.

My nipples hardened at the finality in David's tone. I pulled my hand away from his and stuffed it into my jacket. Prolonged contact equaled heightened emotion, I told myself. I'd have to pace myself if I wanted to have a leg to stand on in this relationship. He couldn't have known I was this wanting so early on.

David cocked his head to the side, studying me and my rigid posture when I pulled away from him. But he said nothing until we crossed the threshold of the house.

"Don't wander or lag too far behind." He brushed aside a plastic curtain tattooed with mist from the excessive fog machine.

"I wouldn't dare leave you to fend for yourself." I grabbed onto the hem of his jacket. That seemed a much safer option than skin-on-skin contact.

David led the way like he'd done through every house, rounding each corner with the vigilant eye of a man with every intent to survive. It was regrettably hot, and I found no part of me willing to resist the pull.

I didn't notice the house's first jump scare because I'd been too busy studying his sharp jaw. The green light from above painted shadows across his skin. A fan that was supposed to clear out the fog pushed his spicy cologne into the air.

"Fuck," he said with a low laugh when the second scare actor knocked into us. David looked back at me for a check-in.

"Yeah." I chewed on my bottom lip, trying not to stare at him for too long.

He caught on to me, anyway. "What is it?"

"Nothing." I shook my head and nudged my chin toward the fork in the house. "Which way?"

David wasn't convinced and said, "You pick."

"No, you."

"Are you scared?" He frowned and grabbed my hand.

"Terrified," I mumbled. Of wanting him this much.

"We'll make it out," he promised with a teasing smile.

"Maybe." I took the lead and tugged him into the hall on the right. Perhaps following him was the issue. If I were in front, I wouldn't have the chance to watch this curve on his shoulders or the flexing of his jaw.

Leading worked for a while. I screamed a few times, backing myself into his chest when an actor tried to tug me into a side room. David held onto my waist, refusing to let go until the actor relinquished their grip. I kept leaning into him, exaggerating my panic just to feel his warmth. We were almost at the end of the house when I bumped into him a final time and felt how hard he was against my ass. He didn't say a thing. I'm not even sure he knew I noticed. But by the time we got out of the house, his cheeks burned and gaze wouldn't hold mine.

"Wasn't so bad," he said in a low voice.

"Told you." I was too breathless and hot to properly tease him.

David ran his fingers through his hair, scanning the crowd. "Hungry yet?"

"Not really."

"Then what do you want to do now?" He finally looked at

me, reading the want in my gaze. David shook his head but grabbed my hand. Before I knew what was happening, he led me through the throng of people. It felt like ages before we found a quiet, isolated spot at the back of a hay maze. David's hands held onto my waist as he backed me against the stacked hay bales.

"How about now?" he asked again with his gaze on my parted lips. "Hungry?"

"Getting there." I gripped his jacket collar, pulling him into a kiss. David placed one hand over my shoulder and the other around my waist. He pulled me against him so I could feel the extent of his arousal. The buzz of the crowds faded into nothingness, and we continued to cling to one another as if we were the only people in existence.

"Yara," he groaned against my mouth. The vibration of my name on his lips sent my nerves on fire.

"Yes?" I bit his bottom lip and swiped my tongue across to soothe the assumed sting.

"It's nearly impossible not to touch you." His mouth ventured down to my neck, planting kisses against my pounding pulse. "How did it get this impossible?"

"I'm irresistible once you get your head out of your ass," I joked.

He nipped at my jaw, and I laughed.

"You and that mouth," he murmured, less scolding and more wonder in his voice.

"What about it?" My smile faded when his thumb lightly traced my bottom lip.

"It's been all I could think about for the last four years. Its ability to cut me down while simultaneously—" He pressed my waist harder against his. I could feel him against my clit. "—giving me the best hard-ons of my life."

"Best hard-ons?" I smiled and shook my head. "Sounds frustrating."

"I like the teasing. Build up without reward."

"A little torment."

"A lot," he confirmed.

"How many times have I caused this?"

"A lot," he repeated and kissed me with the desperation of a man in the middle of a desert with no water in sight.

"Promise me something?" he asked, breathless.

"Depends." I smiled against his smile.

"Don't go easy on me. Ever."

I shoved my fingers through his hair, tugging on it a bit. "With me, easy was never in the cards for you."

28

WE WERE in his apartment again, but something had changed since the last time I was here. It was warmer. Softer. There was an orange blanket draped over the back of his couch. A pine-scented candle in the middle of the coffee table. Cushions were on the dining chairs. Another orange throw blanket on the bed. Every recent home good addition was my favorite color. I was all over his space.

David didn't say a word as he took my jacket. I didn't have time to get one in before he started kissing me. He led me backwards until the back of my knees hit his bed. I sat on the springy mattress. David instantly kneeled and kissed down my neck.

"It looks great in here," I whispered between heavy breaths.

"I wanted it to be nice for you."

I gasped when he playfully bit my nipple through my shirt. The fabric was so restraining and pointless now. How I kept it on this long, heaven knew.

He unzipped my pants. "Lift," he ordered.

I did as I was told, too drunk on his kisses to realize what I'd done until it was too late.

"Didn't think you'd follow orders so quickly and well." He smiled, tossing my pants to the side. "I like it."

I frowned. "That doesn't have anything to do with you. I wanted to."

"I know you did." His low, deep voice made my pussy clench in anticipation of him. I couldn't keep any of my thoughts straight. Tonight, David was far better than I in the concentration category.

"How are you so calm?" I wondered. "After all this time, we're here, and you are so calm."

"I'm not." David's fingers hooked onto the hem of my underwear. "But I've wanted you badly enough to learn how not to show it."

"Show it," I said. "I want to see it."

"It's not that simple."

"I dare you." I kissed him, parting my mouth to let him in, to show that I wanted him there. "I dare you to show me how badly you want me."

He groaned against my mouth. "It's not your turn."

I pulled back and pouted. "I've been good to you tonight, though, right? Helped you through the alien house."

I spread my knees wider, calling attention to the wet spot already soaking through my underwear. The sight I offered him earned me a deep, longing groan.

"Can't I get one pass?" I kissed him.

David bit my lip before tugging my underwear off. "Fine. I'll make an exception just this once. Which version do you want? The one where I'm gentle? Or the one where I don't hold back?"

My stomach jumped at the idea that he'd imagined options. Imagined him and me doing this. "Give me a little of column A and B."

"You sure?" His thumb traced my lips. I open my mouth, sucking on the tip. David watched in agony as I took more into my mouth. I held his gaze as I released him. My hand guided his thumb between my thighs, and we let out a shared moan as it slipped inside of me.

"More of column B." I arched into him.

"You're not going to see the outside of this room for a while," he warned, switching out his thumb for his index and middle.

"That a promise?" I chewed on my bottom lip, trying not to moan too loud. Dorm room walls were thin. We didn't need a noise complaint and an RA scolding. If we wanted to remain isolated and uninterrupted, we'd have to tread lightly. But, damn, I needed to make some kind of noise. Especially when he bent down to take my clit between his lips.

I fell back onto the bed, my lower body trembling against his mouth. David began with gentle kisses, then moved into heated licks. My body didn't know whether to lean into him more or pull back because of how stimulating it all was. I laced my fingers through his hair, tugging a little because it was all that kept me grounded on this plane of existence.

"David," I whispered, not really needing anything but wanting to taste his name. I'd hope it'd provide some sort of stability, but it led to him offering me his darkened gaze. The lust in his eyes was a perfect match to what he was doing with his tongue. And I'm pushed off balance all over again. The peak was within arm's reach, and just as I felt it coming, he pulled away.

"David." The name's a curse this time. I'm half-naked, ruining his brand-new comforter, and being denied a climax.

"Your top." He nudged his chin toward me.

"You've got to be joking. You stopped for this?" I tugged off my top, skin hot in frustration.

"Need to see all of you," he explained and reached up to

unclasp the front of my bra. Instead of removing the straps, he left them there, the black, lacy cups dangling.

"Leave it," he ordered when I reached to finish a job he'd clearly thought was done. "I like how it looks."

My nipples hardened at the statement and his attention. David slipped his fingers inside me again. They were soaked when he pulled them out. The moan I released when he painted my breasts with my wetness couldn't be suppressed. And when his mouth covered my nipples to clean them off, I nearly screamed. He held his hand over my mouth for a second, allowing me to release the sound without fear.

David took his time painting me, tasting me, teasing me. I'd soaked through his comforter. It would be embarrassing if I weren't so blinded by the need for him.

"Turn around," he said after his third round of torturing me. "On all fours."

"Not until you finish what you started."

His chuckle nearly did me in. Was it possible to climax from that kind of vibration? I would find out by the night's end.

"I'm trying, I promise." He nipped at my neck. "Do as I say."

I shook my head. "I'm pretty sure I have all the cards."

His eyes flickered to my swollen clit. "What makes you think that?"

I slipped my hand into his waistband, pre-cum already soaking through the fabric of his boxers. He knew how to swallow a moan, but he didn't know how to tame the longing in his eyes. David had been looking at me like that for weeks, and now I finally had the context to know what it meant.

"You've wanted me like this for a long time, haven't you?" I whispered.

"Maybe." It's a poor attempt at nonchalance. He couldn't keep his eyes from closing as I rubbed him.

"On all fours is how you imagined me, yeah?" I asked, coaxing him to reveal the truth. "Did you touch yourself while you fantasized about it? Was it on this bed? Or the shower? Maybe on the couch? Are you risky enough to do it in your car?"

"Yara," he warned.

"Tell me, and I'll do what you want." I went in like I was going to kiss him but simply held my lips against his. When he tried to close the gap, I shook my head. "Tell me, and I'm yours."

"Every fucking where," he confessed in a hoarse tone. "I've thought about you in every corner of this apartment. I couldn't stop. I never will now. I don't want to. There's not one inch of my world that you haven't become a permanent fixture."

I hadn't expected the hot desperation of his confession or the ache in his tone. As much lust as there was, there was also uncertainty. There was a real fear that I wouldn't respond in the way he needed. He worried I'd find him to be too much and leave.

Words wouldn't work with David. He'd been given enough promises for a lifetime. I kissed him instead. Offering my promise in the pressure, the silence, the desire.

"You did good," I praised, and that seemed to do something for him. He pulsed in my hand. "Very good."

"Yeah?" he asked.

I nodded. "Since you were so good, I'm all yours."

We kissed one more time before I turned over and positioned myself on all fours. David's breathing went shallow, and he rid himself of all remaining clothing. The springs squeaked when he climbed onto the bed behind me. His hands gripped my hips, carefully massaging circles onto my skin.

I gasped when I felt his warm breath against my pussy. He

parted my lips and licked up the wetness with a kind of reverence one may associate with salvation. I rest my cheek on the bed, fully enjoying the joy of being eaten out from behind. My hands gripped the sheet as his fingers played with my clit.

"Go ahead," I permitted when I felt him stop himself from licking too far up. "Only if you want."

"You sure?" he asked, unable to mask his desire.

"Mm." I nodded, already delirious from the thought of him even wanting to taste me all over.

David teased me a little longer before reaching my ass. I moaned when his tongue made contact. He pushed two fingers inside my pussy and used his other hand to completely focus on my clit. David simulated every area with equal focus and attention. His fingers worked in harmony with his tongue. No one had ever eaten me out with this much dedication.

"David," I whispered, over and over, barely able to hold on. I didn't want to finish too soon, desperate to linger in this moment for an eternity. "I need you so bad. Please don't stop."

He listened to the command, keeping his rhythm up. My muscles squeeze around his fingers. The climax came on like a thunderstorm, loud and uncontainable. I forced myself face down on the mattress, screaming his name into the sheets. David didn't slow for a second, eating like it was the meal he'd been craving all his life.

"David," I said again once I recovered enough to speak again. "I'm...that was..."

"The sexiest thing I've ever seen," he finished for me and playfully bit my ass cheek before pulling away.

I flipped over, out of breath but wanting more. When he caught my gaze, he raised a brow.

"You okay to keep going?" David asked. "We can wait for you to catch your breath."

"I don't care about my breath." I inched down on the bed,

closer to him, to prove I wanted him to finish what we'd started.

"One second." He leaned over to his nightstand and rummaged around. I propped myself up on my elbows when it took him more than a few seconds to grab what he was looking for.

"Shit," he muttered.

"What?"

David sighed and gave the drawer one final, just-in-case check. "I don't have any condoms."

I fell back onto the bed, groaning in disappointment. "How do you not have any condoms?"

"It's... been a while."

My eyes widened. "How long?"

"That's private information."

"You don't get more private than this," I teased.

David scoffed, deciding instead of indulging me to disappear into the bathroom and clean up. The tap turned on, harmonizing with his electric toothbrush. My body continued to buzz as I waited between the sheets that smelled of him and the warmth he left behind.

Once David reappeared, I arched a brow at him, a wordless, *what now?*

"I wanted to clean up for you so I could do this," he said, climbing onto the bed and kissed me. I wrapped my legs around his waist, urging him close enough to feel how much I still wanted him. David let me have my fun for a bit. I rocked my hips back and forth, feeling him get hard against my thigh.

"I'll go to the pharmacy?" he said, voice strained.

"It'll take too long," I said and pointed at my stomach. "Just finish here."

"Are you serious?"

I widened my thighs, so he had a better view of my fingers circling my clit. "We'll finish together."

His expression darkened. "Yeah?"

Instead of answering, I reached for him. David moaned when I spent a moment coaxing pleasure from both of us. He eventually joined in, but instead of reaching from himself, he touched me. Two of his fingers slipped inside, and his thumb took care of my clit. I leaned my head back, body on fire as his speed kicked up a notch.

I tried to match his rhythm. He'd gotten bigger since we started. What was already impressive in length became that much more heart-stopping. I played with his tip, spreading the pre-cum around so stroking became nice and easy.

David watched me stroke him, eyes hooded in ecstasy. When he couldn't hold on any longer, he leaned forward, kissing me with hard determination.

"You're the most beautiful person I've ever seen," he whispered against my lips. "You know that?"

"It's hard to trust the flattery of the person I'm jerking off," I teased.

David nipped at my bottom lip. "So, I'll tell you after I finish. Tell you every fucking day. Show you I know how incredibly lucky I am to be with you even for a second."

"I want more than seconds," I said.

"Then that's what you'll get." David kissed me again. His thumb slowed down, the long, torturous circles offering me another orgasm. I moaned into his mouth, and he swallowed the sound, acquiring a rabid taste for my pleasure. He continued to eat said pleasure as I came again. I don't know how he lasted this long without finishing, but I was in no mood for making this a competition. As soon as he pulled away from my mouth to make sure I had my fill, David glanced down at my hand still stroking him.

"Still okay with me finishing on you?" he asked, his fingers digging into the sheets on either side of my head. "Because I'm so fucking close."

"Look at me when you do. I want to see you." My request was the final push. He locked his eyes on mine, his hand cupped my cheek, the touch an anchor for both of us. Months of unspoken and ignored desire clouded our vision. The chance to finally satisfy each other made my heart stop. David moaned as his cum painted me with hot and sticky strokes. His thumb traced circles on my cheek, bringing some softness to the hard, erotic moment.

"Yara..." he whispered, unable to say anything else. I laughed after he buried his face in my neck, kissing me as he continued to finish. I continued to stroke him through it all, enjoying every drop on my skin.

"Good?" I asked when he lowered himself down beside me.

David let out a heavy, contented sigh and nodded. "You're dangerous."

I laughed. "You already knew that."

"I did," he agreed with a smile. "But this is a whole other level."

We lay side-by-side, watching the spin of the ceiling fan as we caught our breath. Now and then, I'd sneak a glance at him. He had his eyes closed. The small, content smile on his lips made my stomach flutter. He reached for my hand, his eyes still closed, and squeezed it as we enjoyed the quiet.

Eventually, David pushed himself up to go to the bathroom. He returned with a warm, soapy washcloth. I lay still as he cleaned me up.

"I don't know if you understand how beautiful you are," he whispered, with one hand caressing my cheek and the other wiping off the mess we'd made. "How well you did."

I smiled, basking in the praise. David massaged my inner thigh, coaxing relaxation into the strained muscles. "Tell me."

"The kind of beauty that makes it hard to think straight when I desperately want to argue," he teased and kissed me.

David tossed the washcloth toward his hamper before pulling me into his arms. I nestled my head right in the crook of his neck, enjoying the warm cuddle and abundant attention. Being loved before sex was incredible, but post-sex meant even more to me. The affection David offered was confirmation that I wasn't a means to an end. This time in his bed wasn't a temporary experiment.

"You give so much." He kissed my forehead. "And take it so well."

I sighed, relaxing in his arms. Protection felt like David's warm embrace. His heartbeat drummed steadily in my ear. I pressed my nose to his skin, breathing in familiarity. The thought of ever having to leave made my chest ache with sadness.

"Will you stay here tonight?" David asked, reading my mind.

I smiled, nodded, and clung to him harder. "Since you asked so nicely, yes."

29

THE FOOTBALL STADIUM reminded me of a living thing, pulsing with every roar of the crowd. I'd only been to three games in the whole time I'd been at Westbrooke. The first time was freshman year, when I thought happiness lay in experiencing every clichéd college moment. The second time was the water bottle incident. Third, when I was experiencing one of my bouts of homesick moments and knew I'd find David on the field. Unconsciously, I'd looked to him for distraction through the years. And his gift of distraction had evolved into one of comfort.

The Angels were ahead by three, their kicker winning them enough wiggle room to still have a decent shot at a victory. Tension was high considering we were up against the Mendell Hawks, the school that poached not one but two of Westbrooke's best offensive players and one offensive coordinator.

"Think a fight will break out?" Haven had to cup her hand around her mouth as she whispered in my ear. Typically, the stadium was divided with the fans on their respective team's side. And typically, home teams could expect way more fans than away teams. But Mendell had shown up and out, decked in their forest greens, mountain logo tees, and yellow foam fingers, claiming number one. There was a particular group of rowdy Mendell guys a couple of rows down who would cheer until their faces were red anytime Mendell so much as touched the ball. And their faces went blue anytime a referee called a play against their precious Hawks.

"If it does—" I eyed one superfan as he whipped off his shirt, twirling it in the air. "—we'll exit stage left. No hesitation."

Haven nodded and grabbed hold of my hand as if she were ready to bolt in a heartbeat. I squeezed her fingers, grateful she'd agreed to join me.

I'd said 'yes' to attending this game for David while hopped up on post-sex calm. David wanted to see me in his jersey. His number.

"Paint it on your cheeks," he'd whispered to me this morning between kisses along my collarbone.

"What's in it for me?" I'd asked.

His chuckle had sent my body aching despite having come twice. "Always negotiating."

"It'd be a waste not to. How else will I be satisfied?"

"I can think of one guaranteed method." He'd disappeared underneath the sheets and had me promising to paint his number anywhere else he wanted within a matter of seconds.

I untangled myself from the image of David in bed, replacing it with that of him on the field. He played focused. David didn't find himself in the arguments fueled with a competitive venom that'd plagued most of today's game. When the Angels and Hawks clashed post-play, David found himself outside the circle, either talking to one of the assistant coaches on the side of the field or Nathaniel, who (expectedly) also kept his frustration (if it existed) internal.

It was a relief to see David not taking the bait of fights. It was also a joy to see him in those tight white pants, and his muscles hardened whenever he got his hands on the ball or tackled a man in blue. The sun was setting, and within a couple of minutes, we'd be at some celebration party, counting down the moments until we got to sneak out for some alone time. I was counting down the seconds. But prepping for such a night proved to be a jinx after a Mendell lineman somehow got his hands on Weston. The crowd collectively gasped and winced at how hard the quarterback went down. And the angry uproar that followed was born from the lineman yanking Weston back up before slamming him into the ground again.

My gaze immediately found David. He'd been the one to shove the lineman off of Weston. And he didn't stop there. The fury on the field flooded into the crowd, dyeing our clean waters red.

"Yara." Haven tugged me behind her when the guys from below started shoving a couple of people in protest of the thrown flag.

Someone broke a beer bottle, and the shattered glass made another person scream. And so began the avalanche of highly charged fans who wanted nothing more than their chosen football deity to stand firm at their altar.

Haven's ironclad grip made it impossible to unlatch, no matter how many times a wayward person knocked into us. My wrist screamed in protest of being twisted at all kinds of angles, but I didn't consider letting go for a second. I could barely think straight, wide-eyed and fearful in all the chaos. One could get trampled to death in this kind of crowd. My sides ached from hard elbows and aggressive shoves. What happened above, happened below. The football field was in shambles. Coaches and referees in the mix, trying their best to break up cluster after cluster of guys.

"When I run, you run," Haven called over the crowd. She had only time to glance back at me for a second. "Okay?"

"Okay!" I said as loud as I could.

There was a brief opening in the crowd where Haven and I could slip through. We didn't waste a second, bolting to our escape. Haven tripped over the bottom of her skirt. I tugged her upright before she reached the ground. We continued running, hand in hand, until we were past the concessions and near the gate that led to the parking lot.

Cop cars lined the lot, their lights blinking. We ducked into the darkness of a row of cars, sensing even more trouble on the horizon.

"Are you okay?" I asked through heavy breaths when I noticed a cut on her elbow. Dark blood trickled down her arm.

"Fine." She peeked over the hood of a rusted truck, trying to suss out the vibe before we moved forward. "Next time you convince me to come to one of these things—"

"Not happening," I told her with a humorless laugh. "Nothing is ever this serious."

"To them, it's life." She sighed and shook her head. "Did you see what they did to Hart?"

"What? No." I'd been too focused on David, too worried about how he'd lost his helmet at the beginning of the fight.

"His arm looked broken." She squeezed her eyes shut for a second, as if trying to rid the image from her brain by sheer willpower.

My heart sank into my stomach. "Really?"

Haven gave me a solemn nod, mouth pulled down in a frown. She gestured me forward. "Hate this kind of energy. Bad omens all around."

———

NO MATTER how many times I tried, I couldn't get David or Hart to answer their phones. The school's social media blasted updates and safety alerts for everyone on campus. Warnings about probation and potential expulsion for vandalism and violence were the focus. I got caught in an online rabbit hole of other students recounting tonight's events with far more information than Haven and I'd been privy to in our section of the stands.

"Hart answered," Haven finally updated from her seat on the couch. She'd been chewing on her nails, trying to get in contact with him for the past hour. "He's in the hospital. Doing good. His shoulder just had to be popped back into socket."

"Thank God." I sighed, grateful at least one person on my list of worries was okay. After learning Indie and Covee had been somewhere in the crowd too, my anxiety heightened in fear for their safety. Neither of them was answering their phones either.

Weston, the last person I'd thought would contact me, sent a simple text:

WESTON

Can you get to David's dorm in the next half hour?

My heart jumped, and I immediately responded:

Of course. Is he okay? He's not answering his phone.

WESTON

Rough shape. I need to go check on Nat and Hart. But I can't leave him alone like this.

I was already tugging on my jacket and asking Haven for a

ride. It took us longer than usual to get to the other side of campus because of post-game traffic. Haven couldn't find on-street parking, so she let me off at a red light close enough that I only had to backtrack a couple of yards.

> Here! Will you let me in?

Weston came down in less than a couple of minutes, pushing the door open for me. He smelled of grass and looked like a train wreck. Someone had haphazardly taped the cut above his eye, his bottom lip was purple with early signs of swelling, and his knuckles were red and bloodied as though he'd rubbed them against a cheese grater.

"Has he told you about freshman year?" Weston mashed the elevator button multiple times until the doors opened.

"Freshman year?" I hurried in behind him, heart rate rising when I saw how his hand shook when he pressed the number for David's floor. "No, I don't know... are you okay? What happened out there?"

"I want to say what usually happens," he began, trying to smile. "But those guys... that was rougher than usual. David's been good at avoiding fights like this up until now."

I tugged at my sleeves, resisting the urge to pluck at the loose hair curling around my temples.

"He's going to be fine," Weston assured quickly as the elevator door dinged open. The floor was cold, empty, and eerily quiet. He led the way toward David's front door. "He's just... and that stuff in high school and then, freshman year—"

Weston stopped so quickly in the middle of the hall that I nearly bumped into him. "What?"

"If he hasn't told you yet, I don't think it's my place to talk about it. But it was hard for a lot of us new guys in our freshman year. Toxicity runs deep in this sport."

I scoffed, almost upset at how casual his tone was. How accepting he'd become of the fact of the matter. "That's an understatement."

"He needs... time," Weston said. "Right now, he's in what we call the loop. And he knows how to get out of it on his own, but I don't like leaving him to do that alone. He deserves to have someone. I want to stay, but Hart's with Nat and... he's in worse physical shape than all of us. I need to check on him."

I nodded, admiring his dedication to them. "I... I don't know if I'll be of any help to David, but I will do everything I can."

Weston's gaze softened. "It's not always like this. David's... not going to always be like this. He just needs more time to heal."

"Go find Nat and Hart," I ordered. "I got this."

"Are you sure?" Weston lingered at the cracked door, unconvinced as he studied me.

"Of course, I'm sure." I pushed open the door, stepping inside. "Where is he?"

"Bathroom." He studied me for a second longer and decided something about my determined gaze was trustworthy. "He just went in when I went to get you. Don't let him stay there for too long. Call me as soon as you feel in over your head. I'll be back as soon as you need."

"Okay." My back straightened as I readied myself for heaven knew what.

"Promise?" he asked.

I nodded, adamant. "Swear it."

"Thank you," Weston whispered before disappearing back down the hall.

I shut and locked the door behind him, turning around to an empty, dimly lit room and the sound of running water in the bathroom. Someone had stripped the bed bare. There were no dishes in the sink. The air smelled of Clorox. It looked as if it were move-out day, the space void of any sense of life. The thought made my throat tighten.

"David?" I called as I hurried over to the closed bathroom door.

"Damn it, I told him not—one sec," he said, voice muffled by the noise of running water.

I waited. One minute turned into two, and five, and ten. The water kept running. My jaw tightened as a sinking feeling weighed down my stomach. "David?"

No response this time. I banged with my fist and pressed my ear against the door. A million and one scenarios were running through my mind. None good, or healthy, or happy. When he didn't respond to the banging, I tried the doorknob. It turned, allowing me in with little effort.

The bathroom was bright with harsh white overhead lighting that hurt compared to the low lighting in the room. I blinked a few times, trying to reorient myself.

The air was heavy and hot with steam. David stood bent over the sink, washing his hands. A pair of black sweats hung low on his waist. He was shirtless, dots of purple bruises formed underneath his ribcage. David leaned over the sink as if he needed to get closer. As if something had fallen down the drain and he'd risk it all to retrieve it.

"David?" I asked again.

"One second." He didn't look up. I moved closer, standing near his elbow. My gaze fell on his hands, and the hot water ran over them. His skin screamed red, raw from the heat and scrubbing. David scraped a bar of soap across his palm, between his fingers. He didn't waver for a second, as if on a mission to rid his skin of something that wasn't showing up to the naked eye.

"David," I repeated softer. I wanted to reach for him, but the tightness in his shoulder made me hesitate. Despite his height and muscle, David looked as though he'd shatter if disturbed.

"I just need a minute," he said, still scrubbing with intense focus.

"I've given you a lot of those," I joked in a low voice, threading carefully.

"You're not supposed to be here." David looked up at me through the mirror. His brow glistened with sweat, eyes rimmed red from exhaustion. There was a sense of hard desperation in him that pierced through my chest. His armor shed, and from the looks of it, not of his own volition.

"You should go," he said, trying (with no success) to make his voice harder.

I shook my head, refusing. "Weston called me; he didn't want you to be alone. I didn't want you to be alone."

David's chuckle was devoid of all humor. He started another round of scrubbing, this time employing his nail to scrape the skin. "I don't want you here. I don't want you to..."

He took a deep breath as if there wasn't enough oxygen in the room. My brow furrowed at the hot steam engulfing his bruised fingers. I moved close enough to turn off the tap. David's hand gently covered mine before I could switch it off, fingers on fire as he said, "I'm not done."

"You're done," I insisted, placing my free hand between his shoulder blades. The muscles underneath my palms flexed with tension.

"I'm not." He met my gaze, icy determination in his dark eyes. "Please, Yara, let me finish. Please."

This was more than just a different side of him. It was a truth underneath the well-laid concrete. The darkness shoved into the basement of the boarded-up house.

My mind raced, wondering how I could pull him back toward me when he was tugging in the opposite direction. I felt so unprepared, so ill-suited for providing the support and comfort. I knew exactly what he was doing. Exactly how deep his mind had buried logic underneath the rubble. I understood so deeply I could almost feel the burn of the water myself.

"How many rounds do you have left?" My stomach twisted at having to ask. At the thought of him going on for any longer than he already had.

Color drained from his face when he realized I knew exactly what was going through his mind. Shame latched itself onto his jaw, making movement near nonexistent.

"I don't know," he whispered, turning his gaze to the running water. His hands returned to the burning stream. "I don't know."

He sounded determined to stay trapped, as if this was all he could become and all the world would allow him to be.

"You know," I urged, ignoring the tightening in my throat. "How long? Give me minutes. Or rounds. Something."

"It's... I'm not..." He shook his head as if to shake off the weight of it all. "Go, Yara. Please. You weren't supposed to be here and see this. I never wanted you to see this."

He looked at me when he whispered the last part. His shoulders dropped in defeat. He looked so much younger and isolated, like the middle-school version of himself, just trying to get through the day. Not knowing why he needed to count the cracks in the sidewalk or tap the edge of his desk before getting up. My heart felt like it'd shatter into a million pieces, but I barely blinked. He couldn't have me breaking down. I was of no use to him in shambles. It was his turn to be looked after. My turn to love him through this.

"I don't want you here," David's cold order had morphed into a quiet plea. "Not when I'm like this."

"Well, that's too bad." I wrapped my hand around his arm. The skin-to-skin contact gave us both something to find shelter in. "Because my plan was to stay here the entire night.

And you know how much I hate a change of plans. So tell me how many."

He swallowed; his neck bobbed as he stared at the soap in his hands. "Until it stops hurting. I can't stop until I stop remembering or else..."

"Or else what?" I snuck my hand closer to the faucet as he spoke, moving as slowly as my trembling fingers would allow. Much like my picking, the burns on his hand were the punishment he never deserved. My eyes burned with frustration with his foster parents. He never deserved to be this alone and to feel this helpless.

"Or else I won't make it." David released a shaky exhale. "I'll be stuck in New Harbor. I won't make the team. I won't figure out how to stand up to Mary or that other asshole in my nightmares. I will die on a concrete floor at the bottom of a staircase he pushed me down, and no one will find me. No one will... want me. I'll be nothing. If I don't learn how to live with this pain, I will be nothing."

I bite the inside of my bottom lip to keep it from trembling. There were no words that'd undo the pain and horror that had latched onto his soul for over a decade. But I could pull him into me. I buried my hands in his hair, coaxing him to rest his forehead on mine as I whispered, "None of that's true. It never was, never will be."

David shook his head. His frantic breath was hot against my skin.

"You are everything to me, David," I said firmly. "I need you. I want you. That's not going to change anytime soon."

My words gave him pause.

"Hurting yourself like this will not ensure your ticket out of New Harbor. You've already done that. You made West-brooke's team. You figured out how to stand up to more than just those assholes." I cupped his jaw, urging him to open his eyes and meet my gaze. "You figured out how to live. That's not nothing, David. It's everything."

His hands went slack, fingers curled around the edge of the sink. I took advantage of his retreat. The air buzzed with silence when I shut the water off. David frowned at my hand on the faucet handle but said nothing. He let me wrap my arms around his neck and bury my face in his collar. David's shaking arms wrapped around my waist, pulling me tight against him. His heart continued to race, pounding hard enough that I vibrated along with him.

"It's everything," I promised over and over again.

30

I GOT David into bed and crawled underneath the sheets with him. The night was quiet, most of the campus either asleep or abandoned thanks to the upcoming weekend.

David rested his head on my chest, tightly fisting my shirt as he tried to calm his breathing.

"I'm sorry," he murmured after almost half an hour of silence. "I'm so sorry, Yara."

I frowned, my heart aching at the pain in his tone. "You have nothing to apologize for."

"I do." He held onto me tighter. "I never meant to be like this in front of you."

"If you can't be like this in front of me, then who else?" I buried my fingers in his hair, trying to distract myself from the blur of tears in my eyes. "We're together, aren't we?"

He remained quiet. The hum of the heater turning on, filling the cracks in between our conversation.

"Aren't we?" I repeated, feeling a little more desperate as I nudged the top of his head with my nose.

David readjusted, pushing himself up so that his head rested beside mine on the pillow. "I want to be."

I tucked my hands underneath the side of my face, trying to make out the outline of him in the darkness. "So then, we are."

"Is it that easy?" He spoke so low I wanted to reach out and touch the curve of his lips to feel the words.

"Why wouldn't it be?"

"Because nothing ever really is."

"We could be," I whispered. "Don't you think?"

The hope in my voice couldn't be hidden, nor could my uncertainty. The decade between us had proven one thing and one thing only: we were very good at being each other's villain.

No hint of fondness had snuck its way in between us until this semester. The ground on which we tread was untested. We couldn't stake promises here. He was too logical to stake dreams. And I was too cowardly to stake hope.

Instead of answering, David kissed me. It wasn't hot and desperate like the ones before. This kiss revealed an ache for something deeper, a longing for something that may never come to fruition.

I answered the pressure of his lips with evidence that I wanted him, this, and us, that I would never hold what I saw tonight against him. His pain wasn't something I stocked up on to be used as ammunition any longer.

"I think this part of me," he said against my lips. "Will be difficult for you. If you see me like this enough times, you'll get lost in the dark along with me. We can't help each other if we're both lost."

I shook my head, rejecting his reasoning. "I'd rather be lost together than alone."

"I'd rather be alone than hurt you anymore than I already have."

My eyes stung at his confession. "So... what the hell does that mean? Are you... are we..."

David pulled me into his chest. It wasn't until my cheek pressed against his shirt that I realized my tears had finally shed. The damp cotton softened underneath my confusion.

"Let's sleep." David rubbed my back, trying to calm my trembling. "We need rest."

"I can't sleep." I gripped his shirt, pulling it closer to my nose so I could breathe every bit of him in. This may be the last night he let me do it, the last time he let me in.

"I don't know how you could right now," I said, resentment sharpening every word on my tongue. "How could you even consider sleep after what you just said?"

"I'm not taking this lightly." David matched my tone. "I'd never take this lightly—"

"Then why would you say something like that?" I pulled out of his grasp and sat up. My hands shook as I shoved off the blanket, the heat of the bed too much to manage along with my anger. "Why would you ever say something like that and expect me to close my eyes and wait for the resolution tomorrow? David, do you understand what you've done to me this year? I can't wake up without wanting to hear your voice. I can't read a book without wanting to know what you'd think. I can't laugh without wanting you to do the same."

I sucked in a breath, so ashamed at how quickly I'd fallen or how deeply these feelings for him had rooted within my core. Uprooting would take years. Healing the wound would take longer.

"Yara," David said firmly. He'd sat up too and cupped my cheek, turning me to him. A sliver of light from outside outlined the edges of his face. Seeing the hurt in his eyes was as sharp and painful as laying my hand on a burning stove. "Every part of me belongs to you, which is why the second I heard you on the other side of the door, I needed to be okay. I wanted to be okay because I can't stand the thought of you feeling like you need to fix me. I'm not whole, and I can't expect you to take that on. I'm not worth being with—"

"Stop trying to make the fucking decision for me," I snapped. "You're not the smartest in the room just because you can process and accept logic. Just because you can siphon off emotion. And you don't need to be fixed."

He shook his head as he brushed away a few rogue tears on my cheek.

"Then tell me I'm broken too," I challenged.

David frowned and didn't say a word.

"Go on," I continued. "Tell me I'm broken. Tell me my anxiety disqualifies me from finding someone who'll care for me. Tell me my hair-picking makes me impossible to love."

His jaw ticked, upset over my bait. "You're not. It doesn't."

"Then what makes you so different? So unique that the rules change for you?"

He looked ready to protest, but let out a low, exhausted chuckle. "You won't ever make this easy."

"I promised you, remember? I never will."

Something broke within him at those words. David closed the distance between us, his mouth crashing against mine. We found ourselves on our backs again, legs entangled in the cotton sheets.

"I need you to know that I'm going to give this my all," he said, breathless and resolute. "And maybe that won't be enough, but I will do it."

I didn't know if he meant us, his recovery from his disorder, or surviving the rest of this season. Either way, I nodded and told him, "I know."

———

I WOKE to the chill of early morning seeping through the windows and the tempting smell of bacon. David stood with his back to me, shirtless, in the kitchen area as he transferred a pancake to a stack. The second I rustled underneath the covers, he looked up.

"Morning." David's smile was small, but it lit up his eyes in such a way that they provided far more warmth than the mountain of blankets I was under. He clicked off the burner and stacked one last pancake before coming over.

"I was going to make you something," I whispered as he crawled back into bed beside me.

"Got to wake up—" He took his time kissing me. I tried to pull back because of my morning breath, but his groan in protest was too convincing. "—earlier than this to beat me to it."

"How are you feeling?" I pulled back to get a good look at him. An image of him scrubbing away at the sink flashed across my mind. David's brows tightened, probably thinking of the same thing.

"Be honest," I told him when he shook his head, ready to brush the question off. "It's just me."

He kissed me again, parting my lips gently to offer a hint of tongue. I lay back down with him on top of me, my thighs wrapped around his waist.

"And don't distract me." I laughed against his mouth.

"Demands, demands," he tsked, his body relaxing into mine. "Is this how every morning is going to be with you?"

I stilled at the thought of getting so familiar with David's bed and feeling like it was as much mine as his. My stomach fluttered, wanting that vision for the future so badly.

"Every," I said, trying to keep my voice light and gaze without too much meaning. Too much desire.

"Good," he whispered into my ear before playfully

nipping at the lobe and sitting up. "Want me to make you a plate?"

"Only if you talk to me after we eat," I bargained. "Really talk."

David brushed his thumb across my chin before nodding and climbing out of bed. "Alright, Daredevil. You win this round."

"I've won them all."

He chuckled. "What's this revisionist history?"

"A victor's right."

"You mispronounced 'wrong.'"

I laughed. David came back to bed with one plate, which we shared, and a glass of orange juice for just me. He cut the pancake into triangles before I could touch it. And he made sure the bacon stayed out of the syrup. I kept looking up at him between bites, my mind just now catching up to the fact that I wasn't just on good terms with someone I'd routinely argued with for years. I was in bed with him, having breakfast, and wishing time would slow to a stop because the minutes were already moving too fast for my liking.

"What does really talking sound like?" he asked after dumping our dishes in the sink. David came back to bed with a warm, wet washcloth. I froze when he reached for my hand and carefully wiped the sticky parts of my fingers.

"Like you telling me what happened," I spoke quietly because being too loud could risk waking yesterday's fears, and I needed them to fall asleep for good. "Why it happened?"

"It's... a lot goes into it." He cleared his throat, still focusing hard on cleaning me up.

"I can handle a lot. You've seen my family," I reminded him. "I handle a lot."

He smiled at me but shook his head. "I don't know how to do this. Talk to someone I like in a romantic sense."

"Just start with what Weston couldn't tell me," I tried with a gentle squeeze of his hand. "Start with the coaches' freshman year."

Red stained his neck, branching up to his cheeks. "Freshman year?"

I nodded. "Just the parts you can share. The parts that aren't too hard."

"It's all hard." He stopped wiping my fingers, pulling his hands back into his lap where he stared.

I allowed the silence to wash between us, waves lapping up all his hesitation. If it took hours, days, months, or years, I would wait. However long it took for him to feel safe enough, I would wait.

David eventually took a deep breath. He tossed the towel inside his bathroom door and leaned horizontally across the bed. His gaze was trained on the ceiling as he said, "As a freshman on the football team, you expect a bit of hazing — it's technically not condoned, but that doesn't really matter. Not if no one speaks up. And we're conditioned not to speak up. Especially those of us who have little left off that field."

I bit my tongue and ran my fingers through his hair, brushing it off his forehead.

He closed his eyes as he continued, sinking himself into a dark world because maybe that made sharing this with me easier. "There were two particular staff members who fed into it with the senior guys. They were younger, so the line between staff and player was blurred. Lukas was one of them. I was... they were... it was the most bruised I'd been in a long time. Far worse than anything my aunt's boyfriend could have done."

My gaze flickered to his chest. White scars crisscrossed his skin like the pattern of a chain-linked fence. I remember him telling me not to push him. How it was a trigger. I pressed a kiss to his forehead, and when I pulled away, his eyes were open and on me.

"I didn't tell anyone for the first few months." He rubbed a hand over his face. "Very... pathetic."

"Afraid," I corrected in a hard tone. "Hurt. Mistreated. Not pathetic, David. Never pathetic."

"What kind of person stands there and lets someone..." He sucked in a breath and shook his head, no longer meeting my gaze. "Hurt them. Hurt them over and over and over."

His chest rose and fell more quickly as he spoke. I brushed circles across his cheeks, trying to keep him calm.

"A person who's trying to survive in the only way they know because they've been doing it this way all their life." I cupped his cheek and turned him back to me. "Being quiet was how you learned to protect yourself. You don't deserve blame for that."

"I just wish I could have been better."

My jaw tightened at the thought of those men taking advantage of their power and wielding that power against the man who lay before me, a man who was brilliant, thoughtful, and vulnerable. The man who'd closed himself off in fear of being hurt again by those he wanted to trust the most.

"You didn't have a job or a family you could count on," I said. "No power. No expectations. David, all you should have had to worry about was playing a game you loved and finding yourself at university. You should have been worrying about crappy cafeteria food and shared bathrooms."

He laughed through the hurt and covered his hand over mine.

"When I look at you, David," I said. "I see a guy who fought tooth and nail to be here, who didn't let the external or internal stop him from being extraordinary. I see a guy who opened himself up to me even though his past told him that was the most dangerous thing to do. David, I don't see what anyone did to you. I see only how incredible you've become."

"I want to believe that." He squeezed my hand and kissed the palm. "I really do."

"You will," I promised. "One day you will. For now, I'll believe it for both of us."

31

"We should get you a change of clothes," David suggested after his second time going down on me. I groaned into the pillow still covering my face. Pulses from my climax made it too hard to think, let alone plan a trip outside our four walls.

He chuckled, massaging the inside of my thighs like the tormentor he was. "I know you love it, baby. But it's Sunday. We've been marathoning for over twenty-four hours. And I need to feed you more than just pancakes."

I snatched the pillow off my face and sat up. "Did you just... call me baby?"

David shook his head, brows raised. "Not if you didn't like it."

"I hated it," I teased with a smile and tossed the pillow at him. He dodged it with little to no effort.

"Really?" He wrapped his hands underneath my thighs and tugged me down the mattress so my ass met his knees.

"That may be the cheesiest pet name of all time," I murmured, breath catching when his thumb found my clit. How blood still rushed to the spot, I didn't know. All I knew was that I'd seen so many stars in the past couple of hours, I may as well be in another solar system.

"Then why did you get wetter after I said it?" David leaned closer but kept his mouth just out of reach.

"Correlation's not causation."

"I beg to differ," he whispered in my ear and slipped two fingers inside me to match the gentle teasing of his thumb.

"I wish you would." I pressed kisses on his bare shoulder.

"Mm?" he hummed with his eyes half-closed. He did that a lot, seemingly as satisfied with my pleasure as I was. David's concentration was unmatched, as was his ability to push me over the edge. I should have known from the second we started arguing with one another that his mouth could make me frustrated in more ways than one.

"Beg." I tucked my hand behind his head, fingers curling around his hair, and I pulled him into a kiss. His fingers moved faster as he swallowed my moans.

"I don't do that unless I'm being fucked," he confessed against my parted lips.

My heart jumped at the look in his eyes. David's fingers were soaked with me, and I clenched around him as I asked, "Would you let me do that then?"

"Fuck me?" David let out a ragged breath, in disbelief and utter excitement. "Only if you want. *Really* want to."

"I want to," I promised. The thought of me fucking him opened up a whole new door of pleasure. My vision dotted as I came onto his fingers while imagining what he'd sound like when I pushed into him.

"You sure?" he asked, searching my eyes when I came back down from the climax.

I nodded with a lazy smile. "Unbelievably."

"Have you ever done anything like this?" He spoke faster, excited by this new prospect.

"Used a strap-on a couple of times," I whispered,

exhausted from the multiple orgasms but more than willing to push through it all for more. "With a girl, though."

He nodded and kissed me. As soon as he pulled away, he said, "I'll walk you through it."

David pushed off the bed to retrieve the toy. I used the small window to brush away the tears of ecstasy that'd painted the corners of my eyes and tugged on my hair tie that'd gotten lost in my twisting and turning.

"It's new," he said when he came back. The dildo was purple, long, and veiny. My hand strained around its circumference. I sighed at the weight. At the weight of all of this.

"Lie down," I told him.

"I could help you —"

"David." I took the toy, claiming it for my own. "I got it. Just speak up if I do too much."

"Alright..." He followed orders well enough, but there was a teasing hint of uncertainty in his voice.

"Just relax." I swung my leg over his midsection when he settled onto the bed and lowered myself onto his stomach.

He folded his arms behind his head, hard muscles flexing. The guy looked like a dream. I got tunnel vision, realizing I wanted to be his for as long as time exists. I leaned down to kiss him, and he responded with equal dedication.

"Yeah, I know," he whispered when I pulled back, breathless and scared. "That's how I felt when I saw you from this angle. Why did you think 'baby' slipped out?"

I laughed, grateful for some humor to crack my shell of nerves. "Because you liked it. You're some secret softie who likes terms of endearment."

David's chuckle faded into a moan when I kissed my way down his jaw and neck. Before I got to his chest, I paused and asked, "Is this okay? Kissing here? Touching here?"

My gaze lingered on his soft white scars.

"It is." He nodded, but before I could touch them, he

caught my hand and pulled it up to his mouth. David kissed each of my fingers and then my palm. My breath shuddered when he pressed a final one on my wrist, right on top of my pulse.

"Thank you." He met my gaze. Sincerity warmed his dark eyes. "For asking."

I smiled, ignoring the sad tug of my heart at the reason behind having to ask. I pushed away the thought, centering myself once more on this moment and promising myself I'd do whatever I could to keep him in the present, too.

My lips brushed across his skin lightly. I kissed every scar twice over before moving down his stomach. Once I got to his waistband, I took longer, breathing in the mix of his bar soap and natural scent. I could see the hard imprint against his blue boxers. I ached to feel him inside me, but longed to push inside him even more.

"What are you doing?" he asked when I kissed him through the fabric for longer than necessary.

"Getting you ready," I said between kisses.

"I've been ready."

I shook my head and tucked my hand underneath his dick, pressing it into the fabric so my kisses were all the more frustrating.

David laughed through his moan. "You're cute."

"I know." I kissed him long enough for an impressive amount of pre-cum to darken the cotton.

When I finally pulled away, David sighed in protest. I pulled myself onto my knees, securing the harness.

"Off," I said, nudging my chin toward his underwear while still trying to get comfortable with the strap-on. With it secured, applying slight pressure on my core, an ache burned through me. My nipples hardened at the sight of the toy attached to me and the very hard, very patient David. I forgot how much I loved the high of offering pleasure.

"Sit up for a second," I said.

David sucked in a breath, impatient but willing. When he pushed himself up, I moved back to stand at the foot of the bed. I gestured with my fingers for him to follow, sitting on the edge. With his face aligned with the toy, I cupped his cheeks and said, "Take me in."

His neck bobbed as he swallowed.

"Look at me while you do it." I tugged on his hair, tilting his head up so his gaze would meet mine. "Okay?"

"Okay." David's hands wrapped around my hips, holding me steady. I held the toy level with his mouth. David parted his lips, taking in inch by inch while keeping his eyes locked with mine.

I couldn't tell who was more turned on by his mouth taking the toy in. But I knew we were equal in the sexual frustration of being this close and this trusting.

David's hands moved to my ass as I urged the toy further into his mouth. I pulled it out for a second to give him a break before pushing it back in, deeper.

"Can you take it?" I whispered with half of it buried inside. "All of it."

He nodded, moaning around the length.

"You sure?" I pulled back.

David's eyes pleaded with me, grip tightening for me to continue pushing.

I shook my head and pulled out. "My speed. My terms."

He sighed, swallowing a retort and nodding instead. I smiled at this rare hint of obedience.

"You're being so good," I complimented and pulled one foot up to place on the bed.

David's breath hitched at those words. He closed his eyes when I ran my fingers through his hair.

"And here I thought only saying mean things would garner this kind of reaction."

"Don't get used to it." David looked up at me. "I only enjoy the switch-up in bed."

"So do I." I pressed the dildo onto his mouth again. He parted his lips.

Despite wanting to see if he could actually handle the whole thing, I worried about pushing him too far, too fast.

"How do you know you can take it all?" I asked while brushing his hair off his face so he could focus on sucking the tip. "Do you practice?"

David smiled and released the dildo from his lips. It's downright criminal how sexy his mouth looked while being fucked, or how hot he was when he was taking it. I would never look at his mouth in the same way when he was talking back to me. And I didn't want to.

"No, I don't practice," he said simply. "I'm just trying to be good for you. Trying to impress."

"I'm impressed," I assured and guided him back to the dildo. This time it went even deeper. David held my gaze as he relaxed his throat and took nearly every inch in.

I'm soaked seeing the feat. Dying with the need to pull out and claim that mouth with my own while he took the dildo inside.

"Where's your lube?" I asked in a hoarse breath.

David's energy met mine, his dick veiny with the need to release. He'd lasted through two of my orgasms. I thought impressed might be too light a word for how I felt about him now. I couldn't say that without the risk of making his head even bigger. I'd have to deal with his ego after this.... so no matter how hazy sex made me, I had to remember that.

He moved to the top of his bed, reaching into the drawer of his bedside table. I accepted the bottle, pouring the lube onto my fingers and rubbing it across the toy. David touched himself while he watched me prep, barely hanging on. I offered him the lube next, and he prepped himself as best he could.

"You ready?" I asked.

He nodded and could barely get out the word, "Yes."

"Positive?"

"Yara." David's jaw tightened. He wrapped his arm around my waist and pulled me against his mouth. The kiss was hot and hungry, tongues clashing. "Give it to me."

"That's not how you beg."

"Please."

"With a little more humility." I kissed his nose and pulled back.

"*Please*, Yara. I need... I need you to give it to me."

"How?" I raised a brow, balancing myself on my knees above him.

"Like you're the only person who will ever be able to until the sun burns out."

"Do you want to be mine forever?"

"With every part of my fucking being," he pleaded, fingers tugging on my waist. "I want you to take so much of me, I'll never be able to think of anything else when I'm horny. When I'm alone at night, I want to remember you. I want to touch myself, thinking of the fantasy that is you. Please, Yara. I'll do anything for one second of being like this with you. I'll crawl on my knees. Let you have the next thousand dares. Fuck your pussy until you can't take it anymore. Whatever you need, I'll do it with so much pleasure. I want to give you so much. But I'm selfish enough to want to receive too."

"It's not that selfish," I said, breathless as I lowered myself, aligning with him. David relaxed when he realized he'd won me over. When he realized his begging was satisfactory.

"Thank you," he whispered.

"So polite," I mused with a smile. "Nice work."

He moaned at the praise, grabbing hold of my hand to

place it in the middle of his chest. I was hesitant about applying pressure at first, taken aback by his conscious placement.

David shook his head as if he could read my thoughts. "I want to feel you. I want to make new memories. Could you do that with me? Can we do that together?"

I took a deep breath, centering myself amid the heavy emotion bubbling to the surface. "I can try. I will try."

He smiled, grateful. "That's all I ask."

We kissed before I pushed inside him. It was a slow process that left us both buzzing. I glanced down for a second, watching the toy enter him. The moan that escaped my lips made his dick pulse between us.

"Okay?" I asked before sliding the rest of it inside.

David nodded, leaned forward to capture my nipple between his lips. I screamed out in pleasure, my nails digging into his shoulder blades. My breasts muffled his reply. As soon as I was completely inside him, I began moving my hips. David's tongue licked faster and harder, mimicking my motions. My hand found his dick, and I stroked up and down, finding a mind-numbing tempo that had us both crying out for more.

"Am I...?" He tried to speak through the strokes but couldn't get the words out.

I searched his gaze, finding what he wanted through those hooded eyes. "You're taking it well. So damn well. Just keep breathing."

"I want to last, but... you... you're so..." He closed his eyes, resting his head back on the sheets.

"There you go," I encouraged. "Breathe."

"Yara, I..."

I speed up a little, working my hand and hips in tandem. "You've got this. You got me."

"I don't think I can..."

"You did," I promised. I felt him reaching his peak. Pre-cum beaded at the swollen head. "You did enough. It's enough. You're enough."

My encouragement and praise broke the last barrier between us. David's gaze locked on mine as he proved I possessed every part of him.

"Fucking hell," he groaned out when his hot cum spilled across my hand and his stomach. "Fuck me."

I nearly come from the sight of him completely open, unbound by any judgment, sense of time, or place. He kept whispering my name, the syllables a prayer on his lips.

"I know," I said as I leaned forward to kiss his neck. "I know, baby."

David nearly choked with laughter. His grip around me tightened. I laughed when he flipped us over so that he was on top, far too amused at the red in his cheeks.

"I know how to wipe that little smirk off your face." He smiled as he threatened me.

"Thought you said we should get me a change of clothes," I teased.

"No point in doing that yet if I'm just going to take them off of you," David said as he undid the straps around my waist.

3 2

At 9 p.m. on a Sunday, David and I found ourselves drunk on chai lattes and in a maze of a home goods store.

"These places always smell like pine needles." David wrinkled his nose as we turned down yet another aisle of wicker baskets and half-priced ghost mugs. "And cinnamon."

"*You* always smell like pine needles and cinnamon," I retorted as I picked up another basket and tossed it into our stacked cart. David had made the mistake of driving me to the side of town where all the families lived and rich people invested. We'd come for Thai food and stayed for hand-dyed rugs.

"Then I don't know how you stand me," he lamented.

"I hold my breath in increments." I went to dump another basket in only for David to catch my wrist. The smile I offered made him laugh.

"You can't be serious." He kept hold of my wrist even though I successfully dropped the basket into the cart. His grip was more than welcome. I didn't know how we'd done it before, not touching. It seemed impossible now.

"I don't need this much stuff." David frowned at all the

items in the cart—most of which were hand-picked by yours truly.

"You told me you wanted your apartment to feel more like a home." I poked out my bottom lip, feigning offense. To be honest, I didn't care how sanitized David wanted to keep his place; I just liked the excuse of being able to spend more time with him. As the new week quickly approached, so did my responsibilities on the opposite side of campus, and his on the field.

"Yeah, and I bought some stuff that made it feel like that."

I raised a brow. "A couple of throw blankets and decorative pillows?"

"They're shaped like leaves."

I snorted. "Your eye for interior decorating is enviable."

"You love leaves."

"Is that why you bought them?"

David frowned, tugged my wrist to his mouth to give it a gentle bite that meant, fuck off.

"It is. And the blankets, they're there because that's my favorite color, right?"

He let me go and released an exaggerated sigh. "The world doesn't revolve around you, would you believe it?"

"Your world does." I poked his side, and he started pushing the cart again. "Doesn't it?"

There was no response, but the faint smile on his lips revealed a simple, velvet truth. I continued teasing because I didn't want him to see the thrill in my eyes. The excitement that undoubtedly made my smile too wide.

The guy liked me. Of course, the sex was an obvious indicator. But lots of people could have sex with someone —even someone they hated. Changing their lives was another story. And the more I thought about it, the more I realized just how much he'd changed for me.

"Yara?" David hooked his fingers around my jean hoops,

holding me back from running into another person's cart in the cross traffic of the aisle. "You okay?"

"Yeah." I blinked and looked up at him. "I'm good."

"Where'd you go?" he asked. Worry pulled at the corners of his mouth.

"Sorry about that! That was my bad," the owner of the other cart interrupted.

I turned to see a dark-skinned girl in a tight, long-sleeved training top that hugged an impressive curve of muscles and a pair of baggy black sweats. Her smile was apologetic, hair freshly braided, and her cart full of everything from purple bedding to specialty popcorn bags.

"See? What I tell you?" a guy as built and beautiful as her with his dark brown skin and an easy smile offered a teasing reprimand. He turned the corner with his own cart, full of everything she had, but in a different range of colors. "Told you not to race."

"You agreed to it." She rolled her eyes, but the teasing curl of her lips hinted she didn't feel an ounce of malice. The smile triggered a memory of someone I'd seen online.

"Are you..." I looked at the guy, recognizing him from her social media too. "Aderyn? Aderyn Jacobs?"

Her smile faltered a little as wariness set in. "Yeah... that's me."

"Uh oh," her boyfriend murmured with a grin. "You're in trouble now."

She waved him off.

"I'm Yara." I pressed my hand to my chest. When she blinked, confused, I added, "Emmy's friend. From the Black Women's org on campus. We've been emailing. I wanted you on a panel."

Realization softened her features. "Yara. Oh, man, I've been meaning to ask if you wanted to meet up before the panel. Talk shop. And maybe talk me off a cliff."

"Stage fright," her boyfriend explained when concern tugged at my brows.

"I'm not used to talking to people without a visor blocking my way." She waved her hand in front of her face. "This is Sam, by the way."

He gave me a wave. "How's it going?"

"I've been emailing you, too," I smiled. It was one thing to see their beauty online and another to see it in person.

"I promise to answer back." A bit of guilt bled through his tone. "Change of scenery's been hectic."

Aderyn and Sam were hockey players who'd transferred to Westbrooke from their old university, Mendell. A power couple in every sense of the phrase, it wasn't just the talent and the skill, but their sheer confidence that made it vital I work with them. They were so wholly themselves in a sport so commonly dismissive of them. The wisdom they had about being a Black person in a predominantly white space was invaluable. And if the org had nothing to glean from them, I surely did. I'd been lost at sea, wondering how to fit in. Watching a few interviews with them made it clear they never worried about the how, but instead fit in on their own terms.

"Is it okay if we exchange numbers?" I pulled out my phone, hand trembling mostly from excitement, partly from nerves at making a decent first impression. "Maybe we could get coffee on campus?"

Aderyn smiled and nodded. "I'd love that."

David rested a hand on my back, brushing light circles on the sliver of skin that peeked through my top. His small smile indicated he knew I was nervous. I tilted my head when meeting his gaze, a wordless challenge. There were butterflies in my stomach when he simply shook his head, showing this wouldn't be used as ammunition. No, this time he was quiet support. My stability.

"This is David," I introduced, finally with some of my bearings once more. "My boyfriend."

I expected some internal resistance after saying that for the first time and really meaning it. The label wasn't fake any longer. But resistance never showed. The label was a seamless fit. A transition that felt as natural and familiar as the rising sun's warmth against my skin. When I met his gaze, I knew from the softness in his eyes that he felt the same. My boyfriend felt the sunrise.

"I DON'T THINK we've gone a day without talking since the dares started," I mused Monday morning when we ruefully untangled ourselves from one another after the most cathartic weekend of our lives.

"I know we haven't." David was in the steamy bathroom, trying to see through the fog from my recent shower as he shaved.

I snorted. "You don't know that."

"I know it." He turned on the tap to rinse off his razor. His gaze remained on me through the mirror, watching as I tugged on my underwear and pants.

"Yeah, well, according to you, you know everything," I muttered under my breath.

"What was that?" He raised an amused brow and turned off the water to hear me better.

"Nothing." I shrugged on my jacket with a smile. Messing with him would always be my favorite pastime, no matter how many times we slept together. In fact, the jabbing made sex more fun. It'd taken me over a year, but I'd willingly admit to having a fetish for back and forth. Pushback would always be my favorite brand of foreplay.

"There's never nothing with you." He stepped out of the bathroom, clean-shaven and smelling like spring.

"I have to go." I sat on the couch and tugged on my socks, ignoring the look on his face when he came closer. "I have a lot of work to do."

David kneeled in front of me. "So do I."

His hand cupped my chin, guiding me toward his lips.

"You're not acting like it," I murmured right before he kissed me. David took his time, pulling me far away from my ever-looming task list so I was weightless for a moment.

"Aren't I?" David teased me with one last kiss and unlaced my boot for me to slip my foot in.

I fought the urge to tug him back to bed as he tied both boots.

"All set." He tapped the toe of the boot before pushing off the floor to go back to the bathroom.

I swallowed a sigh and pretended not to be annoyed at his ability (or at least, acting chops) to walk away without so much as a glance over his shoulder.

"What have you got planned this week?" he asked from the bathroom.

I pressed my fingers to still-tingling lips as I packed my bag. "The... my org's masquerade."

"This Saturday, right?"

"Right." I pulled the bag over my shoulder.

"See you then."

I froze, but he added nothing else as he unloaded his cleaning supplies from underneath the sink.

"See me then?" I asked.

He made a noise of approval, and I laughed.

"Oh, come on." My smile faded. "You're joking."

David looked at me then and shook his head. "That's a mean thing to joke about."

I laughed. "You've joked about worse."

He tilted his head from side to side. "Alright, sure."

"You're actually coming?"

"Why wouldn't I?"

"Because we've only just started sleeping together, thus making me the newest entry on your list of things you can tolerate."

"You're not giving yourself enough credit." David leaned against his counter, abandoning the cleaning supplies and lending me his full attention instead. "You've been an entry since Weston's birthday party."

"What an honor," I teased.

"When did I become an entry for you?" he asked.

I knew that slight twist of his mouth. The crossing of the arms nearly hid the flexing of his fingers. David was fishing for something vital. Some assurance amidst uncharted waters. I was too wrapped up in him to deny a simple request.

"When you met my family," I said. "When you told me you liked how mean my brother was to you because that meant I had someone to protect me."

"I'll take it." David nodded with a smile. "It's a little later than expected, but I'll take it."

I laughed. "I'm glad you approve."

33

THE RAIN POUNDED against the metal roof of the warehouse like a budding threat. Dark clouds had taken up residence this morning and continued unpacking until late in the evening. The unusual wet winter storm felt like a bad omen. I didn't say as much out loud when I shed my rain jacket and flicked on the lights of the warehouse.

"How's it looking?" I asked Haven, who'd been uncharacteristically nose deep in her phone all morning. I continued to flip on lights and straightened up a couple of tablecloths as I waited for her answer. The rest of our org members were en route, ready to put a couple of final touches on the space before we opened the doors tonight.

The other orgs failed to send people to help with set-up and went ghost in our group chat. Fury burned through my veins these last couple of days as we did our marketing push and barely got so much as a repost on anyone's end. But I couldn't let it drag me down. I focused on doing whatever it took to make them regret not believing in us, or this, or me. My road to non-vengeful, non-petty thoughts was long and full of hazards.

"Haven?" I stopped in front of the makeshift stage when I realized she wasn't following me. Her glossy lips and red-stained cheeks did wonders in emphasizing her dismay. My stomach dipped, mind racing to solve a problem I wasn't yet briefed on.

"I haven't checked the ticket sales in a couple of days." She looked up, eyes wide as tonight's full moon. "It was getting so dire."

My shoulders sagged. "Okay… that's fine. What is it now?"

We couldn't survive with low numbers this late in the game. My face burned at the thought. I held my head high and considered everything I put into this event. I hadn't gone down without a fight, and that was something to be proud of.

"Yara, we're sold out." Haven came to my side, holding her phone so I could witness it for myself. But even with the screen brightness turned all the way up and the font large and clear, I couldn't make out a thing.

"Three hundred and fifty." Haven bit down on her bottom lip, holding back a squeal.

"This is a cruel joke," I whispered.

"It's the truth." She swatted my arm with the back of her hand. "Log in to your phone and see."

I did just that and saw the same beautiful number. "Holy… what happened?"

Haven shrugged. "Covee's brilliant marketing push? Indie's work on word of mouth? Your boyfriend?"

"My boyfriend?" I frowned, confused about how David, a complete left turn, had anything to do with this.

"See this spike in stats right here?" She pointed to a line stretching past the thousand-view mark. "David posted about it on his socials."

"You follow David on his socials?" I laughed, amused as I studied her.

"Yeah, after you refused to, but still wanted to look for dirt." She playfully poked her elbow into my side. "Remember?"

"Oh, right." That was eons ago, sophomore year, before I built up the courage and fuck-it mentality to just text the guy. "He didn't tell me."

"You know what this means?"

I blinked, lost in a daze of gratefulness for David and my girls. "What?"

"At sixty a head, my love, we're looking at over twenty thousand." Haven's eyes were aglow with the knowledge I wouldn't be going into debt over a student organization. My heart jumped at the realization as well. Twenty grand, in addition to our fundraising, put us smoothly in the realm of paying off all our debts, treating the girls, and leaving an impressive cushion in the savings account for next semester.

I pulled Haven in for a hug. We squeezed each other as we spun around.

It wasn't life-changing work. We wouldn't be remembered as the women who raised a quarter of a million for health research or donated enough money to fund a soup kitchen for an entire year. But getting the org out of debt was something. It was enough to lighten the load of the women who came after us. Enough to set them up for success.

"I..." I tried, then laughed, before nearly crying. "I think that was truly stressing me out."

Haven pulled back to make sure I wasn't too far gone in the depressed department before joining me in laughter. "You think, love?"

We continued laughing.

"God, I need to break and just..." I said through my laughter.

"Just?"

"Finally, take an art class." The rest of the weight on my chest disappeared. "I'm awful at it."

"Don't say that."

I tilted my head to the side, giving her a 'come on' tilt with my brow.

"It's a challenge for you," Haven tried and tucked a few of my fresh goddess braids off my shoulders. "A big challenge. But you'll get there."

I continued to smile, feeling far more warmth than sting from her assessment. "It'll lead nowhere, but it's fun. And that's okay, right? Having fun. Not doing things just because it'll lead to something bigger than that?"

"Of course." Haven's expression sobered. "You deserve to enjoy life, Yara. Stop with all the full steam ahead and take an art class. Be bad at something and see that the clock keeps ticking."

———

THE WAREHOUSE'S walls glowed blue, and the air was warm enough to shield us from the persistent cold outside. Our grunge fairytale had been embraced coming off the tail end of Halloween–just as I hoped. The crowd comprised a mix of masquerade masks and black tulle. My elbows and shoulders continued to be tapped and tugged, with a pairing of congrat-ulations.

"You pulled through." Anthony stopped me on my second round of the room. Each time I'd looked for David, and each time I'd failed. There'd been a large group of football players that'd filtered in soon after the doors opened, but he hadn't been among them. And he hadn't been answering his phone. Worry pinched at my stomach, but I tried to keep breathing and keep positive.

"Yeah." I scanned the room. The music was loud enough

to get the blood pumping, but not so much so that we'd get a noise complaint... yet.

"It's impressive," Anthony continued. "You should be proud."

"I am." I nodded, still distracted. I found Hart, Weston, and Nathaniel near the refreshment table and nearly dipped in that direction. But before I could make any ground, Anthony said,

"We should meet and plan something for next semester. A BSU and BWD event. It'll be great."

I turned back to him. Once upon a time, that would have been music to my ears. Not an outright approval, but definitely as close as I would get from him.

"I've been emailing you about a joint event for years." I kept a neutral tone even though my insides were buzzing from the vindication. I'd worked for three years to earn a second glance from every org president on this campus. I knew it was all about numbers; it's always been that. But deep down, I thought if I showed them who I was and how smart the people in my org could be, then maybe, just maybe, that would be enough.

"And now you've proven you can put something together," he said with a half-shrug. "So? Are you free for a chat next week?"

I touched the tip of my tongue to my top lip, nodding as I considered. "I'll get back to you on that. For now, enjoy the party."

I would email him. Most likely tomorrow. But tonight, I wanted to soak in the small win and petty upper hand I'd gained. Turning the other cheek was great and all, something I was raised to do, but giving someone a taste of their own medicine was too satisfying to ignore. I'd grow up... one day.

"Hey," I greeted the guys. My smile was bright as I rode off the high of leaving Anthony without a definitive plan. "You guys enjoying yourselves?"

"Top tier." Hart gestured to the room. "You've outdone yourself."

I laughed. "You've never been to one of my events."

"It's an educated assumption," he promised. "You always outdo yourself. Of that, I'm sure."

"Impressive," Weston agreed. "I wouldn't expect any less."

"It is very nice," Nathaniel said. I could barely hear his low, deep voice over the music. His small smile made me feel more accomplished. Tonight would be a record for wins, I was sure of it.

"Have any of you seen David?" A simple question that left them speechless. I went from zero to ten in suspicion. "Well?"

They exchanged subtle looks, reading one another's minds for clues on how to avoid revealing to me what appeared to be buried.

"I'm sure he's around here somewhere..." Hart scanned the room like he was looking hard.

"Definitely." Weston nodded and had a look himself. "In the meantime, tell us how you figured out this whole renting and zoning thing for orgs."

"This had to cost an arm and a leg," Hart agreed. "Maybe even your firstborn."

"You want to talk shop?" I asked flatly.

"We love a good location," Weston attempted to smooth over their kinks. "Hosting parties is kind of our favorite pastime."

"Sure," I said, not believing a word. "For your secret society, right?"

"Secret society?" Weston asked, brows knitted in confusion, while Hart simultaneously said, "Right."

I snorted when Hart tried to discreetly nudge Weston with

his elbow and get him on board. I scoffed and turned to the one person I knew wouldn't lie to my face right now.

"Where is he?" I asked Nathaniel. "Do you know?"

Nathaniel scratched the back of his head, but at least ignored the guys' looks of warning. "There was an emergency."

"An emergency?" I asked, blood pressure rising.

"Not anything major," he promised quickly. "Something to do with people sneaking in alcohol and underage attendees and cops."

"An emergency that involves cops at my event?" I pressed my hand to my chest. "That I didn't know about?"

"Covee, Indie, and David wanted to handle it," Weston said, talking slow and calm like it'd relax me amid the budding crisis. "They wanted you to have fun."

"We all do," Hart chimed in.

"And you were for a moment." Weston pointed toward the dance floor.

"Very interesting moves," Hart assured.

"It was... my song." My cheeks burned at how people had been watching me throw caution to the wind for the first time, and I had no idea.

"David told us to wait until he texted and then alert you," Nathaniel said. "Tonight's a big deal; he wanted to lighten the load."

My shoulders relax slightly. I took a breath because this wasn't worth getting upset over. This was what I'd dreamed of —someone who anticipated my needs and looked out for me before burnout came to collect the debts I so willingly and consistently raked up.

"And it looks like they've done their job," Weston noted, glancing over my shoulder.

David, Covee, and Indie made their way through the

crowd. Indie, the most energetic, with a glass in one hand and her shed jacket in the other.

"We're not going to jail," she sang, danced, and kissed both my cheeks.

"Hooray," I said. "So happy. I didn't even realize that was an option."

"Not anymore." Covee reached out to squeeze my hand as a greeting before taking a spot next to Weston. She looked shy and unsure by his side, but he didn't seem hesitant in the slightest with how quickly he wrapped his arm around her waist and pulled her into him. Indie started chatting Nathaniel's ear off, and Hart jumped in as if he wanted a stake in the game.

"I have questions," I said to David. Not all for him, but he'd have to be the first lamb to slaughter.

"I may have answers on two conditions." He was dressed in a dark blue sweater and jeans. The second his aftershave hit my nose, I was taken back to his apartment, and that weekend and every kiss we'd had in between. My mouth went dry, and the curl of his smile hinted he knew exactly where my mind had gone. This wouldn't do. Not long-term. I'd have to get used to being with him if I wanted even the slightest chance of standing my ground.

"No conditions..." A lump caught in my throat when he cupped my cheek and stepped in close to kiss my forehead. David kept his lips pressed against my forehead for a couple of seconds as he breathed me in like I'd done with him.

"Condition one: You thank me for saving you a headache. An asshole was trying to get your party shut down," he murmured into my ear.

"Was it really that bad?" I pulled away enough to see his face. The outside world may as well have been streetlights cloaked in fog. The music, once blaring, now turned into a soft background lull, as if relenting to David's deep voice.

"You have enemies, you know that?" he asked with a teasing smile.

"So many," I joked. "You were number one, remember?"

He nodded with a chuckle. "Once upon a time."

"And now, you protect me from them."

David hummed in agreement. "I'm going to make a career out of it."

"So, I guess that deserves a thank you." My smile came easily. "Thank you for fixing a problem I didn't need right now. And for helping bring in this crowd. For looking out for me. Thank you, David."

"Was that so hard?"

I pressed my lips to his, surprising him only for a second before he relaxed into me. "Horribly."

"Well, get used to it," he whispered against my lips. "We're going to be very polite to one another moving forward."

"Cordial," I agreed.

"Chivalrous."

"Kind."

"Open," his voice softened.

"Loving," I tried, heat rushing to my cheeks as I waited for the taunt, tease, brush off.

"Loving," he agreed without hesitation. "Next condition."

I sighed as if I weren't full of the kind of joy that could solve every single one of my aches. "What is it?"

"You accept my dare," he said.

"I always do."

"I dare you to run away with me. After this semester, just you and me."

"Okay."

He laughed. "That's it? No inquiries about where we're going? If I planned to bring you back?"

I shrugged. "I don't need to know where we're going. And

I trust you enough to know you understand how important school is. How important my family and friends are. We'll be back in the spring."

David sighed, giving up a rouse that only lasted a split second. "Fine. You're right. I'll bring you back so we can walk across the graduation stage together again. But after that, well, I plan on taking you anywhere and everywhere for far longer. New Harbor's too small for you, Yara. I want you to grow. Stretch someplace where you aren't knocking limbs with family members and small-town gossips."

"I love my family members and small-town gossips." I smiled.

David chuckled. "You know what I mean."

I nodded. "I do. And I agree. I want to grow. To stretch out and see the world with you."

"That's a yes?"

"I told you, when the time comes, you'll be the one to forfeit," I promised before giving him another kiss.

34

WINTER BREAK

WE HUGGED the coastline for most of the drive. The waves and mountains sandwich us on a half-empty highway. Everyone else had flown south for the winter. David and I agreed that going further north was better.

"I have to think of something horrible for your next dare. I refuse to continue being soft," I said with my arm stretched outside the window, the cold air like pinpricks against my skin. David turned the heater to full blast because he knew I liked the windows down, despite the risk of hypothermia.

"Why not be nice?" David had one hand on the steering wheel and the other on my thigh. I kept glancing down at his grip as he applied the exact right amount of pressure. "You know, like I've been."

"I'm way nicer than you'll ever be."

"State of delusion give you the keys to the place yet?" he asked. "Need help going over the lease agreement?"

"Only if you're co-signing," I said sweetly.

David chuckled and squeezed my thigh. He turned on his blinker for the next exit, pulling off onto an abandoned gas station parking lot. I frowned when he unbuckled his seatbelt. The car stayed on as he opened the door.

"What are you doing?" I asked.

"We're switching." He got out of the car before I could protest, coming to my side to open the door for me.

"We're on vacation," I said, not moving an inch. Unfortunately, I couldn't cite my lack of a learner's permit because I'd spent two hours at the DMV last week to get it.

David's breath came out in small clouds, his cheeks splotched with red. Despite his thin sweater and gloveless hands, his smile was effortless, with patience firmly in place.

"Doesn't mean you shouldn't seize a learning opportunity," he said. "Come on, you need to get used to driving in the snow. Now that we're off the highway, it'll be less risky."

I frowned but unbuckled my seatbelt. My yielding came mainly from guilt about how red the tips of his ears had gotten. If he froze to death because of my stubbornness, I'd never forgive myself.

"Okay," David said once we'd settled into our respective spots. "Quick review before we go: what do you do if you hit a patch of black ice?"

My stomach dipped at the thought. I'd forgotten that was even a possibility. "I'm not going to."

"It's a what-if scenario."

"There's no what-ifs about it." My hands squeezed the steering wheel as if we were spinning out-of-control right now.

"I thought we worked through this not being in control of everything?" he asked.

"Progress isn't linear."

He laughed. "Fair enough, Daredevil. What you're going to do is avoid slamming on the brakes. That'll feel like the natural response, but it's not."

I swallowed. "I know."

"If you skid, turn in its direction." He covered his hand over mine, turning the wheel and squeezing me for a second before letting go. "Pull off to the side of the road once you've gained control, and we'll figure out our next steps. Keep breathing the entire time; you'll be fine. You got this."

My shoulders relaxed a bit at his vote of confidence. "You're not scared I'm going to get us in a serious accident?"

He shook his head. Trust made his dark brown eyes kinder. "Your capabilities are endless."

I snorted and put the car in drive. "Oh, how flattering."

"When I compliment you, I get flak. When I offend, I get flak," he mused. "What can I do that'll earn me something nice?"

"You don't like me nice." I pulled us out of the parking lot with timid hesitation. There were no cars on this stretch of road, and yet, I looked for any and every chance of interference.

"I like you in all kinds of ways," David promised.

I had to focus hard not to give him the satisfaction of a laugh. "Shut up. I have to focus."

"In case of fire and flood," he promised. "You've got it."

We were silent for a long stretch, the wind from the cracked windows and low hum of old Christmas music filling in the gaps between us. I kept my eyes on the road, grateful for David's reassuring hand on my thigh when I reached a slight curve as we made our way up the mountains.

"You're doing great," he said in a low voice as if he were afraid to disrupt my flow.

"I know."

I could hear the smile in his voice when he said, "I told you so."

I rolled my eyes but let him have it. And let me enjoy the gentle warmth of support. The quiet returned for a beat before David broke it again with,

"Nice work."

My smile was instantaneous. "Right?"

He hummed, thinking for a second before saying, "And because of that, I can't help but wonder when you are going to talk to your sister?"

The smile disappeared. "Which one? And about what?"

"Logan. About the accident," he said simply.

My gaze strayed from the road for a second to hunt for the punchline. "What?"

"It could help you get over some of your fear." His tone was serious and somber. "Help you get better at something you're more than capable of doing."

"I... no, I don't think I'm going to bring it up again." I winced and readjusted in my seat. David removed his hand, giving me space to try to manage my discomfort. "That would hurt us both."

"Or maybe it's exactly what you two need?" he asked in a low, unassuming tone. "Maybe if you talk to her, you'll see you didn't ruin her life. She loves you, Yara. That was more than clear when I met her. Your whole family does. And if they knew how much guilt you took on. How much you were hurting yourself—"

"I'm not doing that anymore," I interrupted and nudged my chin to my pack of gum in the car's cup holder. "I'm... doing better."

"So much," he agreed. "But this part of recovery could help with all the rest. I just think you should consider it."

I glanced at him again, only to find pure hopefulness in his eyes. As much as the idea of talking to my sister about old haunts made my stomach churn, David's concern counteracted the discomfort. I didn't feel half as hollowed out and lonely as I would if I had to face the possibility of talking to Logan on my own.

"I'll consider it," I promised.

His smile made the car warmer and brighter. "That's my girl."

I laughed like the words didn't give me a surge of pride and a sense of achievement. "Shut up."

———

I GOT us to our final destination without so much as a hint of a mistake. The weight on my chest vanished as soon as I pulled into a spot shielded by the trees of the dark, windswept forest.

"This is it?" I got out of the car and marvelled at the two-story log cabin that glowed from the inside with orange lights.

"Ours for a grand total of three days." David smiled. He'd been watching me since I pulled into the drive, tracking every change of my expression. "Not the runaway of our dreams— these are shockingly more expensive than I hoped— but it's something. It's a start."

"What do you mean? It's perfect." I grabbed his hand and squeezed.

His smile faded slightly. "I wanted someplace where we could stay longer so you could just relax in peace. But... well, let's just say once I get signed to a team, I'll make it up to you. We'll spend months in nice places."

I frowned and placed a hand on his cheek. "Hey, I would have stayed in your dorm with you and would have been perfectly happy. There's no reason for you to spend a ton of money."

"I know, but I want to. You're used to stuff like this, and I want to keep it that way." His confession pulled back a layer of insecurity. "You deserve it to stay that way."

I kissed him. My fingers tangled in the hair at the nape of his neck. I'd never expected David to keep up with the Joneses. Or for him to make enough to reach the level my parents found themselves. But having him so earnestly want to both mended and broke my heart.

"I'd be with you if you never got signed, you know that, right?" I whispered against his lips. "If you wanted to work some crappy job or live in a small apartment with noisy neighbors and awful water pressure."

"You would not." His laugh felt like a cool breeze on a perfect evening.

"I would." I brushed my nose against his. "I also would probably go home to take a decent shower now and then, but that's beside the point."

David continued to laugh and pulled me closer, so my cheek rested against his collarbone.

"You don't have to impress me," I promised, voice muffled from his shirt.

"Maybe not." He pressed his nose into my hair. "Regardless, I'm going to."

"Why are you so stubborn?" I playfully pulled away and shoved him in mock-disapproval.

"Learned from the best." He reached for my hand again. "Come on, I want to give you a tour."

Our weekend getaway had two bedrooms, a roaring fireplace, a fully stocked fridge, and a hot tub with a mountain view. The place was beautifully decorated, covered in browns, greens, and reds. Shag carpets felt like sinking into a layer of velvet. After a walk-through, David let me stay inside while he grabbed our bags. It hit me then: I was away on a trip with a guy I could barely stomach being in the same room with for more than an hour at the beginning of this year. And now, watching him go back and forth between the car and the house to bring in all my luggage had me fantasizing about spending years to come in plenty of vacation homes with him. And eventually, some permanent place where we could argue over furniture, wallpaper, and couch placement. I wanted to wear any and every jersey of his team, and come home to him after a long day at work, just to vent about how much my feet hurt and how exhausted my bones were.

"All good?" David closed the door, untangling his scarf and running a hand through his hair to brush off the lingering snow.

I nodded, heart skipping from holding onto all these wishful imaginings and realizing they could come true. I trusted David enough to believe every one of my dreams could come true. "What should we do first?"

"Whatever you want," he permitted with a shrug.

"Hot tub?"

"Already trying to undress, I see," he teased.

"I am." I smiled. "It was a long drive. And you've been ordering me around all day. Why did you think I kept read-justing?"

"You serious?" His jaw tightened at the thought of me turned on and ready for him.

"This time," I warned. "Don't think it'll always work."

"This time is enough for me." He shed his jacket and nudged his chin toward the hot tub. "Lead the way."

I laughed and did what I was told.... this time.

35

THE MAGNOLIAS WERE IN BLOOM, so Rose and Ren wanted to have the rehearsal dinner in our parents' backyard. The colors were orange, pink, and white. And the day shone brightly enough to burn away the remaining cold of winter. David and I arrived early enough that most of my family hadn't made it out to the backyard. My mom and Rose were the only ones buzzing around the tables, making sure the people hired to help set each table with the right amount of flowers and name cards.

"People from town will be here," David reminded me in a whisper. We stopped at the garden entryway, taking in the painting before committing to being in it.

"And?" I straightened his perfectly straight pink tie just to have an excuse to touch him. The white button-down and black slacks he wore were tailored to perfection thanks to yours truly. He'd protested the bill, but I presented a counteroffer of letting me ride shotgun all semester, and he folded.

"We'll be official." He looked down at me. "No takebacks."

"I can't change my mind after one measly wedding rehearsal dinner?" I raised an eyebrow in mock-horror.

"No, you can't; those are the rules," he joked.

"Well, in that case..." I kissed him. "Full steam ahead."

"But seriously." David brushed his thumb lightly across my jaw. "When they see us together, we're cemented in this story. Before now, we could have been a rumor. But after this, when we become small town official, anytime you go to the corner store, and they'll ask you how I'm doing."

"Sounds like my kind of story."

"Yeah?"

My smile faltered a little. "You disagree?"

"Even if this all ends in flames—"

"You're such a pessimist to even think that." I frowned.

"—I would have rather gotten a glimpse of a life with you than nothing at all. I don't mind being forever linked to you in story or otherwise. In fact, I downright prefer it."

Breathing became easier. I pressed my hands to his chest, feeling the steady heartbeat of a man I'd slowly but surely fallen in love with. "Good, because I'd hate to fight on a day like this."

"You're such a liar." He kissed me this time and bit my bottom lip before pulling away. "I'm going to go in the front and help your dad and Adam unload that truck."

"Alright." I nodded, disappointed to have to detach from him but grateful he was attempting to to be a part of something.

David wasn't used to this family thing. And after a handful of dinners with my family, I realized just how hard the change would be for him. But I also realized how willing he was to unlearn his lone wolf mentality and let people see him. Allow people close enough to love him.

"I really love seeing you two together." Logan appeared at

my elbow with a box of unsorted flowers stuffed inside. "You're always more present when he's here."

My cheeks burned, but I nodded. "He's grounding. Humbling. Annoying."

"All the makings of a perfect partner." Logan smiled and gestured with her elbow to a nearby table. "Want to help me sift through these? We're supposed to give them as gifts with the baskets."

"Those overstuffed, raffle-prize equivalent baskets?" I pointed toward a table holding baskets that were probably worth upwards of ten thousand dollars in merchandise.

Logan sighed and nodded. "One and the same. Rose wanted to impress."

"The gold water fountain wasn't enough? Or the Michelin star chef? Maserati getaway car—which isn't really a thing during rehearsals. They're supposed to drive away after the wedding."

My sister laughed. "Of course, none of that's enough; how could you be so silly?"

"How could I?" I agreed and followed her to the table. She unloaded the flowers and handed me the twine to cut for our ties. We worked in silence for a bit, and my nerves picked up like they usually did when I was alone with her with nothing to distract my mind with. Her fingers moved quickly and effortlessly. A small scar wrapped around her thumb from the accident, barely noticeable yet still screaming at me.

I'd been building up the courage to broach the topic of the car accident with her for weeks after David suggested it. My therapist agreed that I'd benefit from this conversation, no matter how hard it'd get.

My fingers itched to touch the top of my head. But I was two months into no-picking. And doing so now would only trigger a spiral in which I'd shift focus onto myself and not the issue at hand.

"Lo?" I asked.

She hummed in acknowledgement, not taking her eyes off her tying.

"Can I talk to you about something?" I swallowed, keeping my gaze on my task but not registering what my hands did.

Logan stopped working and glanced over at me. "Of course. Is everything okay?"

I nodded and tried to smile. "Mostly."

"And the small part?" she teased.

I took a breath, filling my lungs until they protested and emptied them until they ached. "I've been thinking about the accident. Our accident."

Her brow furrowed, but I couldn't read her eyes. "Really?"

"Yeah... well, I always think of the accident," I confessed. "Especially when I'm around you."

Logan's shoulders sagged. "I'm sorry, Yara."

"No, no," I hurried. "You shouldn't apologize; I'm the one who needs to."

"You have. You've done that so many times—"

"I know, but you deserve to hear it again and again. Look, I don't think I can ever forgive myself for what happened to you. I nearly... we nearly lost you because of my mistake. I should have been driving more slowly and more carefully. I should have stayed calm, and maybe it wouldn't have been so bad. We could have been fine. You could have graduated on time and done all the big things you had planned. And I... I just wish I could change it all. Every day I wish I could change it all. I'm so sorry."

Logan moved to my side in an instant and pulled me into her arms. It wasn't until my cheek pressed against her shoulder I realized I was crying. She was crying too, but her voice was far more stable than mine.

"I didn't realize this was affecting you," she said as she rubbed my back. "I didn't know you were holding on to this so tightly."

"It was the only thing I could do," I confessed. "The only way I knew how to serve penance."

"Yara, listen to me carefully." She pulled back to look me in the eyes. "I have not and will never hold the accident against you. I love you too much to ever expect you to pay for one mistake. When I look at you, I see the one of the people I love most in this world, and everyday I think of how lucky I am to call you my sister. Nothing will change that. My love for you will never change."

I cried silently now, but just as hard. Logan pulled out a tissue to dab away my tears. Her words nestled into my chest, medicine to a cold I'd been harboring for ages. The shame wouldn't go away completely, but it wouldn't burn through me like a fever any longer.

"Are you sure? I wouldn't hate you if you weren't. I love you forever."

Logan smiled and nodded. "I'm surer of this than anything else in life."

I sniffed and pulled her into another hug. She rubbed my back and let me take all the time I needed to calm down. When I finally pulled away, I almost started crying again because my makeup had ruined the soft pink fabric of her dress.

I groaned. "I'm so sorry."

She laughed. It was a light sound that made me smile and thank the heavens I got to hear her. To know her and be a part of her journey, wherever it may take her. "It's just a dress. This moment's more important than just a dress."

———

WE HAD our first batch of fireflies of the season. They lit the sky and could be easily admired through the clear event tent. Their lights made the toasts and well-wishes more magical.

David didn't leave my side for a second after he helped with unloading. He'd seen my puffy eyes and ruined makeup and tried to figure out the issue without alerting people around us. I whispered to him that I would tell him everything once we got some alone time. He could barely keep still ever since.

I placed my hand on his knee after my dad gave the last speech, and the band started playing what I assumed was Rose and Ren's song. We all watched the couple dance on their own for a moment before people began joining in. I stayed seated, enjoying the view of the people who I most days I couldn't stand and every day adored.

"I miss our friends," I whispered to David.

He leaned in to kiss my temple. "Just one more week."

"I miss you," I teased and turned to him.

"I'm right here." He kissed my lips then. "Till you get sick of me."

"Never," I promised and stood. He raised a brow at my outstretched hand. "Do I have to waste a dare?"

"I don't dance," he reminded me.

"We'll sway."

He sighed. "That's somehow worse."

"David." I waved my hand. "Come on, just two seconds, and we'll brood in the corner like you always did during school dances. It'll be like old times."

"I didn't brood." He got up, though, and accepted my hand.

"Then what would you call it?" I led us to the edge of the dance floor. We were close enough to be included but far enough to feel like we had our own space. We were on our own time.

"I believe the word is judging." His hands wrapped around my waist, pinning me against his hips.

I pursed my lips and flickered my gaze down at my midsection. I could feel how hard he was.

"What can I say?" He offered me a crooked smile. "I missed you, too."

I laughed. "Why did you go to those dances if you were just going to judge?"

He offered me a one-shoulder shrug. "To see you, of course."

"Very cute."

"Don't go getting a bigger head." He brushed his nose across mine.

"Too late."

"You have always been an incredible distraction. Doesn't matter which side of the fence I'm on," he noted.

"I'm nothing but proficient in everything I do."

He nodded. "What happened when I left you earlier?"

David touched my cheek, noting the lack of blush I had so clearly applied in his car.

"I talked to my sister." My arms tightened around his neck.

"How did it go?" he asked, concern clouding his eyes.

"We both cried, and she told me she'd forgiven me forever ago." I let out a breath, remembering all my anxiety over the past few years, how it'd almost eaten me alive. Those feelings lingered in my bones because my body had been their home for far too long. But they occupied a smaller unit. And I'd learn how to co-exist with them. Time was an excellent teacher.

David's smile expressed the pure joy I thought only family could offer a loved one. An unabashed, loving care I thought I wouldn't deserve unless I became an incredible doctor or a brilliant lawyer.

"I'm so proud of you," he whispered between kisses. "So incredibly proud."

I laughed against his mouth. "I couldn't have done it without you. Wouldn't have."

He shook his head. "You needed more time, but you would have done it. I know you well enough to understand you don't need me. But you want me, and that's all I could ever ask for."

"We'll argue about semantics till the day we die, won't we?" I asked.

"There's no doubt about it."

"I look forward to it," I said honestly.

He nodded. "Me too. Especially since I have such a brilliant and beautiful opponent."

I smiled. "Brilliant and beautiful? Dare you to keep up that energy for as long as we're together."

"You've got yourself a deal."

EPILOGUE

DAVID

YARA'S SIDE of the bed was cool to the touch. I moved my hand around, reaching to pull her close. But there wasn't even an imprint in the sheets indicating her absence could be a temporary setback.

My stomach twisted, and my eyes strained to make out shapes in the near-dark. The silence of the room buzzed, a loud warning. I sat up, examining the space. The only bit of light in our bedroom came from the cracked bathroom door. I waited, listening for movement behind the door. The only sound was the hum of the air conditioning.

A nightmare had woken me up. I had one of my recurring ones where Yara and I were separated. Her side of the closet was empty, her toiletries gone, and a simple note reading "this isn't working" on the countertop.

I knew it wasn't real. It would never be real. But the heavy weight that bore down on my chest was bent on convincing me otherwise.

"Yara?" I called and reached for my phone to check the time. One AM. The world was quiet, cloaked in black. I tossed off the tangled blankets and started out of the room.

Yara was a heavy sleeper. A *I-always-get-eight-hours-every-night* sleeper. So, for her to be up and gone at this hour made my chest burn with what-ifs.

I beelined downstairs, automatic lights illuminating every step I took. Our apartment was too big for just two people. There were too many places for an intruder to hide. Too many dark shadows that could harm my wife.

"Yara?" I called again, adrenaline readying me for whatever or whoever.

When I got to the kitchen entryway, I found evidence of rummaging. Boxes of cookies, bags of chips, and an empty pickle jar on the kitchen island. A half-full glass of water and an empty mug of coffee. My heart rate slowed a little, seeing the telltale signs of a woman with late-night cravings. I didn't feel completely satisfied until I entered the living room.

And there she was, lounging on our L-shaped sofa with a yogurt cup in one hand and her laptop resting in her lap. She wore noise-cancelling headphones that covered her ears, so she had zero awareness of my heavy steps.

I took a deep breath, lingering in the living room's entryway just to admire her for a second. Yara had tucked her hair under her favorite pink bonnet. The silk robe she wore hung off her shoulder, revealing her soft, dark brown skin. She slipped the spoon between her perfect lips, holding it there as she typed something up.

Six years. Six years with this woman and I still couldn't stop feeling like I was so incredibly unworthy, yet wholeheartedly needy.

"Yara," I said, more gently and understanding as I moved to the end of the couch.

She looked up, sensing movement in her periphery. Her eyes went wide for a second before realizing it was me. The smile that broke across her face set my skin on fire. I sat in front of her and gently tugged the headphones off. She set the empty yogurt cup aside, giving the spoon one final lick.

"You're nervous." I reached for the laptop, but she moved it away.

"I don't get nervous," she said, a teasing glint in her eye. "Why are you down here? Did I wake you?"

"No, but I wish you had." I tried to grab the laptop again, and this time she didn't put up a fight. "How long have you been down here?"

She shrugged. "Not long."

"Your trail of snacks says otherwise." I gestured for her to move over. She obliged, allowing me to sit next to her and wrap my arm over her shoulders. I pulled her to my side, kissing the top of her head a couple of times.

"What's going on, baby?" I whispered and laughed as she elbowed my stomach.

"I wanted to work. Can a woman not work anymore?" She stretched her legs over mine, and I couldn't resist helping myself. I brushed my hand up and down her skin. It was winter, and she always let her hair grow during the colder months, citing the need for extra warmth. I didn't care what the reason was; I loved the soft bit of hair prickling across the palm of my hand. I loved that she could fully relax into me and understand I wasn't going anywhere.

"Not when said woman has been working her ass off for the past month," I said.

Yara worked for a children's television production company as their Head of Communications. They were bringing on a new series this year. One that didn't hold back on teaching kids about things like poverty, war, and mental health.

"Nothing you do in the next couple of hours will change the fact that this project's going to be a total touchdown because of you," I promised.

"You don't know that."

"I do." I kissed her temple. "Now, please, come back to bed. You know I can't sleep unless you're there."

"You're so needy," she teased, smiling up at me.

I pulled her tighter into my chest. "I am. Desperate, too."

"Desperate, you say?" She raised a brow, something brewing in that beautiful brain of hers.

"Don't," I warned, even though I loved it when she looked at me that way. Loved how her challenges made me want her even more. I'd do anything to make this woman smile. Crawl on my knees (check), beg (double check), offer her the sun, moon, and stars (triple check). I lifted her hand to kiss the ring on her finger. The shining sunstone that tied me to her from now to eternity.

She's mine, I repeated, still trying to get used to the reality because I never thought this would happen. That Yara Every could fall for me as hard and deeply as I had fallen for her.

I kissed her hand again and then her wrist, right where her heartbeat drummed, and then her exposed shoulder.

"David," she said. It's supposed to be a warning, but her breathy sigh made it an anthem of desire.

"Yes?" I asked, trying to sound clueless as my hand cupped her cheek to turn her face to me. I kissed her, trying to melt away all her anxieties.

"I'll go back to bed with you on one condition," she said against my lips.

"Anything," I promised, not even opening my eyes because I was so lost in her voice.

"Tell me who you were dating."

I laughed and pulled away to see her face. Yara lifted her brows, tilting her head to the side. She'd been asking me this question for the past few weeks after she found one of her journals from our senior year in college.

"Yara, come on," I said, holding out only because I enjoyed

hearing her guesses. Seeing her try to put the puzzle pieces together. "Really?"

"Really." She poked my chest. "Why are you so secretive about it?"

"I'm not. I totally forgot about it until you started bringing it up."

"David, please." Yara crossed her arms over her chest, offering the prettiest pout I've ever seen. I groaned. It was impossible to deny her anything.

"You are so gorgeous," I mused, taking her face between my hands and pulling her close enough so that my forehead pressed against hers. "You know that."

She grinned. "I do. Now stop stalling."

"Fine, fine. But only because I'm exhausted and need to get up early tomorrow." I exaggerated a sigh. "I was... seeing you."

Yara laughed and pointed at me. "I *knew* it! I knew you didn't have anyone."

"Hold on, hold on." I held up my hands. "No, you did not. There's no way you knew that."

"I did! You were so obsessed with me, you couldn't have been dating anyone else." She was buzzing with vindication.

I playfully bit the finger she pointed at me. Yara snatched it back and used her other finger to carry on its blaming legacy.

"*Obsessed* with me," she repeated with a laugh.

"Was not." I grabbed her waist, trying to pull her back into my lap. Yara put up a fight, and we ended up wrestling until she was lying underneath me on the couch.

"Not fair." She wiggled out of breath and full of laughter. "You're not allowed to use pro-football moves. We agreed."

I snorted. "That was hardly a pro-move. You should see me on the field."

"I always see you on the field." Yara had never missed one

game. Whether she had to take her laptop for work into the NFL suite or not, she was there, cheering me on.

"Sure, but are you ever paying attention to anything other than my ass?" I asked.

She was silent for a moment before letting out a huff of surrender. "Fine. I yield."

I grinned. "You yield?"

"Yes, for now." She squirmed some more before I got off her.

"I just..." I laughed under my breath a bit, remembering how caught up I'd been in image and trying to hide the parts of me I didn't want her to see back then. "I said I was seeing someone so you wouldn't think I was waiting around for you all the time."

She sat up, readjusting her bonnet with a bright smile on her face. "But you were."

"When I wasn't practicing." I ran a hand through my hair. "Sure, I guess."

"Sure?" Yara laughed and crawled into my lap. "That's all I get? A sure? I guess?"

"Fine. Yes, then," I said, voice hoarse as she lowered herself onto me. I knew she felt how hard I was from how her pupils dilated. "I didn't realize it, but I was obsessed with you. Seeing you. Hearing you. Wanting you. You were the best part of every moment. Still are and always will be."

"Why couldn't you just say that?"

"And ruin all the fun we had?" I shook my head. "I wouldn't dare."

Yara leaned in closer, her lips hovering over mine. "You're really a piece of work, you know that, Mr. Evans?"

I nodded. "But you love, don't you, Mrs. Evans? You love me."

"Till my final breath," she promised. "What about you?"

"Till my final breath," I agreed. "And many millennia after."

Yara shook her head, smiling. "Always trying to one-up me."

I kissed her, tattooing the promise on her lips so she'd memorize the taste of it.

The feel of it.

The truth of it.

ALSO BY DEANNA GREY

Mendell Hawks

Sunny Disposition

Team Players

Safety Net

Standalones

Outdrawn

Oasis

The Case of Elmwood Ranch